Make Room for Family

Michael Embry

A Wings ePress, Inc.

Contemporary Novel

Wings ePress, Inc.

Edited by: Jeanne Smith
Copy Edited by: Joan C. Powell
Executive Editor: Jeanne Smith
Cover Artist: Trisha FitzGerald-Jung

All rights reserved

Wings ePress Books
www.wingsepress.com

Copyright © 2021 by: Michael Embry
ISBN 978-1-61309-548-5

Published In the United States Of America

Wings ePress Inc.
3000 N. Rock Road
Newton, KS 67114

What They Are Saying About
Make Room for Family

Michael Embry's engaging John Ross series about boomers negotiating the demands of community and family in their retirement years hits new heights with *Make Room for Family*. John must cope with his son's opioid addiction, his daughter's cancer, his wife's forgetfulness, his mother-in-law's cantankerousness, his in-law's self-righteous intrusions, and white supremacists moving into the neighborhood.

Embry is wonderful at catching the rhythms of everyday life, as John takes his dog Whiskers out for walks to escape the tumult and tension in the household and as he constantly feeds family members and houseguests. That feeding of others becomes indicative of John's nature as his consideration is marked by both good manners and a generosity of spirit. He needs that spirit to address all of the concerns on his plate, particularly as he watches his son Brody's struggles with addiction.

Among these rhythms of domesticity emerges an intriguing story about a new neighbor who starts proselytizing throughout the community. When racist graffiti soon follows in the neighborhood, John becomes increasingly involved in trying to uncover the mysterious goings-on at that evangelical house. While Embry artfully weaves and resolves the threads of the story, the greatest pleasures of *Make Room for Family* derive from his realistically capturing the interactions that accompany everyday stress. The exchanges between John and his mother-in-law Geraldine are an absolute hoot. Throughout, John's wry sense of humor buoys this novel even when the tension builds.

Make Room for Family is such an enjoyable novel that sometimes the reader loses sight of how telling and relevant

Embry's comments are about life in America in the early Twenty-First Century. For its head and its heart, I highly recommend *Make Room for Family*.

—Michael Hartnett, author of *Blue Gowanus,*
The Blue Rat, and *Fools in the Magic Kingdom*

Readers may find in this most recent in Michael Embry's series of John Ross Boomer Lit novels a fictional corollary of the constraints they've accepted as the price of survival during the worst pandemic in living memory.

For many of us, daily life has become a hamster wheel of dull interactions with the same small cast of significant others, all of us confined to the same physical space by the surrounding mortal threat. That experience should prepare readers of *Make Room for Family* to admire the grace and equanimity that John Ross displays toward his drug-addicted son and his self-centered in-laws. Readers might also find that their own recent history sharpens their sense of how much teeth-grinding effort John must exert to put up with those invaders of his household.

After they have vacationed together in Budapest, Hungary—an interlude chronicled in Embry's novel *New Horizons*—John and his wife Sally agree that he should return home to Lexington, Kentucky, while Sally stays on in New York to support their daughter, Chloe, who is undergoing treatment for ovarian cancer. In the interim, John must deal with four extra family members who constantly complain, demand that food be fetched or prepared to their specifications and occupy all the available bedrooms, leaving John to sleep on a couch.

A reader might decide within the first few pages of this novel that its title could have been the one tacked over the gate of Dante's inferno: "Abandon hope all ye who enter here." But give John and Sally Ross enough time in any seemingly hopeless situation, and hope will win out.

—Michael Jennings, author of *Ave Antonia*

Dedication

This novel is dedicated to my sweet, loving, and precious
niece
Cynthia Marie Brohm
(April 5, 1976-June 22, 2020)

"Those we love don't go away, they walk beside us every day.
Unseen, unheard, but always near; still loved, still missed
and very dear."
–Anonymous

* * *

In Memory of
Great and Talented Friends

John Asher (1955-2018) - Louisville, Ky.

James "Poncho" Easterwood (1936-2018) - Wingo, Ky.

Patricia Gill (1946-2019) - Lexington, Ky.

Garry Jones (1954-2019) - New Albany, Ind.

Jim O'Connell (1953-2018) - New York, N.Y.

Michael Schillhahn (1952-2018) - Gdansk, Poland

Billy B. Smith (1933-2017) - Campbellsville, Ky.

Richard Stroud (1941-2018) - Philadelphia, Pa.

Fred L. Waddle (1937-2019) - Campbellsville, Ky.

Gwendolyn Jenetta Young (1931-2020) - Edmonton, Ky.

"There are some who bring a light so great to the world that even after they have gone the light remains."

—Unknown

One

John Ross felt a nudge against his shoe as he read a crumpled *New York Times* he'd picked up in the boarding area at Newark Liberty International Airport. He continued reading, then felt another slight bump, knee against knee. He lowered the newspaper, turned his head to look at the person, and grinned.

"What are you doing here, you old hoot?" Brandon Wilkes, a longtime friend and retired sports columnist from Lexington, Kentucky, stood in front of him, holding a small carry-on bag and a large cup of coffee.

John folded the newspaper, leaned forward and shook Brandon's hand. "Heading back to God's country after a week or so in Europe and a couple days in the city visiting my daughter. And you?"

Wilkes sat next to John and crossed his legs. "Business trip. I'm supposed to have a book published in the fall, so met with an editor to go over final edits. But I'm not holding my breath. These things can drag on forever. Or so I've been told."

"Sports book?"

"Yeah, that's about all I know. Or at least that's what people think. Once a sportswriter, always a sportswriter, if you know what I mean. But the book is about horse racing."

"Well, congratulations. I never had the time to do anything like that. Too busy with other things. How's the wife?"

"Doing great," Brandon said. "Clarice is still working in PR, mostly as a consultant. She'd like to retire but still makes a pretty nice paycheck. Allows me to carry on my writing follies and helps pay for our health premiums. Everything well with Sally and the kids? I guess they're not kids anymore."

"Maybe not kids, but still our children. You never stop being a parent. As for Sally, she stays busy."

"Problems with kids? It's Chloe and Brody, right?"

"Good memory." John stared up at the arrival and departure screen. "No problems other than the usual stuff we all go through at one time or another."

"Sally's back in Lexington?"

"She's with Chloe. Decided she wanted to spend a week or so with her and our granddaughter."

"Wow. Surprise! I didn't know you guys were grandparents," Brandon said, arching back in his seat. "I'm really out of the loop."

"You need to join our little morning group at McDonald's, near Palomar." John was relieved to steer the conversation in a different direction rather than divulge Chloe's cancer and Brody's drug problem. "Just bunch of old farts from the paper. You probably know most of them. We opine about everything under the sun, and then some. Lots of reminiscing about the so-called good old days."

"I may just do that," Brandon said, tapping a foot on the tile floor. "After I finish this darn book. You'd be surprised how much time I've spent on it and I bet I won't make more than a couple thousand dollars."

"If you don't mind me asking, then why do it?"

"First of all, they contacted me. They offered a nice little advance, so I couldn't refuse. And I suppose it was a vanity thing as well. I've always wanted to write a book, so this was the opportunity. I just didn't realize it'd be this difficult."

"The writing?"

"The writing was a breeze. I've been writing all my life. It's dealing with the rewrites and endless edits. Just when I think I'm finished I get an email from my editor suggesting a few changes."

"So the end is near?"

"I sure as hell hope so." Brandon took a deep breath with a crooked smile. "At least that's what they told me yesterday. The only things are a few photographs they want me to caption and write an acknowledgment and a forward. So yes, the end is near. But we'll see. I've heard those words before."

"And to think I'll actually know someone who'll be in the Library of Congress," John said.

"Yeah, along with a several other million writers. It's not so elite or unique anymore."

"But it's still a fine accomplishment."

Brandon shrugged. "That'll be our secret."

The airline clerk announced first boarding for the flight, which would make a stop in Detroit before touching down in Kentucky. John was surprised when Brandon stood. "That's me."

"You must be doing okay," John said, grinning, "Flying first class."

"Thank my publisher," Brandon said. "They handled all the details. If it were me paying for it, I'd be in economy. See you back in Lexington."

"Don't forget McDonald's," John said.

"Send me a reminder, if you can remember." Brandon smiled and got in line with the others in first class.

John glanced at his watch, grabbed his carry-on, made a quick stop at the men's room, and returned to the boarding area with a few minutes to spare.

He took out his cell phone, remembering there was one more thing he needed to do before departing; he tapped the quick dial for Sally's number.

"Where have you been?" she asked with concern in her voice. "I've been worried sick about you."

"Sorry 'bout that. I got busy and it slipped my mind. I made it safely to the airport, then ran into Brandon Wilkes, an old sports writing friend from Lexington. I'll be boarding my plane in a few minutes. Just want to let you know I'm on my way back home."

"Try not to forget to call when you get back."

"I'll try not to."

"You better do more than that."

John noticed the boarding officer about to close the gate. "Love you, sweetie. Gotta go." He hurried toward the attendant, waving his boarding pass.

John hurried down the ramp to board the 737. He shook his head in mock disgust at Brandon as he passed through the first-class section. Brandon flicked his brows and smiled as he lifted a glass of orange juice. John found his seat on the aisle near the rear of economy.

~ * ~

A young woman with a gold nose ring wearing black yoga pants and a frayed, bulky black sweatshirt with the sleeves pulled up to her bony elbows and revealing scrawny, tattooed arms, was already nestled next to the window. Her eyes were closed and earphones dangled through her stringy red-streaked, shoulder-length black hair. There was no sign she was aware of John's presence. He stowed his carry-on in the overhead compartment, trying not to spoil her siesta.

John smiled to himself, eased back in his seat, fastened the seatbelt, and closed his eyes, only to disturbed seconds later by a rotund woman tapping his shoulder. She didn't say anything, simply raised her brows and pointed a stubby forefinger toward the empty seat in the middle.

John maneuvered from his seat, having to take a couple steps backward. The woman jammed two pieces of luggage in the overhead bin, assisted by John tugging on his own carry-on to make enough room. She grabbed the top of the two seats in front of her, causing the occupants to shift forward and turn their heads around to see what was going on. They scowled with piercing glances. She ignored them and plopped into the seat. The young woman next to the window squinted and glowered at her as she edged away, if only an inch or two, then turned her head and stared out the window as if to make her seatmate fade away.

John glanced at the floor at an overstuffed carry-on and picked it up. "Yours?" he asked the large woman.

"Oh, yes, please." She took it and set it on her lumbering legs stuffed into navy blue leggings like a bulging burrito. She wore a beige shawl over a tight tunic top, unable to suppress her thickness rolling over the armrests as she wriggled into the body-hugging space.

John slid back in his seat, forced to lean toward the aisle, his right arm crossing his lap. Moments later, he was jarred from his position when the woman began digging through the carry-on. She eventually pulled out a cell phone, giving John a hard jab to his ribs in the process. John grimaced and attempted to rearrange his rear end on the seat, hoping to gain some relief, but not as much as he wanted as the woman's fluid form seemed to move in unison with him like gelatin.

John turned his head on the left side of the headrest and watched several passengers get situated before takeoff. He lifted his head a bit higher and glanced around the cabin to see if there were any vacant seats offering an escape from his compact quarters. He felt another jolt on his side and heavy breath on his cheek.

"Excuse me, sir. I need to get one of my bags." The woman in the middle began to ooze up from her seat. The gal next to the window turned her head with narrow eyes and tight mouth. John noticed "Wiccans Rule!" and an ankh symbol emblazoned across the front of her sweatshirt. He wondered if he'd been cursed.

Before the large woman could move toward the aisle from her upright position, and grasp the seat in front of her, John slipped out and held up his hands. "Why don't you let me?" he asked.

Her bloated rosy cheeks puffed out as she held her hunkered over position and gazed at John for a moment. "It's the pink one, I believe, sir."

As John tugged at the small bag, a male passenger with a jammed backpack pressed against his body without saying a word. John eased in front of his seat and waited for the man to pass before retrieving his seatmate's belongings. She waggled back into the seat, placing her other carry-on on the floor beneath stubby legs, and took the pink bag from John.

The stewards began making their way down the aisles, slamming shut the overhead bins, making sure passengers had fastened seatbelts, and properly placed belongings under the seats in front of them as the airplane was about to taxi to the runway. John sat back down, nearly sideways, as he crossed his legs and leaned toward the aisle.

"Ma'am, you'll have to move the bag under the seat," the steward said to the woman in the middle. She bent as much as her body would let her but couldn't reach the bag. She shoved it with her pointy, purple-sequined heels, but to no avail.

"Let me help," John said as he slinked from his seat. He kneeled and pushed the bag, but it wouldn't go completely under the seat. "Be careful, sir," the woman whined. "I just bought it and I don't want it scuffed."

A small smile slipped across John's bedraggled face as he rose and stared at the woman. He asked the steward, "Are there any vacant seats?"

The steward pointed toward the restroom five rows back, where there was one empty seat across from the door, next to an older woman in a maroon jumpsuit and white hair in a fuzzy perm.

"I'll take it."

"You'll have to wait until after takeoff." The steward glanced at John's crowded condition and frowned. "Oh, go ahead. It'll be our little secret."

John breathed a sigh of relief, smiled, and strode directly to the empty seat. He only nodded at the elderly woman and plonked in his seat, fastened the seatbelt, and without saying a word, closed his eyes.

~ * ~

Ten minutes later, the 737 roared down the runway and soared through the puffy white cumulus clouds. John glanced over to where he had been sitting and noticed his former seatmate hadn't budged from her middle seat. He could only imagine how the thin gal next to the bulky frame must be coping with the physical spread. Perhaps conjuring some sort of curse? He took a deep breath and leaned back, hoping to get some shut-eye as the plane tilted toward Detroit.

Passengers streamed toward the restroom seconds after the seatbelt light went off, standing in line for their chance to empty their bladders or bowels, or both, or whatever they needed to do at thirty-thousand feet. The door opened and closed every few minutes. John turned his head toward the center, keeping his eyes closed to avoid the light from the restroom. Seconds later, he almost dozed off.

"Where are you going?"

Hazy-headed from his nano nap, John concentrated for a moment to see where the high-pitched voice was coming from before realizing it was the lady next to him. He turned his head and opened his eyes to see a tiny earnest face with puffy rouge-smeared cheeks staring directly at him.

"Kentucky," he muttered.

"Me, too," she said in a cheery tone. "Where in Kentucky?"

"Lexington."

"I love Lexington. I went to UK back in the 1950s and got a degree in home economics. I was a high school teacher in Madisonville. By the time I retired, there were hardly any home ec courses in high schools."

"I would guess not." John grinned. "Lots of things have changed since then."

"Did you go to UK?"

"Eastern Kentucky."

"What did you study?"

"Journalism."

"So you're a journalist?"

"Retired."

"Did you write for a newspaper?"

"Yes, ma'am. The Lexington paper."

"Oh, how interesting. I love to read newspapers."

"I wish there were more people like you. They seem to be dying out." He immediately regretted the last remark, adding, "Uh, I mean newspapers are dying out."

She seemed unfazed. "What did you write about?"

"I was a sports editor."

"Oh, my goodness. I love sports. Have you heard of the Madisonville Maroons?"

"Yes, ma'am," John said with an earnest smile. "The high school has a good sports program."

The conversation abruptly stopped when a middle-aged man in a dark gray business suit stepped out of the restroom. A pungent odor drifted with him for several rows. Several passengers covered their noses or waved their hands in front of their faces. A young boy bellowed, "Phew-wee!" which brought some muffled laughter. If the suspected offender noticed the commotion, he didn't let on as he hurried to the middle of the plane without looking back.

John lowered his head and clenched his mouth, holding his breath until the rancid smell began to dissipate in the tight quarters. An older teen-aged girl stood outside the restroom, hands on her hips, declaring she wasn't going to enter until a steward sprayed the place with air freshener.

A steward showed up a minute later, stepped inside the restroom with an aerosol can of air freshener. The prolonged spray made the confined area smell like a bed of a thousand roses, causing passengers to cough as the quarters went from fart infested to floral overload.

John gazed at the woman next to him, who held a tissue over her nose.

"Are you okay?" John asked.

"A real stinker, wasn't it?"

John chuckled. "It makes you wonder if something died in there."

The old lady giggled.

John leaned back in his seat and closed his eyes again with the intention of taking a short nap before landing in Detroit. It didn't happen as stewards began making rounds, handing out snacks and taking drink orders.

He straightened up in his seat and plugged in earphones in the front console, pushing various buttons for music selections until he noticed his seatmate staring at him. He removed his earphones.

"Yes?"

"I get so bored on these flights," she said, tilting her head. "Hardly anyone wants to talk anymore."

"I guess because we're all strangers."

"But you don't get to know others unless you converse with them. That's why we're all strangers. People seem afraid to get to know others."

"I suppose so."

"Don't you want to talk?"

"I'm just a little tired."

"Then why are you fooling with the display?"

"Just finding some quiet music. It helps me relax."

"Did I tell you I'm a widow?"

"No, ma'am." John's brows furrowed. "Sorry to hear that. For very long?"

"I've been on my own for 'bout fourteen years. My late husband was a school principal. Erthel was a football coach and physical education teacher when we got married. He loved sports."

"Interesting."

"My name is Alma."

John forced a smile. "It's nice to meet you Alma."

"What's your name?"

"John."

"Nice to meet you too, John. Are you married?"

"Yes, I am. My wife's a retired schoolteacher."

"Oh, how sweet." She patted the top of John's hand. "Just like me. We have something in common, don't we?"

"I guess we do."

"So we're not really strangers, are we?"

"What do you mean?"

"We're both Kentuckians who like sports and you're married to an educator. So we have connections."

"I never really thought of it in those ways, but I can understand what you're saying."

Thirty minutes into the flight, Alma was nonstop jabbering about all sorts of things—her children, grandchildren, and great-grandchildren—providing the name, approximate age, and interest of each one. And then she recounted her years as a teacher in Madisonville. John listened with a frozen expression, nodding, and smiling on occasion.

"Did you know Madisonville is the best town on earth?" she asked.

"That's debatable," John said. "I'm sure lots of towns feel the same way."

"I'm serious, John. It's on signs when you enter the city. The U.S. Postal Service has even been known to deliver mail to addresses with 'The Best Town on Earth.'"

"You learn something every day."

"You should visit."

"I'll give it some thought."

"You can bring your wife and I'll show you around. By the way, what's your wife's name?"

"Sally."

"What a sweet, old-fashioned name."

"I guess so."

"Are you changing planes in Detroit?"

"No, ma'am. I'm going on to Cincinnati, then to Lexington."

Her mouth drooped. "That's too bad. I have to board another plane to Nashville."

John smiled to himself. "Sorry to hear that."

As the 737 approached Detroit Metro Airport, Alma reapplied her glossy red lipstick, puckering her mouth and smiling several times in the compact. She glanced at John and wriggled her brows. "Now I look presentable."

John nodded. "You look very nice, Alma."

Minutes later, the plane touched down on the runway. Nearly half of the passengers scurried from their seats to remove their luggage from the overhead bins, despite pleas from stewards to wait until the jet came to a complete stop. When the plane parked next to the terminal, they pressed their way past others to the front exit, creating a logjam. The stewards stepped aside, knowing it was beyond their control.

John stepped out in the aisle and removed Alma's wheeled hard-shell pink luggage, pulling out the handles for her. He grasped her hand to help her rise from her seat, realizing her small and petite stature. Standing next to him, she only reached his chin.

"I'm so glad we got to sit next to each other," she said. "I usually have people who put those plugs in their ears and close their eyes the entire flight. They can be so rude and inconsiderate."

"It was a pleasure meeting you," John said, shaking her thin, manicured hand. "I hope you have a safe trip back to the best town on earth."

Alma beamed. "Oh, you remembered." She stood on her tiptoes, clutched his shoulders, forcing him to lean over, and pecked his cheek. John felt his face blush as she grinned at him.

She grabbed the luggage handle and eased up the aisle, turning around midway and waving her tiny fingers. John noticed a wet spot on the back of her pants as she disappeared among the passengers converging at the exit.

"Damn." He ran a hand over his head.

About to sit down, John noticed a small damp area where Alma had been sitting. The stewards were near the front of the plane, so he removed a blue blanket from a plastic wrapper and covered the soiled cushion.

John scooted back into his seat and closed his eyes, catnapping until awakened by the bustle of passengers dawdling down the aisles to locate their places for the flight to Kentucky. He looked at his cellphone to see if there were any messages, but the battery was drained since he had forgotten to recharge it in Newark.

John was startled when he sensed someone scrutinizing him. He glanced up at a twenty-something man with scraggy chin whiskers and a bleached-orange buzzcut, wearing baggy black gym pants, a tight-fitting pullover shirt with a large Confederate flag emblazoned on the front.

"That's my seat," the young man said, pointing to Alma's seat.

"You don't want to sit there," John said. "It's—"

"I'll sit wherever I fuckin' well please. So get up, boomer."

"I beg your pardon?"

"You heard me," the man snarled. Before John could slip out of his seat, the man stepped over his feet, and plopped next to him.

John turned his head and bit his tongue.

The man shuffled deep in his seat, then yanked the blanket out from under him and smelled it. "What the fuck!"

John lifted his palms. "I tried to tell you."

The man rose, his reed-thin legs stepped back to the aisle and he marched to the stewards' station, dragging the light blanket on the floor. John snickered when saw the man's damp rear end.

"Boom," he said, pointing a forefinger like a pistol.

Passengers craned their heads to see what the commotion was all about as the wild-eyed dude waved the blanket back and forth like a flag, finally tossing it over the head of a steward while spewing several expletives in her direction. An unassuming man in a navy blue sports coat and gray slacks from the middle of the economy class creeped behind the furious passenger, and after a brief scuffle, dropped him to the floor with a swift two-finger punch to the neck. A steward closed the ruffled curtain to their quarters.

Minutes later, the dazed and limped-legged passenger was hauled down the aisle, handcuffed, by the unsmiling air marshal.

To John's relief, the remainder of the trip proved to be uneventful. On a short and brisk layover at Cincinnati/Northern Kentucky International Airport, John noticed Brandon Wilkes heading toward the exit for the parking area.

"Getting some fresh air?" John asked.

"Hardly," Brandon said, shaking his head. "My first-class flight ends here. I have to drive the rest of the way. Whoever booked my flight thought Lexington was a suburb of Cincinnati."

"Drive safely. And don't forget the gang at McDonald's."

"And don't forget to remind me."

John boarded a small commuter jet for the connecting flight to Blue Grass Airport in Lexington.

He took a deep breath as he stepped out of the terminal under cloudless, soft blue sky. It felt nice to be in Kentucky. He strolled to long-term parking and located Sally's SUV. It had collected several weeks' worth of bird droppings of varying levels of muck. He ran the wipers and windshield spray several times, smearing the surface with light pale streaks. John put on sunglasses, backed out and headed home as the Beatles' "The Long and Winding Road" played on the radio. His shoulders slumped from fatigue as the weight of the journey began to take its toll.

As John turned the corner toward his house, he waved at Bert Reliford, who was putting down mulch in a flower bed with a hoe. Bert didn't miss a stroke with the hoe but managed a slight nod while squeezing in a smile.

John parked in front of his house, as an unfamiliar car was in the driveway. As he walked across the lawn to the porch, he heard Whiskers barking on the other side of the closed front door. The dog's yelps brought a bright smile to his face, making him forget how tired he was from his travels. He glanced at the car in the driveway, a black Ford Escort station wagon. He figured it was probably one of Brody's friends.

As John reached for the doorknob, the door swung open, nearly causing him to lunge forward before bracing himself against the jamb. Whiskers leaped into his arms, almost knocking John backward, and began smothering John with slobbering licks over his face and neck.

"Hey there, little buddy." John patted his furry friend behind his ears, oblivious to the person holding the door open.

"Hello, John." The voice was formal with little inflection, almost robotic. Wendell Corman, Sally's younger brother, faced John with an ingratiating smile.

John stiffened like a statue before cracking a weak grin. "Well, hi, Wendell. What a surprise. I didn't expect to see you."

Wendell stepped aside as John entered the house with the wiggling Whiskers secure in his arms.

"Libby and I arrived a few days ago." Wendell led John to the den as if it were his house. His mother-in-law, Geraldine, was perched in the recliner, watching a soap opera, and ignoring the two men. When a commercial came on, she looked at John, expressionless, and said, "Finally decide to come home?"

John sauntered over and kissed her cheek. "Glad to see me?"

"Where's Sally?"

"She's still in New York with Chloe," John said. "She wanted to stay a few extra days with her."

"She could have alerted me. I may have had plans."

John glanced over at Wendell, who appeared to be in suspended animation with his arms crossing his chest and staring at his mother.

"Some things came up," John said. "Maybe she told Brody."

"Brody has been in and out of the house so much I couldn't tell if he was here or there," Geraldine said. "And always asking for money. When is he going to find a job? That's what I want to know. Enough is enough. When are you going to say something to him about it?"

"We can discuss it later, Geraldine. If you don't mind, I think I'll go up to the bedroom and take a short nap and get refreshed.

I'm a bit exhausted. If anything, get out of these clothes and into something else."

"Uh, John." Wendell, clearing his throat, emerged from his slight stupor. "Libby's in your room, resting her eyes."

"Oh."

"I hope you don't mind, but we've been using your bedroom. Brody said we could sleep there since you and Sally weren't around. I hope that's okay with you."

"That's fine." John flashed a grin. "There was no sense in letting the room go to waste."

Geraldine looked up from the TV. "It would have helped if you could have given us some notice as well."

John and Wendell glanced at each other and then looked at her.

"I'm talking to you, Wendell. You dropped in unannounced."

"But Mama, we hit some traffic jams in Nashville and there was a terrible accident on the interstate near Elizabethtown. We got here as quickly as we could. I told you we were thinking about coming to see you after you fractured your hip. It just takes time to make all the arrangements."

"Did you break a finger?"

Wendell's pallid face turned crimson. "I apologize, Mama. We just didn't think."

"That's an understatement. You're just like your father. He seemed to think he could just show up and everything would be fine and dandy."

John set Whiskers on the floor. "I guess I'll get something to drink. Coffee anyone?"

"How about dinner?" Geraldine said. "We do need to eat around here. I'm famished."

"What would you like?" John asked. "Pizza?"

"Heavens no! That's all Brody had around here all week. I think I'll vomit if I see another pizza."

"Maybe John could order some White Castles?" Wendell said. "You always loved them. And it's been a while since Libby and I had some. What do you think, Mama?"

Geraldine clenched her jaw. "Whatever. Just don't take all night long."

"Well, White Castles it is," John said. "How many?"

"Please, John," Geraldine said. "We have four adults here. Maybe Brody, if he shows up. So do some calculating. It shouldn't be difficult. And don't forget fries and drinks."

"Yes, ma'am," John said, cocking his head. "No desserts?"

Geraldine grabbed the side lever and pulled the recliner to an upright position with a thump. "John, please go. We can talk about it later."

"I'm going to feed Whiskers before I leave, if that's okay."

"Wendell can handle that. I hope. Just get us something to eat."

"I guess I can change my clothes after I get back."

Two

John remembered his cell phone needed to be recharged and went to the bedroom. A squeal filled the room as he opened the door. Libby stood in front of the dresser mirror, fastening the rear clasp of her bra, and suspended for a moment by the innocent intrusion. The only other coverup was a pink bikini panty revealing the top crack of her flat butt.

"Oops!" John raised his shoulders and shut the door. He turned as Wendell approached, brown eyes bulging with curiosity over the sudden commotion.

"What in the world's going on?" Wendell asked, twisting his head to look past John. "Libby, are you all right?"

"I accidentally walked in on her while she was getting dressed," John said, lowering his eyes in embarrassment. "I forgot you guys were using it."

Libby peeked through a two-inch opening of the door, her eyes vertical from turning her head sideways. "I'm okay, Wendell," she murmured.

"I apologize," John said, standing to the side and out of Libby's sight. "I was going to recharge my phone."

"I'll be out in a few minutes," she said.

"Would you mind plugging the phone to the cord?" John said, facing Wendell. "It's on my nightstand, the right side of the bed."

"Sure. No problem."

John handed Wendell the phone as he stepped to the doorway and slipped the phone through the crack in the door. Libby took it and closed the door. Wendell stood still as if waiting for a command from someone on what to do next.

"I guess I better be going," John said.

John dashed to the kitchen and picked up the landline phone on the wall between the bar and the counter. He dialed Sally's phone, but no answer. He left a voice message but didn't mention Wendell and Libby, believing Sally already had enough on her mind without having to fret about unexpected company.

"You still here?" Geraldine sauntered into the kitchen, pecking the floor with her cane like a harried hen.

"Getting ready to leave," John said as he hung up. "Just made a call to Sally."

Geraldine sat at the counter. "You couldn't have called her from the airport, after you got back?"

"My phone was dead."

"Everything seems dead around here."

Whiskers ran to John, placing a paw on his pants leg, a gesture he needed to go outside and relieve himself.

"Okay, little buddy," John said, bending and patting the top of the pup's head. "Let's go do our business."

Geraldine took a deep breath.

"What's the matter?" John asked.

"Are we ever going to eat? I told you an hour ago I was hungry."

"It's only been fifteen minutes."

"Well, it seems like an hour."

"I need to take Whiskers out. It'll only take a minute or so," John said.

"And what was all the ruckus upstairs?" She tapped her fingers on the counter.

"Ruckus?" John pinched his nose. "Oh, I was just saying 'hi' to Libby."

"If you say so." She took another deep breath.

"Anything else?"

"I thought Wendell was going to let your mutt out?"

"He needed to give Libby a hand with something."

"Oh?"

"This'll only take a minute or two. I'll be right back."

Geraldine grimaced, shaking her head. "You always say it won't take long and it takes forever."

"I think you're exaggerating, Geraldine. But I'll do my best to get back as soon as I can."

John flashed a smile and hurried out the front door with Whiskers, who darted to his favorite dumping grounds at the side of the house. He stood on the porch as Whiskers took his time, behaving as if it had been a while since he was outside for an extended amount of time.

When John returned to the kitchen, Wendell and Libby were seated at the counter with Geraldine. Wendell's head rested on his long, thin hands while Libby's arms were crossed under her ample bosom as if she were giving them more support. Libby didn't make eye contact. Geraldine sat tight-lipped as if she were about to explode.

John refreshed Whiskers' water bowl and refilled the food dish, sensing their eyes following his every move.

"I'm leaving now," John said. "Anything else you folks need while I'm out?"

Wendell and Libby looked at each other, shrugged, then at Geraldine.

"Don't get lost on the way," Geraldine said.

Wendell slid off the stool and stood next to John. "I'll think I'll go with him."

"No doubt it takes two men to do what one woman could do," Geraldine said. "Just hurry up." Libby giggled, prompting a dismissive smirk from Geraldine.

"Don't get lost," Geraldine said as they left the house.

Wendell followed John to the car, getting into the passenger side and fastening the seat belt before John had got in the vehicle.

"Let's get out of here," Wendell said, looking straight ahead as John pulled the seat belt strap over his shoulder. "Mama's been on the warpath."

John let out a feeble cough. "Oh really?"

"She's been this way the past few days. You'd think she'd be happy to see us."

"You'd think."

"I hope you don't mind the intrusion."

"Not a problem," John said, smiling, as he tapped the accelerator and pulled into the street. "Family's always welcome."

"Maybe Mama will settle down since you're here."

"We'll see."

"She always liked you."

"Really?"

"She likes the way you take care of Sally. I think that's the big reason."

"That's understandable. We all want the best for our children, regardless of age."

"She's never cared much for Libby."

"Why do you say that?" John asked.

"She thought I could do better."

"Really?"

"Yes, really, John," Wendell said with perturbed expression.

"I always thought you and Libby were a good match."

"I'm not sure if that's a compliment or not, John."

"Believe me. It's a compliment. And furthermore, I've never heard Geraldine speak ill of Libby."

"I'm not sure you're being totally honest with me, but that's okay. She has to me."

"And?"

"She thinks Libby bosses me around. She also believes Libby gets carried away with religion. To be honest, they've never hit it off. Libby's not crazy about Mama either, so it works both ways."

"You might be right. I've read there is always a degree of tension between in-laws and couples. But I think it's exaggerated with all the mother-in-law jokes and so forth. Like I said, I get along fine with Geraldine. We have our differences, but so what? We're different people. I have differences with most everyone I know but I try not to let it cloud my overall opinion of them. I just try to accept people for who they are."

"I try to do the same, but it's not always easy."

"Do you get along with Libby's parents?"

"They're long gone now, so I get along with them great." Wendell's head jerked back as he let out a laugh.

"Okay, did you get along with them?"

"For the most part, I think. We didn't see much of them, especially her dad. He was the type who wouldn't come around unless he had an invitation. And her mom seldom did anything without him, so we didn't see a lot of her either. But overall, I guess I'd say they were good people, if a bit strange. You know what I'm saying?"

John shrugged. "I suppose so."

"You didn't think my dad was strange?"

"He was different in a few ways, but I thought I got along with him just fine."

"He thought you were odd."

"Huh?"

"I'm not saying he didn't like you...he thought you seemed a bit aloof."

"I always tried to treat him with respect. Maybe I came across aloof because I'm basically a reserved person. I'm more of a listener and observer."

"I guess the old man just misread you."

"He's probably not the only person to do that."

"I probably shouldn't have said anything."

"Don't worry about it. I find it interesting to learn those things."

"There's more I can tell you."

"That's okay. I have good thoughts about Harry so let's leave it there."

Wendell tapped John's shoulder. "Sure thing."

~ * ~

When they returned from White Castle, John's car Brody used while he and Sally had been away on vacation was in the driveway. Sally didn't trust Brody to use her SUV for fear he would take it to places unknown. John didn't notice any undue wear and tear on his vehicle other than needing a good washing. It wasn't something he expected Brody to do, since it wasn't *his* car.

John questioned if he had purchased enough hamburgers, since Brody had a voracious appetite, regardless of how the food was supposed to be parceled so everyone would get a fair share. Me first, then everyone else, was Brody's philosophy.

Geraldine, Libby, and Brody were seated at the dining room table, glasses filled with ice cubes and paper plates placed in front of them and their faces like eager children waiting for a special treat. There were even places set for John and Wendell.

"Hi, Dad," Brody said with a wide-eyed smile. "I'm starving."

"Good to see you as well, son," John said, angling his head.

"Oh yeah. Welcome back."

"Thanks."

Wendell set two sacks of burgers and fries in the middle of the table while John went to the kitchen.

"It sure took you long enough," Geraldine said as Brody tore into the sack. "I hope they're not cold and you bought enough."

"I'm not hungry," John said.

"Did you buy any soft drinks?" she asked, her brows raised.

"Er, no. We don't have any in the fridge?"

"I wouldn't have asked you if you purchased any if we already had some. Don't you think our glasses would already have soft drinks in them?"

"I wish someone had said something. I haven't been here in several weeks, so how was I supposed to know?"

"You could have asked."

"Mama, please," Wendell said with a frown. "John hasn't been home long."

"Wendell, sit down and eat," Geraldine said, pointing to an empty chair.

John had bought a dozen burgers and six orders of fries. Brody had already taken six burgers and a container of fries. Libby grabbed three burgers, leaving three on the table.

Wendell looked at Geraldine. "Go ahead, Mama. I'm not very hungry."

Geraldine took two hamburgers and fries. Before Wendell could take the remaining burger, Brody snatched it. Wendell took a box of fries.

"I didn't think you were hungry, Uncle Wendell," Brody said between munches on his burger. "You gotta be fast around here."

"Apparently," Wendell said as he dipped a fry into ketchup and nibbled on it like a rabbit.

"Brody, watch your manners," John said, his voice rising. "You know better."

"That's okay, John," Wendell said. "I'm not hungry either."

Brody placed the hamburger back on the table. Wendell, glancing first at John, reluctantly put it on his plate.

"Apparently I didn't buy enough," John said, raising his shoulders.

"You think?" Geraldine said.

John opened the door to the garage and picked up a two-liter bottle of Pepsi next to the steps. He carried it to the dining room, holding it high as if it were an expensive French wine for everyone to see.

"Pepsi anyone?" he asked, flicking his brows.

"Where did you find that?" Geraldine craned her neck.

"I remembered Sally always keeps a few inside the garage."

"I wish you had remembered before we started eating. We're about finished now."

"Better late than never."

"For you, perhaps, since you're not eating." Geraldine pursed her lips for a second. "But go ahead and pour me about a half a glass. It might help wash down everything."

John walked around the table, pouring soda in their glasses.

"Hey, Dad," Brody said. "We've got a new neighbor. Some bitch moved into Georgina's house."

"Brody!" Geraldine glared wide-eyed at him. "Watch your tongue!"

"Sorry, Grandma."

"You need to think before you say things like that. Wendell and Libby are fine Christians and they don't want to hear vulgar language either." Libby sat back in her chair with a righteous glow on her round face.

"Sorry, Aunt Libby," Brody said. "You too, Uncle Wendell. But anyways, she was something else."

"What do you mean, Brody?" John sat at the table. "How do you know her?"

"I was walking Whiskers a few days ago and he took a dump in her yard. The next thing I know she comes running out the front door and giving me all kinds of shit." He glanced at Geraldine with cagey eyes. "Sorry, Grandma."

"You should have had a doggy bag with you," John said. "I can't say I don't blame the neighbor for being upset. I always carry one in case Whiskers does that."

"Now you tell me." Brody raised his hands.

"I've told you in the past."

"Really? I guess I forgot."

"Does she have a family?" John asked.

"I'm not sure. She's kind of dumpy looking. Hair down to her waist and dressed old-fashioned. Real religious like. You know, sorta like the Amish."

Libby turned her head toward Brody with narrowed eyes.

"Well, Aunt Libby, that's what she looks like. I didn't mean to hurt your feelings."

"Do I look like her?" Libby stretched out her arms and looked from hand to hand while thrusting out her bosom. "Christians can be fashionable as long as they are modest."

"Let's move on," John said. "What's her name?"

"Cathy Gibson," Brody said.

"How did you find out?"

"Bert told me."

"Figures." John laughed. "He's probably recruiting her for Neighborhood Watch."

"I don't know about that. He said she was kinda nasty to him, too. She told him she didn't want any solicitors and wouldn't let him explain he was just welcoming her to the neighborhood."

"Poor Bert." John said, then looked at Wendell. "He's our unofficial neighborhood greeter."

"So Mom didn't want to come home?" Brody asked. "Is she pissed about something?"

"No, she just wanted to stay a bit longer with Chloe and Whitney." John smiled at Wendell and Libby. "I'm sure she would have returned with me if she knew who was here."

"It was supposed to be a surprise," Brody said.

John grinned. "Well, it sure surprised me."

"Me, too," Geraldine said.

"We sure didn't want it to be a big deal about coming here," Wendell said. "We thought Sally would be home."

"So it was a surprise for us when she wasn't around," Libby said. "Uh, you too, John."

"I'm glad you're here," John said. "And I'm sure Sally will feel the same way when I tell her."

"You've haven't told her?" Geraldine asked, raising a brow. "You didn't say anything about it when you talked to her?"

"Er, I didn't talk to her. I left a voice message I was here," John said, feeling his face get warm. "And besides, I had to get you folks something to eat."

"If you say so," Geraldine said, shaking her head. "Men!"

~ * ~

Geraldine was the first person up from the table, padding to the den and sitting in the recliner she had claimed during John's absence in Europe. Wendell and Libby followed like sheep, sitting on the couch. Geraldine also controlled the remote, so they waited to see what they'd be watching on TV. Brody retreated to his bedroom, leaving John to clear the table and tidy the kitchen.

The phone rang, and John grabbed it on second ring, anticipating it to be Sally returning his call. His big smile evaporated.

"Just checking up on you, old buddy," came the familiar voice on the line John recognized as Frank Finsterwald, his obnoxious friendly nemesis during the trip to Budapest. John palmed his forehead and closed his eyes. *Why me, Lord?*

"What a surprise," John said, trying to sound uplifting but falling a little flat.

"Dorothy and I were thinking about you guys today and she said I should call and see if you made it back home all right."

"I'm here." John sighed. "I returned early this afternoon. A little tired, but in one piece. I think I'll survive."

"How's the pretty little lady?"

"She's still in New York with our daughter and granddaughter. She wanted to spend a few more days with them before coming back."

"That'll give you some time to have a little fun on your own. Eh?"

"I'm here with my son, mother-in-law, and brother-in-law and his wife." John realized it sounded like he was making an excuse for staying at home.

"Doesn't sound like much fun, if you know what I mean." Frank let out a boisterous laugh, forcing John to move the phone about a foot from his ear.

"When you called, I was thinking it might be Sally," John said with a light chuckle, hoping Frank could take a hint.

"Sorry to disappoint you, old buddy." Frank belted out another laugh. "You got handsome old Frank instead."

"I was getting ready to take the dog out for a walk as well."

"Hold on a sec," Frank said.

A moment later, Dorothy was on the phone.

"Hi, John!" she gushed. "I just wanted to make sure you guys are back home all safe and sound. We miss you. We really do. We had such a wonderful time in Budapest."

"Sally's still in New York with our daughter and granddaughter."

"Oh, really? I should make a trip across the river to visit her. We could have so much fun."

John cleared his throat. "You might want to wait on that. She's busy with a lot of activities and doesn't see them often. I'm sure you understand."

"Maybe we could have a girls' day out. I could ask my daughters and see if they'd want to join us. It'd be fun. Mothers and daughters."

"Why don't you put it on hold? But I'll pass it on to Sally."

"No need to do that, John. I have Sally's phone number. Remember? I'll call her in a few days and see what she thinks." She giggled. "I'm getting excited just thinking about it."

John realized he wasn't going to talk Dorothy out of doing anything she wanted to do. At least it might give him time to warn Sally about any unwanted calls. "Give her a few days. Like I said, they're really busy now. They have a lot of catching up to do. And you know how precious granddaughters are."

"I'll do that," Dorothy said. "But not for long. Oh, well, I guess we should be getting off here now. It's so nice to hear your voice and know everything's okay. You guys are the greatest."

"It's mutual." John looked at the clock on the wall and tapped his foot several times on the floor. "Thanks for calling, Dorothy."

"Oh, by the way," Dorothy said. "We've been looking at the calendar about possible dates to reconnect with you guys."

John closed his eyes. "Really?"

"I'll send Sally a text or discuss it with her in a few days."

John placed his hand over his mouth and sighed. "That'll work."

"Bye John," she said. "Love you guys."

"Take care." John placed the phone back on the receiver in case Frank came back on, then sat at the counter, cradling his head in his hands.

"What's up, Dad? You look a little frazzled."

"A long story. I'll tell you about it later."

"No problem."

John noticed Brody had his laptop tucked under his arm. "Checking on jobs? Sending out resumes?"

"You know it," Brody said with a soft laugh.

Rather than question Brody about employment prospects, or the probable lack thereof, John picked up Whiskers and carried him to the front door. "Let's go for a walk before it gets dark, little buddy."

"Don't forget to take a poop bag," Brody said from the kitchen. "You might get hollered at if you don't."

"Thanks for the reminder, but it's something I always do," John said as he hooked a leash to the dog's collar. He stuffed a plastic bag in his back pocket.

The fading sunlight glinted through the leafy oak and maple trees as John and Whiskers headed toward Shipley Memorial Park, their usual destination since he had rescued the pup the previous year. John glanced at his new neighbor's house, noticing a two-foot tall white plaque in a flower bed near the front porch. He couldn't make out the words as Whiskers jerked him along as if in a hurry to get to his next marker.

By the time they reached the park, streetlights flickered and traffic increased as folks were returning home from work, school, and other activities. Whiskers relieved himself next to a trash receptacle as they turned around to go back to the crowded house.

As they walked in front of Cathy Gibson's home, she stepped out on the porch and smiled, hands positioned on her ample hips. John glanced at the tall rectangular plaque, realizing the Ten Commandments were inscribed on the tablet-shaped sign.

"Evenin'," John said with a small smile as Whiskers halted on the sidewalk, poking his nose in the lawn.

"Evenin' to you, sir," she said, her squinty eyes peering at Whiskers through wireless granny glasses. "Another blessed day."

John held his breath for a moment as to what Whiskers might be planning, then gave him a slight tug, and they continued walking down the street.

When they reached the street corner to turn around, Bert sauntered from the side of his house, wearing bib overalls and pushing a wheelbarrow of soil with a small shovel lying across in the middle.

"Howdy stranger," Bert said, a finger tucked under a shoulder strap as if he were an actual farmer. "Glad to be back after your world travels?"

"You've got it right," John said. "A little travel-logged, if you know what I mean."

"Never been to Europe, but I get the idea. How's Sally? Haven't seen her around today."

"She's with Chloe and granddaughter Whitney for a few weeks."

"Nothing serious, I hope." Bert lifted a foot on the side of the wheelbarrow. "That's a long time to be away." John almost expected him to chew on a wad of tobacco.

"Giving her a hand with a few things. We don't see her often as we'd like."

"If you say so."

"Anything up with you and Wilma?" John asked.

"Same ol, same ol. You know us. Nothing much ever changes except the seasons, and the fact we're growing older by the day." Bert laughed.

"I see you're getting your lawn in shape."

"Yeah, it's my passion. It's a never-ending job, but I love it. I love to work my hands in the earth. It's almost a spiritual thing with me."

"You've got the best lawn in the neighborhood."

Bert blushed. "Aw shucks, John."

"You know you do."

"I try," Bert said, raising his shoulders up and down. "Maybe set an example for the rest of the folks."

"Speaking of being spiritual, I see we've got a new neighbor."

"I met her the other day. Believe it's Cathy Gibson. Seems like good people, but kind of a religious zealot, if you know what I mean."

"I suppose so."

"Gave me some religious pamphlets. I haven't had time to read them. Even helped her set a Ten Commandments sign in her yard."

"I saw that."

Bert raised a finger and grinned. "And I talked to her some about Neighborhood Watch. She seemed interested."

"Brody told me she gave you a hard time."

"Nah, not really. She just thought I was some kind of salesman at first. You know people can react that way when someone knocks on their door. But she seemed interested. So we kinda traded materials."

"That's good to hear. You can't have too many people involved in Neighborhood Watch."

"I hope you show more interest now you're back home. And don't forget you're the person who got it started here."

"I couldn't have done it without you."

Bert nodded, stern-faced. "Probably so."

"Once things settle down a bit more, I'll get more involved. I still have mother-in-law at the house."

"I thought I saw a couple there the other day."

"Oh, I forgot, brother- and sister-in-law, visiting from Alabama."

"Going to be staying very long?"

"I really don't know. As long as they want to, I guess."

Wilma, Bert's wife, flicked the front-porch lights on and off three times.

"Dinner time." Bert grabbed the handles of the wheelbarrow and began turning it around and pushing it up the driveway. "Can't keep the little lady waiting."

"Have a nice evening." John hoisted Whiskers into his arms and carried him back to the house.

~ * ~

John stepped inside and unleashed Whiskers, who dashed to the water bowl. Brody was stretched out on the living room couch reading the newspaper, head bolstered on a throw pillow, feet crossed on the armrest. "Mom called while you were out. She said everything's okay but if you want to call, she'd be up a few more hours."

"I'll give her a call after I feed Whiskers," John said. "Anything else going on?"

Brody rose from the couch and stuffed his hands in the front pockets of his jeans. "I'm going over to the rehab center for a meeting in a few minutes. It's more of a social thing where we drink coffee and eat snacks and talk. It lasts about an hour or so."

"Maybe we can talk when you get back."

"About what?" Brody's forehead puckered.

"Your rehab, son," John said. "I'd like an update. But we can do it tomorrow."

"Oh." Brody raised his brows. "Tomorrow is probably best. I may go over to Ashley's place after the meeting."

"Ashley?"

"She's a gal from the rehab center. We've gotten to know each other the past few weeks."

"I see." John studied Brody's face for a moment. "It seems like you mentioned someone while we were in Budapest. Just get back at a decent hour."

"No problem," Brody said as he put on a windbreaker. He turned at the door. "See you later. Can I have the keys for the SUV?"

"Reminds me of a Harry Chapin song."

"Who's that?"

"Never mind," John said as he tossed the keys to Brody.

John peeked into the den and saw Geraldine, Wendell, and Libby watching *Jeopardy!* on television. He tip-toed the remainder of the way to the kitchen, greeted by Whiskers' pitter-patter on the hardwood floor.

"I need to trim your nails, little buddy," John said. "You could probably use a grooming, too."

Whiskers stared at him for a moment, then proceeded with him to the large bag of kibble under the sink.

After pouring food into the dog's dish, John noticed Brody had left his laptop open on the counter. John tapped the enter key and the screen came to life, showing an employment site. John smiled to himself, glad to see his son was finally trying to find a job. But then he discovered the posted positions were in Chicago, where he formerly worked before his opioid addiction.

"Damn," John muttered.

John was stirred from his thoughts when he heard the tinny taps of Geraldine's cane coming up behind him. He closed the laptop and turned around and smiled.

"Did Brody tell you Sally called?" Geraldine stood next to him, a hand on the counter.

"He told me when I got back."

"Have you called her?"

"I will in a minute. I had to feed Whiskers."

She pressed her lips together. "I think you like your mutt more than anybody in the family."

John shook his head. "Now, Geraldine, you know better than that."

"Well, are you going to call her?"

"Brody said she'd be up for a few hours, so there's no hurry."

"Men!" She took a deep breath.

"Ya'll need anything before I call? Getting hungry?"

"We can wait. I don't think anyone's going to starve. Did you notice Libby's belly?"

John gazed at Geraldine for a moment, his thoughts back to the accidental intrusion on Libby in the bedroom. "My phone should be recharged. I'll go to the bedroom and give Sally a call."

"Why don't you use the phone on the wall?"

"More privacy on my cellphone."

"You got some secrets?"

"Please, Geraldine. You know what I mean."

"Well, let her know I asked about her," Geraldine said. "And Chloe and Whitney."

"And Sam?"

"Go make your call," Geraldine said as she shuffled back to the den.

"Did someone mention my name?" John heard Libby ask as he watched Geraldine sit back in the recliner.

"Why would anyone do that?" Geraldine said. Libby puckered up while Wendell patted her knee.

John sighed before going to the bedroom. Sally answered on the first ring. John heard the television in the background.

"How's everything, sweetheart?" he asked, sitting on the side of the unmade bed.

"It's been a relatively quiet day," Sally said, sounding relaxed. "Chloe seems to be feeling better. Sam took Whitney to school and I picked her up this afternoon. It's nice here. Lovely day. How about there?"

John chuckled. "We have visitors."

"We don't have mice, do we?"

"What?"

"You know I don't like mice in the house."

"Dear, we don't have mice."

"Then who is it?"

"Wendell and Libby."

"You've got to be kidding me. When did they arrive?"

"A few days ago. Remember when we thought things were a bit odd when we called Brody while in Budapest? I believe that's when they showed up. I'll try to find out more."

"If I'd known, I may have come back with you for a few days. I hope they understand why I'm not there."

"I think it was supposed to be a surprise. You can imagine my surprise when I got home."

"Tell them 'hi' for me. How's Mother?"

"About the same."

Sally let out a small laugh. "Lucky you."

"Tell me about it. Oh, she said to tell you she asked about you and everyone."

"Even Sam?"

"Let's not get carried away. You know better than that."

"Be sure and tell her I miss her and love her."

"I guess Brody's the same, for better or for worse. I'm not sure yet. He does have a lady friend now."

"I talked to him for a few minutes," Sally said. "He sounded upbeat but didn't mention a girlfriend. I kinda recall him telling us about a girl he met at the rehab center."

"I think he said her name is Ashley. I'll keep you posted on how everything goes."

"I really wish I could be there," Sally said, a shade of sadness in her voice. "I must admit I'm a little homesick. I miss my bed."

"I do too," John said.

"What do you mean?"

"Wendell and Libby are using our love nest."

"Where are you going to sleep?"

"Den? Living room? A tent in the backyard? I haven't decided yet."

"Poor baby. Anything else I should know?'

"I almost forgot. I talked to your new best friends this afternoon."

"Don't tell me. Frank and Dorothy?"

"You guessed right."

"My goodness."

"One more thing?"

"What's that?"

"Dorothy plans to call you and perhaps pay a visit."

"You can't be serious."

"Just alerting you so you may want to think twice before answering your phone."

"Maybe if I tell her why I'm here and don't want to be disturbed."

"That's your call, if you think that'll work. But I wouldn't count on it. Those Finsterwalds are one of a kind."

Sally sighed. "I'll give it some more thought."

"I need to go check on our guests. You let me know if there's anything you need."

"I could use you, but it can wait."

"Give Chloe and Whitney a few hugs for me and a hug for Sam, too."

"I will," she said softly. "I love you."

"Love you, too."

~ * ~

John glanced several times at his cell phone as he sat in the den with Geraldine, Wendell, and Libby. He struggled to keep his eyes open while a reality show squawked on the TV.

"Expecting a call?" Geraldine asked, her eyes drowsy as she tilted her head toward him. "You keep looking at your phone."

"Just looking at the time."

"You know a watched kettle never boils. That's what my dear sweet mother told me when I was a child."

"I heard the expression from old folks." John stifled a yawn. "There's probably some truth to it."

Wendell and Libby held hands on the couch, their vacant faces focused on the television like robots. Whiskers lay at John's feet, letting out an occasional snort that didn't help John's sleepless state of mind.

"Why don't you go on to bed?" Geraldine said. "You haven't been much company."

"I had things to do," John said. "Plus, I want to talk to Brody when he gets home."

"Good luck with that. He comes in at all hours of the night. Sometimes I wonder if he even comes in at all since he met that little Mexican gal."

"Mexican?"

"Her last name is Garcia. It sure sounds Mexican to me." Geraldine pushed out her lower lip. "I wonder if she's one of those illegals?"

"Who knows? It could be Hispanic heritage," John said.

"You never know. I saw a lot of them back in Arizona."

"We had a few in 'Bama," Wendell said. "Most worked on farms. They kind of stayed to themselves."

"Maybe because they spent most of the day in the hot sun and rested at night," John said.

"They're taking jobs and spreading drugs," Libby said, her head bobbing. "America ain't as safe as it once was."

"They do some hard jobs in Kentucky a lot of people don't want to do, such as working in tobacco fields, landscaping, and putting on roofs. I'm thankful they're here."

"I've heard some bad things."

"You need to be careful what you watch on TV," John said.

"I beg your pardon, John," Geraldine said. "I'll watch what I want to. I don't tell you what to watch." Wendell and Libby nodded in agreement.

"Okay, okay," John said, palming his hands in the air. "So has Brody's girlfriend been here?"

"Not to my knowledge, unless Brody snuck her to his bedroom after I went to bed."

"I doubt if he'd do that." John looked at his house guests, who had returned to their robotic states.

"Wake up, John. After what he did in Chicago and under your nose during the holidays?"

John rubbed his right temple, not wanting to think about Brody's opioid problems or anything else. "Please, Geraldine. It's too late to have this discussion. And furthermore, he does live here and he's not a child."

"So you're saying it's all right for him to bring girls here overnight?"

John pressed his lips together for a couple of seconds, then let out a breath. "I'm not saying that."

"Sounds like it to me."

John let out a deep breath and pushed himself up from the couch. "Good night, everybody. I hate to leave good company, but it's late and I'm going to bed." He forced a weary smile.

"Be that way," Geraldine said.

"I'm not going to argue with you, Geraldine. It's been a long day and it's too late and I'm tired. So please forgive me."

"You're forgiven." Her spry smile came and went like a flicker from a lightning bug.

Wendell stared at Libby for a few seconds and they rose from the couch in unison. Wendell stretched out his arms and let out an inflated yawn. "I think we're going to bed, too."

"So everyone's abandoning me." Geraldine gripped the armrests.

"Mama, we're tired too," Wendell said meekly. "We're all tired."

"Well, I'm not tired." Geraldine clenched her jaw and sat up straight in the recliner. "I'm going to stay up and finish this show."

Wendell moseyed over to Geraldine and kissed her bony cheek while Libby stood a couple feet away, a faint smile on her round face. They nodded at John as they departed for a good night's sleep in *his* bed.

John proceeded to the closet in the hallway, pulling out a sheet and blanket from the linen shelf, and headed to the couch in the living room. Whiskers leaped to the end of the makeshift bed after John spread the covers.

"I know you're sleepy too, little buddy."

Several minutes after turning off the lamp on the end table, John heard the clickety sound of Geraldine's cane. Instead to going to her bedroom, she went to the kitchen. John lay still, taking shallow breaths, trying to determine what she was doing.

Geraldine shuffled back to the den five minutes later. John heard her changing channels on the television. He tried to ignore the sounds, longing to fall into a deep sleep. But every sound in the house seemed to be magnified. He wished he had the throwaway earplugs from the plane to block everything out. At least Whiskers seemed snug and relaxed, even letting out a few extended snorts.

When quietude finally arrived, the doorknob turned, bringing Whiskers to his feet with low growls. A light flicked on, causing John to pull the covers over his head.

"Hey, Dad," Brody said. "What are you doing?"

John groaned. "What does it look like?"

"Looks like someone is still up in the den since a light is on. Must be Grandma."

"Why don't you check it out," John said, pulling the blanket up to his neck while Whiskers curled by his feet. "I'm sure she'd like the company."

"Didn't you want to talk tonight?"

"Son, it has to be almost midnight."

"Actually, it's about two."

"We can talk in the morning."

"Sure, Dad. I'll see you then." Brody took a couple steps toward the den.

"Uh, Brody."

"What?"

"Turn out the light."

Three

A soft glow shimmered through the drawn beige curtains the next morning. John turned over to face the cushiony back of the couch, pulling the covers over his head. He gave up after a few minutes when Whiskers tapped gently on his shoulder several times, his way of informing John it was time to go outside and take care of some urgent doggy business.

John swung his legs over to the floor, rubbed his sensitive eyes for a few seconds, then walked over to the easy chair and put on his wrinkled pants. He pressed his hands against his lower back, swayed back and forth a few times, and groaned before opening the front door. Whiskers sprinted to the side of the house to relieve himself; John felt like taking a leak but had to wait his turn.

John sauntered barefoot across the damp lawn and fetched the newspaper, glancing at the headlines while waiting for Whiskers to finish doing his thing. He meandered over to his car Brody had been using for nearly two weeks, saw it was locked and peeked inside. He was comforted to see nothing out of the ordinary, recalling the occasion before Christmas when he discovered a packet of heroin Brody had inadvertently dropped on the floor of the car.

John returned to the house, making a detour to the bathroom before refilling Whiskers' food and water bowls. He prepared a carafe of coffee and sat at the counter with the newspaper. He turned first to the obituary pages, a habit he always dreaded because of the sad news it had the likelihood of delivering, especially as he was growing older with the passing of friends, acquaintances, familiar names, and even a few foes. It was a daily reminder of the uncertainty of life.

This morning was no exception as he looked at the face of a longtime coach in the region, someone he had known during the early years of being a sportswriter. He slowly moved his head back and forth while reading the tribute listing the woman's list of accomplishments in basketball and golf, as a player and coach. He felt a sense of sadness wash over him because she didn't leave an immediate family and died at a nursing home, perhaps neglected and alone. There would be no funeral, only a memorial service to be announced later. *Will it even happen*, he thought? *Or would she be forgotten in old age, outliving her contemporaries?* He made a mental note to call someone at the newspaper to see if there was a place to which he could donate money in her name. Then John grabbed a pen from the end of the counter and circled the notice because he knew he'd likely forget.

John perused the remainder of the ever-shrinking newspaper, then poured a mug of steaming coffee. He hoped the black brew would lift him out of the morning melancholy which had enveloped him much too often since he retired. He folded the newspaper, setting it aside for someone to read, and stared, unfocused, across the room. Obits seldom unsettled him, so he thought it was a combination of things—Sally being in New York, his daughter Chloe's ovarian cancer, the new houseguests, dealing with Brody and Geraldine again, and perhaps the new neighbors. It didn't feel comfortable being back in the neighborhood.

John went to the den, refreshed coffee in hand, to watch the early morning news. Whiskers was a step behind, his ever-present shadow. John was surprised to see the lamp on the end table was on. Then he saw Geraldine sprawled on the recliner, legs apart and arms slackened over the sides, head turned away from him. And silent.

He froze for a few seconds, unsure what to do. He stared at her small chest to see if there was any movement; he held his breath. He glanced at Whiskers, who let out a sharp bark.

John tried to shush the pooch, but it was too late.

Geraldine jolted from her sleep and pulled the recliner to an upright position. Her glazed eyes blinked several times.

"What time is it?" she asked.

"A little after six."

She grabbed her cane propped against the side of the chair and stood. "Why did you let me sleep here last night?"

"It wasn't my decision. I slept in the living room. You saw me go to bed. Remember?"

"Then who turned off the television?"

"It automatically shuts off after four hours. That's probably what happened."

"If you say so." Geraldine veered past John. "Any coffee left?"

"Almost a full pot."

"Can you fix me a cup? I need to go pee. I'm about to pop."

"Certainly." John turned and followed her out of the den, with Geraldine springing to the bathroom and him to the kitchen counter to pour the coffee. When she returned a few minutes later, John noticed she had brushed through her reddish hair and may have applied some rouge to her cheeks.

"Thank you." She sat on the stool and spooned creamer into her coffee.

"Sleep well last night?" John asked, immediately regretting his question.

"What do you think? Every bone in my body is sore. I wish someone had woke me up."

"If I had known, I would have. I guess Brody went straight to his bedroom instead of the den when he returned last night."

"Oh, he finally came home."

"About two o'clock."

Geraldine took a sip from her cup. "I sure didn't see much of him while you and Sally were away. Either at those meetings, seeing his girlfriend, or using your computer. At times I thought he might be avoiding me."

"I think he's trying to find a job."

"A job? I caught him one day looking at one of those dirty pornography, what do you call it?

"Website?"

"That's right. Filthy. He slammed the computer shut so hard I thought it might break."

"Really?'

"He surprises me all the time. He can be so sweet, then he just turns his back on me. I just don't understand him. And all I've done for him."

"We all have trouble understanding him from time to time."

"And why hasn't Sally called me? I am her mother, you know. Has she forgotten about me? I'm not going to be around forever."

"You know she's been busy with Chloe. We're all concerned about her. Cancer is scary. You know how you'd be if Sally had cancer."

Geraldine stirred her coffee for several seconds, lost in thought. She looked at John with heavy eyes. "You're right. She needs to be with Chloe. But it still wouldn't break her finger for her to call, if only to see how I'm doing."

"I'll call her later this morning and put you on with her."

"That'd be nice."

"How about some breakfast?" John asked, arching his brows. "I can go out and buy some pastries. I'm sure the others will be getting up soon."

"That'd be nice. Libby isn't much of a cook. I never understand why she didn't learn, because Wendell enjoys a good home-cooked meal. I always had home-cooked meals for him when he was growing up. But she never had an interest in it. Some women just don't want to please their husbands like they used to."

"Times change," John said. "They've been married a long time, so I think Libby's doing a lot of things right for him. They do have five children."

Geraldine covered her mouth with her scrawny hand and giggled. "That, too."

"Were you surprised when they showed up?"

"I didn't have a clue. It was out of the clear blue when they knocked on the door. I thought it might be some kind of salesperson and I almost didn't answer it. But your little mutt started barking like crazy so I finally did."

"I'm sure it's nice to have them visit you."

"Don't forget they're visiting you and Sally, too."

"I'm glad to see them. I just wished I'd been told by Brody. It was quite a surprise to see them when I got back."

"I don't know how long they're going to stay."

"Not a problem. They're family."

"Be careful what you say, John. You might regret it."

"At least I have you here to keep an eye on everybody and everything."

She winked. "Yes, you do."

~ * ~

John drove to the bakery and purchased an assortment of pastries. He considered getting a dozen, but after thinking about their appetite for pizza and White Castles, especially with Brody at home, he decided on two dozen. When he returned, Wendell and Libby were sitting at the bar with Geraldine, drinking coffee and chatting. They had paper plates and napkins in front of them, ready to devour the sugary overload. Brody was still in bed, and probably would be for another hour or so, giving everyone an opportunity to make their breakfast choices before he gobbled the goodies.

They ate and conversed, mainly about Geraldine's recovery from her fractured hip. It was pleasant, especially after the brief disagreement about illegal immigrants the previous evening.

Geraldine relished the conversation, since it revolved around her condition. John was about to add that Whiskers came to her rescue but thought against it because it might set off another quarrel.

"Mama, I'm so happy you're doing so well," Wendell said. "We were so worried we would lose you when we first found out about it. It just pained us being so far away."

"Then why didn't you come here sooner?" Geraldine asked. "It's not like I was going anywhere. And it's not like you live in Timbuktu."

"Things just came up and we couldn't get away."

"But we kept you in our thoughts and prayers, day and night," Libby said with a warm smile.

"I've heard it before," Geraldine said, shaking her head.

"I think it worked. God was watching over you."

"I'm glad someone was."

"Well, folks, I hate to leave good company but Whiskers and I need to take our morning walk," John said.

"The way you act around him, I wonder if he's part of the family," Geraldine said.

John flashed a wide grin. "He is."

John hooked the leash on Whiskers and headed out the door to Shipley Park, their usual destination when the weather was pleasant. The streets were relatively quiet since most neighbors had left for work and children had already walked or boarded buses to school. Whiskers dallied along, lifting his leg at familiar trees, fire hydrants, and lampposts, as John took in the fresh spring air of blossoming flowers and the shimmering sunshine through the mature trees. It was the one activity he missed when away. He figured Whiskers felt the same by the bounce in his stride.

When they reached the park, John sat on a bench near the large pond and unleashed Whiskers. Without fail, as he'd done many times, Whiskers darted toward the ducks and geese. The fowl squawked and flapped to safety on the still water, creating gentle ripples across the sparkling surface. Keeping an eye on his energized friend, John took his cell phone from the pocket of his light jacket and called Sally.

"How's everything in the Big Apple?" he asked.

"It's been interesting," she said. "Chloe seems a little stronger. She just walked out the door to take Whitney to school. Sam left a couple hours ago. So it's all quiet here. I'm just sitting on the couch, enjoying a cup of coffee, and watching a home-and-garden show on TV."

"I guess I caught you at a good time then. I'm at the park with Whiskers on this beautiful morning."

"I talked to Chloe last night and she told me why she and Sam had problems during the holidays."

"I hope it wasn't anything too serious."

"Sam had a one-night stand—with a man. She saw him a few more times but swore to Chloe they didn't go all the way. I guess she meant sex. I'm not sure what to think about that."

"So everything's going all right now?"

"Sam's been seeing a therapist. She's still confused about what she did."

"And Chloe?"

"She seems to have shrugged it off," Sally said. "She says she has more on her mind dealing with the cancer right now. But I'm not sure she'd be totally forthcoming about how she feels. You know how she keeps some things to herself. She'll probably tell me more as time goes by."

"I sure hope things work out for the best, for both of them."

"Chloe thinks Sam is trying to understand her behavior and will be with her through the cancer treatments," Sally said. "After that, it's wait and see."

"I guess that's all you can do."

"I'll keep you updated on how things go between them."

"I wonder if Chloe should see a therapist as well?"

"First things first. After the cancer treatments."

"You're right," John said.

"How's everything? Is Mother behaving herself?"

"She hasn't been too bad. You need to give her a call. She's upset you haven't checked on her."

"I know I should. I'll try to call her this afternoon. How's everyone else?"

"Brody is Brody. What else can I say? And Wendell and Libby have been keeping your mother company, for the most part. I still don't know exactly why they came to visit, especially since it all seems out of the blue. I sense there's more going on with them."

"Wasn't visiting Mother supposed to be a surprise?"

"But four months after your mother fell?"

"That's odd. But again, they're a bit odd."

John chuckled. "You said it, not me."

"Chloe just returned," Sally said. "I should be getting off here and do some things around the apartment."

"Give her a hug for me," John said. "I need to be heading back. I'll talk to you later. And don't forget to call your mom. I won't hear the end of it until you do."

John walked in front of Cathy Gibson's house on the way back. She sat on a rocking chair on the front porch, reading a black book John assumed was a Bible. He waved but didn't receive a response as her head was bent as she rocked back and forth like a metronome in slow motion.

When he stepped into the house, Geraldine was in her bedroom while Wendell and Libby were in the den, watching a barely audible western on television.

"Mama complained about not getting a good night's sleep, so she's taking a nap," Wendell whispered, a forefinger in front of his mouth for added emphasis. "We're trying to keep it quiet for a while."

"She slept on the recliner last night." John sat on the rocker. "She was a little stiff this morning."

"She didn't tell us that."

"Poor baby," Libby said, scrunching her brows. "No wonder she was a little cranky this morning."

"Wendell, I'm going to McDonald's a little later this morning to see some of my old buddies. We meet there several times a week. Care to go with me?"

"Sure," Wendell said. "It'll get me out of the house for a little bit."

"And leave me here by myself?" Libby said, pushing out her lower lip. "That's not fair."

"Mama will be here." Wendell patted her knee. "You can keep her company."

Libby grimaced for a moment, and after glancing at John, a slight smile emerged. "I'll look after her."

"We won't be gone long," John said. "I just want to let the guys know I'm back in town."

"Maybe I can go for a walk around the neighborhood," she said.

"You should," John said. "It's beautiful out there today. There's a park down the street if you go to the right."

"Is it safe?"

"It shouldn't be a problem. I see folks out there every day taking walks or sitting by the large pond. It's my favorite spot when I walk Whiskers."

"I may do the same."

"You might want to take Mama with you," Wendell said. "She could use some fresh air."

Libby glared at him. "I don't think so."

"Just a suggestion, sweetie."

"It might be difficult for her because of her hip," John said. "Her mobility is pretty good but that'd be quite a hike for her to the park."

"That's right, John," Libby said. "My thoughts exactly. We don't want to overdo it."

Wendell gave her a blank look.

"Is Brody still in bed?" John asked.

"We haven't seen him, so I guess he is," Wendell said.

"That's good." John looked at Libby. "He'll be here to look after Geraldine if you decide to go for a walk."

"You are so right," she said with a saccharine smile. "I certainly wouldn't want to leave her all by her lonesome."

~ * ~

Brody ambled barefoot into the kitchen, wearing baggy lounge pants, his long dark hair flowing in all directions. He plopped down at the bar, yawned, twisted his neck, and rolled his shoulders.

"Mornin' son," John said as he sorted through a sizable stack of mail which had accumulated while he was away on vacation. "Sleep well?"

"Yeah," he muttered. "Any coffee left?"

"Should be some in the pot. The light's on, so it should still be hot."

"Can I have a cup?"

"Sure, son. You know where the cups are, so help yourself. I believe there's a few pastries left as well if you're hungry." John pointed to the white rectangular box on the counter.

Brody eased off the stool, gave John a dismissive glance, sauntered to the counter and poured a cup of coffee. He picked up the box of pastries and carried it back to the bar. He gave John another glance, curling his upper lip, before opening the box.

"Where's everybody?" Brody asked before taking a large bite of a chocolate long john.

"Grandma's taking a nap and your uncle and aunt are getting dressed. We've all been up for several hours. What are your plans today?"

"Nothin' at the moment." Brody shrugged. "I'll probably give Ashley a call and see what she's up to later on."

"Any job prospects?"

Brody dropped the pastry on a napkin and slumped his shoulders. "Dad, I wish you'd quit harping on the job thing. I'll let you know when I find something. It's difficult to do much while in these fuckin' rehab classes. How many times do I have to tell you? That's not exactly a selling point to an employer. It's not something I can put on a résumé. Okay?"

"Believe me, I understand," John said. "But you need to be sending out your résumé to companies so you'll start getting some responses in the next three to six months, or however long it takes. I'm not expecting you to find something right off the bat. I've been involved in hiring people at the newspaper. I know it's not an overnight thing. And it would be good to look for places around here. Okay?"

Brody planted his elbows on the counter. "What's that supposed to mean?"

"I looked at the laptop yesterday and noticed the job searches in Chicago."

"You are spying on me?"

"C'mon Brody, you know better than that. Furthermore, that's my laptop you're using, so I have a right to see what's on it."

"Maybe I just need to use my smartphone then."

"Quit being childish. You know what I'm talking about."

"If I'm being childish, it's because that's the way you treat me. Ever since I came back, you and Mom haven't shown any trust in me."

"You know better than that," John said. "Didn't we leave you here with your grandmother while we were in Europe? And we haven't kept you on curfews or anything like that. You pretty much come and go as you please—on our dime. We've only asked you to let us know where you're at and when you'll be home. I don't think that's asking too much, considering what you've been through. Make that, what *we've* all been through. It's become a family thing. Wouldn't you agree?"

"Oh, whatever." Brody pushed back the stool, leaving a half-eaten apple Danish on his napkin. "I'm going to take a shower. And then I'll give you a damn detailed list of everything I'll be doing today."

"Let's not get carried away, Brody." John shook his head. "And try to show a little respect."

"It works both ways." Brody strutted out of the room, his hair flopping, without uttering another word. He charged past Wendell, standing at the doorway, as if he weren't there.

"Is everything okay, John?" Wendell said as he warily entered the kitchen.

"Nothing out of the ordinary," John said as he put the cover back on the pastries. "Sorry you had to witness his tantrum."

"Mama mentioned something about drugs."

"He's had a problem with opioids and other drugs. He's been in rehab for several months. I think he's getting things under control, then he starts going off the wall. I need to talk to the counselors and make sure he's following their protocol. There's always the fear about relapsing. It's frustrating for all of us."

"I wish there were something I could say or do to help him. I know it's not easy being a parent."

"Always a parent," John said. "I suppose it never ends."

"I hear ya."

"And then you're a grandparent," John said with a laugh.

"Mama says Chloe's a dyke."

John tilted his head. "She did?"

"She said it in passing. Kinda surprised Libby and me. We always thought your kids were so clean and perfect."

John's back stiffened. "I don't know of any perfect family. As for Chloe, we don't consider her sexual orientation as a problem. It's who she is."

Wendell raised his hands. "Please, John, no offense intended."

"No offense taken," John said.

"But it didn't surprise you? I know Libby and I would be shocked if we discovered it about our kids."

John shrugged slightly. "I suppose we were at first. We didn't have an inclination, or perhaps we were blind to what was going on. It doesn't make any difference. We have gay friends, worked with gays and so forth, so after some thought, it wasn't an issue. Like I said, it's who she is. We love her regardless."

Wendell rubbed his chin. "Interesting."

John placed the cups in the dishwasher. "About ready to head over to McDonald's?"

"Our kids called it Mickey D's."

"I'm old-fashioned. It'll always be McDonald's to me."

"Do we plan to eat again while there?"

"Only coffee, unless you want to order breakfast or whatever. Are you still hungry?"

"I was just wondering."

"Let me wipe off the bar and counter and we'll hit the road."

"Sure, just let me tell Libby." Wendell said. "It'll only take a few seconds."

Libby wore dark green leggings and a bright yellow blouse, looking like a dandelion in full bloom when she entered the kitchen.

"Wendell's brushing his teeth," she said. "He'll be down in a minute or so."

"Seconds to minutes."

"Huh?"

"Are you looking forward to your walk?" John asked. "You sure look springy."

"I think so," she said, looking at several framed family photos on the wall. "Do you think later I could go to one of your malls?"

"It shouldn't be a problem. Maybe you could get Brody to take you. I don't think he has too much on his agenda."

"I'll ask him after he gets dressed."

"Geraldine might be interested in going as well."

Libby puckered her brows "I'll think about it."

Wendell bounded down the steps with a wide-eyed smile. "Ready?"

"What are you so grinning about?" Libby asked.

"Nothing really. Just looking forward to going out and getting some fresh air. I'm ready whenever you are, John."

They heard Geraldine stirring in her bedroom, the tapping of her cane, and then the door creaking open.

John looked wide-eyed at Wendell. "It's time to go."

Libby, her lower lip protruding, gave them a dirty look. "Aren't you going to say 'goodbye' to Mama?"

John and Wendell stopped in their tracks midway to the front door, then turned and watched as Geraldine come down the steps.

"What's going on?" Geraldine asked.

"John and I are going to Mickey D's," Wendell said. "We won't be back soon. Right, John?"

Geraldine glanced at Libby, standing a few feet away with a pitiful expression like an abandoned child.

"That's nice," she said with a specious smile. "Take your time. Libby and I will find something to do. Right, Libby?"

"Yes, Mama," Libby said, going to the kitchen with her head lowered.

John and Wendell headed out the front door without saying another word.

~ * ~

John took a long route to the McDonald's, giving Wendell a mini-tour of Lexington as he drove through the University of Kentucky campus and the downtown area, pointing out several government buildings, Rupp Arena, and the state arboretum.

"It's certainly not the town I moved to back in the 1970s," John said as an oldies station played softly on the radio. "Back then, it was more of a sleepy college town surrounded by horse farms. While the city has grown, I must confess I preferred it back in my younger days."

"It's still an interesting city," Wendell said. "If Libby and I didn't prefer a warmer climate, it's a place we'd relocate to if we were a few years younger."

"Thinking more of Florida?"

"Not really. We have our Gulf Shores."

"That's certainly a nice area."

As they pulled into the McDonald's in Palomar Centre, there were more cars lined up at the drive-thru than in the parking lot. John spotted several of his buddies seated in their usual place at the rear of the dining area. He waved as he and Wendell went to the counter to order coffee.

"Welcome back, stranger," Curtis McKenzie said as John and Wendell sat at the table strewn with napkins, wrappers, cups, and food scraps.

John introduced Wendell to everyone and told them about what had transpired in the time he'd been in Budapest and New York. They provided updates on their lives, but from what John could gather, not much had happened, other than health issues or the passing of a few friends and colleagues. Some things never seemed to change much and was a primary reason John found comfort spending time with old friends.

The geriatric group tried to avoid political and religious topics because the guys wanted to keep everything light and friendly. But there always seemed to be something to draw them into a heated discussion, however innocent it would appear at first. Regardless, for John it was an informal group he at first was reluctant to join but now looked forward to as a place of friendly refuge even if he had heard some of the stories or jokes more than a few times.

"It was terrible about the school shooting down south a few weeks ago," John said. "When will it ever end?"

"Part of the social fabric since it's been going on for so long," Mel Snider said. "Lots of folks kinda shrug and go on like it's not a big deal anymore. From Columbine to Sandy Hook, and everything before, between and after. It's a damn shame."

"Makes me sick in my stomach, all those children dying for no good reason," Frank Lopez said, tightening his lips.

"Hey, they're sending those 'thoughts and prayers' to the victims' families," Curtis said with a chuckle.

"Yeah, you can see how that's done a lot of good," Frank said.

"I believe it provides comfort to the families." Wendell clasped his large coffee cup in both hands as if it were a chalice. "And I think it's a way to let them know people are thinking about them in times of grief."

John glanced at Wendell, surprised he'd spoken, since he used to be reticent about expressing views, especially in public.

"I understand what you're saying." Frank nodded with a gentle smile. "My point is more should be done after these kinds of horrendous incidents. Those thoughts and prayers may ease the pain temporarily, but some stringent gun control measures might keep those kinds of tragedies from happening in the future."

"I have to disagree," Wendell cocked his head. "I'm a staunch supporter of the Second Amendment and I don't think taking away guns is going to end the situation. People kill people, not guns."

A thick cloak of silence permeated the table as everyone in the group eyed each other. John knew it wouldn't last with this outspoken bunch of boomers.

"Are you fuckin' kiddin' me?" Curtis blurted, red-faced and with seething eyes. Customers at nearby tables turned and stared for a moment before returning to their meals, some shaking their heads at the outburst.

"Can we change the subject?" John asked in a conciliatory tone.

"Sorry if I offended anyone," Wendell said. "Only expressing my opinion."

"That's a hot topic," John said. "We generally stay away from those things."

Curtis sat tight-lipped, wrenching his hands on the table as if reining in his anger.

"So be it." Wendell took a sip of his coffee. "But God does work in mysterious ways."

"My apology. I shouldn't have brought it up."

"There's no need to apologize, John," Mel said. "And Wendell has every right to express his opinion."

Curtis let out a short breath. "I need to apologize. I didn't mean to lose my temper, Wendell. I'm sorry."

Wendell nodded with a nervous smile.

"How 'bout them Cats?" Frank said, a common expression of University of Kentucky sports fans, looking to break the tension. "Looks like a great football season coming up."

"That's what everyone says until Big Blue Madness," Curtis said, referring to the first practice unofficial start of basketball season. "Maybe it'll change this year."

"That's what they say every year," John said. "Some things never change for UK."

"It's all football where I'm from," Wendell said. "Roll Tide."

"Yup," Mel said a quick grin. "Now that's football country."

"Well guys, I hate to leave good company but I need to be going." Curtis pushed his large body up from the chair. "I've got a few errands to run for the wife. Those endearing honey-dos."

"I should be going as well," Mel said. "I've got a doctor's appointment in forty-five minutes."

"Nothing serious, I hope," John said.

"Old age crap," Mel said. "Drawing blood to check my triglyceride and cholesterol levels."

"You probably didn't help yourself by eating pancakes and sausage," Frank said.

"I'll give a sob story to my doctor and tell him I'll try to do better. It's been working for years."

"I'm sure your doc can see through your excuses," John said, laughing.

Mel shrugged with an impish grin. "I know, but it gives us something to talk about other than enlarged prostate, hearing loss, fading eyesight, and a limp dick."

Everyone burst out laughing.

"I believe I'll leave on that note," Curtis said.

"I've got to run as well," Frank said, glancing at his watch. "Need to have the car serviced."

They all smiled politely and nodded at John and Wendell, still seated, before walking out single file at the rear exit.

John and Wendell stared out the large windows as the others walked, or hobbled, across the parking lot to their vehicles. They stopped next to Curtis' Ford truck, all glancing back at John and Wendell for a moment before going to their vehicles.

"I don't believe your friends like me," Wendell said, his cheeks a pale red.

"Nah," John said with a shrug. "I should have warned you beforehand there are some subjects we don't discuss because of what happened. It was my fault. I wasn't thinking."

"They must be liberals."

"I beg your pardon?"

"You know, always making excuses or wanting to change things. Never satisfied with the way things are. And not very Christian-like, if you ask me."

John's legs bobbed under the table. "I don't know about that. They're good friends. Don't most folks want to make the world a better place?"

"Sure, but it's all in the Bible."

"What's in the Bible?"

"Oh, never mind, John. You wouldn't understand."

John closed his eyes for several seconds and took a deep breath. "You shouldn't say something and not explain yourself."

"Some other time," Wendell said as he rose from his seat.

"Are you about ready to head back? I bet Libby and Geraldine are wondering where we're at."

Wendell said. "It's been kinda nice being away from them for a while. But that's between you and me."

"Would you care to see anything else around town?"

"You're the host and I'm the guest, so you can choose. I don't want to take up all your time."

"You're not," John said. "It's been a while since we spent any time together."

"I don't remember ever doing it."

"You may be right," John said as he picked up trash on the table left by his buddies and placed it in the receptable by the rear exit. "Sometimes life gets in the way."

"So where to next?" Wendell said.

"Maybe drive over to Keeneland Race Course and by a few horse farms?"

"You're the driver."

They got into the car and drove to Keeneland, about five minutes away. John parked near the clubhouse and they entered the gates and strolled around the pristine grounds splashed in green, from trees to buildings to benches. They watched several thoroughbreds being washed down in the barn area.

After walking for fifteen minutes, they sat on one of the benches next to the homestretch rail in front of the clubhouse, observing a horse galloping on the track.

John turned toward Wendell and asked, "I'm curious as to why you visited."

Wendell drew his head back. "Huh? You want us to leave?"

"Of course not. You can stay for as long as you please. I was just surprised to see you and Libby when I returned from vacation."

"I called Mama to see how she was doing, and she went on and on about Brody leaving her all by her lonesome at the house with your dog. You know she's not exactly fond of Whippers."

"It's Whiskers," John said. "And she likes him more than she lets on."

"If you say so."

"So what about Geraldine?"

"Oh, anyways, Mama cried about sitting in the house all day with your mutt and told me how she missed her friends back in Arizona. It was pitiful. Even brought tears to my eyes. I told her I'd pray for her. So the next thing I knew, Libby announced, 'Let's go see Mama!' So we did and here we are."

"That's interesting, Wendell. I'm glad you were able to get away and help take care of her. As I said, you stay as long as you wish."

"It may not be too long."

"Why's that?"

"Mama asked if I would drive her back to Arizona. I told her I'd have to think about it, and I'd want to discuss it with you and Sally. It has to be a family decision. I want to pray on it, too."

"Absolutely."

"So when will Sally be coming home?"

"Honestly, I don't know. It could be several days or a few weeks. It depends on Chloe."

"She ain't got AIDS, does she? I heard Mama and Brody saying something about treatments."

"She's going through cancer treatments. She was diagnosed with ovarian cancer while we were in Europe. Sally wants to be with her while she recovers."

"That's understandable. I'll be praying for my sweet niece as well."

"That's thoughtful of you."

"We all need thoughts and prayers in times of sadness and distress."

~ * ~

Geraldine was sitting on the recliner in the den watching a soap opera when John and Wendell returned to the house. Everyone knew not to disturb her when she was engrossed in a favorite show on TV, especially *Days of Our Lives*. If Geraldine knew they were back, she didn't let on.

Wendell went to the bedroom and came back, sitting at the kitchen bar. Whiskers sniffed his shoes and John refreshed the dog's water bowl. Wendell flicked his foot at the dog to make him leave, which John caught in the corner of his eye.

John clapped his hands several times and Whiskers jumped to his open arms. He stroked the back of the dog's neck and gave him several hugs while glaring at Wendell, a silent reminder that no one should mess with his little buddy. And letting Whiskers know how he felt by giving him a peck on the top of his furry head.

"I wonder where Libby is?" Wendell asked. "I thought she'd be here. I checked the bedroom, thinking she might be reading or taking a nap."

"Wasn't she going to take a walk?" John said.

A look of concern washed over Wendell's face. "I hope she didn't get lost."

"It'd be kind of hard to get lost in this neighborhood. Does she carry a cell phone with her?"

"She has one, but she's not good about taking it with her."

"Give her a call anyway."

Wendell punched in the number, and a second later they could hear a distant gospel-music ringtone coming from the bedroom. "See?"

Seconds later, the clickety-click of Geraldine's cane grew louder, signaling she was approaching the kitchen. "Did you two finally decide to come back?"

"You were lost in another world," John said.

"Are you trying to be funny?"

John chuckled. "I gave Wendell a mini-tour of the city."

"That's more than you've ever done for me and I've been here five months."

"You've never asked."

Geraldine sat next to Wendell. "Why should I have to ask? You should know I don't like being cooped up in the house."

"I apologize," John said. "But don't forget you've been somewhat immobile while recovering from the hip fracture."

"It doesn't mean I couldn't sit in a car."

"I have taken you to the hospital and physical therapy."

"John, are you still trying to be funny?"

"We'll go for a drive in a few days. Okay?"

"Don't do it on account of me."

"Huh?"

"Mama, he's just offering to take you out," Wendell said.

Geraldine smacked Wendell's arm. "Oh, be quiet! No one jerked your chain."

Libby fluttered through the front door and entered the kitchen almost unnoticed except for Whiskers padding over and smelling her sandals. She whooshed him aside with a brush of her foot. "Shoo."

Wendell's eyes lit up when he saw her. "We were wondering where you were. Did you get lost, sweetheart?"

Libby walked to the bar carrying several pamphlets and eased on a stool next to John. "I went for a nice walk and met the most delightful person."

"Sounds like Bert," John said. "Or Wilma."

"Bert? Wilma? Who's Bert and Wilma?"

"Neighbors down the street. He usually talks to anyone in the neighborhood. A retired teacher. She's his wife. The children had him when they were in school. Good people."

"Well, it wasn't your friends Bert and Wilma. Her name is Cathy Gibson. She said she's only lived here a few weeks. I think she moved here a few days before we arrived."

"Sounds about right."

"Anyhoo, she was working on a charming flower garden in her front yard when I walked by and she complimented me on my outfit. We talked for a little bit and then she invited me into her house for iced tea. It was really sweet of her."

"She must have moved into the house where the old woman died," Gertrude said.

"Georgina's place," John said. "Georgina always had flowers, one of the prettiest lawns in the neighborhood. I miss her. Brody liked her, too."

"It's a shame you don't feel the same way about your own yard," Geraldine said.

"Maybe we could work on it together?" John winked at Geraldine.

"You're trying to be funny again," she said, pressing her lips.

"Anyway, you were at Georgina's house," John said, turning his attention to Libby.

"I don't know about that," Libby said, "but Cathy gave me these brochures about Bible study and the church she attends. They're going to have a gospel-tent meeting next week and she invited me to go with her."

"What'd you say?" Wendell asked.

"Of course I will," she said, handing the multi-colored tri-folds to him. "And I told her you will, too."

"Oh."

"How about you, Mama? Would you like to go with us? I bet you haven't been to church since you've been here," Libby said as she glanced at John with a dismissive smile. "We try to go every Sunday and Wednesday and never miss a revival. Praise the Lord! Am I right, Wendell?"

"Yes, honey, we do our best."

John picked up the leaflet with an image of Jesus, children, and sheep on the cover. He noticed everyone was white.

"Interesting," he said.

"I thought so, too," Libby said. "Very inspiring."

"Does she still have the Ten Commandments in front of her house?" John asked.

"Oh yes," Libby said, her eyes twinkling. "And inside she has the most awesome painting of Jesus surrounded by baby lambs and little children on her living room wall. She lives such a simple life. It's inspiring just to talk to her."

"What's so inspiring?" John asked, furrowing his brows.

"She says we need to put the Ten Commandments in every school and public place. She believes it would help eliminate crime because it would be a constant reminder to people. She says we need to have the Bible taught in schools. And we need to make this a Christian nation again."

"Has she ever heard of separation of church and state?" John asked.

"Quit being a smart aleck, John." Geraldine glowered at him. "She doesn't know what you're talking about."

"I was just asking.' John cupped a hand over his mouth to hide a grin.

"I don't think it really matters," Wendell said. "Good Christian people will make good laws for everyone, especially if they use the Bible as the guidepost. It's pure and simple."

"It hasn't worked in the past," John said. "Why do you think the Pilgrims and others fled England? What about the Holy Roman Empire?"

"That was then, and this is now," Wendell said. "Things change. Times change. We're modern. We won't make those mistakes."

"Really?"

"Anyhoo, Cathy says she'd like to set up weekly Bible studies," Libby said. "It's on one of those brochures."

"Interesting," Wendell said, flipping through the leaflets and pulling out the one about home study. "Good stuff."

"I'm going to go out with her this week and hand them out to people on your street," Libby said, looking at John. "We'll be spreading the word."

"Good luck with that," John said.

"Now what do you mean?" Geraldine asked, her head jutting forward like a lizard.

"I mean lots of folks around here work and they may not be at home."

Geraldine shook her head. "Sure."

"We'll go in the late afternoon or early evening then," Libby said. "I'm so excited about it. It'll give me something to do instead of sitting here in the house watching those TV shows."

"And what do you mean?" Geraldine asked, her eyes squinted.

"Uh," Libby stammered. "I've seen them before. That's all I'm saying. I want to do something new."

"Maybe you can do the same in Arizona," John said.

"Now what are you talking about?" Geraldine said

"Wendell told me they may be driving you back to Arizona."

"That's only an option," Geraldine said. "I'll probably end up flying back. It's faster."

"But Mama, I told you we'd be more than happy to take you back home. Anything your heart desires."

"Do you realize how long it would take to drive there? Especially with you behind the wheel? And I'm not sure your car would make it that far."

"I'd get it serviced."

"John, why did you bring that up?" Geraldine scowled.

John rolled his shoulders. "Just making some suggestions."

"As much as I want to go back, I'm not going anywhere until Sally gets back here. I want to see my daughter. So you're stuck with me until then." Geraldine had an odd look of satisfaction with her proclamation, grinning from ear to ear. Then she stuck her tongue out at him.

"As long as you need to stay," John said with a warm smile. "Our home is your home."

"And we'll stay here for as long as you need us, too, Mama," Wendell said. "Ain't that right, Libby?"

"You might want to run that by Sally and John," Geraldine said.

"Of course they can stay here," John smiled at her. "Anything for you."

Geraldine grimaced. "Thank you, John. You're so considerate."

"Maybe we can start our own Bible study, too," Libby said with a glowing grin. "Right here in the dining room or den."

"Amen." John steepled his hands in front his face.

Libby's expression turned from sweet to sour as she gave him a disbelieving look.

John glanced at the others, merriment in his dark brown eyes, then picked up Whiskers. "Ready to go outside, little buddy?"

~ * ~

While John let Whiskers out the front door to take care of potty business, Wendell and Libby retreated to the bedroom, saying they were going to take a short nap.

John stepped out on the front porch and surveyed his yard, certainly a standout in a negative way. He had to admit Geraldine was right about his lawn. Dandelions sprinkled the lawn like yellow bubbles and crabgrass threatened to become the dominate growth between the dead spots. There was a lot of work to be done to bring it up to par with the rest of the neighborhood as it was a rough in a row of landscaped greens. Whiskers ran to him as if to assess the surroundings. They glanced at each other for a moment and returned to the house.

Geraldine was in the kitchen, thumbing through the brochures at the bar. John took care of Whiskers' bowls, then sat across from her.

"You're right about the yard," he said. "It does look kind of threadbare."

"Kind of?"

"I'll get to it now I'm back from vacation. It'll give me something to occupy my time."

"Maybe you could go with Libby and hand out leaflets in the neighborhood."

"Now you're being a smart aleck."

"So you agree with me about your yard?"

"I'm not the best yard man."

"Maybe you could ask Brody to give you a hand. He doesn't do anything around here. It'd do him good to get his hands dirty."

"Good idea."

"You could hire a landscaper."

"Nah, that's too much trouble."

Geraldine tilted her head. "Or too much money?"

"Are you implying I'm a tightwad?"

"If the shoe fits."

John tipped his head and grinned. "Maybe I'm just selective in my spending."

"Oh, John, I'm just teasing you. Furthermore, you need the exercise. I've noticed you've developed a little belly since your vacation."

John glanced down at his midsection. "Well, that does it. I'll do my own landscaping."

"And don't forget, with Brody."

Brody returned from rehab class, and seeing Geraldine and John in the kitchen, and without saying a word, dashed to the den to claim temporary control of the television.

"His ears must have been burning," Geraldine said, pushing out her lower lip.

"Sure seems like it," John said. "But I'll talk to him about it. He's got a stronger back than I do."

Geraldine closed a brochure, and then arranged them in a neat stack. John walked to the refrigerator and took out a beer. "Care for anything to drink?"

"No, thank you," she said.

Geraldine twisted her head slightly and stared at John as he sat down.

"What?"

"John, why in the world did you bring up about Wendell driving me back to Arizona?" Geraldine asked, her brows creased.

"That's what I heard from him."

"I only said it was an option. Do you really think I'd want to sit in their little car for several days with Libby blabbering about everything under the sun? She'd drive me crazy. I don't think I'd make it all the way. It'd kill me."

"Then why did you say anything?"

"I only mentioned it in passing. I wasn't serious."

"At least you've got time to back out since you said you wanted to see Sally before you left."

"I'm not even sure I want to go back now," she said somberly.

John's forehead crinkled. "What?"

"I've been here so long it's beginning to feel like home. And who knows who's died since I've been away from there. I could have a whole new set of neighbors. That's depressing, if you know what I mean."

John stroked the side of his beard. "I don't know what to say."

Geraldine's voice softened as she looked at him with sad eyes. "Unless you think I'm too much of a burden."

"No, no, no." John waved his arms. "You're not a burden at all. You just surprised me because you've been saying all along about how much you want to return to your place."

"I gave it a lot of thought while you and Sally were in Europe," she said. "And with Wendell and Libby here, I realized how much I miss being around my family. I'd hate to be way out there and kick the bucket."

"That'd be a pain."

"A pain? What do you mean by that, John?"

"I mean, you know, handling the funeral arrangements if you were two thousand miles away. It could be difficult for all of us."

"So you're saying it would be easier if I dropped dead here?"

John let out a nervous laugh. "That's not what I mean, Geraldine. Quit trying to put words in my mouth."

"It's the truth, isn't it?"

"Of course, but that's beside the point. What I'm trying to say, and not doing a good job at it, is saying you need to be here. Like you said. With family. We can take care of you."

"So you think you need to take care of me now?"

"I mean if you got ill or something. Like when you fractured your hip. We were here for you."

"I just want to make sure. I never want to be a burden on you and Sally."

"You just get that thought out of your mind. Understand?"

"That's sweet of you."

"Consider this your home now."

Geraldine's eyes began to water, then she looked away.

Brody sauntered into the kitchen, opened the refrigerator for a few seconds, and slammed it shut. "Is anyone going to the grocery? There's hardly anything to eat."

"I'll go later this afternoon," John said. "Is there anything in particular you want?"

"Anything edible. Maybe some fruit. I'm going to get back into my exercise routine. The counselor says a person should be focused on doing the right stuff, so I want to start eating healthy food again."

"Makes sense," John said.

"Maybe you could help your dad with the lawn," Geraldine said. "That would be good exercise."

"What's wrong with the lawn? Looks fine to me."

"Just some minor yardwork," John said. "We'll discuss it later."

"Your father is saying he'd like for you to help him fix up the yard," Geraldine said. "He's not a young man anymore. He needs help with it."

John gave her befuddled look and shook his head.

"Sure," Brody said. "Whatever."

"Now was that so difficult, John?" Geraldine asked, tipping her head. "All you have to do is ask."

Brody sat at the bar next to Geraldine and picked up the pamphlets in front of him. "What's this shit?"

"Brody! Watch your mouth." Geraldine squinted like a startled cat and clutched his hand.

"Sorry, Grandma," Brody said. "Some religious nut drop by this afternoon?"

John glanced at Geraldine, pressing his lips together. Geraldine did the same.

"It belongs to your Aunt Libby," Geraldine said.

"Aunt Libby? What's she doing with this crap?"

"A neighbor gave them to her," John said.

"The weirdo down the street who lives in Georgina's house?"

"Let's be careful with name-calling," John said. "But yes, it was Ms. Gibson."

"Libby wants to have a Bible study," Geraldine said. "I told her you'd love to do it."

"You what?" Brody rose from his stool, eyes flaring.

"Gotcha!" Geraldine said with a devilish grin.

John broke out in laughter. "That's a good one, Geraldine."

Brody couldn't resist grinning. "Yeah, you got me all right."

~ * ~

John wanted to change clothes and take a quick shower before going to the supermarket. Wendell and Libby were still in the bedroom, so he went to the den, sat next to Brody on the couch since Geraldine had reclaimed the TV remote and was watching another of her endless favorite programs.

"How's rehab going?" he asked Brody, who was reading the sports pages in the newspaper.

Brody kept his eyes on the paper. "About the same. I still hear testimonials from former junkies which are supposed to scare you. Every few days we have a new person join the group and another who falls off the wagon."

"I hope you're getting something out of it."

"I guess so. I haven't taken any drugs, if that's what you're implying, so I suppose it's working."

"That's the idea."

"I saw Arnold Pomeroy the other day."

"And?"

"He just asked me how I was doing. He wants to get together sometime."

"I hope you told him it wasn't going to happen."

"C'mon Dad, what we did was a long time ago. Everything's cool now."

"It was only five or six months ago. And giving you cocaine isn't being a friend."

"Arnie feels bad about it."

"As he should."

Brody folded the paper, placed it between them and stared straight ahead. "Whatever."

"You need to stay positive."

"You're making me feel like I'm in another rehab class. I like to have a break from it once in a while. Especially here. You make it difficult to be positive."

"I'm sorry, Brody, but I am your father and as strange as it may seem to you, I do care about you. And I don't like to be kept in the dark about what's going on."

Brody shrugged. "Whatever."

Geraldine turned toward them and sneered, "Shush. Would you be quiet? I'm trying to watch TV."

"Sorry 'bout that, Geraldine," John said. "I'm just trying to have a conversation with my son."

"Well, you don't have to include me!" She turned back to the TV.

"I'm going for a walk." Brody pushed up from couch. "Want me to take Whiskers?"

"Go ahead. He needs the exercise. One more thing."

Brody's slumped his shoulders. "What is it?"

"Take a doggy bag."

Brody shook his head and let out a deep breath. Seconds later, the front door opened and closed, and all was quiet except for the television. John picked up the newspaper, turning to the comics, hoping to find something to lighten his spirits.

"I'll probably go to the supermarket in a few minutes," John said to Geraldine. "Anything you want me to get?"

Geraldine held up her hand. "Wait a minute. Something important is happening."

"No problem."

Wendell sauntered into the den, sat in the rocker, and stretched his arms. "I slept longer than planned."

"I know what you mean," John said. "I usually get in an afternoon nap. Kinda comes with age."

"Would you keep it down?" Geraldine asked.

"Oops," John said. "I forgot. Let me know when it's safe to converse with Wendell."

"Is something the matter?" Wendell asked.

John pointed to the TV, then placed a forefinger over his mouth. "Important stuff happening on TV," he whispered.

"Okay," Wendell said, smiling. "I see."

They sat quietly for two minutes until a commercial blared. "Now you can talk," Geraldine said.

"Thanks," John said. "The suspense was killing me."

"Are you trying to be funny?"

"With you." John flashed a sycophantic smile.

Geraldine shook her head. "So where's Libby? Still sleeping?"

"Libby should be out in a few minutes. She had to fix her face."

Geraldine looked deadpan at Wendell. "Is that all?"

Wendell glanced at the ceiling and shook his head. "Now, is that nice, Mama?"

Geraldine turned her attention back to the television.

"Anything you'd like from the grocery?" John asked.

"We really don't care," Wendell said. "We're not picky eaters. But you should ask Libby just in case."

"You can't make that decision?" Geraldine asked, her eyes still focused on the TV.

"Please, Mama, let's not fuss."

"Have you decided on anything, Geraldine?" John asked.

"Some more of those cheese crackers, potato chips, spinach dip, and veggie sticks."

"You eat like a bird, Mama."

"Maybe you should try it. It's worked for me nearly ninety years."

Libby entered the den, smiled at everyone, and sat on the couch. "Am I missing something?"

"John's going to the store," Wendell said. "Do you need anything?"

"Perhaps some more soft drinks," she said. "I like the diet drinks. I think we need some breakfast items like those pastries you got the other day."

"I'll get some eggs, bacon, pancake mix. It looks like we need about everything."

"You finally figured it out?" Geraldine said.

"Just for that, no goodies for you," John said, raising a forefinger. "Except for bird seed."

"Oh, you'll do it because I'm Sally's mom."

John nodded with a smile. "You got me there."

"I'm getting hungry now," Geraldine said. "Can you order a pizza?"

"I thought you were getting tired of it."

"I wouldn't mind some pizza," Libby said. "Can you add soft drinks to the order? Remember, I like diet."

"Sure thing," John said. "But first, I want to shower and change out of these clothes. I'll call in the pizza when I'm finished."

"How about Brody?" Geraldine asked.

"What about Brody?" John cocked his head.

"Don't you want to know what he wants?"

John rose from the couch. "Brody'll eat anything I bring in the house. You know that."

"Please don't look around in the bedroom," Libby said. "It's a mess."

"I'll try not to," he said, wondering what to expect when he entered *his* bedroom.

When he opened the door, it appeared the way the rooms he and Sally used on their vacation, although Sally was more orderly. Clothes were piled on opened luggage, an unmade bed, and toiletries scattered around the sink and top of commode in the bathroom. He noticed a jar of female lubricating gel on the nightstand. John thought they must really feel at home.

John grabbed a pair of cargo pants and pullover shirt from the closet and placed them on the bed, then shaved and took a hot shower. It was nice to feel clean again.

He ordered two large pizzas, a meat lover's and vegetarian, before returning to the den. Brody was sitting on the couch, nuzzling Whiskers on his lap.

"Pizzas should be here in about thirty minutes," John said.

"Did you remember the soft drinks?" Libby asked.

"Damn!"

Libby appeared disappointed and lowered her eyes like a disappointed child.

"Sorry 'bout that. I'll make another call."

"What kinds of pizzas?" Brody asked.

"Meat lover's and veggie."

"I was kinda hoping you'd order a double pepperoni."

"I told you to wait, John." Geraldine had a look of satisfaction on her face.

"Okay, I'll order a medium pepperoni."

"I think I could eat a large one," Brody said. "I'm famished."

"You're always famished."

"Please?"

"Okay, a large one."

"And don't forget the soft drinks," Libby said with a cheeky grin. "Diet for me."

"Thanks for reminding me, again."

John called the pizza place and updated the order, then covered the phone mic with his hand. "Anything else?"

"How about breadsticks and sauces?" Brody said.

"That'd be nice," Libby said, with a bright smile. "I like ranch."

"Buffalo for me," Brody said.

"I prefer honey mustard," Wendell said.

"How about you, Geraldine?" John asked.

"Just go," she said in an exasperated tone. "I'm hungry."

John got back on the phone and completed the order. "I guess I'll go to the supermarket now. Save a slice or two for me."

"Aren't you forgetting something?" Brody asked.

John stared blankly at him. "What now?"

"How are we going to pay for it?"

John glanced around the room at everyone, then took out his wallet and handed Brody two twenty-dollar bills. "There should be enough for a tip."

"I forgot to tell you," Brody said, stuffing the money in his front pocket.

John frowned. "Not something else."

"Nah, the weird lady down the street. She stood on her porch and watched me and Whiskers walk in front of her house. What a freak! I guess she was worried Whiskers would take another dump in her yard. I almost wished he would of."

"Now, Brody. Let's try to get along with our neighbors."

"Tell her that."

"Who are you talking about?" Libby asked.

"Your Cathy clown a few doors down."

"She's a sweet woman, full of love and grace. A godly woman."

"You can't be serious."

"Oh, well, I need to be going," John said. "Anything else from the grocery?"

Everyone looked at him with pensive expressions.

"Diet soda?" Libby blurted with wide eyes.

John nodded with a tiny grin, then escaped the house before there were any more good requests or discussion about the new neighbor.

~ * ~

John stood in the frozen-food section, looking over the array of family meals behind the glass-door enclosures. A few might pass the slapdash demands of his family and house guests who preferred pizza, pastries, and pop. He quickly learned healthy content wasn't a priority for them.

As he pondered what to put in his grocery cart, someone came up from behind, and in an impersonal, deep feminine voice, asked, "May I help you, sir?"

"No, I'm good." John didn't turn around, his eyes sweeping over the various brands on the shelves. Then he saw a reflection in the glass of Kate Washington and whirled around to face her. The recognition brought sunny smiles to both their faces.

"What a surprise!" he said. "I didn't identify your voice."

"I did it on purpose to see if I can still disguise it. My bad."

"I guess so you can still nab those criminals out there. You sure fooled me."

"It's so nice to see you," Kate said, her formidable voice back to the one he remembered. "Are you making some difficult food decisions?"

"Yeah," John said with a shrug. "We're out of a few things so they sent me to the store. We have some visitors as well, so I need to get a few things to satisfy all the tastes. They lean toward junk food."

"Sally's got you trained well."

"Sally's not home, so I've been assigned to this duty. Lucky me."

"I hope it's nothing serious with Sally."

"She's visiting our daughter in New York," he said.

"Expecting her back soon?"

"I hope so. Chloe's been undergoing chemo for ovarian cancer. Sally's been helping her and taking care of our granddaughter. She should be back soon if all goes well."

"I'm sorry to hear about your daughter. I hope she has a speedy recovery."

"It's stage one cancer, so doctors are hopeful for a complete recovery. She seems to be doing well, considering."

"That's good to hear."

"What have you been up to lately?" John asked. "You're out of uniform, but I assume you're still doing the same assignments for the police department?"

"Pretty much the same." Wearing tight jeans, and a low-cut tunic, with her brown hair touching her shoulders, made her look more like a delicate model than a tough street cop. "I've applied to become a detective, so we'll see how everything goes. There are other applicants for two positions."

"I'll be pulling for you."

"How's your son? Brody, isn't it?"

"He did the drug rehab and now he attends classes several times a week. So far everything is working out for him. He's staying clean. But we keep our fingers crossed."

"Be mindful of relapses. I've seen it happen time after time. It's heartbreaking."

"We're trying to keep tabs on him but sometimes it's difficult with an adult child, if you know what I mean."

"I certainly do. Addiction touches all ages. Let me know if there's anything I can do for him."

John chuckled. "Can you find him a job?"

"Are you serious?"

"No, I wouldn't ask that. He's a big boy and can find his own job. He hasn't been enthusiastic about it."

"If I hear of something—"

"Hey, I was just making a comment. I wasn't serious. He can find his own job."

"Well, okay."

John glanced at his watch. "I need to finish up here and get back. If you don't mind me saying, you look great. I need to get on your exercise regimen." He patted his belly.

"You look fine, John."

"It's been great to see you."

"Same here, John," she said with a narrow smile. "Maybe we can meet for coffee again someday and catch up on everything."

"I'll let you know when I can free up some time."

"I'll be looking forward to hearing from you."

John put out his hand, but Kate responded with light hug, surprising him for a moment. She stepped back, beamed, and with a bounce in her step, walked away holding a small basket of groceries.

John turned back to the frozen foods but couldn't help but glance at Kate as she rounded the corner and disappeared toward the checkout lanes. He rushed through the remainder of his shopping, realizing he'd probably miss a few items. Geraldine and Brody would let him know.

When he returned, Geraldine, Wendell, and Libby were parked in their usual places in the den, the TV booming *Dr. Phil.* Brody was nowhere to be seen.

John carried four sacks of groceries into the kitchen, then went back out to the car to get the remaining three bags and a gallon of milk. Whiskers followed him, perhaps seeking relief from the din inside the house.

When he went back, everyone was still in their places. John took his time putting the groceries away in the refrigerator and cabinets.

After closing the freezer door, he turned as Wendell entered the kitchen. "Need any help, John?"

"I think I've got it all under control," John said. "How was the pizza?"

"It was okay. Not the best in the world but took away my hunger pangs. Brody seemed to like it, though. I think he left you a piece."

"Wow," John said, lifting his shoulders. "What a surprise."

Libby walked in a minute later, put an arm around Wendell's waist and grinned. "Did you remember to get some diet cola?"

John shut his eyes for a few seconds. "I knew there was something I forgot."

Libby pushed out her lower lip. "Maybe you can pick up some tomorrow?"

"I'll try to remember," John said as he sat at the bar and opened the pizza container. Wendell was right...only one slice of pepperoni pizza remained, along with a greasy breadstick. He picked off the pepperoni and took a bite as they stared at him.

"Oh, I forgot to tell you Sally called," Wendell said. "She talked to Brody for a minute or so."

"Any messages?"

Wendell shrugged "You'll have to ask Brody. I didn't talk to her. I guess she didn't want to talk to me."

Libby stiffened her mouth and gazed at Wendell with sad eyes.

"Is Brody here?" John asked.

"He left after eating," Wendell said. "Didn't say where he was going. Didn't even say good-bye. Just up and left."

"Did you buy any desserts?" Libby asked, flicking her eyelashes with a broad grin. "I always like something sweet after a meal."

"I bought some ice cream and breakfast pastries."

"What kind of ice cream?"

"Chocolate."

Libby frowned. "I like butter pecan."

"I'll try to remember to get a carton tomorrow," John said. "Give me a list if you think of anything else."

"Just the diet soda."

Geraldine toddled into the kitchen and sat at the counter. "Took you long enough."

"I had lots of groceries to buy," John said. "And I'll go back tomorrow for a few things I missed." He flashed a smile at Libby. "Let me know if there's something you need."

"I've been wanting some yogurt," Geraldine said.

"I'll pick some up when I go back."

"Make sure it's the Greek yogurt. It's supposed to be good for a person's constitution. I haven't been regular for the past week."

"Maybe I should go back out now and buy some?"

"There's no hurry. Another day won't matter."

"I want to make sure."

"Did you get any ice cream?"

"Chocolate."

"I told him I prefer butter pecan," Libby said.

"You shouldn't prefer any ice cream," Geraldine said, her eyes scanning Libby from head to toes.

"Now Mama, that's not very nice," Libby said, her forehead creased.

"I'm just being honest. Go look in the mirror."

Libby pressed her lips together, and fighting back tears, darted to the bedroom. Wendell shook his head at Geraldine and followed Libby.

Geraldine looked at John with an innocent expression. "Can you fix me a dish of ice cream? I love chocolate."

Four

Several days later, everything in the house was calm and relatively quiet except for a game show on TV. Geraldine was in the recliner; Wendell, Libby and Brody were nowhere to be seen or heard. John took the rare opportunity to call Sally, creeping to his made-up makeshift bed in the living room, away from the TV. Whiskers followed and curled in for a snooze next to his sock feet.

"Chloe's a little nauseous at times but other than that, she seems to be doing fine," Sally said. "You know she's not one to show weakness unless she's really down. The doctor is pleased with how she's responding to the treatments. She seems to be getting stronger, little by little, so we're all encouraged."

"Everything okay with Whitney and Sam?"

"Whitney's been going on like nothing's happened. She's a happy little girl. As for Sam, she takes off from work whenever she's needed to be with Chloe or Whitney. She's been helpful and attentive."

"Any idea when you'll be coming back home?"

"Miss me?"

"Of course, I do, sweetheart. It's not the same without you being here."

She laughed. "Mother must be driving you crazy."

"Seriously, she hasn't been too much trouble at all. Maybe I've grown used to her sarcasm. It's been more Wendell and Libby, and Brody to a lesser extent. I guess I'm just not used to having someone else in the house. I miss our empty nest. It seems like I'm going to the grocery every day because you can't please all of them. I think I'll need another vacation after they leave. I'm glad I have Whiskers to keep me company. He's earned the title as man's best friend."

"I wish I could be there," she said, with a longing in her voice. "If things go well after the next two treatments, then I may. Chloe's been urging me to leave, but I'm not ready to right now. I know you understand."

"Give me a couple of days' notice so I can go out and buy a hide-a-bed or something. I'm still sleeping on the couch. It's not the most comfortable way to sleep."

"Any idea when Wendell and Libby will be leaving?"

"If I knew, I'd be counting the days. Wendell says your mom wants them to drive her back to Arizona. She told me she wants no part of that."

"Didn't you tell me she wouldn't mind staying with us?"

"Yep, that's what she said. And surprisingly, she hasn't talked much about missing her home and friends in Arizona."

"She must have toned down a bit since I've been away."

"I think so. But you seem to bring out the ornery side in her."

She snickered. "Thanks for reminding me. Maybe I'll just stay here indefinitely."

"She knows I won't put up with her nonsense like you do."

"Because she's my mother."

"So poor Wendell and Libby have to put up with the brunt of her scorn."

"Oh, dear."

"Oh, by the way, you hurt Wendell's feelings the other day when you called."

"What did I do?"

"It's what you didn't do. He mentioned you didn't want to talk to him."

"Where did he come up with that?"

"His imagination?"

"Is he there now?"

"Nope. Only me, Whiskers, and your mother. I have no idea where he is."

"I'll try to talk to him the next time I call."

"Any other news?"

"I almost forgot," she said hastily. "I got a call from Dorothy Finsterwald a day or so ago."

"Lucky you. What did she want?"

"Oh, just to chat for a few minutes. She wanted to know if she could drop by some day, but I told her Chloe didn't need to be around others because of her reduced immunity. She seemed to understand. At least I hope so. I certainly don't want any surprise visits."

"Just be sure to see who buzzes at the door before you answer."

"I'll try to remember that."

"She and Frank made for a memorable trip to Budapest. Something I'll never forget, no matter how much I try."

"She did say she and Frank are definitely looking forward to getting with us later in the year."

John groaned. "That's not good to hear. I really didn't have to hear that."

Sally giggled. "Something for you to look forward to."

"Don't remind me. Please."

"We'll cross that bridge when we get to it, honey."

"Always bridges to cross, whether you want to or not."

After goodbyes, John stepped outside on the porch. He glanced down at Cathy Gibson's illumed house. Three cars were parked out front and four in the driveway. He figured she was having a Bible study. He was startled for a moment when Wendell and Libby walked out the front door, holding hands, along with several other couples. They were all smiling and chatting back and forth.

John retreated inside the house, escaping to the garage with Whiskers. He sat on a stack of cardboard boxes filled with clutter, collected through the years. Clutter on top of clutter.

His cover was blown when Whiskers suddenly began barking at the door to the kitchen.

The door creaked open, with light from the kitchen revealing John's whereabouts.

"What are you doing out here?" Wendell asked, standing in the doorway, and casting a shadow over John. "Hiding?"

"I've got a slight headache." John rubbed the side of his head. "I thought I'd sit here in the dark until it passes."

"Anything I can get for you?"

"I'm good," John said with a weary smile. "Thanks anyway. I'll be okay in a few minutes."

"Are you sure?"

"Yes, Wendell." John bit his lower lip. "I'm sure."

"Okay then. Want me to take your pooch?"

"Whiskers is fine," John said, stroking his buddy's furry back. "He's my therapy dog."

"Therapy dog?"

"Just a figure of speech, Wendell."

"Well, okay." Wendell closed the door. John cradled Whiskers in his arms for a few minutes before the door opened again.

"You feel okay, John?" Geraldine asked, bending forward with squinted eyes. "Wendell said you were hiding out there sitting in the dark."

"I'm fine, Geraldine," he said evenly. "Just wanted a little peace for a few minutes. Slight headache. It's been a long day. And I'm not hiding."

"I may have to join you."

John stared at her clutching her cane, her pencil-thin body silhouetted by the light. "Why?"

"Libby's driving me crazy. She and Wendell just returned from Bible class down the street and she's talking non-stop about it."

"I'll pray for you."

"Don't be a smart aleck, John."

"I'm sorry. I didn't mean it that way."

"Why don't you come back in and save me from her?"

"You need to be saved?"

"There you go again, John."

John rose slowly from the cardboard seat and walked in her direction. "On one condition."

She stepped to the side as he entered the house. "What's that?"

"You save me from her as well."

"So we'll both be saved."

"You're getting the hang of it, Geraldine."

"Now how about fixing me another bowl of chocolate ice cream?"

"That I can do."

~ * ~

After dropping two scoops of chocolate ice cream in a bowl for Geraldine, John tried to avoid Wendell and Libby, first going to the bathroom and then to his makeshift bedroom, sitting on the couch and reading a magazine in silence. He heard Libby and Wendell's passive voices in the den, and after several seconds of quiet, they appeared into the living room with pensive expressions.

Wendell sat at the opposite end of the couch while Libby went to the easy chair near the door. John, sensing they wanted to discuss something, closed the magazine, and set it between him and Wendell.

"What's up?" John asked, glancing with a bright smile, first at Wendell and then Libby.

"Can we speak to you for a few minutes, if you're not too busy?" Wendell asked politely.

"I'm only going through a pile of magazines before Sally gets back and tosses them out. Whatcha want?"

"Are we being a burden?" Libby asked, tilting her head forward with doleful eyes. "I know we've only been here for a short time, but we don't want to infringe on your kindness. We don't want to be taking advantage of your Christian hospitality that's been a blessing to us."

"It's not a problem," John said. "You're visiting Geraldine. Besides, Sally and I always believed in having an open house for family and close friends. Family matters. So, no, you're not a burden. You stay as long as you need."

"We truly appreciate that," Wendell said.

"You know sweet Cathy Gibson from down the street?" Libby asked.

"Yes, I met her a week or so ago."

"She's offered to let Wendell and me live in her house," Libby said. Wendell nodded and smiled.

"Interesting," John said. "You must have gotten to know her well."

Wendell cleared his throat. "She wants us to help in her neighborhood ministry."

"Neighborhood ministry?" John stroked his short beard. "Really?"

"Reverend Cathy has a calling to spread the Lord's word and believes we are the vessels to help her sacred mission."

"Reverend? Vessels? Sacred?"

"She's a blessed person," Libby said. "And we feel anointed by her."

"And exalted," Wendell added with a solemn smile.

John glanced at them again, trying to say something they wouldn't find offensive. It took several sluggish seconds. "When did you become, uh, vessels?"

"We started tonight at the Bible study," Libby said. "She filled our souls with the spirit."

"Interesting." John drummed his fingers on the cushioned armrest. "And when will you move in with her?"

"She's going to move some things around in her house in the

next few days," Libby said. "It won't be very long."

John gazed at Wendell. "What about your job in Alabama?"

Wendell turned red-faced and lowered his head like a child who had been shamed for disobedience.

"Wendell hasn't worked since a little after Christmas," Libby said in a somber tone.

"I wasn't aware of that."

"Yeah, I got laid off," Wendell's mouth twisted as if he were holding back tears. "They let quite a few of us go, especially the older ones."

"I'm sorry to hear that," John said. "Are you in financial difficulty?"

"We got a six-months' severance package," Wendell said. "We still have some funds to cover things the next few months. It hasn't been easy."

"I'm sure it hasn't. So you've been a victim of invisible discrimination."

"I've never heard of that. What is it?"

"It's a way companies try to cut back their workforce without drawing attention. You and the others were probably let go because they could hire replacements at a lower salary and maybe with lesser benefits."

"That sure sounds like what happened to me."

"It happens in similar ways to ethnic groups, women, gays."

"Oh," Wendell said. "Never thought about it, but I see it being done to get rid of people."

"Are your kids still in Alabama?"

"Four of them," Libby said. "Wendell Junior's in Atlanta. We haven't heard from him in ages. He thinks he's better than we are. Ever since he became a high-falutin' lawyer. You know, he won't admit it, but he's embarrassed to be seen with us. It breaks my heart in two after all we did for him."

"I certainly hope the others are okay."

"Marcy's a preschool teacher, Wendy's a busy housewife with

four little ones under her feet, Randy's a security guard," Libby said. "And Bobby bounces from one job to the next. But they're all good kids, for the most part. Even Wendell Junior." Libby wiped a tear from her face.

"Bobby's been in a jail a few times, but nothing serious," Wendell said. "Mostly child support. He's trying to get his life in order, but a couple exes are making it difficult. He may be facing some of the so-called invisible discrimination you mentioned. He just can't find a decent job."

Libby glared at her husband. "Now you don't need to be telling him our family secrets."

"Honey, John's family," Wendell said meekly.

She crinkled her nose. "You know what I mean."

"If I can help in any way, let me know," John said, hoping he wouldn't regret the open-ended offer.

"We appreciate that," Libby said in a sugary tone.

"I've been looking for a job around here," Wendell said. "I check the paper every day. Even asked Brody for advice."

"He's probably the last person you should ask," John blurted.

"Oh?"

"Never mind. I thought you wanted to return to Alabama," John said. "You said something about the weather being nicer in the South."

"You have to take what you can find," Libby said. "We think maybe the Lord's calling on us to do His work here in Kentucky."

"What about Geraldine? Weren't you going to take her to Arizona?"

"John, you sound like you don't want us to stay," Libby said, arching a brow while slanting her head.

"No, no, no," John palmed his hands. "Wendell mentioned it to me the other day."

"Well, Mama seems content to stay here," Wendell said. "If she insists on going back, then I'll do whatever it takes to make her happy."

"Didn't she fly in before Christmas?" Libby asked.

"Yes, she did," John said.

"Then she can go back the same way," Libby said, nodding her head.

"But it was before she fractured her hip."

"She seems to be getting around simply fine. Just sayin'."

Geraldine, who seemed to have radar when she was subject of conversation, stood at the entryway to the living room, near the steps to the den. "Are you talking about me?"

"Come over, Mama, and sit between John and me," Wendell said warmly, tapping the cushion. She didn't budge.

"We were just talking about you going back to Arizona," Libby said.

"Who says I'm going back to Arizona?" Geraldine said, tapping her cane twice on the floor.

"Only if you want to, Mama," Wendell said. "We're not going to force you to do anything you don't want to do."

"You ain't forcing me to do anything. Understand?"

"Oh, Mama."

"Don't 'Oh, Mama' me. I'll do what I want."

John raised a hand. "Geraldine, Libby told me they may be moving in a few days."

Geraldine's eyes widened. "Back to Alabama?"

"Down the street," Libby said. "We'd still be neighbors."

Geraldine's shoulders slumped. "Oh."

"Won't it be nice?" Wendell said, his brows raised halfway up his forehead. "We could still come here every day and visit you and things like that."

Geraldine stared at Wendell for a few seconds, ignored Libby, then turned around and went to the den.

Wendell shrugged with a weak smile, not making eye contact with John or Libby. "I guess she's okay with it."

"I didn't hear an objection," John said, rising to his feet. "Come here, Whiskers, let's go outside so you can potty." Whiskers scampered from the den to the living room and followed John out the front door.

Libby and Wendell sat in stunned silence.

Five

Two weeks later, Libby and Wendell hadn't moved to Sister Cathy's holy abode. Brody was spending time in rehab classes and at his girlfriend's apartment. Geraldine appeared content in front of the TV. John's purpose in life was taking care of family, highlighted by trips to the supermarket and pizza orders, although he did flee on a few occasions to huddle with his buddies at McDonald's.

Other than daily walks with Whiskers, John's main escape was reading the newspaper in the quiet of the morning while everyone else was asleep, and getting lost in books when the others were out and about spreading the gospel or listening to lectures about the evils of opioids and such. Except Geraldine, of course, but she got lost in her TV land.

John was startled from a deep read of a Chris Helvey noir novel while lounging on the couch when his cell phone vibrated in his pocket.

"Damn!" he said as he swiped the screen without looking to see who was invading his personal retreat.

"I'm coming home," Sally said brightly. "Chloe's had all her chemo treatments and she's doing great."

"Are you sure?" John bookmarked the page and pulled himself up in his temporary bed.

"Don't you want me back?" she purred.

"Sweetheart, you know what I mean. I just want to make sure Chloe's going to be fine."

"John, you know I wouldn't be leaving if I had any doubts. Sam's been wonderful for her since you left. Everything's fine. Don't worry. It'll probably be next week."

"That's the best news I've heard in ages."

"We're going to celebrate tonight. Remember the pizza place we went to when you were here?"

"The time we all got drenched by a torrential thunderstorm?"

"That's the one. Whitney wanted pizza, so we'll be going there after I get off the phone."

"You know, it seems like ages since I last saw you," John said.

"I know it has. And I can't wait to sleep in my own bed."

"I'll change the sheets and tidy up the bedroom once our houseguests move out."

"I'm surprised they're still there."

"Not as much as me!"

"I guess things around the house will be somewhat quiet after they're gone."

"I'm sure they'll pay a visit every day to visit Geraldine and you when they're not on one of their missions. And they'll find time to eat and watch TV with her. About the only difference is we'll have our bed to sleep in. And it'll be nice to have our bathroom back as well. Knock on wood."

"You sound anxious for them to leave."

"I wish I could count the days."

"How's Mother handling it?"

"What do you think? Now she complains about the possibility of them dropping in to see her."

"Whitney's calling for me to join her, so I guess I should be going," Sally said. "I'll let you know about the flight plans and everything in the next day or so."

"Give her a hug for me."

"I always do."

"Love you, sweetie. Can't wait to have you back in my arms. And back in bed."

"You naughty man!"

"Love ya."

"Love you, too," she said before the phone went silent.

John left the room and glided to the den as if walking on air. Geraldine sat in her usual place, feet propped up in the recliner while watching an early *Law and Order* episode on TV.

"Guess what?" John asked as he sat on the couch.

"I'm not in the mood for games, John," Geraldine said above the droning sound of the TV.

"Sally's coming back home."

"I figured she would eventually."

"I mean, probably in the next few days."

Geraldine grabbed the side lever, tugged the recliner to the upright position and lowered the volume with the remote. "Well, it's about time. I thought she'd forgotten about us and was thinking about staying up there permanently."

"Now, you know better than to say that." John said. "You would be doing the same thing if the roles were reversed."

"I know," she said. "But it's about time for me. I need a break from the holy couple."

"I thought you were religious."

"I am but I don't want it crammed down my throat all the time. That's all they talk about, especially Libby with her chirpy laugh. It's going to drive me to an early grave."

John tried to hold back a cough.

"Anyway, Chloe's doing much better. She's completed her treatments. Everything appears to be under control."

"That's because Sally's been with her."

"And Samantha."

Geraldine took a deep breath and gazed at the ceiling. "Whatever."

"Maybe things will start getting back to normal around here."

"I sure hope so. I sure miss Sally."

"I've got an idea," John said, bright-eyed.

"I'm almost afraid to ask what it is."

"It's entirely up to you."

Geraldine shook her head. "Don't play games, John. What is it?"

"How about we go to Orange Leaf for frozen yogurt and celebrate Sally's impending return? Just the two of us."

Geraldine pulled the side lever on the recliner and stood. "Let's go."

<h1 style="text-align:center">Six</h1>

John's early morning walk with Whiskers was disrupted by light rainfall and rumblings of thunder after they reached the park. Instead of a few peaceful minutes on the bench while Whiskers romped by the grassy banks of the pond, John tucked his little buddy under his arm and hurried back to the house, just before the dark billowing clouds unleashed a torrent of rain.

All was quiet except for Brody, slumped at the bar in the kitchen, reading the sports section in the newspaper, sipping coffee in lounge pants and a faded gray Chicago Bears T-shirt.

"Where's everybody?" John asked, heading to the counter for coffee.

"Got me," Brody muttered without looking up. "Haven't heard a peep. And suits me fine."

"Problems?"

"Not really, just tired of having to tip-toe around here because of Uncle Wendell and Aunt Libby."

"They'll be leaving soon."

"You've been saying that for weeks. Are they going back to Alabama?"

John laughed. "Down the street."

"Huh?"

"To live with your new friend."

"You're kiddin' me. The religious nut?"

"That's their plan."

"I bet it won't last long."

"We'll see. The Lord works in mysterious ways."

Brody raised his hand. "Please, Dad, I hear enough pious crap from Aunt Libby."

John sat across from Brody and stirred creamer in his coffee. A heavy silence filled the room for a minute before Brody belched. John was thankful his son at least had the courtesy of covering his hand over his mouth.

"Mom's coming home soon."

"Chloe's doing better?"

"Everything seems to be going well for her. She's finished her treatments and Mom is going to stay a few more days."

"That's great."

"Chloe's fortunate, I should say we're all fortunate, her cancer was detected early."

"I wish I could go up there and see her."

"Maybe we can arrange for you to visit her after Mom gets back."

Brody's eyes sparkled. "Really?"

"She's been here for you, hasn't she? You need to be there for her. We're family. Remember?"

A wide grin spread across Brody's stubbled face. "Damn. Now that's something to look forward to. I can't wait."

"Now hold your horses. Let's wait until Mom gets back and work things out. We need to discuss it with Chloe as well. There's not a lot of room in her apartment."

"Seems to have been enough for you and Mom."

"We slept on the couch."

"Just like you've been doing here."

"Touché," John said with a sigh. "And don't think I'm not looking forward to having my bed back."

"You don't have a clue when Uncle Wendell and Aunt Libby are moving out?"

John shrugged. "That's the sixty-four-thousand dollar question."

"Huh?"

"Never mind. You wouldn't understand."

"Okay. If you say so."

"I need to speak to them about their plans. I've been putting it off, not wanting them to think I'm trying to push them out."

"You know, it's hard to believe Mom and Uncle Wendell are related. They're so different from each other."

"I agree. Kind of like you and Chloe."

"Meaning?"

"Siblings have differences."

"He's kind of full of himself. A know-it-all except when Aunt Libby is around. Then he's a wuss."

"Now, don't be so harsh," John said. "Wendell's not a bad guy, and Libby is, well, Libby. I've known them for more than forty years. They haven't changed much through the years."

"That's scary."

"C'mon, son, most of us get into daily habits, or ruts, which are difficult to break."

"At least you and Mom are somewhat open-minded about things."

"That's probably the key. We've tried to be open to most everything, although I'm sure there are a few things we haven't questioned. Sometimes it's easier to go with the flow. Life is difficult enough without creating more conflicts than necessary."

"Same with me."

"Besides, Wendell is out of work," John said. "He was laid off."

"He was probably fired."

"Now, Brody, you don't know that. Regardless, you should know how stressful it can be being out of work. Right?"

Brody averted eye contact. "Uh, sure."

As much as he wanted to ask, John resisted inquiring Brody about job prospects, since he probably knew the answer. And he didn't want to create another thorny conflict in his knotty retirement years. He knew he was being a wuss as well.

~ * ~

John was jolted from his afternoon nap on the couch by sharp raps on the front door. He peered through a slender gap in the curtain, startled for a moment by Bert tipping his head at him. John nodded and opened the door.

"Anyone home?" Bert muttered.

"Geraldine and I," John said. "She's watching TV in the den. Come on in."

"Can you step outside for a few minutes?"

"Sure, but hold on a second." John called for Whiskers, who jumped off the end of the couch and scurried out the door and to the side of the house.

John followed Bert down the walk to the driveway. Bert looked furtively up and down the street. "There's something fishy going on in the neighborhood."

"More crime?"

"No, I think I've got everything under control with Neighborhood Watch. Which reminds me, we have a meeting in three days. I hope you can be there."

"Count me in." John grinned. "Anything else?"

"You know that gal who moved into Georgina's house?"

"Ms. Gibson. We discussed her a few days ago. Remember?"

"Oh, yeah," Bert said with a befuddled look.

"Is there something you want to tell me?"

"She's been canvassing the neighborhood with a few folks about Bible studies and such."

"So?"

"It's come to my attention from the Patels and the Martins that they've been targeted with some hate literature."

"What does that have to do with our new neighbor?'

"She's involved in a group called Christian One."

"Never heard of it."

"I'm told it's a white supremacist group that excludes dark-skinned races as well as alternative lifestyles, if you know what I mean," Bert said.

"I know what you mean. Gays, lesbians, transgenders."

"They preach about cleansing the church and making it so-called pure again."

"Have they caused any trouble?"

"The Patels and Martins told me they've had some minor vandalism of their houses."

"Have they called the police?" John asked.

"I told them to, but they don't want to draw any attention to it. They say they've encountered these things before and they pass over time."

"I don't know what to say."

"Don't you have some family members involved?"

"Well, er, yes. They've never mentioned any of those things. It's been mostly fundamental stuff you usually hear from Baptists, Pentecostals, and such. Never any hate messages. But I confess I haven't read the literature."

"Ms. Gibson dropped by my house about a week ago and talked to Wilma for a few minutes. It was cordial enough and she invited the wifey to one of the Bible studies."

"Maybe you should go to one of them," John said.

"Are you kidding?" Bert took a step back. "I'm a Lutheran."

"Be an undercover agent."

Bert touched his chin. "Hmm. Never thought of that."

"I'll let you know if I hear anything from my in-laws. I know Geraldine isn't involved. She escapes to the den and turns up the TV's volume when Libby begins to spout anything from the Bible."

"Works for me."

John glanced down the sidewalk and saw Wendell and Libby three houses down the street. "Here they come."

"I should be going," Bert said, loud enough for them to hear. "Wilma's probably got supper on the table. Stay in touch."

"I'll keep you informed if I hear anything."

"Thanks. And don't forget our Neighborhood Watch meeting on the twelfth."

"I'll mark it on the calendar."

Bert waved at the couple and headed toward his house.

"Getting in an afternoon walk?" John asked as Wendell and Libby reached the driveway. "Great day to be out."

"A glorious day," Libby said, beaming. "We've been out spreading the word."

"I hope it was a good day for that."

"Sister Cathy says it's something we must be diligent about if we're going to save lost souls. She says never get discouraged because we'll be rewarded in the end."

"Sister Cathy?"

"We call her sister now," Wendell said. "We're all brothers and sisters."

"Interesting," John said. "I suppose she's the big sister."

Wendell and Libby gave him a hard stare without saying anything.

"Just a little joke," John said. "By the way, have you approached the Patels next door? Nice family."

Wendell glanced at Libby as if she would provide an answer. "Not yet," he said. "But we will. We've been working in other parts of the neighborhood."

"Let me introduce you to them," John said. "I believe they're at home."

"John, I've really got to go to the bathroom," Wendell said with a nervous laugh. "I've been holding it for the last block."

Libby looked flustered, then blurted, "I'm about to pop, too," and dashed past Wendell, who followed her inside the house without looking back.

"I hope you make it," John said to himself. "Brother Wendell and Sister Libby."

John walked to the rear of his house where Whiskers was bouncing up and down under an oak tree, yapping at a gray squirrel teasing him from a wobbly limb.

"Whiskers sure gets excited about the squirrel."

John noticed Manny Patel standing at the end of the fence separating their yards.

"Hi there," John said as he walked toward him. "I think the squirrel is just playing around with him."

"Probably."

"Mind if I ask you something?"

"Shoot," Manny said a smile.

"Bert told me you and your family have been subjected to some vandalism."

Manny's smile vanished like a vapor. "A few times. We've had our trash cans turned over and someone keyed my car."

"Keyed your car? Are you serious?"

"I'm not sure if it happened here, work or some other place."

"Have you called the police?"

"I've given it some thought. I'm going to give it a little time and see if it blows over. When you're a minority, you kinda expect these kinds of things once in a while. You don't like it, but you learn to live with it."

"Minority or not, it shouldn't happen to anyone."

"I agree but—"

"Let me know if there's anything I can do," John said. "I know some folks at the police department. There's no reason for you to have to put with those kinds of things."

"I appreciate the offer, John. I'll think about it."

"Don't think about it too long. It might get out of control if you do."

Manny nodded, waved, and went back to his house. John watched Whiskers for another minute until the pooch gave up on the squirrel and ran to his side.

Returning to the front of the house, John noticed Sister Cathy watering her lawn. He went inside and took care of Whiskers' needs in the kitchen, where Wendell and Libby were seated at the bar, going over a sheet with addresses, presumably from their canvassing the neighborhood for Christian One.

John couldn't resist glancing over Wendell's shoulder, noticing it was also a checklist that included items such as visited, whether or not at home, numbers in family, and race.

"I don't mean to be nosy," he said. "Just curious to see what has your attention. That's quite a list you have there."

"It gives Sister Cathy a feel for the neighborhood," Wendell said, looking up at John. "And we have a record of homes we need to go back to if residents aren't there. It's quite useful."

"Interesting," John said.

"We combine our lists with others," Libby said. "Sister Cathy keeps a master list that grows with all input from ministry workers like us. It's a lot of work but she hopes to see the fruits of our labors."

"I'll let you get back to your data input," John said. "I'll be down the street for a few minutes. Don't work too hard."

There wasn't a response from his houseguests, who were lost in their paperwork.

John strolled to Cathy Gibson's house. She was still watering her yard and didn't notice him approaching from the driveway. She glanced in his direction with a surprised expression before shutting off the water.

"You startled me," she said, touching her chest.

"Sorry 'bout that. I should have said something."

"Is there something you want?"

"Not really," he said. "You've been here about a month or so and I thought I should introduce myself."

"I've seen you and your little doggie walk past the house a few times," she said as she wiped her damp hands on her skirt. "I'm Cathy Gibson. And you?"

"John Ross. My wife, Sally, is away in New York right now. My son and mother-in-law live here while my brother- and sister-in-law have been visiting for several weeks. They're Wendell and Libby Corman."

"Oh, I've been blessed to know Wendell and Libby," she said with a glowing grin. "They're a divine couple."

"They've told me they'll be moving in with you."

"One of these days, God willing," she said. "I've had so much going on with the ministry I haven't had time to make room for them. And then my son recently showed up, so it's been kind of chaotic around here."

"Wendell and Libby have mentioned your ministry," John said. "Christian One?"

"We put Christianity as the number one priority."

"That's interesting. Have you had much success around here?"

"Not as much as I'd like," she said with a puckered brow. "So many people have rejected the word, so it's been a lot of work. Wendell and Libby have helped with our Bible studies. You should join them some evening."

"I'll give it some thought after my wife returns," John said. "Thank you for the invitation."

"I need to go back in the house to check on a roast in the oven. It's been nice talking to you, Mr. Ross."

"Same here," John said. "By the way, you've got a lovely yard."

She smiled. "It's all part of God's grace."

~ * ~

John grabbed the leash for Whiskers and headed to Rufus Martin's house down the street the following afternoon. He tapped on the door several times.

"Who is it?" A woman's soft voice asked on the other side of the door.

"John Ross."

Tanya Martin opened the door about six inches, making sure he was who he said he was. A tired smile crossed her face as she welcomed him into her dimly-lit home.

"Rufus is still at work," she said as they walked to the entryway to the living room. "He should be back at any time. Won't you have a seat?"

"Thank you, but I can only stay a minute," John said, clutching Whiskers in his arms. "I need to ask you something."

"What is it?"

"Have you received any kinds of racist threats, taunts or anything in the past few weeks?"

Tanya squeezed her lips as her eyes turned watery. "We've had a few things happen. The other day someone turned over the trash cans. My car was keyed and it's in the shop being repaired. And someone spray-painted the 'n' word on the garage door."

"Have you notified the police?"

"Rufus called and they're investigating it as a possible hate crime."

"Has anyone else in the neighborhood been victimized?"

"Two other black families on the next street over. The Crawfords and Parkers. They had the same stuff as we did. And I was told a Muslim family had a rock thrown through their front window. I don't know their name."

John shook his head. "I hate to hear that. The Patels have experienced some vandalism, too. We've never had those things happen around here. It seems unreal."

"We have a few times in the past, when we first moved here, but it's been relatively quiet until the past few weeks. Remember the Summers?"

John frowned. "Very much so. They moved after we caught their son breaking into the home of Bert's neighbor. They haven't been missed."

"What's going on now is very upsetting to us. I don't like being here alone. I don't feel safe. Can you understand?"

"I don't blame you. We felt the same way after our house was vandalized last year. There's no reason for these kinds of things to be happening to anyone. Especially the graffiti. It makes me sick to my stomach."

"Rufus has talked about moving. We had hoped for this to be our last home. I'm not so sure anymore."

"I'm going to check with the police," John said. "I've talked to Bert and perhaps we can get the Neighborhood Watch group on the lookout for vandalism and, uh, racism."

"Thank you, John," she said. "We love this neighborhood, but I don't know if we can take much more of this kind of behavior. I'm scared."

"By the way, have you heard from any religious group in recent weeks?"

"There was a woman who stopped by the other day dressed in one of those granny dresses. Remember them? I'm not sure if she was from some church, but she had some flyers in her hand."

"What did they say?"

"I don't know." Tanya laughed. "She said, 'wrong house,' and walked away. It was kind of strange."

"Was she by herself?"

"There was an older couple waiting at the end of the driveway. I've never seen them before."

"Interesting." John's brows furrowed.

"Do you know them?"

"Maybe. I'll be getting back with you. I'm trying to get a handle on all this. Please let me know if anything else happens."

As John walked home, several cars were parked at Cathy Gibson's house; he assumed for a Bible study. He stopped across the street and heard the faint sounds of "Blessed Assurance" coming from the dwelling.

When he returned, everyone except for Brody was in the den, sitting silently as one of Geraldine's favorite TV shows filled the room with canned laughter. Whiskers scampered to the water bowl while John joined the others.

"Sounds like they're having an old-time gospel hour down the street," he said to Wendell and Libby from the rocker.

"Were you there?" Libby asked, turning her head.

"No, I just heard it while walking by. How come you're not there?"

"We'll go later this evening. They have several studies."

"I met your Sister Cathy yesterday," John said.

"You did?" Wendell said.

"She's been here a while so I decided to drop by and introduce myself. She thinks a lot of you and Libby."

"We think a lot of her," Libby said. "We feel blessed."

"She said the same about you guys. It must be a mutual admiration society with her Christian One congregation."

"How did you know about that?" Wendell asked.

"You've been spreading the word and it got around to me."

"We're doing the Lord's good work," Libby said.

"You must be doing a good job at it," John said, grinning.

"We start after breakfast and work straight through to supper," Wendell said.

Geraldine turned her head from the TV. "Did I hear someone mention supper?"

"It's about time," John said.

"I'm getting a little hungry myself," Wendell said, patting his spongy paunch.

"Me, too," Libby said, her brows in a delightful arch.

"We do have food in the refrigerator," John said. "Has anyone looked inside, perchance?"

"Maybe if Libby would put her Bible down once and do something, or stop going on those so-called neighborhood missions, she could prepare some meals once in a while," Geraldine said, glowering at her daughter-in-law. "It wouldn't hurt you to lift your finger around here."

Libby covered her face with her hands and began sobbing.

"Mama, you didn't need to be so mean." Wendell wrapped his arms around his slouching wife. "She didn't do anything."

"That's right. She doesn't do anything."

"Now you know that's not true," Libby said, wiping tears from her cheeks. "I washed a load of clothes the other day."

"But they were your clothes."

"But still—"

"You two seem to think you're on vacation," Geraldine said. "Don't think I haven't noticed. You eat, sleep, watch TV, and whatever racket you make in the bedroom."

Libby's weeping turned to wailing as she bolted from the Wendell's loose embrace and scuttled to the bedroom.

"Now look what you've done," Wendell said. "Mama, you should be ashamed of yourself talking in a hateful manner. She's my wife. She's family."

"Maybe you and Libby should do something around here," Geraldine said, rapping her cane on the floor. "Has it ever occurred to you? And you should be ashamed of yourselves."

"Now everyone settle down." John stood and waved his hands back and forth in an attempt for a degree of peace.

"You hold your horses, John Ross! Ever since you came back from your vacation, you've done about everything while they've sat back and watched. Libby can prepare meals. If she can read a Bible, she can read a cookbook. And you could help, Wendell, instead of sitting around on your rear end. John even has to mow the lawn."

"That's okay," John said, trying to ease the familial friction. "I can handle everything. It's not a problem."

"I'm not finished," Geraldine said as she rose from the recliner with knitted brows. "Sally will be here tomorrow, and she doesn't need to come back to this mess. Understand, Wendell? You and Libby can do some dusting and things like that. Maybe empty the trash and clean the bathrooms."

"Did Sally call?" John asked.

"What do you think?" Geraldine snapped. "Smoke signals?"

John chuckled. "Just asking."

"I'm going up to my room and rest. Let me know when supper's ready. I don't care what we eat," Geraldine said, "or when we eat."

Geraldine exited the den as fast as her bony legs would carry her, a look of triumph on her stern face as she carried the cane like a baton.

"I don't know what to say, John," Wendell said softly. "We haven't been trying to take advantage of you. I hope you know that."

"I understand. I think we're all getting on each other's nerves just a tad. It'll blow over after Sally gets home."

"You just let me know if there's anything Libby and I can do. And I'll be honest, Libby's not much of a cook. Never has been. That's why she hasn't done much in the kitchen. But she's good at other things."

"Not a problem, Wendell. I enjoy cooking. It's become a little hobby of mine since I retired."

"Is there anything else we can do?"

"Like Geraldine said, perhaps cleaning up around the house before Sally returns."

"We're on it," said Wendell, who headed to the bedroom to comfort Libby, stopping briefly to flash John a thumbs-up.

John nodded with a feeble grin.

"Oh, by the way," Wendell said. "When's supper?"

Seven

John met Sally at the baggage-claim area of Blue Grass Airport the next afternoon, kissing her on the cheek along with a gentle hug. They sat on a bench while waiting for her luggage to roll out on the conveyor.

"It seems like it's been ages since I last saw you," he said as they held hands.

"I know." She squeezed his hand. "But you know I want to be with her when she goes back to her doctor in a few weeks for her long-term prognosis."

"I'll go back with you," he said. "I want to be there as well."

"How are things? Or should I ask? You know you're not the most forthcoming person on the telephone."

"You know I've always preferred face-to-face. That's just me. Anyway, I haven't had much privacy and you've been busy as well. It's been difficult to connect the past few weeks."

"I hope things aren't too bad."

"Are you sure you want to know?"

"Probably not, but I need to be somewhat prepared before we get there. You know I don't like surprises."

"You know Wendell and Libby are still at the house," he said. "I'm not sure when they're going to move in with Sister Cathy."

"Sister Cathy?"

"I think I've mentioned her to you a few times. She's the gal who conducts the Bible study in the neighborhood," he said. "She's put them on hold for a few weeks."

"And Mother?"

"She's turned her wrath on Wendell the past few days, so you may be safe for a while."

"Poor Wendell."

"She's turned on Libby, too."

"Seems fair."

"Sometimes I sense it's deliberate to get them to move out."

"I hate to say it, but I wouldn't put it past her. Once you get on her bad side, it's difficult to get back on her good side. She holds grudges."

"I've noticed," John said. "For a long time."

"How's Brody?"

"Honestly, he comes and goes so much I can hardly keep up with him. I believe he's keeping his nose clean, so to speak."

"That's good to hear."

"He still doesn't have a job. I'm not sure he's trying to find one in Lexington."

"One thing at a time. Maybe it'll help if I talk to him."

John shrugged. "It sure couldn't hurt."

"Anything else?"

"We've had some hate crimes in the neighborhood ever since Sister Cathy started spreading her understanding of the gospel. I'm not sure if there's a correlation."

"What do you mean?"

"It's more of a white supremacist philosophy excluding others," he said. "It even has Bert up in arms. He plans to get Neighborhood Watch involved."

"It must be serious if Bert is riled up about it."

Her two pieces of luggage appeared, which they reached in and grabbed between the throng of passengers standing next to the horseshoe-shaped area. They hurried to the short-term parking lot and drove home in light traffic, hardly saying a word while an oldies station played the Eagles' "Take It to the Limit" in the background. John glanced at Sally, eyes closed behind her sunglasses and breathing lightly. He knew she was probably mentally and physically exhausted. He turned down the volume to barely above the hum of the tires on the road.

Pulling into the driveway, they were surprised to see Geraldine standing on the front porch, both hands gripping the cane handle. Then they spotted Whiskers at the side of the house.

John collected the luggage from the trunk as Sally, mustering a tired smile, went to the porch, giving her mother a soft hug and kiss on the cheek. Whiskers dashed to Sally, lavishing her with wet kisses after she picked him up.

"You look great, Mother."

"You're the first one to say that," Geraldine said as she led the way into the house. "I wish I could say the same about you."

"What?"

"You look simply worn out, Sally. Haven't you been getting any sleep? You've aged ten years."

"I've been sleeping on Chloe's couch. It hasn't been quality slumber. I hope to catch up on some sleep now I'm back."

"Good luck, since your brother and his wife have taken over your room. I'm beginning to think they're moving in permanently. John shrugs every time I mention it to him. He's a pushover."

"Hey!" John said with a laugh. "How did I get mixed up in this?"

"It's your house," Geraldine said. "It's not their vacation home."

Sally responded with a crooked grin as she noticed the neatly stacked covers on the couch where John had been sleeping. "They're company, so that's fine."

"The couch isn't too bad, but it may be a bit packed for two people," John said, raising his brows.

"We'll manage," Sally said. "We'll sleep on the floor if need be."

"It's your house, so it's none of my business," Geraldine said. "But I know I wouldn't put up with it."

"Where are they?"

"They left about thirty minutes ago to do their so-called missionary work. They didn't want to wait for you. I don't know what to think anymore."

"It'll give us a little time together, Mother," Sally said.

Geraldine's eyes brightened. "That's good. I never thought of it that way."

Sally and John followed Geraldine to the kitchen. They sat on the bar stools in silence for several seconds as Sally looked around as if to refamiliarized herself with her surroundings after being away for so long.

"Everything looks so nice," Sally said with a pleasant smile.

"It should after I told your brother they needed to do some things around here to earn their keep. They spent several hours tidying up the den, kitchen, and living room."

"Cracking the whip," John said.

"Don't be a smart aleck, John. Someone has to tell them. You and Sally can be softies."

"I don't deny that."

"Then you need to say something."

"In time."

"Well, John, I think the time is now."

"How about a timeout right now?" he said. "Let's let Sally get adjusted to being back."

Sally flickered a meager smile and didn't say a word.

"Later then," Geraldine said, glancing at Sally.

"I'm tired, Mother. Do you mind if I take a short nap?"

"I haven't seen you in more than a month, but that's okay. We can talk later."

"Are you sure?"

"I have a program coming on TV soon. I'll be all right. I'll let you know when I'm ready."

"Thanks, Mother."

Geraldine padded to the den, got situated in a comfortable position on the recliner, and turned up the volume on the television. It was almost as if Sally were back in New York.

~ * ~

John grabbed Sally's luggage and followed her to their bedroom. "Oh, my goodness," she said, wide-eyed after opening the door. "Wendell and Libby didn't get to this room. It's a mess."

Clothes were tossed in the corner, two pieces of opened luggage lay on the dresser, and the bed was unmade as the comforter was pulled over rumpled sheets and pillows. She glanced in the bathroom, where towels draped over the side of the tub and toiletries stacked on the counter. And for some reason, several of Libby's panties and bras and Wendell's boxer briefs were slung over the top shower railing.

"They've made themselves at home," John said with a light laugh. Sally didn't have the same response.

"That's an understatement." Sally planted her hands on her hips. "You'd think they were staying at a motel."

"Yeah, the Ross Motel," John said. "And rent free."

"Doesn't she know we have a washer and dryer?"

"Maybe she's trying to save us a little money on the utilities."

Sally cringed. "How much longer are they going to stay?"

"I thought they would have moved in with Sister Cathy by now. That's what they told me a few weeks ago. In other words, I don't have a clue."

"What are we going to do?" Sally pursed her lips as she continued to survey the bedroom.

"Should I change our mailbox to Ross-Corman?"

"That's not funny," Sally said, trying to suppress a grin.

"I don't think it'd be the proper thing to kick them out. Or should I say evict. But I'm tempted."

"Let's discuss it with them when they return."

"Eviction?"

"Please, John, I'm trying to be serious."

"I suppose I need to come up with an exit strategy for them."

"We can talk about it some more. Maybe I'll have a different opinion after I give it more thought. I just didn't anticipate this."

"Want to go out and get a bite to eat?"

"I think I'd like that," Sally said. "Maybe get something to drink to settle my nerves. I'm a bit upset right now."

"Where do you want me to put the luggage?"

"Just stick it in the closet. There's nothing I need at the moment."

John opened the closet door and took a step back. Stacks of pamphlets, Bibles, and boxes of assorted materials covered the floor. "You might want to see this."

Sally peeked inside and picked up a pamphlet showing a Jesus in a white robe surrounded by angelic white children. She took another one, with an image of a glowing Jesus looking heavenward, in the center of pristine people, all white. "There's something strange about this," she said.

"You could say that."

She tossed them back in the closet and slammed the door. "Let's go. This is really upsetting me now."

"I'm sorry." John touched her back. "I didn't mean to get you worked up."

"I'm fine, honey. I'd rather know than be kept in the dark. I'm just amazed they've drifted to such an extreme. I knew they were fundamentalists, but this is crazy. And scary."

"I guess it'd be safe to say you've seen the light."

"That's not funny, John," she said, frowning. "Let's go."

They closed the door to the bedroom and went to the kitchen, where Geraldine was perched at the bar sipping on one of Libby's diet soft drinks.

"We're going out to eat," John said. "Care to join us?"

"I'm not really dressed to go out in public." She glanced down at her floral top and loose black leggings. "Can you give me a few minutes to change clothes?"

"That's not a problem," John said. "I can feed Whiskers while you're getting dressed."

After Geraldine retreated to her bedroom, Sally gave John a questioning look. "I'm surprised you asked her to go with us."

"I'm surprised she accepted. But we couldn't just leave without asking her if she wanted to come along."

"That's sweet."

"You might say your mother and I have bonded while you've been away."

Sally shook her head. "If you say so."

"Now, if she doesn't take forever getting dressed, I'd like to get out of here before Wendell and Libby get back to the house."

"Are you worried they'd want to join us?"

"I know they'd want to join us. And I'm not in the mood for their company."

"I feel the same way," Sally said. "And I haven't seen them in ages. I know that's a terrible thing for me to say."

"You're tired. That's understandable."

"I hope so."

Geraldine returned to the kitchen, wearing a bright pink jumpsuit and matching tennis shoes, while John was putting kibble in the bowl.

"You remind me of someone," John said.

"Who?"

"I don't know. You just triggered a memory."

"Let's go," Geraldine said. "I'm hungry."

"I said I wish Wendell and Libby were here to go with us," Sally said.

"Be careful what you wish for," Geraldine said as she headed out of the house.

John glanced at Sally and covered his mouth to keep from chuckling out loud.

~ * ~

Backing out of the driveway, John and Sally noticed Wendell and Libby leaving Sister Cathy's house.

"Should we wait?" John asked, glancing at Sally.

"Wait for what?" Geraldine said, tilting her head from the backseat.

"Let's go," Sally said. "I can see them later."

"Oh," Geraldine said after catching a glimpse of her son and daughter-in-law. "Better hurry then."

John drove the opposite direction from them, noticing in his rearview mirror Wendell waving his hand in the air as they headed down the street. He quickly focused on the road ahead.

"Damn."

"What's the matter, honey?" Sally asked. "Forget something?"

As he turned the corner, and Wendell and Libby were out of sight, he said, "It was nothing."

They went to O'Malley's Pub, one of John's favorite casual places to eat. He didn't bother to ask Geraldine if she had a preference, figuring she would have them going all over town while trying to decide where and what she wanted. She seemed content peering out the window.

Although the pub wasn't crowded, it was a bit noisy as Garth Brooks' "Friends in Low Places" streamed through the speakers. To John's amazement, Geraldine didn't seem to mind as she glanced around at the surroundings after they were seated in a booth, tapping her fingers on the table to the beat of the country tune. He was even more surprised when she ordered a glass of red wine, and they actually had it available. John and Sally got Samuel Adams draft beers.

"Sally, it's so nice to have you back," Geraldine said, after taking a small sip. "I've really missed you."

"Why, thank you, Mother." Sally beamed. "It's nice being back. I admit I was getting a little homesick. And I missed you, too. As they say, there's no place like home."

"Did John tell you I've been giving some thought about staying in Kentucky?"

Sally smiled at John. "Yes, he did. You have no desire to go back to Arizona?"

"I've been gone from there for so long," she said. "I have mixed feelings. If I go back, I don't know who'll even be there, because people kick the bucket all the time. It's depressing to me."

"I understand," John said. "I often get depressed when I read in the newspaper the passing of people I know."

"You can imagine what it's like for me because most of the people I know are near the end. There's nothing more depressing than to see someone on her deathbed."

"Have you ever called your friends?" Sally asked. "I'm sure they'd like to hear from you."

"Well, they have my number. If they want to talk to me, they're capable of calling me."

"I guess you're right." John nodded and took a swallow from his mug. "It's a two-way street."

"Anyways, I don't know who's dead or alive back there, since I've been away for so long. And I'd rather not know." Geraldine took a sip of her wine, her eyes casting a blank stare for a moment as if lost in thought. "Some of them had memory problems so they've probably forgotten about me."

"Can we change the subject?" Sally asked. "This is making me depressed."

"Me, too," Geraldine said.

"Live in the present," John said, lifting his beer as if a toast.

"Speaking of the present, have you had a nice time with Wendell and Libby?" Sally asked.

"No," Geraldine said without hesitation. "I never realized how much Wendell was like his father. At least Harold loved to travel. That's one thing we had in common. But Wendell seems content to sit around the house, watch TV, and comment about everything under the sun. Even when I tell him to shut up, he starts it back up a little later."

"What does he say?" John asked.

"When I tell him to shut his trap?"

"I guess."

"I thought Harold was conservative," Geraldine said. "Wendell's way out there. What do you call it? Ultra? Extreme? Whatever it is, that's what he is."

"He's never talked politics around me."

"Because he knows how you feel about things."

"Oh, really?"

"He knows you have black friends and you give to charities. He knows about Chloe. He also notices what you watch on TV. He sees what you read. He's not stupid, especially since he's staying at your house."

"Never realized that."

"At least he's keeping it to himself rather than arguing," Sally said. "There's enough tension in the world without having to deal with it in one's own home."

"But I have to," Geraldine finished her glass of wine. "And it gets on my nerves."

The waiter returned with their orders, including refills on their drinks. Geraldine chomped on her hamburger and onion rings as if she hadn't eaten all day. Sally was nearly as famished, munching away on a plate of cheesy nachos. John sipped his beer, enjoying the relative peace before having to return to his hectic home.

A few minutes later, when the waiter asked if they needed anything else, Geraldine lifted her glass for more wine.

"Mother, do you think you need that?" Sally asked after the waiter left.

"Who's the mother here?" Geraldine snapped. "I think I know when I've had enough."

John sensed Geraldine was gradually becoming her old self around Sally. "We're in no hurry," he said, defusing the situation.

"How's Brody been while I was away?" Sally asked, dipping a fry into ketchup.

"Brody comes and goes," Geraldine said. "I gave up on trying to keep tabs on his whereabouts. He's going to do as he pleases."

"From what I can gather, he's still involved in the rehab," John said. "We're thankful about that."

"Have you checked to see if he is?" Sally asked.

"No, I haven't. I'll make a call tomorrow and get a progress report. Thanks for the reminder. Sometimes I take things for granted when it comes to him. I should know better."

"I hope you've checked your computer," Geraldine said. "He doesn't need to be looking at naked people. He's too old for that."

"Naked people?" Sally asked. "What are you talking about?"

"It's naughty porno stuff," Geraldine said. "Disgusting."

"I'll say something to him," John said.

"One evening I walked in on him in his bedroom and I could swear he was playing with himself."

"Mother!"

"Well, it sure looked like it," Geraldine said. "He covered his hand over his pants and yelled at me to leave."

"Did you knock before going in the room?" John asked.

"No."

"Maybe you should have?"

"I can tell you I never did it again."

"I don't know what to say," John said. "I'm sure it was embarrassing for him."

"Him? What about me?"

"Okay, it was probably embarrassing for both of you." Sally said. "I hope things are better now."

"He acted like it never happened," Geraldine said.

"Maybe you need to do the same."

Geraldine finished her wine in two swallows. "I'm ready to go."

"Me, too." Sally said.

"Let's go," John said, easing out of the booth. He paid for their meals while Sally held her mother's hand as they walked to the car.

After everyone fastened their seatbelts and John turned on the ignition, Geraldine asked, "Do you think we can go to that leaf place?"

"Leaf place?" Sally said.

"We went to Orange Leaf the other day for frozen yogurt," John said. "Sure, I wouldn't mind having a dish."

"That'd be a nice dessert," Sally said. "Maybe we should swing around home and pick up Wendell and Libby."

"That's fine by me," John said.

"But what if they aren't there?" Geraldine said. "We might be wasting our time."

"It's only five minutes away."

"I'm really not hungry for it now," Geraldine said. "I think my stomach is a little upset from the wine. Do you think we could just go home?"

"Are you sure, Mother," Sally asked. "Yogurt sounds good right now."

"Well, why don't you just drop me off at the house and you and John go by yourself."

"Hey, let's do it tomorrow or another day," John said. "When Geraldine feels better. And I know it's been a long day for you, Sally. I'm sure you want to see Wendell and Libby."

"You're right, John."

"Well, we're not going to get there if we stay parked here," Geraldine said. "It'll be dark soon."

"Home, John!" Sally said with a laugh.

~ * ~

Sally rushed over and hugged Wendell and then Libby, catching them by surprise as they sat in the den watching a bombastic preacher on a religious program on TV. They barely moved on the couch, speechless and their faces flushed at Sally's spontaneous show of affection. Geraldine claimed her usual place in the recliner, eyeing the remote control next to Wendell, while John stood to the side with his arms crossed.

"It's so good to see you," Sally said as she nudged the rocking chair near the couch and sat. "You guys look great. It's been so long. How's everything?"

"We're doing fine, Sis," Wendell said, his voice soft and quivering. "Trying to look after Mama while you were away."

Geraldine turned and scowled at Wendell. He probably sensed not to make eye contact with her.

"We may be staying for a while," Libby gushed with a broad smile. "We've met some nice people here."

"That's what John told me," Sally said, leaning forward in the rocker. "And I understand you might be moving in with a woman down the street?"

Wendell's shoulders sagged. "I think it fell through."

John's shoulders slumped as well. "Uh, what happened, Wendell?"

"We're not sure but I think there've been some complaints about Sister Cathy's ministry."

"What a shame," Geraldine chimed in, her face contorted in mock sadness. "So you'll be staying here?"

"Only if John and Sally are willing to keep their doors open for us." Libby pursed her mouth for a few seconds. "At least for a little while longer."

"Of course you're welcome to stay here," Sally said. "Until you find a place of your own."

"Thanks, Sis," Wendell said. "We'll try not to be a burden."

"That's what family is for," Sally said, sitting back in the chair. "To be there for one another. Right, Mother?"

"And you can help around the house," Geraldine said. "I didn't raise a freeloader."

"Now, Mama," Wendell pressed his lips together. "We cleaned up today."

"After I told you to."

"That's okay, Mother," Sally said. "They're our guests."

Geraldine wobbled her head and turned her attention back to the TV where the bloated evangelist was pleading for donations to help his ministry.

"Can I have the remote, Wendell?" Geraldine asked. "How can you stand to watch this nonsense?"

"He's a man of God," Wendell said, cocking his head.

"Hogwash! He's a conman."

Sally turned toward Geraldine. "Let's not argue, Mother. Please?"

"Then let me have the remote so I can put something decent on the TV."

"Like one of your soap operas?" Wendell said. "Do you think we all want to sit around and watch your programs all the time?"

"Now watch your tone," Geraldine said, pointing a finger at him. "Don't get mouthy with me. I'm still your mother."

Wendell handed the remote to Sally, who passed it on to Geraldine. He sat erect, jaw clenched, and face turning a light red as Geraldine clicked through the channels before stopping on a soap opera. She turned up the volume a notch as if to make a point. John lowered his head to hide a grin.

Libby twirled a finger in her hair with a timid face like a child who had avoided a maternal scolding.

Seconds later, the front doorknob clicked and the door creaked open, prompting a yap from Whiskers in his cushion. They turned their heads in unison toward the entryway. Brody appeared, eyes sparkling, and holding hands with a twentyish woman with a shy smile, a half-step behind.

"Hey guys, I'd like you to meet Ashley," he said.

Ashley, wearing a multi-colored African tunic and purple leggings, waved her hand. "Hi," she said, her brows arched.

John stepped toward her and shook her hand while Sally rose from the rocker and walked over to her. "It's a pleasure to meet you, Ashley," she said with a warm smile.

"Now this is a surprise," Geraldine said, rising up in the recliner. "Pleased to meet you, dear. Brody's talked about you, but we weren't sure you were for real."

"Now, Grandma," Brody said, blushing. He then introduced Ashley to Geraldine, Wendell, and Libby.

Wendell and Libby's faces drained of color as they sat on the couch with their mouths agape.

"I thought we'd stop by for a few minutes since you're back," Brody said to Sally.

Brody placed his hands on Ashley's waist and guided her to the couch, forcing Wendell and Libby to move over so they would have room to sit. Whiskers ran up to Ashley, who leaned over and rubbed between his ears.

"Are you from Lexington?" John asked.

"Louisville," Ashley said. "I got my degrees in social work from UK. I'm working on my doctorate now. I hope to finish next spring."

"She's brainy," Brody placed his arm around the back of the couch and patted her shoulder.

"Just good study habits," Ashley said. "It's not that big of a deal."

"It sure impresses me," Geraldine said. "I don't know many black folks with degrees."

"Mother!" Sally said, eyes wide open.

John surmised Brody must have warned Ashley about what could come out of his grandmother's mouth since she appeared amused by the comment.

"That's okay, Mrs. Ross," she said. "My father's a surgeon and mother's a school administrator with a doctorate in education. My siblings have advanced degrees as well."

"Your family should be proud," Geraldine said. "You're a credit to your race."

"Please, Mother," Sally said, shaking her head.

"We've all been supportive of each other," Ashley said. "My mother and father set good examples for my family."

"I guess I didn't do such a good job," Geraldine said, glancing at Wendell.

"I don't hear anyone calling you doctor," Wendell said. "At least I went to college."

"Are you guys hungry?" John asked as he stepped between Geraldine and Wendell.

"What do you have to eat?" Brody asked.

"I can order a pizza."

Wendell broke his silence. "Sounds good to me."

"Nah, that's okay, Dad," Brody said, making a cursory glimpse at his watch. "We really need to be going. I just wanted to see Mom and introduce Ashley to everyone."

Brody and Ashley stood, his hand on her shoulder. "It's nice meeting everybody," she said.

"Please come back and visit anytime," Sally said. "Our house is always open to Brody's friends."

Wendell and Libby nodded with awkward smiles.

After Brody and Ashley left, Geraldine leaned back in the recliner with her feet up. "Brody never mentioned his girlfriend was a colored girl. I thought she was Mexican."

"Mexican?" Sally asked.

"He told us her last name was Garcia."

"That could be anything," John said. "Does it make any difference?"

"I don't know what to say," Wendell said, shifting his body and gripping Libby's hand.

"You don't need to say anything," Geraldine said. "Nobody asked for your opinion."

"Please, Mother," Sally said, playing her role as peacemaker. "Let's not argue."

Wendell lifted two fingers.

"Something else you want to say?" Sally asked.

"I was wondering if John was going to order pizza," he said, his brows lifted. "Libby and I wouldn't mind some." Libby nodded in agreement.

"No problem," John said. "Anything in particular on it?"

"Lots of meat," Wendell said.

"Wendell's a meathead," Libby said, tapping his thigh.

"You're right," Geraldine said before turning up the volume on the TV and changing the channel to *Jeopardy!*

~ * ~

After dinner, Wendell and Libby slipped away to Sister Cathy's house for a fellowship meeting while Geraldine retreated to her bedroom, declaring she needed a break from everyone. While the others didn't express sentiments, they may have needed a break from her as well.

"We have the television if we want it," John said to Sally as they sat at the kitchen bar with two pizza boxes, near-empty glasses, paper plates and napkins scattered everywhere.

"I'm not in the mood for TV," Sally said. "To be honest, I'm tired and want to get some sleep."

"Why don't you go get our bed ready in the living room while I clean up this mess?"

"Couch or floor?"

"There's more room on the floor," John said. "But if you think it'd be too hard sleeping on the floor, the couch works."

"Don't we have a foam layer stashed away from a long time ago when we went camping?"

"I think we do," John said. "I believe it's in the garage."

John found the foam, rolled and tied in an overhead bin, and carried it back into the house. Sally was already unfolding the sheets and cover in the living room when he returned and placed it on the floor. He went back to the kitchen, and when he returned five minutes later, Sally had their bed covering the middle of the floor.

"How's that?"

"Looks inviting," John said with a wink. "I can't wait."

"Now don't you get any crazy ideas, silly man. We've got company."

"It didn't stop us in the past."

"It was forty years ago, before Chloe and Brody came along," Sally said.

"And probably a reason they did come along."

"Could be."

"My how time flies."

"I'm going to go change into my sleepwear before Wendell and Libby come back."

"While you do that, I'll take Whiskers out one more time before we call it a night."

John fastened the leash on Whiskers and headed out the door and down the street. Sister Cathy appeared to have a full house, with lights on upstairs and downstairs. He stopped for a few seconds when he heard shouts of, "Amen sister," "Amen brother," "Praise the lord," and "Hallelujah" filling the air.

"I think it's time to move along, little buddy," John said as he tugged on the pooch's collar and hurried down the street. When they returned, Sally was sitting on the couch reading a book.

"There's some old-time religion going on at Sister Cathy's," John said as he unleashed Whiskers. "They're really getting into it."

"You didn't want to join in?" Sally asked, lowering the book to her lap.

"Maybe if you were with me."

She closed the book and placed it on the end table. "Let me sleep on it."

Moments later, Wendell and Libby opened the front door, their eyes ablaze and faces flushed with wide smiles.

"You guys all right?" John asked. "You don't look so well."

"Oh, John, our souls are filled with love," Libby said breathlessly. "We just had the most wonderful experience at Sister Cathy's."

"You might want to sit down and relax before you fly off to the heavens," John said.

"That's how we feel now," Wendell said. "Heaven bound."

"I hope you get there. We're headed to the land of nod."

"Huh?" Wendell asked.

"Sleepy town."

"Oh, I didn't notice your stuff on the floor."

"It's been a long day for me, so we decided to get to bed," Sally said. "I hope you understand."

"Sally, why don't you let us sleep there and you and John take back your bed?" Libby said. "I know you must be exhausted. You're not going to get a good night's sleep there."

"We're good. The arrangements are fine for now."

"Oh, well, if you insist," Libby said. "But let us know if you ever want to switch."

"Well, good night, ya'll," Wendell said as he and Libby turned toward their bedroom. "We'll see ya in the morning. God bless!"

"Same to you," John said.

After hearing the bedroom door close, Sally took off her bathrobe and slipped under the sheets. John turned out the lights, then took off his clothes and snuggled next to her.

"It feels good having you next to me again," Sally cooed.

"I've missed you, too," John said. "I hope you get a good night's sleep."

He kissed her cheek, and within a minute, she drifted off to sleep. Whiskers found a spot between their feet.

~ * ~

In what seemed like a few minutes, but probably several hours, John and Sally were jarred from their deep sleep by Brody's return with the quick on and off of the light switch.

"Sorry 'bout that," Brody whispered as he tip-toed past them to the kitchen. He flicked on the lights, casting a glow through the entry into the living room. He opened and closed the refrigerator door with a slight thump. The microwave kicked on for a minute and the door slammed shut.

John pushed himself up from the floor as quietly as possible, slipped on his pants, and toddled to the kitchen. Brody sat at the bar with a bottle of beer, munching on a slice of leftover pizza. John poured a glass of water and sat across from him. He glanced at the clock on the wall: one twenty.

"What did you think?" Brody asked casually.

"About what?"

"Ashley."

"She seems like a nice young woman. Is she the person you met at rehab?"

"Yep."

"I thought they would be prohibited from having any involvement with patients."

"I think they do, but technically, she's not a counselor."

"Please don't tell me she's there for treatment as well."

Brody chuckled. "She's observing what goes on. It's part of the doctoral program she's in. I guess I'm a case study."

"Oh, I see," John said. "Are you getting serious?"

"No way," Brody said. "I've only known her a couple of months. We're more like good friends right now."

Sally drifted into the kitchen, clutching her robe at the neck and kissed Brody on the cheek.

"What's that all about?" Brody asked, twisting his head.

"Just that I've missed you and that I love you." She sat next to him. "I hope that's all right."

Brody blushed. "Love you too, Mom."

"Your girlfriend seems pleasant," Sally said.

"Eh, we're just good friends right now," Brody said with a shrug. "It's cool."

"Mother says she didn't see much of you while we were away."

"She wouldn't know if I was at home or on the moon. All she does is watch TV in the den. You know that."

"She does do that," John said. "At least it keeps her out of your hair."

"John!" Sally said. "That's not a nice thing to say."

John tried to suppress a grin. "I didn't mean it that way."

"If you say so."

"Uncle Wendell and Aunt Libby are kinda strange," Brody said. "If you haven't noticed."

"How so?" Sally tilted her head.

"They either sit around in the den with Grandma or hang out in your bedroom. They don't have a lot to say."

"You probably wouldn't want to hear what they had to say," John said.

"John! There you go again." Sally reached over and lightheartedly tapped his hand.

"Well, it's true."

"That's beside the point."

"Are you going to get your bedroom back?" Brody asked.

"Eventually," Sally said. "We're going to discuss it with them."

"You can use my bedroom, if you like. It wouldn't bother me to sleep on the couch in the living room or den. I've done it before."

"We may take you up on that offer," John said. "I'm not sure if my back can take sleeping on the floor if it goes on very long."

Brody took a swig of beer. "Dad says I can go visit Chloe."

"I said that's a maybe," John said. "Let's wait and see how things are going with her. And how things are going here for you."

"I'm sure she'd love to see you," Sally said. "She's finished with her treatments. Now we're waiting to see how her body responds. I'll probably go back for a few days in a week or so. Maybe you could go with me?"

"I was kinda wanting to go by myself." Brody took another swallow from his bottle without making eye contact with either of them.

"What difference does it make?" John asked. "It would probably be more convenient if you went at the same time."

"Isn't the apartment small? And wouldn't it be too cramped with both of us there?"

"It's cramped with two people," Sally said. "But we'll see how things are going."

"Did you have other plans?" John asked.

"What do you mean?" Brody said.

"Other things to do in New York?"

"I have a few friends who live there I'd like to see. Maybe I can check out the job market."

"Son, you don't need to be looking for a job in New York. You need to get your life together here before moving on."

"Whatever."

"Believe it or not, I'm on your side," John said.

"Damnit, I'm almost thirty-nine and you treat me like a child."

"Who's fault is that?"

"Okay, I slip up a few times. Can't you let go? I'm tired of hearing your shit over and over."

"Brody, we just don't want to lose you," Sally said. "I don't think you understand. It's because we love you."

"Sometimes a person can show their love by letting go, you know? I can take care of myself."

"You're getting there, one step at a time," John said. "Don't take it personally."

"What do you mean by that? Personally? It's me you're talking about. I'm going to take it personally."

"Okay, bad choice of words. I just meant for you to understand it takes time and let's work through this together. Believe it or not, I'm looking forward to the day when you're back to being self-sufficient again. We didn't raise you to be dependent on us. You know that."

Sally tapped Brody's hand. "Brody, I wish you'd try to understand our side as your parents. You're not a child, but you're our child."

Brody moved his hand away from her. "I'll just be glad when this shit is over with."

"Me, too." John said faintly.

Brody eased off the stool, smirking, and headed to his bedroom without another word. John and Sally looked at each other, shaking their heads as a gloomy silence suddenly filled the room.

"What are we going to do with him?" John asked. "All we've done *for* him and he seems to believe we're doing something *to* him. It makes no sense at all. I'm getting damn tired of it. I came close to telling him he can forget going to New York."

"Don't do that, honey," Sally said, placing her hand on his forearm. "There's no telling what he'd do then."

"I know. He'd go back to his old ways and then blame it all on us."

"Be patient," she said. "He does seem to be doing better, at least from what I can tell."

"I agree with that; I just don't want him to blow it."

"John, we can't keep him here. If he wants to go to New York, Chicago, or wherever, it's his decision. I want us to have an environment that won't drive him away."

"That's what I want as well, but I'd like for him to get it through his stubborn, thick skull we want the best for him. I wish he'd realize that."

"Honey, I believe he does. We just can't force it on him."

"And I'd like for him to show us at least a small degree of respect. Am I asking too much?"

Sally's eyes began to water. "I know, honey."

"I didn't mean to upset you."

Sally picked up a napkin and dabbed her eyes and nose. "We'll discuss it later."

John sighed. "Ready to go back to bed? I mean, the floor?"

"I'm exhausted," she said, sliding off the stool.

John kissed her cheek. "I'm sure you are, mentally and physically. And I didn't help matters."

"It's not you. You know that."

John took her hand as they headed to the living room.

"Would you mind if I slept on the couch?" she asked in a hushed tone. "The floor's killing my hips."

"No problem," he said. "I know you're worn out. Would you care if I go to the den and sleep on the couch or recliner?"

"I don't mind. We both need our sleep."

"My problem is I'm not sure I can get back to sleep. Brody waking us up and then his mini-temper tantrum. I may have to read, watch TV or do something."

"What's all the racket about?" They turned around and there stood Geraldine in a pink bathrobe and slippers. "It's almost two a.m."

"I'm sorry, Mother," Sally said. "Brody woke us up when he came in."

Geraldine crept past them to the kitchen counter. John and Sally followed, both stifling yawns. "He woke me when he went to his room, mumbling to himself, and practically slamming the door. I'm surprised it didn't wake up Wendell and Libby. He can be so inconsiderate."

"He's just frustrated," Sally said.

"If you say so. I think he needs to grow up. You baby him too much."

"And you don't?" John said.

"I'm his grandmother so I'm entitled to do that. You're the parents. It's your responsibility."

"It's too late, or too early, to argue with you," John said. "I'm going to bed."

"See what I mean?"

"What are you talking about, Geraldine?" John said, a trace of irritation in his voice.

"You don't want to discuss his problems, that's what."

"Not at two in the morning. Okay?"

Geraldine, grimacing, sidled off the stool. "If that's what you want." They watched her shuffle to her bedroom, shaking their heads when they heard her bedroom door close with a thump.

"My hip suddenly feels a little better. Would you mind sleeping with me on the floor?" Sally asked.

"Only if you snuggle up close."

"That's why I want to be with you."

After John flicked off the lights, Sally took his hand and led him to the living room. She removed her robe while John took off his pants. They cuddled under the covers, falling asleep in each other's arms. Whiskers was curled next to their feet again.

Eight

"My, don't you two look cozy."

John's head wobbled as he opened his sleepy eyes. Geraldine sat in the easy chair, a toothy grin on her face. Sally rubbed her eyes, squinted, and yanked the covers over a bare leg sticking out of the sheet.

"Good morning, Geraldine," John grunted with a strained smile.

"It's a shame you have to sleep on the floor while Wendell and Libby share your comfy bed," Geraldine said. "I bet they slept well. You need to put your foot down."

"Please, Mother. It's too early in the morning to discuss this. We'll deal with it later."

"By the way, what time is it?" John muttered, his head burrowed in a pillow.

"Nearly seven."

"Didn't we see you about five hours ago?"

"But it's morning now. I was hoping for some coffee."

"Didn't you drink coffee while we were away?"

"Don't be a smart aleck, John. You know I like your coffee."

John groaned. "Gee, thanks. Give us a few minutes and I'll put on a pot."

"Don't take too long. Wendell and Libby should be getting up soon."

"They can't make coffee?"

"Please, John, don't be difficult. I prefer yours. Now don't fall back asleep."

"As if I could."

Geraldine puttered toward the kitchen, the rat-a-tat of her cane on the floor until she reached the bar. Whiskers crawled out from under the sheet and followed her, and seconds later, John could hear Geraldine refilling the pooch's bowls.

"I think we're getting your mom somewhat trained," John whispered, slipping on his pants. Sally put on her robe and they went to the kitchen. John prepared the coffee, then let Whiskers outside and bent down to pick up the newspaper in driveway.

The streets were quiet except for the occasional barking of a dog in the distance. A dark gray overcast sky formed a glum view for a Sunday morning.

Sally had a cup of coffee waiting for him when he returned. She appeared upset, with pursed lips, probably from some rant by Geraldine.

"I thought you went to the store the other day," Geraldine said, her mouth tight.

"I did," John said. "What's the problem."

"The problem? There's nothing to eat!"

"Do you want me to go to the bakery?"

"That wouldn't be a bad idea. We do have to eat around here."

"Do you mind if I finish my coffee?" John lifted the cup to his mouth.

"Mother, we have eggs, bread, cereal. I can prepare something for you."

"That's too much trouble," Geraldine said. "You've been busy for the past few weeks and you shouldn't have to fix breakfast. You need to rest and relax for a few days. You deserve it. Right, John?"

John nodded before taking a sip of coffee.

"It's not a problem, Mother," Sally said. "I've been doing it most of my life."

"I'll go to the bakery." John eased off the stool. "I'm sure the others will want something when they get up."

"I like those cream-filled long johns," Geraldine said.

"I'll try to remember that."

"You might want to write it down."

"I think I can remember long johns."

"Cream-filled long johns."

"Okay, okay, I won't forget."

Geraldine took a deep breath. "If you say so."

When John returned twenty-five minutes later, Wendell and Libby were seated at the bar, dressed in their Sunday best, a light-blue suit and red tie for Wendell and a spring-floral dress and black pumps for Libby.

John set the box of pastries on the bar. Libby opened it, and when Wendell reached in to take a long john, Geraldine smacked the top of his hand.

"That's mine!"

Wendell flinched. "Sorry, Mama. How was I to know?"

"John got the long johns especially for me." Geraldine cocked her head with a fawning grin. "Right, John?"

John hesitated for a few seconds. "Sure, Geraldine. But I bought several so others could have one."

"Thanks a lot." Geraldine scrunched her nose.

Wendell and Libby each took a plain glazed donut, wanting to avoid Geraldine's wrath. Sally stared at the remaining pastries, smiled at Geraldine, and seized a long john in an apparent act of defiance. Geraldine stared at her for a moment, took another long john and laid it next to her other uneaten pastry.

John ran his hand over his head. "There's plenty for everyone. Even Brody." He reached in and took a chocolate-glazed donut.

They ate their sugar-laden breakfast in silence for a few

minutes. Whiskers even sensed the tension, leaving the room for his padded cushion in the den.

"You folks look awfully nice this morning," John said to Wendell and Libby. "What's the special occasion?"

"It's Sunday," said Wendell, who had a napkin tucked under his neck. "We go to church on Sundays." Libby's wide grin revealed donut crumbs on her chin.

"Down the street?"

"No, we're going to a traditional church today," Wendell said. "I found an interesting congregation about a mile from here. It's more of a community-type church."

"Doesn't Sister Cathy have church services?"

"Only Bible study."

"Where does she go to church?"

"I really haven't a clue."

"You've never asked her?" John asked. "You're not curious?"

Wendell flashed a snooty grin. "I'm not the nosy journalist like you. Furthermore, it's really none of my business where she goes to church as long as we worship the same God."

"You should come with us," Libby said, eyes gleaming as she looked at the others one by one. "It would make for a glorious day."

"Maybe some other time." John took a sip of his coffee. "How about you, Geraldine?"

Libby's smile evaporated into a frown. Wendell's lips stiffened.

"You mind your own business, John, and quit being a smart aleck," Geraldine said, brows drawn. "I don't know what's got into you since you went on vacation."

John raised his palms chest-high. "I was just thinking of you."

"I can think for myself, thank you," she said. "And if I wanted to go to a church, I sure wouldn't pick some Bible-thumpin' place."

"Now, Mama, that's not nice," Wendell said, sitting upright. "You used to go to church with us years ago."

"That's before you got goofy," Geraldine said. "I can get more religion watching the Sunday morning shows on TV."

"That's not the best way to praise the Lord," Libby said, raising her right brow. "You need singing and prayers and fellowship and everything like that. You need to get filled with the spirit."

"You praise the spirit the way you want to, and I'll do it my way." Geraldine scowled at Libby, who lowered her head. "I don't need to hear some racket from a band to fill the spirit. It gives me a headache."

"Can we talk about something else?" Sally suggested. "It's too early in the morning for this."

"That's fine by me." Geraldine took a bite from her long john, part of the creamy filling oozing from the corner of her mouth.

Brody bounded into the room, barefoot and wearing lounge pants and a T-shirt. "What's all the commotion down here?"

"We're discussing religion," Geraldine said.

"Jesus Christ!"

"Now watch your tongue." Geraldine pointed a finger at him. "I won't stand for that kind of talk. We used to call it blasphemy."

"Whatever." Brody walked to the coffee carafe and poured a cup. "What's for breakfast?"

"I saved you a long john," Geraldine said brightly.

"Thanks, Grandma," he said, pecking her on the cheek. "At least someone thinks about me."

John glanced at Sally, placing a finger over his mouth, although he realized she knew from experience it was better to remain silent than to open another sarcastic outburst from her fearsome mom.

"You guys going to a funeral?" Brody asked Wendell.

"No, we're going to church," he said.

"Why don't you go with us?' Libby asked. "You've got time to get cleaned up."

"I don't think so," Brody said with a slim smile. "I've got some things going on today."

"You know you have an open invitation," Wendell said.

Brody took a bite from a long john and munched on it for several seconds. "I'll think about it. But thanks, anyway."

"It might help you," Libby said.

"Help me with what?"

"Oh, you know, with some bad things you've been experiencing."

Brody stuffed the rest of the pastry in his mouth and chewed slowly. "That's none of your business, Aunt Libby."

Libby's face flushed. "I didn't mean it that way. I'm only trying to help. I'm sorry."

Brody forced a smile. "That's okay. Thank you for your concern, but I'm doing things my way."

"Just like the Lord says," Wendell said.

"What are you talking about?" Geraldine said.

"The Lord helps those who help themselves. It says so in the Bible."

"I don't think so," Geraldine clenched her jaw. "Where do you hear that nonsense?"

"We'll discuss it later, when I get back from church."

"Figures."

"Any more long johns?" Brody asked.

Geraldine hovered over one on her plate, slowly wrapping her hands around the corners as if to hide the coveted sweet concoction. She glanced at the open box, which contained a few jelly-filled and glazed donuts, and at the others' plates with partially eaten pastries.

"I don't think so," she said with a prim smile.

Everyone finished their sweets in silence.

~ * ~

"Let's go for a walk, Whiskers," John said as he reached down and stroked the pooch between the ears.

"Is it getting too hot in the kitchen?" Geraldine asked. "You always decide to take your little mutt for a walk when things get a little heated."

"You ought to try it, Geraldine," he said. "It's good for the heart and soul.."

Geraldine grabbed her cane and tapped it on the hard on the floor. "Does it look like I can go for a walk?"

"Calm down. If you ever want to go to the park with me, we can make it happen."

"I'll think about it," she said.

"You just let me know."

"I will." Geraldine said boldly as she picked up the long john and took a small bite. The others looked at her, expecting another comment. But she took another bite, signaling the conversation was over.

John needed to escape from the tense surroundings for a while despite being greeted by gray skies when he opened the front door. Whiskers appeared eager to do the same, his tail wagging as he scampered across the yard for his daily journey to the park.

The street was quiet and peaceful as they headed out the door. Newspapers, what few neighbors were still subscribing, were scattered on several of the dew-covered lawns. Whiskers took his time, as always, leaving marks along the way. John didn't mind because it was Whiskers' time and he was tagging along for an unhurried Sunday morning stroll. He learned that having a doggie into his life was a great way to unwind, something he never anticipated in retirement.

John walked to the park bench where he usually sat, and unleashed Whiskers to romp and aggravate the fowl minding their own business by the pond. He was lost in thought, staring across the still water, when startled by a hand on his shoulder. He turned around, and Sally stepped around the bench to sit with him.

"I hope you don't mind," she said, smiling. "I needed some fresh air as well. I couldn't take much more at the house."

"The bench is a little damp," John said, running his hand over a dewy spot for her to sit.

"I can see why you come here so often," she said as she sat next to him. "It's so peaceful."

Whiskers saw her and scampered to her feet. She patted his head for a few seconds, then he scurried back toward the pond to torment the birds.

"This has become my favorite place," John said, taking hold of her hand. "Even when things aren't so crazy at home. It's my special sanctuary."

"Do you mind sharing it with me?"

"Anytime," John placed an arm around her shoulders and scooted closer.

"And Mother?"

"Your mother?"

"I think she's getting stir crazy."

"When all you have is TV, it's bound to happen to a lot of folks," John said.

"I hope we can take her out more, like we did to the restaurant and yogurt place. She seemed to really enjoy it."

"I'm all for it.

"You're good to her."

"I try to be, although I must admit it can be a strain," he said with a light chuckle. "What's on your mind? I know you didn't walk all this way to commune with nature."

"Everything." She let out a weak laugh. "I almost wish I were back with Chloe. At least there the only commotion was Chloe rearranging things in the cabinets and closets. There's always something going on here. If it's not Mother, then it's Wendell and Libby. Or it's Brody."

"Or me?"

"Now, you know better than that. You're my rock."

John gently squeezed her shoulder. "I try, but it's not easy at times. But I know what you're saying."

"Like minds."

"It'll all soon pass."

"You really think so?"

John chuckled. "Maybe it's optimistic thinking on my part. But doesn't it eventually? Nothing goes on forever."

"What are we going to do about Mother?"

"What do you mean?"

"Most of her belongings are in Arizona. How are we going to get them here?"

"Guess I'll fly out there, pack everything in a rental truck, and drive back."

"You're too old to be doing something like that."

John angled his head. "Thanks a lot. You make it sound like I should be confined to a rocking chair or moseying about in the yard with a walker."

"You know what I mean."

"I'd like to think I have a few more good years left in me. Furthermore, I could take Brody with me. I don't think he'd object to getting out of Lexington for a week or so."

"That's a thought. Maybe Wendell could go along as well."

"Let's not get carried away. Wendell would be more of a supervisor, watching us work."

"That's Wendell."

"I do think Brody and I could handle it. Or maybe hire a couple hands out there to help out."

"We'll see."

"We'll need to talk to your mom first. Maybe she'd want to give most of it away to a charity."

"That's a thought. I'll ask her when I think the time is right."

"Good idea. You don't want to catch her on a bad day."

"And then there's Wendell and Libby. Are they ever going to leave? I'd really like to be sleeping in my own bed, in my own bedroom, with my own bathroom. They've hardly mentioned about taking over our room. It makes me feel like an outsider in my own house."

"Libby has brought it up," John said. "But I wonder how serious she is about it."

"I'm beginning to wonder as well."

"Maybe because we're still treating them like guests."

"John, I don't want to be mean, but it is my home. I wouldn't go down to Alabama and take over their home. I'd like to think we'd stay at a motel or find some long-term accommodations if we were there in a similar circumstance."

"He's without a job so we have to give them some slack."

"I know, but how much?"

"Let's give it some more thought," John said. "As you've mentioned, they're family."

"And as for Brody, I'm concerned about him, regardless of what you may think. I wish we knew what's going on when he's not home. He just seems so cavalier about everything, like he's getting something over on us."

"Maybe the drugs short-wired his brain."

"Is it possible?" Sally asked.

"I don't have a clue. Maybe it's something we can discuss with his counselor. Or girlfriend."

"I'd prefer discussing it with the counselor."

"It would be nice if he had a job," John said. "I'm not sure his intentions for visiting Chloe are on the up and up, since he told me he has friends there. Maybe we should set an appointment with his counselor and get an update on everything."

"It probably wouldn't hurt. And I'd like to know about his girlfriend."

"Check on that, too."

"Oh, I forgot to tell you the class reunion will be in August."

"What class reunion?" John asked.

"Yours, silly. Don't you remember receiving the notice before Christmas?"

"Yes," John said. "And I didn't do anything with it."

"Chloe did."

"What?"

"Don't you recall her saying how nice it would be for us to go to your reunion, just to get away from it all?"

"I vaguely remember that, but I didn't do anything with the RSVP."

"Chloe also mailed the registration fee and paid for two days in a motel."

John raised his arms. "Why in the hell did she do that?'

"Because she loves you and wants us to enjoy retirement."

"But I hardly remember any of them."

"It might be fun."

"Yeah, and it might be a disaster."

"John Ross! You always look at the negative side."

"Because I know that's always a strong possibility. I didn't spend all those years in the newspaper business being a Pollyanna."

"But they were your friends."

"If I had wanted to see them, I would've made visits back there through the years."

"Oh, John."

"And they would have tried to stay in contact with me. You know, it's a two-way street."

John stared off in the distance.

Sally touched his hand. "I understand."

"There are some things I just don't care to revisit, such as my life fifty years ago."

"Do you have any secrets you've been hiding from me?"

"Oh, sure," John said with a chuckle. "Deep, dark secrets."

"I can't wait to hear them! Maybe I'll learn some new things about my mysterious husband."

"It won't be interesting."

Whiskers sprinted back to the bench, jumping up to Sally with wet paws and wagging tail. She stroked his back for a few seconds before setting him next to John and standing, looking out over the pond.

"I guess you're ready to head back," John said, pushing up from the bench and fastening the leash to Whiskers' collar.

"Maybe Wendell and Libby will be at church when we get back," Sally said.

"That'd be a blessing."

Sally elbowed him in the side.

~ * ~

Activity in the neighborhood was picking up as Whiskers led with numerous stops along the way. Several neighbors were placing mulch and ornamental plants around their houses, a few boys and girls were riding bikes toward the park, and other folks were probably heading to church, supermarkets, golf courses, and other weekend destinations as bright sunshine replaced the gray overcast sky.

John noticed Wendell and Libby had left as well as Brody, since their vehicles weren't parked in front of the house. He waved at Bert, who was pruning a small Bradford pear tree. Bert nodded and continued his chore without missing a snip.

"It looks like we may have some peace and quiet," John said as he opened the front door for Sally. They were greeted by a religious program blasting "Bringing in the Sheaves" from the television. Geraldine warbled along with it, lost in heavenly bliss as she was unaware of their presence at the entry.

Waiting until the song was almost over, they entered the den as Geraldine tapped her right foot to the bouncy beat of the tune. When the music ended, she lowered the volume, smiling to herself.

John and Sally sat on the couch while Whiskers scurried to his pad.

"I always loved 'Bringing in the Sheep'," she said with a sunny smile. "Makes me feel good all over."

"Mother, I believe it's 'Bringing in the Sheaves.'"

"Sheaves? What in the world are sheaves?"

"They're plants bound together, like wheat," Sally said.

"I think sheep makes more sense," Geraldine said. "It's like bringing in the flock of sheep."

"Whatever makes you feel good, Mother."

"Like the Bible says, sing with joy in your heart. And you seemed to be doing that," John said. "Filled with the spirit."

Geraldine, sitting rigid in the recliner, glowered at him for a moment. "Are you being a smart aleck?"

John chuckled. "Please, Geraldine. Give me a break. I was simply commenting on how much you seemed to enjoy the song. I think saying sheep is irrelevant to what you were feeling."

"Well, that's okay then," Geraldine said, still giving him a wary look.

"You should have gone to church with Wendell," Sally said. "I've heard they have a band and there's a lot of singing and hand clapping."

"I don't need all that racket in church, especially those loud bands. I prefer to hear people singing"

"Everything's changed since you were younger," John said. "They want it to appeal to younger generations."

"It doesn't mean I have to like it." Geraldine said.

"I'm not saying you do," John said. "Maybe we can find a more low-key church for you to attend, one focusing on traditional services. Would you like that?"

"I'd prefer staying here in the house and watching it on TV," she said, her sharp chin protruding. "That way I don't have to be with a bunch of hypocrites."

"That's fine, too."

"Thanks for giving me your stamp of approval."

"Now, don't be sarcastic," John said. "I'm only agreeing with you."

"I can even send donations to my favorite preachers."

"I understand some people do that. Have you?"

"I have a few times, when I feel moved by their sermon."

"I didn't know that," Sally said, rising from the couch. "How long have you been doing that, Mother?"

"You don't know everything I do," Geraldine said. "As a matter of fact, I've done it for several years. I have some money sent every month to several ministries."

"It's your money," John said with a nod.

"Oh, really? Thank you for letting me know that."

John raised his palms. "There you go again. I'm only agreeing with you, Geraldine. Don't be so sensitive."

"Are you worried about your inheritance?"

"No, Mother," Sally said, the corners of her mouth turned downward. "We've never brought up any of that with you. And you know that."

"Wendell has."

Sally sat in the rocker and leaned toward her. "How so?"

"He asked me how much I had in savings," Geraldine said. "He's also asked me about my will."

"What did you tell him?"

"I told him it wasn't any of his durn business. You should have seen the look on his face when I said that." Geraldine grinned from ear to ear like she'd won a game of Bingo.

"I know it's none of our business, but let us know if you need to see a financial or estate planner," John said.

"How stupid do I look? Don't you think Harry and I did that years ago?"

"I'm not saying you're stupid, Geraldine. Quit being so defensive. People go back and review their retirement plans and wills from time to time, especially after the passing of a spouse. We do. Just to make sure everything's in order. That's all I'm suggesting."

"I'll let you know if I need your advice on my money."

"Can we change the subject?" Sally began swaying back and forth as if it might defuse the tension in her body.

"Chloe called while you were gone," Geraldine said evenly.

"What did she have to say?" Sally asked, leaning forward.

"Nothing much. She said she's feeling better. We talked for several minutes. She even put Whitney on the phone."

"Does she want me to call back?"

"She didn't say anything about it. I guess she was content speaking to me."

"I'll give her a call a little later."

"If you were sick like Chloe, I know I'd get right back to you."

Sally took a deep breath and rose from the couch, her mouth pressed tightly. "You're right, Mother. I'm going to the bedroom and give her a call right this minute."

"You mean the living room?" Geraldine asked.

"Yes, Mother," Sally said. "I forgot I didn't have a bedroom. Thanks for reminding me."

"Honey, why don't you go to our bedroom," John said. "Wendell and Libby probably won't be back for a while. You'll have more privacy there."

Sally, flashing a twisted grin at her mother, said, "I think I'll do that. Is that okay?"

"It sounds like a great idea, sweetheart," Geraldine said. "I'll let them know if they return while you're in their room."

Sally shook her head, took a deep breath, and left the room.

"What did I say?" Geraldine crooked her neck.

"I think I'll go out in the garage and check the garden tools," John said. "I feel like working on the yard this afternoon."

Geraldine pushed back in the recliner and increased the TV volume without saying a word. "Peace in the Valley" flowed through the speaker.

~ * ~

John was sorting through gardening tools in the garage when Wendell and Libby returned to the house from church, parking behind Sally's SUV in the driveway. He ducked below the rectangular windows, hoping they wouldn't see him.

John sat on a large box in the front corner, holding a weeder in one hand and a trowel in the other. He stared at them, wondering if he really wanted to go outside on such a gorgeous day and work on the lawn. Other activities seemed more tempting, such as taking a nap, reading a good book, or watching a classic movie on TV—if he could wrest the remote control from tight-fisted Geraldine.

John was jarred from his thoughts by Whiskers' sharp barks. He held his breath as he heard the kitchen door creak open.

"Are you in here, John?" Sally asked, poking her head out the door.

"Over here," John said, waving his hand. "Whatcha need?"

Sally entered the garage with Whiskers and closed the door behind her. "Are you hiding or something?"

"What do people always think I'm hiding in here?"

"What's that supposed to mean?"

"I'm just looking at some stuff." John held up the tools for her to see. "Trying to get in the mood to work in the yard."

"Don't you think you should turn on a light? It's kinda dark in here."

"Nah, it's cooler when the light is off."

Sally grinned. "John, I don't believe you. But that's okay."

"Is there something you wanted?"

"Oh, yes, I talked to Chloe a few minutes ago and she's fine. She told me Brody had called and said he was planning on a visit."

"He's assuming quite a lot," John said. "What did she think about it?"

"It kinda surprised me, but she said she's not ready for him to go up there. Says she has too much going on and too much on her mind. She asked if we could let Brody know without hurting his feelings."

"I'm sure it'll disappoint him, but I'm not ready for him to go either. I sense he's got some ulterior motives for wanting to go."

"I feel the same way," Sally said, sitting on the top step to the kitchen. "We need to see what's going on with him."

"I'll let you handle it."

"Gee, thanks."

"By the way, did you mention the reunion?"

"She got a big kick out of that. She figured you'd react the way you did about going so that's why she went ahead and took care of things."

"I guess we'll make the most of it." John stood, hands tucked in his back pockets. "We can always leave early if it's a bore."

"Now don't start that, John. There's no need to be negative about it before it's even started. It's still a few months off."

"I'm just not into reunions and things like that. You know that."

"But the fiftieth is a special milestone."

"When is your fiftieth?"

"I really don't know." Sally placed a hand on her chin.

"Maybe we should look into it."

"I'm sure I'll hear something."

"Well, just in case, you should find out. It's better to be safe than sorry. You don't want to miss a milestone event. Right?"

"I know what you're doing." Sally pointed her forefinger at him.

"Oh, so you're not interested in attending yours?"

"Okay, okay. If we go to your reunion, then we'll go to mine. I'll make a few calls to some classmates and see if anything's planned."

"And if you don't, I'll mention it to Chloe and she'll take care of things."

"I promise I will."

"I wonder if it's safe to go back inside?" John asked. "I'm really not in the ready for your brother and sister-in-law."

"So you were hiding in here."

"No, no, no. Like I said, I'm thinking about working in the yard."

"Sure," Sally said, shaking her head. "I know you a lot better than you think I do."

"Oh well, regardless, I do need to go to the bathroom."

"And then go work on the lawn?"

"Are you trying to be like your mom?"

"What?"

"Trying to be funny."

"Just curious, honey. I don't want to keep you from doing your chores around the house."

"Now you're being a smart aleck!" he said with a chuckle. "Let's go inside and see what's going on."

"I'm sure they're getting hungry."

"I wonder how long they would hold out if we didn't prepare something?"

"Hard to say. I've noticed someone has been getting into the granola bars and a few other snacks. It's either them or Brody."

"It's hard to say but Libby does have a sweet tooth."

"Mother's probably getting hungry, too. I'll ask her what she would like and go from there. There's no reason to be rude to our houseguests."

"Houseguests? You mean homesteaders!"

~ * ~

Later in the evening, after Wendell and Libby retired to the bedroom and Geraldine dozed off in the recliner, the telephone rang. John looked at Sally for a moment, then dropped the book he was reading on the couch and dashed to the kitchen to answer it before it would disturb others in the house. Sally followed him, carrying a magazine, with Whiskers a step behind like a shadow.

It was a nurse from the University of Kentucky Medical Center notifying them Brody had been admitted after an apparent drug overdose. John, stunned for a moment, made sure the nurse was referring to his Brody Ross, the son who was in rehab and supposedly kicking the opioid habit.

After the call ended, John turned around, a look of disbelief washed over his face. Sally stood several feet from him, tears welling in her blue eyes from the fragments of the conversation she had overheard.

John stood silently for several seconds as in a haze. "No details other than an overdose," he said in an even tone.

"Let me change my clothes," Sally said, barefoot and wearing a T-shirt and pajama shorts. "It'll only take me a minute."

Her oversized blue blouse and black leggings were draped over the easy chair in the living room. She made the switch and slipped on her canvas shoes. They were out the door, leaving Whiskers whining by their quick departure. They did not notify the others where they were going.

Almost. Wendell's car was parked behind Sally's SUV.

"Damnit!" John said as they stood in the driveway. "Why in the hell did he park behind you?"

"Wait here, I'll go ask Wendell to move his car," Sally said as she headed back to the house. A few minutes later, Wendell, wearing a wife beater's shirt and dress pants, followed Sally to the front yard. John was in Sally's vehicle, the motor running and ready to go.

"What's up?" Wendell asked.

"Brody's in the hospital," Sally said. "We think it's drugs."

"Need me for anything?"

"Just move your car," Sally said. "We're in a hurry."

"Oh, yeah."

Wendell got in his car and eased into the dark street while Sally climbed in with John and fastened her seatbelt.

"I was afraid something like this would happen," John said, backing Sally's vehicle out of the driveway. "I just had a gut feeling something wasn't right."

"I don't know what to think," Sally crossed her arms over her chest while fighting back tears. "They told us there was a chance of him relapsing, but he seemed to be doing so well. At least we thought he was."

"That's what he was telling us. We should have known better." John bit his lower lip and gripped the steering wheel. "Damnit! I don't understand him."

"Try to calm down, John. Please."

They drove in silence to the hospital. After John inquired about Brody at the nurse's station in the ER, a stocky middle-aged man approached them and introduced himself as Bill Shelby, adding he had been the person who had notified Fayette County Emergency Medical Service.

"I found him slumped over in a car in front of a strip mall on Lane Allen Road," he said. "I didn't detect any alcohol on his breath, so I assumed it was a drug overdose. There's a lot of bad stuff going on now."

John clenched his jaw for several seconds. "Brody's been in rehab the past five months. My wife and I are at a loss for words. We've tried to keep close tabs on him. We're floored by this. I feel like I've been punched in the stomach."

"I've read enough about overdoses in newspapers to know it's impossible to watch over them twenty-four-seven," Shelby said.

"We'll do what needs to be done to help him," Sally said, holding back tears.

"I trust you'll get him back in rehab as soon as he's released from here."

John was taken aback by the comment. "That's our plan."

"By the way, I've been through it with my daughter. I know it's an uphill struggle. Just don't give up on him." An apprehensive smile crossed Shelby's lined face before he turned and walked away.

"Mr. Shelby," John said, raising his hand. "Thank you for looking out for our son."

"Please pay it forward. They need all the support we can give them."

A nurse led them to Brody's room. He was groggy, and the sheets were marked with yellow splotches from where he had heaved bile from the overdose. His face was ashen and eyes hollow from the self-inflicted suffering.

"I'm sorry." Brody's dilated eyes brimmed with tears as turned his head away from them.

"We are, too," John said. "We thought you were doing better. I guess we were wrong."

"John, please," Sally said. "Not now."

Brody sniffled and sobbed. Sally took a tissue from the metallic dispenser on the table and placed it in his hand.

"Why?" John asked. "After all this time in rehab."

"I don't know." Brody kept his head turned away from them. "I knew I shouldn't do it, but something just came over me. I can't explain it. I don't know. I wish I knew. I didn't think this would happen."

"This is the first time, is it?"

"What do you mean?" Brody turned around and looked at them.

"You've taken drugs before this."

"Oh, maybe once or twice." Brody blew his nose. "I don't remember. While you were on vacation."

"What did you take?"

"I'm not sure. Someone gave them to me. I didn't ask what they were. Just some pills to get a little high."

"Who gave them to you?"

"I don't know his name. Someone I met a few weeks ago."

"Where?" John asked, raising his voice.

"I don't remember. Some bar downtown."

"I don't know what to say." John took two steps back

"You need to go back to rehab," Sally said, touching Brody's shoulder.

"I know." Brody lowered his head.

"We'll get you back to it tomorrow," John said. "Understand?"

Brody closed his eyes and mumbled, "Yes."

"Does Ashley know?" Sally asked.

"She doesn't have a clue," Brody mumbled. "Anyway, she's visiting with her family in Louisville. She's not going to be happy with me."

Nine

Brody's release from the hospital came just after daylight. He sat in the backseat of the SUV, staring out the window. Sally fidgeted with her cell phone. John clenched the steering wheel to the point his knuckles were white.

"I guess I'll have to ask Wendell to go with me to pick up my car," John said to Sally as he pulled into their neighborhood. "Remember where it's at, Brody?"

"Uh, I think at the Stonewall Center on Clays Mill."

"I can go with you," she said.

"You need to stay at the house." He glanced at Brody in the rearview mirror, still gazing out the window as if in a trance. Sally, as if sensing the tension in the air, squeezed John's forearm.

Brody led the way into the house, going directly to his bedroom without saying a word to his grandmother standing near the front door in her bathrobe with Whiskers at her feet. Sally followed, holding the door open for John.

"What's his problem?" Geraldine asked, arching her thin neck. "He walked past me like I wasn't here. He can be so disrespectful at times. And after all I've done for him."

John and Sally pushed their makeshift and unruffled bed on the floor with their feet, and plopped on the couch, exhausted from Brody's unpredictable caper.

"Well?" Geraldine demanded as she sat on the easy chair with a stiff stare.

"We've been at the hospital, Mother."

"Was Brody sick?" Geraldine softened her tone.

"Yeah, he's sick, Geraldine," John said. "He's been sick for a long time."

"The flu?"

"No, damnit," John said, taking a deep breath. "Drugs!"

"You didn't have to say it so mean!" Her face turned a deep red. "I was only asking."

"I apologize, Geraldine." John sighed. "I'm just frustrated by it all. We thought he was on the road to recovery and then he overdoses. One step forward and two steps back."

Geraldine sat erect on the edge of the chair, clutching her cane with both hands. "I'm sorry. I thought he was getting better, too."

"Please, John." Sally tapped his knee. "We knew this could happen. We shouldn't be surprised."

John shook his head. "I know. I know. But it doesn't make things any easier. Is it okay to be disappointed?"

"So what are you going to do?" Geraldine asked meekly.

"Back to rehab," John said, heaving an overstated sigh. "There's no other choice. We're back to square one."

"Do you think it was the girl he brought over who gave him the drugs?"

"We don't think so," Sally said. "She's supposed to be in Louisville. All we know is a man found him overdosed in John's car."

"Where is the car now?"

"At a shopping center on Clays Mill Road," John said.

"Where's that at?" Geraldine said.

"What difference does it make, Geraldine?" John voice began to rise. "You wouldn't know if I told you."

"Excuse me," Geraldine's back stiffened like a rebar. "I was simply curious. You don't have to bite my head off."

"It's about two miles from here. Anything else you want to know?"

"What if it's been towed away?"

"Please, Geraldine," John said. "We'll cross that bridge if we come to it."

"You asked if there was anything I wanted to know."

"Well, then, that's all I know. Okay?"

"It may cost some money if it's being towed by the police."

"So what?"

"You always seem concerned about spending money."

"No, I'm not." John's face flushed. "Furthermore, money doesn't grow on any of my trees. I can find better ways to spend money. Like for rehab. Okay?"

"You don't need to take it out on me," Geraldine said with a light whimper.

"I'm not taking anything out on you. Okay?"

"Do you need money to get the car?" Geraldine asked, looking at Sally for an answer.

Before Sally could respond, John snapped, "No, Geraldine. We have plenty of money. I was simply making a point about picking up the car. I wish I hadn't said anything."

"But you did," Geraldine said, smirking. "Let's not forget about poor Brody."

"Please, Mother," Sally said, lifting a hand. "Let's not discuss it now. We're rather upset and we need time to gather our thoughts."

Geraldine pulled herself up with the cane, eyed them with a snooty smile, and padded toward the den without another word.

John waited to say anything until he was sure she was out of earshot. "She's pushing my buttons and I fell for it. Sorry 'bout that." Whiskers sensed John's distress and hopped on his lap, then rose and licked around his chin.

"That's okay, honey." Sally rested her head against his shoulder, patting Whiskers' back. "Mother's good at that. We know from experience."

"I should have known better." John leaned over and kissed the top of her head. "I'll apologize later."

"You don't have to. She's the one who brought it on."

John shrugged. "Oh, well."

Geraldine returned to the living room, standing at the entry, and looking at them for several seconds.

"What is it, Mother?" Sally asked.

"Is it safe to open my mouth?"

John leaned his head back and closed his eyes. He was determined not to be drawn back into Geraldine's perceived mistreatment.

"Of course, Mother. What do you want?"

"Well, if it's not too much trouble, it would be nice if someone would put on a pot of coffee and perhaps prepare breakfast."

John rose from the couch and walked toward the kitchen. "I'll make the coffee and you and Sally can decide what's for breakfast."

"You know you should have picked up some pastries on your way back," Geraldine said. "Those long johns the other day were really good."

"Mother, I can whip something up here," Sally said as she went to the kitchen with Geraldine practically on her heels.

"I'll run to the store and buy some pastries," John said, pouring water into the coffee maker. "It'll be quicker."

"Thank you, John," Geraldine said with a self-satisfied smile as he walked past her.

"I'm going to ask Wendell to go with me to pick up my car," John said as he headed toward the stairs. "I shouldn't be gone long."

"I hope it's not too late," Geraldine said.

"Too late for what?"

"It being towed." She looked at the ceiling with an incredulous look. "What do you think?"

John ignored her comment, got Wendell to go with him, and went after the pastries.

~ * ~

Brody didn't make an appearance until mid-afternoon, after Wendell and Libby had left the house to do one of their wandering ministry missions. He tramped to the kitchen, opened the refrigerator for about ten seconds, and closed it without saying a word.

"Good morning, son," John said from the adjoining dining room where he was reading the newspaper. "Or should I say, good afternoon?"

"Whatever," Brody muttered as he opened a cabinet.

"Sleep well?"

"What do you think?" Brody closed the cabinet.

"Only asking, son," John said. "I hope you did."

"I did." Brody opened another cabinet.

"Mom called rehab and made arrangements for you to check back in tomorrow morning."

"Are you shittin' me? Why did she do that?" Brody slammed the cabinet shut.

"As if you don't know. Didn't we discuss it in the hospital?"

"I don't remember agreeing to that."

"You probably don't recall hardly anything from the hospital. Do you even remember being in the hospital?"

"Funny."

"I don't see any humor in it either."

Brody stood in the middle of the kitchen, hands on hips. "Is there anything to eat around here?"

"I'm sure there's something. Look in the cabinets. Freezer."

"I have! Why do you think I'm asking?"

"There's food if you look hard enough."

"Oh, fuck it. I'm not hungry." Brody said.

"If you look on the counter, there's a box of pastries."

Brody opened the box, grabbed a long john, stomped to his room and slammed the door shut.

Sally, who had been napping on the couch in the living room, rushed into the dining room. "What in the world is going on?"

"Brody's not happy about going back to rehab," John said. "And I think it almost took his appetite."

"I'm going to his room and talk to him," Sally said.

"Just wait." John put down the newspaper. "Let it sink in on him a bit. He's pouting as usual, wanting us to relent about helping him. He'll get over it. And if he doesn't, well, he's still going to rehab, like it or not."

"Should I fix him something to eat?"

"He got a pastry. If he wants another one, he knows where they are."

Geraldine's cane tapping on the floor grew louder until she entered the dining room and sat at the opposite end of the table from John. No one said a word for a minute, sitting there in strained silence. John picked up the newspaper. Sally stared out the window to the backyard.

"Did I hear someone ask about dinner?" Geraldine purred.

"I'm going to get something together in a little bit," Sally said, turning around. "Do you have any idea when Wendell and Libby will be back?"

"Are you kidding me?" Geraldine said. "They come and go as they please. And I've noticed they're usually on the go when something needs to be done around here."

"They're guests, Mother."

"Would you do that if you were staying at their house in Alabama?"

"Well, uh, probably not. But that's neither here nor there."

"Sally, you know you wouldn't. You weren't raised that way."

"How about Wendell?" John asked.

"He's like his father. Harry was good about getting out of work."

"Mother, that's a terrible thing to say about Dad."

"Well, it's the truth. You know it."

"And maybe I don't."

Geraldine grimaced. "Oh, sometimes I don't understand you."

Sally shook her head and went to the kitchen. "I'm going to go ahead and get something started. If Wendell and Libby get here late, they can have leftovers."

"Now that's the attitude," Geraldine said, tapping her cane on the floor.

"Thanks, Mother," Sally said, taking a deep breath and opening the refrigerator.

"You need any help?" John asked.

"I'll let you know but I think I have everything under control."

"That'd be a change," Geraldine said.

John lowered the newspaper and glared at Geraldine. "I believe there's a long john or two in the box if you need a between-meal snack."

Geraldine shrugged. "I'm going to the den and watch TV. Let me know when dinner's ready."

~ * ~

As Sally began preparing a dinner of spaghetti, broccoli florets, and a tray of breadsticks, with Geraldine in the den and Brody sulking in his bedroom, John decided it was a good time to take Whiskers for a quick stroll around the block.

Along the way, John noticed small security cameras fastened inconspicuously below the gutters of several homes, thinking they were probably a deterrent to anyone trespassing on their properties. He thought back to when he and Sally had first moved to the neighborhood more than thirty years earlier...it had been considered a safe and friendly area to raise a family. And it was. He realized the situation had certainly changed over the years, with a different attitude toward protection.

Whiskers stopped in front of Sister Cathy's house and lifted his leg on flowers she had planted on the corner of the lawn next to the sidewalk and driveway. He tugged his fur buddy to move along while glancing at the house to see if she was peering from one of the windows. But all he saw was Wendell positioned in a chair near the picture window. Three cars were parked in her driveway so he assumed it was another one of her Bible studies.

When he returned, Sally had plates and silverware on the dining room table. Geraldine had already claimed her chair. Brody was still upstairs, not making a sound. John wondered if he was wallowing in self-pity as he had done in the past.

"You're back just in time," Sally said as she brought spaghetti in a pan to place on the plates with tongs.

"Can I help?" John asked.

She asked him to remove the breadsticks from the oven. He put them in a basket covered with a red-checkered cloth to keep them warm.

"I guess Wendell and Libby are out of luck." Geraldine grabbed a breadstick and took a nibble like a bird.

"I saw them down at Sister Cathy's house," John said. "They're probably at another Bible study."

"Figures," Geraldine said as Sally poured marinara sauce over her spaghetti. John set the bowl of broccoli near Geraldine's plate, from which she spooned several florets on the spaghetti.

"What about Brody?" Sally asked.

"What about him?" John said.

"Aren't we going to ask him to join us?"

John shrugged. "I'll go check on him and see what his plans are."

"Plans?" Geraldine asked. "Is he going back out?"

"Only a cynical comment."

"Figures."

"I'm sorry, but Brody is beginning to think the world revolves around him again," John said. "In case you haven't noticed."

"You need to show him more love."

"Perhaps he needs to do that as well."

"Now what does that mean?"

"Nothing, Geraldine. I'll go to his room and invite him to join us. Unless you want to?"

"You can do it," she said. "You're his father."

"Thank you."

"You're welcome," Geraldine responded, sitting primly and putting a floret in her mouth.

John knocked several times on Brody's door but there wasn't a response. When he turned the doorknob, it was locked.

"Brody open the damn door," John said, raising his voice. "It's dinnertime. Do you want to eat?"

No response.

"Brody, did you hear me? Please open the door! Quit playing silly games. It's time for dinner."

John rapped a few more times, again without a peep from Brody. He went to his bedroom and took a clothes hanger from the closet. He stretched it out and used the straight end to poke into the doorknob to release the lock mechanism.

Brody was outstretched on his stomach, arms extended over both sides of the bed. His breathing was labored. John rushed to him and shook his shoulders.

"Sally! Call nine-one-one!

"What?" she said.

John stepped to the door. "He's overdosed again. Call nine-one-one!"

~ * ~

The ambulance arrived fifteen minutes later with lights flashing. Gawking neighbors gathered in their front yards to see what was going on. Three EMTs, two men and a woman in crisp white shirts and blue pants, carried a gurney into the house, and followed John to Brody's bedroom. They asked John and Sally to remain in the hallway, warning the room could be contaminated. They put on gloves and masks before approaching Brody's listless body. Checking vital signs, they noticed the pin-sized pupils in his eyes and deep breathing.

Sally, standing near the doorway, spotted a small plastic bottle partially hidden under the nightstand. She pointed it to the female EMT, who picked it up, looked inside, placed it in a plastic bag and sealed it.

"It's hydrocodone/acetaminophen," the EMT said to her partners. "Get the naloxone."

One male medical worker took the naloxone injector from the medical case and inserted it in Brody's thigh. The men took hold of Brody, lifting him from his shoulders and legs, onto the gurney. Brody began writhing, his arms and legs thrashing against the restraints and his head twisting side to side. "Leave me alone," he slurred, trying to rise from the tight grip.

The EMTs whisked Brody to the ambulance. Three boys were straddled on their bicycles by the open doors, curious to see the equipment inside the vehicle as Brody's gurney was fastened. The female EMT told John and Sally to follow them to the UK Medical Center in their own vehicle.

Geraldine stood at the front door as John and Sally returned to the house after watching the ambulance dart down the street. Neighbors retreated to their homes like deer slipping into the forest.

"So what's going on?" Geraldine stepped back as they walked into the living room. "Is Brody going to be okay? He looked so pitiful on the stretcher. Poor baby."

"Another drug overdose, Mother," Sally said. "We're going to the hospital now."

"What should I tell Wendell and Libby?"

"The truth," John said. "What else would you tell them? That he stubbed his toe?"

"John, please," Sally said in a mollifying voice. "Mother was just asking what to tell them."

John turned toward Geraldine and took a deep breath. "I'm sorry, Geraldine. I'm tired and frustrated. I don't mean to take it out on you."

"I was only concerned about my grandson," Geraldine said, her eyes watering.

John walked over and hugged her. "I know you are. We're all concerned about Brody."

A caring smile emerged on Geraldine's face. "Tell him I love him."

"Will do," John said.

"I'll put the food away and clean up while you're gone," Geraldine said to Sally. "Don't you worry about a thing. I'll even let Whiskers out and feed him."

John and Sally scurried out the door and got into Sally's SUV. They arrived at the hospital's emergency room several minutes after the ambulance. Standing outside the room where Brody was being examined, they didn't speak, lost in their own thoughts as hospital staff moved in and out the long corridor of rooms to treat patients.

"What are we going to do?" Sally wiped a tear away with a tissue. "I feel so lost right now."

John patted her back. "Rehab. What else can we do?"

A doctor stepped out of the room holding a tablet. "You're Brody Ross's parents?" he asked in a slow Southern drawl.

John nodded as Sally turned around to face the tall, thin intern wearing wrinkled and blemished blue scrubs.

"I see he was here only a few hours ago," the doctor said.

"That's correct," John said. "We took him home and thought everything was settled. Then we discovered he had locked himself in his room and overdosed. And before you ask, we don't have a clue how he got the drugs. I believe one of the EMTs said it was hydrocodone. It must have already been in his room."

"Have you considered rehab?"

"We've had him in rehab, Doctor," Sally said. "In fact, he's still in the program, attending classes several times a week."

"We're going to be taking him there in the morning," John said. "We've already talked to the facility and they have a room ready for him."

"That's good," the doctor said with a tight smile. "Unfortunately, people who are using opioids can relapse. It's an ongoing struggle for most of them. He should be ready to leave here in an hour or so. I want to keep him under observation to make sure there are no other complications."

"Thank you, Doctor," John said. "We hope this will be an eye-opener for him."

"Good luck." The doctor shrugged and headed toward the nurses' station.

"He wasn't very encouraging," Sally whispered to John.

"I bet he goes through this routine several times a week, if not each day," John said. "And should we be surprised by what happened? We've been warned about it."

"I don't know anymore," she said. "I wanted Brody to be the exception."

"I'm not sure if there are any exceptions with addictions."

A nurse stepped out of Brody's room and looked at them. "You can go in now. I'll be back in a little while to see how he's doing."

John grasped Sally's hand and they went inside the room. Brody was propped up in the bed, still in the clothes he had worn to the hospital. His face was pale, his long hair matted, and eyes gloomy and drained.

They had seen it before, only a few hours earlier.

"I don't understand," Sally said. "It makes no sense to me."

"I wonder if he's trying to spite us," John said. "Or perhaps me?"

~ * ~

At the dining room table after returning home, John gazed at Sally sitting across from him as if in a quiet trance. Brody was in his bedroom, sleeping off the effects of his opioid trip. They sat in silence. John noticed the pale purple puffiness under her eyes and the narrow lines creasing her forehead.

"You need some rest, hon," he said softly. "It's been a long day."

"I know, but I don't feel like lying down," she murmured. "There's too much on my mind."

Geraldine came up from the den and sat at the head of the table between John and Sally. If she wanted to say something, she must have thought better of it than to open her mouth at this time. Her eyes flitted back and forth from John to Sally.

"Are you getting hungry, Mother?" Sally asked without looking at her.

"A little later."

"Where's Wendell and Libby?" John asked.

"Probably Bible thumpin' in the neighborhood," Geraldine said. "I haven't seen them all day."

"Mother, I know you want to know about Brody," Sally said. "He's going back into rehab. I'm not sure for how long."

"I kinda figured that. I don't know what's gotten into him."

"I guess we were too optimistic, believing he was getting his life back together," John said. "We were warned he could have a relapse. We were hoping it wouldn't happen. But it did. Now we have to deal with it and move on."

Geraldine studied Sally's face for a few seconds. "You look awful. You need to start taking care of yourself."

John raised his hand. "Please, Geraldine. We've been through a lot in the past twenty-hours. We're both tired and deeply concerned about Brody."

"I didn't mean anything by it," Geraldine pushed out her lower lip. "Just making a comment. That's all."

A tired smile eased across Sally's face as she patted the top of Geraldine's scrawny hand. "That's okay, Mother. I've looked in the mirror. I probably need a complete makeover."

Geraldine giggled. "I need a complete new body."

Wendell and Libby returned to the house, and after whispering something to each other in the living room, entered the dining room and stood next to the table with somber expressions.

"How's Brody?" Wendell asked.

"He's up in his room, sleeping," Sally said.

"Is he going to be all right?"

"We're taking him back to rehab in the morning, so we hope so. It's probably going to take a while."

"We'll be praying for him," Libby said, her chin crinkled like a prune.

"Thank you," Sally said. "He's going through a difficult time."

"I don't know what's so difficult," Geraldine said, her head moving like an agitated hen. "He doesn't do anything except go to those rehab classes. Mostly just comes and goes as he pleases."

"Maybe that's his problem," John said. "He doesn't have any purpose in his life right now."

"You're just making excuses for him," Geraldine said. "That's one of his problems. You and Sally letting him do as he pleases."

"Perhaps so." John raised a hand for her to stop her accusations. "But you're guilty of it as well."

"But he's my grandson, so I have a right."

"Not if you care for him."

"We'll have our prayer group send prayers and blessings his way," Libby said. "The Lord works in mysterious ways, so maybe there's a miracle for Brody."

John glanced at Sally, tight-lipped.

"He's going to need all the help he can get." Sally glanced at Libby with a taut smile. "We hope it doesn't take a miracle."

"Would you like for us to talk to Brody about finding his way through his Lord and Savior Jesus Christ?" Libby asked, her face somber. "We'd be more than happy to share the good news with him."

John turned his head and coughed. "I think we're okay with the rehab at this time."

"But thank you for the offer, Libby," Sally said. "We appreciate it."

"One thing at a time," John said with a small grin.

"Does Brody have a Bible?" Wendell asked. "If not, I have one from our ministry I'll be more than happy to give to him."

"There's one in his room," Sally said. "But thanks anyway."

"Well, you just let us know if he needs any spiritual assistance," Libby said, touching Sally's shoulder. "We love Brody and we don't want to see him suffer, now or later."

"Thank you," Sally said. "That means a lot."

"We'll have Sister Cathy say a prayer for him as well."

John pushed back his chair and stood. "I think it's time to take Whiskers outside before it gets too late."

Whiskers, curled in the corner on his pad, sprang toward John with perked-up ears and bright eyes when he heard the magic word, "outside."

"While you're gone, I think I'll lie down for a few minutes," Sally said. "I've got a terrible headache."

"You want to use your bed?" Libby asked.

"I'll be fine on the couch," Sally said.

"I'm a little hungry," Wendell said. "Is there anything in the fridge?"

"I tried to save some spaghetti and breadsticks from lunch," Geraldine said. "I had to throw most of it out."

"No breadsticks?" Wendell asked.

"There's some in the refrigerator you can heat up."

Wendell looked at Libby. "What do you think?"

"Is there anything else to eat?"

"My goodness, Libby," Geraldine said, raising her voice. "Can't you go over there and look for yourself?"

"Now, Mother," Sally said.

"You just go take your nap, Sally," Geraldine said, her eyes narrowed. "Wendell and Libby can get their own dinner. You don't need to wait on them hand and foot. They can fix a bowl of cereal if they're really desperate."

"Mama," Wendell said, the corners of his mouth down. "That's not nice to say. We've made our own food since we've been here."

"Once or twice?" Geraldine said, lifting a brow.

"You guys settle this," John said, a tired but bemused look on his face as he rose from his chair. "I'll be out front with Whiskers."

Sally said, "And I'm going to be in the living room." She pushed back her chair and sauntered to the couch.

"I'm going to watch TV," Geraldine said as she headed toward the den, her cane poking the floor louder than usual.

Wendell and Libby looked helpless, standing alone at the table, not really sure what to do next. They bowed their heads for a few seconds before going to the refrigerator. They stared inside for a few seconds before Wendell grabbed the milk carton.

"Where's the cereal?" he asked, raising his voice for everyone to hear.

~ * ~

John was relieved to get away from the house, not wanting to hear more gospel according to Wendell and Libby, listen to copious comments from Geraldine, or even to look at Sally's fatigued face. He figured Sally had the same thoughts when she looked at his droopy eyes and scruffy beard.

Whiskers may have even sensed the tension in the house as he practically pulled John out the front door, stretching the leash like a rubber band.

Threatening dark gray skies rumbled in the distance, forcing John to pick up the pace. Whiskers wasn't a happy pooch since he couldn't follow his normal leg-raising and smelling routine along the sidewalk toward the park. While John tried not to yank the leash, a couple of times he flicked on the collar to keep the contesting pooch moving along the uneven and cracked sidewalk.

Only after John sat on a bench near the pond and unleashed Whiskers did he feel the emotional stress flow from his body like small ripples. He closed his eyes and took several deep breaths. The only sounds were the sporadic thunder, Whiskers' snappy barks, and squawks from the oppressed waterfowl.

John was jolted from the temporary tranquility by a lightning bolt illuminating the western sky, followed by a small blast. Moments later, large raindrops pelted the pond as thick, rolling clouds enveloped the area. Whiskers stopped chasing the birds and raced toward John as cascading sheets of rain swept over the area.

John grabbed his canine companion, nestled him against his chest and ran toward a wooded area for dubious cover as the winds whipped against him and lightning lashed across low, menacing clouds. He heard snaps from the canopy of trees as limbs and branches crashed to the ground.

"What in the world are we going to do?' John said to Whiskers, who was quivering in his grip.

He saw an open picnic shelter about one-hundred yards away but realized it wouldn't provide any protection, especially with its aluminum overhead rippling back and forth. Two portable restrooms had been toppled by the heavy winds.

"We'll have to ride it out here," John said, stopping next to a small ditch turning into a gullywasher. After crouching in the gap, a sudden burst of wind twisted through the wooded sanctuary, knocking down several small trees in its path. He hoped he wouldn't be blown away or standing on a conduit of lightning striking a tree.

John knelt for several minutes until the wind bursts finally ceased, then lugged himself out of the tiny ravine through the broken branches. Trickles of blood oozed from his forehead and bare arms. Skies began to clear in the west with a streaky purple cast in the long, thin clouds. He stood and glanced around at the fallen trees, scattered branches, and leaves strewn over the once pristine landscape.

"Sally!" It occurred to him his family could be in danger from the storm which had ended as quickly as it began.

Still clutching Whiskers against his chest, John jogged across the soggy park grounds, splashing water on his pant legs up to his knees. As he drew closer to home, the only damage he noticed were small branches in the street and neighbors' yards.

He bounded into the house, wet and grimy from head to toe, only to hear the television blaring in the den. Geraldine was watching *The Price is Right* while Wendell and Libby were seated on the couch, sharing a Bible and holding hands. Sally was in the rocking chair, reading a magazine, and Brody was still upstairs in his room.

"Where in the world have you been?" Sally asked, head tilted as she rose from the rocker. "You're a mess."

John glanced down at his soiled clothes and set Whiskers on the floor. "You didn't have a storm?"

"Sheesh," Geraldine said, keeping her eyes on the TV. "We're going into the showcase."

"What happened?" Sally asked.

"I don't know," Geraldine said. "They haven't shown the prizes."

Sally shook her head. "Mother, please, I'm talking to John."

"There was a helluva storm at the park. Trees downed. Lightning. Thunder. Winds. Maybe a tornado."

"A storm watch scrolled on the TV, but it only seemed a little windy outside for a little bit," Wendell said with a shrug. "That's about it." He turned his attention back to the Bible as if John had disappeared.

"Unreal," John said. "I didn't think Whiskers and I were going to get out alive."

"Our Lord works in mysterious ways," Libby said, tilting her head and smiling. "He must have been looking over you and your little dog."

"If you say so," John said. "I'm going to get out of these clothes and take a shower."

"Oh, by the way, rehab called and they'll be waiting for Brody in the morning," Sally said. "They said we're lucky they had an opening."

"See," Libby said.

"See what?" John asked.

"We prayed for Brody," she said. "Now the Lord is looking out for him."

"He certainly works in strange ways."

"Now, John." Sally pressed her lips together.

John stared at her for a moment. "I'm going to take a shower."

Geraldine turned around in the recliner with her brows lowered. "Would everybody please be quiet? They're bidding on the second showcase."

"That's really important," John said as he left the den.

Geraldine turned her head toward Sally. "What did he say?"

"Uh, the price is right, Mother."

"How would he know? Is he being a smart aleck?"

"I think you're right."

Ten

John had a restless sleep for several reasons, including the impending trip to the rehab center with Brody. His body was sore from the weather-related escapade from the previous day. Sleeping on the floor didn't help either, even with Sally's soft body snuggled next to him. A glimmer of light sifted through a small opening in the curtain. He eased himself up, tip-toed to the kitchen and prepared a pot of coffee.

John was about to sit on a kitchen stool when Whiskers pawed at his foot, signaling it was time to do his outside morning routine. Whiskers darted to his dumping grounds while John moseyed to the end of the driveway to pick up the newspaper. When he returned to the kitchen, Sally had already poured coffee in their cups.

"I woke up Brody," she said, stirring creamer in her coffee. "He should be down here in a bit. He wants to shower and get cleaned up."

"I'm sure he's excited about it," John said with a touch of sarcasm as he poured kibble into Whiskers' bowl.

"He didn't say anything. I thought he'd put up a big fuss as to why he shouldn't go."

"Maybe sleeping on it made him realize it's the only choice."

"I still can't believe he relapsed so quickly. I thought he was doing so well." Sally puckered up as if she were about to cry.

John walked over and placed an arm around her shoulder. "Honey, we were warned this was a possibility. At least there's still a choice for him."

"I don't understand," she said. "What do you mean?"

"He could have died. Then there wouldn't have been any choices."

"Don't say that, John. That's so cold. I don't want even to let those thoughts enter my mind. He's going to be okay."

"That's what I want as well. You know that. But we've got to face reality. People die every day from drug overdoses. No family is immune. We're not any different. We could say we've been fortunate."

"You news guys can be so practical, and, well, cold."

John let out a small laugh. "I suppose we have to be to see both sides of a situation. I wish there were a cure for Brody and all drug users, but there's not. It's an addiction that will stay with him for a long time, maybe the rest of his life."

"Let's not talk anymore about it right now. You're upsetting me." She sipped her coffee, her eyes fixed as if lost in deep thought.

Brody sauntered up to them, his long dark hair damp and slicked back, and wearing jeans and light pullover shirt. He carried a small travel bag, the same one used on his previous trip to the rehab center more than five months earlier.

"Sleep well?" John asked as Brody sat next to Sally.

"As well as could be expected," he answered with a slight shrug.

"Want some coffee?" Sally asked.

"Please."

"Breakfast?" Sally took a cup from the cabinet.

Brody's head was down and he lightly tapped his fingers on the bar. "I don't have much of an appetite."

"You shouldn't go out with an empty stomach."

"I said I'm not hungry."

John stared at his son, twisting his head to make eye contact. "Anything you want to say?"

"Dad, I really don't want to talk about it." Brody kept his head lowered. "I'm not in the mood."

Sally placed the steaming coffee in front of Brody, then patted his shoulder before sitting down. "You know we love you."

"I know that, Mom." He turned toward her with tear-filled eyes...Sally's eyes beginning to water.

"You don't want to tell us where you got the drugs?" John asked. "Was it from the girl you brought here a few days ago?"

Brody glared at John. "Hell, no. She's not like that. She doesn't even know about this. Like I told you, she's been in Louisville. Okay?"

John held up his palms. "Sorry, son. I'm just asking."

"And her name is Ashley."

"I'm sorry but it slipped my mind. I'll try to remember."

Brody took a short breath. "Dad, the stuff is everywhere. I was stupid to take it. I should have known better. I didn't think it would knock me on my ass. I've learned my lesson. It won't happen again."

"I hope so."

"Please, John, let's talk about something else." Sally wiped her tears with a napkin.

John sighed. "Okay. We can discuss it later."

"How long will I have to stay this time?" Brody asked.

"We'll find out when we get there. I suppose it depends on your progress."

"That place drives me crazy after a week. All the meetings and lectures."

"It sure beats the ER," John said.

"John!" Sally said.

"I know, Dad. I'm just sayin'. Because I'm going there doesn't mean I have to like it. Can't you understand that?"

John wanted to tell Brody it was for his own good, but knew he'd be admonished by Sally and didn't want to magnify the tension he sensed was escalating in the room. He simply nodded and drank from his cup.

Silence enveloped the room like a foggy mist.

~ * ~

Geraldine hugged Brody in the living room as he was about to leave for the rehab center. Libby rushed into the room, waving a Bible in her hand. Geraldine stepped back, clutching her cane with both hands to keep her balance. Libby embraced a bewildered Brody, nearly lifting him off the floor, then handed him the thick black book.

"Carry this with you, Brody," she gushed, pressing the Bible into his hand. "It'll give you comfort and strength. Trust in the Lord."

Brody, back arched, regarded her for a moment, then lifted the Bible and bent his head. "Uh, thanks, Aunt Libby."

"Uncle Wendell and I will be praying for you while you're away," she said. "We have also asked others in our Bible study group to lift you up in prayers."

"I thought he had a Bible," Geraldine remarked, glancing at Sally.

"But this is a new Bible," Libby said. "It'll be with him as he renews his life."

"Heaven help us," Geraldine muttered, shaking her head.

Standing at the open front door, John and Sally watched the interaction, straight-faced and erect like mannequins.

"I guess I should be going," Brody said.

"Where's Wendell?" Geraldine asked, glancing in all directions like a nosy hen. "Isn't he going to say goodbye to Brody?"

"He's on the toilet," Libby said, long-faced. "He ate something that disagreed with him."

"Figures."

"Ready, son?" John asked.

Brody smiled at Geraldine and Libby without saying a word and followed John and Sally to the SUV. Whiskers slipped out the front door and ran up to Brody, who knelt and rubbed the pooch between the nape and withers.

"Back to the house," John said, pointing to the front door. Whiskers let out a wimpy whine and scampered back into the house.

As they were backing out, Wendell lumbered out of the house waving, the back of his shirt hanging over his trousers. Brody lowered the rear passenger window as Wendell reached his hand out.

"We'll be thinking about you," Wendell said, grasping Brody's hand. "We'll be praying for you, too. This is the devil's doin' so you just have to be strong and resist temptation. You can overcome this by the Lord's good grace. Heah?"

"Uh, sure, Uncle Wendell. Thanks again," Brody stammered.

"God bless you, boy." Wendell pointed a forefinger toward the blue sky and beamed like he'd just seen a divine apparition.

Brody managed a crooked smile as he raised the window. John slowly backed the vehicle out of the driveway.

"Get me out of here," Brody said, barely moving his lips as if worried his uncle would hear him. Geraldine, Wendell, and Libby stood on the porch and waved, their hands almost moving in unison. Brody lifted his hand weakly to acknowledge their sad farewells.

Sally turned toward John. "Don't you say a word," like she knew what he was thinking about the exchange. John shook his head with a slight grin to let her know everything was safe.

Hardly a word was spoken during the drive. John turned on the radio to an oldies station, which was playing Huey Lewis and the News' "I Want a New Drug." John noticed Brody grimace in the rear-view mirror and switched it off. Silence prevailed the rest of the way through the pristine countryside marked with stacked-rock fences built by Irish stonemasons dating back to the mid-19th century, and scattered thoroughbreds grazing in the pastures.

When they pulled into the parking lot, John asked, "Anything you need or want to say?"

"No," Brody said, turning his head to avoid eye contact as he clicked open the door latch. "Let's just get this over with."

"I hope your attitude improves."

"Please, John," Sally said. "Brody's got enough on his mind."

John frowned. "Okay."

Brody grabbed his travel bag and walked several steps ahead of John and Sally, who were barely able to keep pace with him. After Brody checked in at the front desk, a counselor appeared in the lobby a minute later, holding a clipboard for them to sign.

Sally embraced Brody, whose rigid body was a like a frozen statue, and kissed him on the cheek. "I love you."

Brody's face tensed as if he were about to shed tears, but he remained stoic and silent.

"We'll see you in a couple weeks, son." John was about to give him a hug but decided against it after sensing Brody's icy demeanor. Instead, he squeezed his son's shoulder. Brody turned without uttering a word, and followed the counselor past the doors leading to the patient wing.

"What was he so pissed about?" John asked after returning to their vehicle. "You'd think we're the ones responsible for this. We didn't give him the drugs."

"You shouldn't be too hard on him," Sally said. "He's been through a lot the past couple days."

"I beg your pardon?"

"Honey, he's trying to get better, but it's difficult."

"He's in rehab because of another overdose. Two in two days. That's his problem. He needs to own up to it rather than acting like a spoiled brat. He's our son but that doesn't mean I have to turn a blind eye to his behavior."

"John, let's discuss it later. We're both upset right now."

"Sally, you don't want to discuss it," John said, raising his voice. "Every time I bring it up, you start defending him. You've enabled him for a long time. It's way past time for him to grow up. And you need to realize it. You're not helping him."

Tears trickled down Sally's gaunt cheeks. She turned her head toward the passenger window.

John gazed at her for a moment in the strained silence before turning the ignition and leaving the parking lot.

~ * ~

"Do you want to stop and get breakfast?" John asked, breaking the dense quiet in the SUV.

Sally, her eyes closed, said, "I'm not hungry."

"I didn't mean for it to come out the way it did about Brody. I was simply trying to make a point and I guess I didn't do a particularly good job. I apologize."

Sally turned and looked at him with forlorn eyes. "Why are you so hard on him?"

"I could turn that around and ask why you are so easy on him."

"I don't think I'm easy on him." She took a tissue from her purse and dabbed her cheeks. "He needs to be encouraged to succeed rather than being put down. That's all you ever do anymore."

"I'm not putting him down. I want him to face the seriousness of what's happening in his life. I don't want continued relapses like we've heard from others. I want him to succeed for his own sake. One of these days we won't be around to pick him up."

"Maybe we should join a support group."

"I'm willing," John said. "Just give me a date, time, and place."

"After you get off your high horse."

"What are you talking about?"

"You make it sound as if you're making a big sacrifice to go to a support group."

"What?"

"Just the tone of your voice. I don't like it."

"My apologies."

"The rehab center recommends support groups so people can learn how to understand and deal with the problem."

"Then we'll do it. Sign us up."

"Thank you, I will."

"How much will it cost?"

"Are you serious, John? Do you have to put a price tag on it?"

"No. I'm simply curious about how much it will cost. Don't you want to know? And believe it or not, we do live on a budget."

"Whatever it is, I think we can afford it. And if we can't, I'll go find a part-time job so we can. Maybe I'll substitute teach."

"Let's not get carried away. Forget I even mentioned the cost. Okay?"

Sally smirked, then looked straight ahead with her mouth squeezed shut.

Not a word was spoken the remainder of the way back. John was tempted to turn on the radio but decided silence fit the mood between them. Sally was first to get out of the vehicle, walking directly to the house without waiting for John or even holding the door open for him.

"How was Brody?" Geraldine asked, standing near the door.

"Ask John," Sally said. "He has all the answers." She tossed her purse on the couch and went to the kitchen.

"Is something the matter?" Geraldine asked as she followed her. "Is Brody okay?"

Sally didn't respond.

John came in the house seconds later, looked in several directions, and headed toward the den until he heard a cabinet door bang shut and dishes clang in the sink. Sally stood motionless, her hands braced on the counter, watching the sink fill with dishwashing suds.

"What's wrong with her?" Geraldine asked.

John shrugged and walked past her.

"Well, excuse me!" Geraldine exclaimed.

Whiskers bounded from his pad and barked several times.

"Let's talk this over," John said in a conciliatory tone, walking toward Sally.

"There's nothing to say."

He stopped several feet from her and picked up Whiskers. "Why are you acting this way?"

"You seem to have all the answers about Brody."

"I've never said that," John said as he stroked between the pooch's ears.

"But you've implied it."

He put Whiskers down and sat on a stool. "I didn't mean to. I'm only expressing my opinion. I want the best for him, just like you."

"Then maybe show more compassion rather than being so judgmental."

"I don't mean to come across that way."

"Brody needs all the support we can give right now," Sally said. "His relapse shows that. Can't you see that?"

"Maybe you're right."

"Maybe?" Sally raised her brows. "Are you serious?"

"Okay, okay. I concede he needs support from us."

"John, he needs support from everyone in the family."

"That's what I meant."

"So we agree."

"But I do think we've shown support for him. Remember Chicago? Remember last Christmas? We've been there for him practically every step of the way."

Sally let out a short breath. "Hungry?"

John realized the discussion about Brody was over. "I could eat a little something."

"I have a blueberry muffin mix in the cabinet. It may take thirty minutes or so."

"That's fine. I'll read the newspaper in the meantime."

Geraldine's tapping the floor with her cane announced her entrance in the kitchen. "Are the fireworks over?"

"Mother, we just had a little disagreement."

"Sure didn't sound that way to me." Geraldine eased herself on a stool.

"Believe it or not, we don't always live in sweet harmony," John said, turning his attention from the newspaper. "We do argue about things now and then. Just not often, especially in front of others. Especially around you."

"It's nice to know you're human. I would have never guessed."

John laughed. "Are you being a smart aleck now?"

"I learned it from the best...you."

~ * ~

Sally shuffled around in the kitchen, peering into cabinets, holding the box of muffin mix.

"What's the matter, hon?" John asked.

"I can't remember where I put the muffin pan."

"Maybe Chloe hid it somewhere when she rearranged everything at Christmas."

"I think maybe she has."

"We've had muffins since then," Geraldine said.

John walked to the kitchen and opened a cabinet door where most of the pots and pans were kept. He found the muffin pan in the rear.

"Here it is." He held up the pan. "Tucked away in the back."

"Oh, thanks." A look of relief came over Sally's face.

"I didn't even see you look in there," Geraldine said. "You know pots and pans are stored there."

"I think I looked inside."

"I don't think so. I was watching you."

"Then why didn't you say something?"

"I didn't want to hurt your feelings."

"Oh, really? And what's that supposed to mean, Mother?"

"It's not a big deal," John said, lifting his hands as if ordering a truce. "We found it and now we can have some muffins for breakfast."

"If she can find the mixing bowl."

"Mother!"

"That's enough, Geraldine," John said. "We've got a lot on our minds."

"I was just making an observation," Geraldine said. "You don't have to get so touchy about it."

"I'll be in the den reading the paper," John said as he picked up the newspaper from the counter and walked away. "Let me know if you need anything, hon."

Sally went about preparing the muffin mix and didn't respond.

Geraldine followed John to the den, padding past him to the recliner as if she were in a race to see who could get there first. John settled for the rocking chair, pushing back and unfolding the paper.

"John?" Geraldine craned her neck. "John?"

John lowered the newspaper and eyeballed her. "What?"

"Did you see Sally look in that cabinet?"

"I wasn't paying any attention."

"She's been a little more forgetful since she returned from New York. I'm worried about her."

"She has a lot on her mind, especially with Brody."

"I think it's more than that."

"You need to give her some slack."

"You need to watch her. You'll see what I mean. Harold got that way. A little ill-tempered, too."

"I'll do that," John said. "But I don't think it's serious. She's just stressed. Hell, I'm stressed. We're all stressed."

"I'm not."

"Okay, Geraldine, everybody's stressed except you."

"Well, excuse me!" Geraldine, tight-lipped, picked up the remote, turned on the TV, and boosted the volume. John shook his head and continued reading the newspaper.

Whiskers ran up to John, tapping his shoe with his right paw.

"I bet you want to go outside, little buddy," John said as he patted the top of the dog's head. He rose and walked to the front door, feeling a sense of relief in getting away from his mother-in-law, even if only for a few minutes.

But he couldn't resist her observations about Sally as he peeked in on her before going outside.

"Everything under control?" he asked.

"Muffins are in the oven. Don't be gone too long."

"I'll be out front with Whiskers if you need me."

"I'll try to remember."

"Huh?"

Eleven

Eight days later, Wendell and Libby walked into the den while John and Sally were relaxing on the couch, reading magazines, and Geraldine was in her usual place watching TV. Whiskers remained curled in his pad, his eyes barely visible after being stirred from his nap.

"We've got good news," Wendell said rather lamely for someone making an announcement.

"Well?" Geraldine asked after muting the TV. "Is this a game? Are we supposed to guess what you want to tell us? I'd like to get back to my program, if you don't mind."

"We're moving out this afternoon," Wendell said with a feeble smile. "Sister Cathy made room in her house so we can help with the ministry."

"God rewards those who do his good work," Libby said excitedly, raising a hand. "Praise the Lord!"

"I'll give an amen to that," John blurted.

"John!" Sally said, nudging his side.

Wendell and Libby turned toward John with perplexed expressions.

"Wow, that's great news," John exclaimed. "Need any help getting your things over there?"

"You're not in a hurry to get them out of the house, are you, John?" Geraldine asked, her thin eyebrows perched high in a spry smile.

John's face turned rosy. "I'm just offering a helping hand. You know, being a good Samaritan."

"You're not fooling anyone. You just want your bedroom back."

John chuckled. "I have to confess, that'll be nice. I'm not sure how much longer my old body can take sleeping on the living room floor." John leaned forward and pressed his hands against his back, his face contorted to emphasize the stiffness.

"I know it's been an inconvenience for everyone," Libby said, ignoring John's pathetic histrionics. "We didn't mean to overstay our welcome."

"You're not overstaying your welcome," Sally said. "You can stay for as long as you like."

John frowned at Sally for a moment before forcing a short laugh. "Sally's right. Our home is your home."

"Better be careful what you say," Geraldine said, her head bobbing up and down.

"It's your home as well, Mother," Sally said. "You know that."

"Haven't you been here since before Christmas?" Libby asked, somehow bolstering some courage to talk back to Geraldine.

"But I was ready to go until my fall."

"But aren't you okay now?" Libby shook her head back and forth with a woeful look that wasn't convincing. "You seem to get around very well, even with your cane."

"What are you implying, Libby? Are you saying I'm a malingerer?"

"No, ma'am. Only that you've been here longer than we have. Remember?"

Geraldine rose in the recliner, back rigid and stern-faced. "But I fractured my hip. Forget?"

"Libby, please," Wendell said, taking her hand. "Mama has a good reason to be here for so long. She's been recuperating."

"Bless her precious heart," Libby said.

Geraldine creased her brows but kept her mouth closed.

"Now let's go pack our suitcases." Wendell said to Libby.

"Again, let me know if you need any help," John said. "It won't be a problem."

"I appreciate it, John, but I think we've got everything under control." Wendell took Libby by the hand and went to the bedroom. John, Sally, and Geraldine sat in controlled silence until they heard the bedroom door close.

"It'll sure be more peaceful with them leaving, even if it's only down the street," Geraldine said.

"It'll give us a little more room, Mother."

"Yes. That too."

"And we'll get our bed back," John said.

"I don't know if it was me, but Wendell didn't seem enthusiastic," Sally said. "He almost seemed indifferent to it all."

"I think you're right," John said. "Maybe he's just overwhelmed and didn't have much to say."

"Oh well, I suppose I should get the living room back in shape," Sally said. "I was concerned we might have someone drop by when the room is in such a mess."

"Oh, honey, it looked fine," John said.

"You say that because you're a man."

"What?"

"Never mind," she said, sighing "You wouldn't understand."

"You're right," he said judiciously. "A man wouldn't understand."

"What about Brody's bedroom?" Geraldine asked.

"What about it?" John said.

Sally shook her head. "I need to change the sheets and everything. It's something I need to do anyway. Thanks for reminding me."

"You might want to write that down or keep a list."

"I believe I can remember that," Sally said.

"Better safe than sorry." Geraldine raised her brows.

"Want me to wash your sheets as well? I can toss them in with Brody's."

"I'll think about it."

"I'll put it on my list," Sally said with a small smile. "Just in case you forget."

"I'm not going to forget," Geraldine said.

"Better safe than sorry," Sally said.

"Sally, you're getting as bad as John."

"Let's not worry about lists right now," John said. "We can do that a little later after things settle down around here."

"I do need to get Brody's room back in shape while he's away," Sally said. "I bet it's a mess."

"Maybe you'll find more drugs," Geraldine said. "You never know."

"I hope not, but we need to look for that as well," John said. "We need to have a drug-free home as much as possible when he returns next week."

"It's hard to believe he's been away that long," Sally said. "I miss him."

"I do too," Geraldine said.

"I wonder if he misses us?" John said.

~ * ~

An hour later, Wendell and Libby lugged two overstuffed suitcases, a crammed cosmetic bag, and a huge handbag to the living room, where John was sitting on the couch reading a book. The breathless couple stood next to the door with outstretched arms by their sides and sweat beading on their foreheads.

John set the book to his side. "Are you sure you don't need a hand with those? They look awfully heavy."

"I think we can handle it," Wendell said, wiping a wisp of sweat above his upper lip away with a forefinger.

"I have a dolly in the garage. It'll make things easier."

Wendell glanced at Libby for a moment as if seeking approval and she responded with a tired smile. "I suppose so," he said. "We have another piece of luggage and a couple boxes of Bible study materials. They are heavy."

John went to the garage while Wendell headed to the bedroom to get their remaining items. Libby excused herself to go to the bathroom. Geraldine hadn't bothered to leave the den, where she was watching TV with the volume turned up and apparently oblivious to everything else going on in the house.

When John returned to the living room, Sally was standing next to the luggage. She raised her fists in a silent salute and grinned.

"Is something the matter?" Libby asked from the entryway.

"Huh?" Sally said, letting out several weak coughs. "Oh, I was just flexing my fingers. Something I read on the Internet says it helps against arthritis."

"Oh, I should try that. My hands and arms have been stiff. Maybe it'd work for me."

"It wouldn't hurt." Sally raised her arms while making fists several more times, even twisting her waist and shoulders to make it appear like a workout routine.

Libby began flexing her fingers while waiting for Wendell to show up with boxes. "I bet you guys will be happy to sleep in your own bed."

"You can say that again," John exclaimed. "I may need some exercises for my back. I'm getting stiff in my old age."

"I recall you saying that a little earlier."

"I've been known to do that."

"I really hate we intruded on your home," Libby said. "It wasn't our intention. And you're not old, John. You get around better than Wendell and me."

"Maybe you should get into exercising."

"It seems too much like work." She glanced at her finger-wriggling hands.

"I guess it can be but it's often worth it." John flexed his forearms. "You know what they say, 'no pain, no gain.' Only twenty or so minutes a day."

"I'll think about it," Libby said, uncurling her fingers. "But we're getting a lot of walking in with our mission work."

"Every step helps."

Libby turned to Sally. "Your bed is really nice. We're going to miss it. It's so firm. I hated using it while you were away. But Brody said it was okay."

"Don't worry about it, Libby," Sally said. "Our home is always open to family and friends. You are always welcome here. Even our bed when you visit."

"You may still see us more than you like."

John's head jerked toward Libby. "What?"

"Our house is always open for you guys," Sally said with a warm smile before John could say anything else.

"Sister Cathy doesn't have a television," Libby said. "There are several shows Wendell and I just love. So we may surprise you a few days a week, if you don't mind."

"Oh, really," John said, taking a deep breath and furrowing his brows. "What shows are those?"

"Anytime," Sally chimed in. "Our home is your home." She scowled at John.

"I wonder what's taking Wendell so long?" Libby said, tapping her foot. "I'd better go check on him. Be right back."

Seconds later, Libby shrieked, "Oh, my God!"

John and Sally hurried to the bedroom, where Libby was stooped over Wendell as he squirmed on his back like a tortoise on its shell. A box of religious pamphlets was next to him, most of the contents spilled on the floor.

"He's thrown his back out," Libby said. Wendell writhed in pain, his eyes closed tightly and lips pressed together.

"Why didn't you say something, baby?" Libby said as she knelt next to him.

"I did," he groaned. "I guess no one could hear me."

Glancing at each other, they realized Wendell's cries for help had been muffled by Geraldine's blaring TV.

"Let's try to lift him on the bed," John said, leaning down next to Libby.

"Now you be careful, John," Sally said. "We don't want your back going out, too."

Libby held his shoulders, Sally took his legs, and John had the midsection before John said, "On three. One, two, three. lift!"

Wendell let out a sharp cry as they hoisted him gingerly onto the bed. "Oh, baby," Libby said. "You're going to be all right."

"Should I call for an ambulance?" Sally asked.

"I don't think so," Libby said. "This happens every few months when he's trying to pick up things he shouldn't. I keep telling him to be careful, but he never listens. He always wants to do things without asking for help."

"You should buy a back brace," John said.

"He wouldn't wear it," Libby said as Wendell let out another groan.

"Is there anything I can get for him?" Sally asked. "Motrin? Advil?"

"Motrin would be nice," Libby said. Wendell lay rigid on the bed as if strapped to a table. "His pain pills are packed in one of the suitcases."

"What's going on in here?" Geraldine asked as she padded into the room. "A person can't take a nap around here with all this commotion."

"Nap?" John asked, before realizing Geraldine had turned off the TV and was probably going to take her daily short snooze in her bedroom.

"Wendell threw out his back," Libby said, blinking her wide brown eyes while trying to hold back tears.

Geraldine shuffled over to her son, placing a hand on his shoulder. "I guess you won't be going anywhere for a while."

Libby looked distraught at Sally. "I'm so sorry. I don't see how we can move over to Sister Cathy's now. It may take a few days until he's over this."

"Are you sure?" John asked.

"Yes, I'm sure," Libby said, glaring at him with narrow eyes.

"That's fine," Sally said, avoiding eye contact with John. "He just needs to get better."

"I'll bring everything back up here," John said as he turned to leave the room. He rolled his eyes at Sally. "I'm glad I got the dolly."

"Maybe you two can sleep in Brody's room?" Libby said to Sally.

"Why don't you and Wendell sleep in Brody's room?" Geraldine glowered at Libby. "Instead of taking their room. Has that even occurred to you?"

"That's okay, Mother," Sally said. "Let's just make do as we have. It's not a problem for us. Another few days won't make any difference."

Geraldine shook her head. "I don't understand you, Sally. I don't care if he is your brother, this is still your bedroom and they've overstayed their welcome. Let them take Brody's bedroom."

"Mother!"

Wendell moaned and turned his head away from Geraldine.

"You'll be all right, baby," Libby said, stroking her hand over the top of Wendell's head.

"I'll get the Motrin," Sally said.

"And I think I'll go take a nap if everyone can be quiet," Geraldine said as she left the room, hammering the cane on the floor as if to make a point.

~ * ~

John followed Sally to the medicine cabinet in the bathroom and whispered, "Did I hear Libby say pain pills?"

"Yes," Sally said as she unscrewed the bottle cap. "Why?"

"Why? Brody had an overdose. Maybe it was Wendell's pain pills he took."

Sally's eyes widened. "John, you may be right. I'll say something to Libby."

"Let's wait until Wendell is resting and your mother isn't around. I don't want any more drama around here if we can avoid it."

They returned to the room and Sally handed Libby two pills and a small paper cup of water. "Let me know if he needs anything else."

Wendell raised up in bed, supported by Libby's soft hand, and swallowed the pills and water. He whimpered before resting his head on the pillow.

Sally and John, rolling the dolly, retreated to their makeshift bedroom and sat on the couch.

"Shit!" John looked at the luggage.

"Now settle down. You don't want to get your blood pressure up."

"It's already there, sweetie," he said with a long face.

"Maybe we should sleep in Brody's room," Sally said. "I can change the sheets and clean it up a bit."

"That's fine with me. If I had to sleep on the floor another night, I might end up like Wendell. Strange bedfellows"

Sally couldn't suppress a grin. "That's funny."

"You know, I can't believe they had pain pills here. Why didn't they say something? They've been here long enough to know about Brody's problem. I don't understand people sometimes."

"I'm surprised, too. They should have known better."

"At least we know now," John said. "I wonder if I should walk down to so-called Sister Cathy's house and tell her about Wendell?"

"It probably wouldn't hurt, unless Libby wants to."

"I think I'll do it. The nosy journalist is coming out in me. I'm curious as to what's going on there."

"Just be careful."

"Careful? Of Sister Cathy? I think I can handle it."

Libby tip-toed into the room and sat in the easy chair. "He's resting now," she said quietly.

"That's good," John said. "I've been down with my back several times and I know the feeling. But tell me something."

Libby twisted her head. "What?"

"What kind of pain pills has Wendell been taking?"

"I believe it's Vicodin. Why do you ask?"

"Because of Brody," Sally said. "Have you been missing any pills?"

"Why would Brody want them? I didn't know he had back problems."

"Libby, he's got a drug addiction. And you know he overdosed. We're wondering if he didn't take them from you."

"Brody wouldn't do that," Libby said.

"Please understand, Libby," Sally said. "Brody has an addiction to opioids. That's why he's in rehab. His resistance is weak. And probably always will be."

"Are you saying Wendell and me are responsible?"

"No, Libby," John said, spreading his hands. "What we're saying is Brody may have stolen the drugs from you. It's part of his addiction. He can't help himself. We're just trying to find out where he got the drugs. We're not blaming anyone. For all we know, he got them from someone on the street. We're asking just to make sure."

"We hide drugs," Sally added. "Even Mother's, after she fractured her hip, we put hers in a secure place. We don't take chances anymore. So please understand we're not accusing you and Wendell of anything."

Libby began to weep. "I'm so sorry. We didn't even think about that. We love Brody and couldn't imagine him going through our things."

Sally walked over and placed an arm around Libby, kissing her cheek. "That's okay. We understand. All we're asking now is when you find the pills you check to see if any are missing."

"I hate to say this, but Wendell asked me when we were packing about the Vicodin because he thought he'd strained his shoulders while we were out doing the ministry, carrying all those pamphlets around with us."

"And?" John asked.

"We couldn't find them. Wendell thought perhaps we had forgotten to get a refill or we'd left them in Alabama."

"I wish you'd said something," John said.

"We weren't thinking," Libby said. "I didn't know Vicodin was an opidoid, or whatever you call it."

"Opioid," John said.

"I'm so sorry." She wiped tears streaming down her cheeks.

John sighed. "I'll carry your luggage back to the room a little later unless you need it now. I was thinking about carting the books to your Sister Cathy."

"You don't need to do that," Libby said. "She may not be at home."

"I can wait until she's there. There's not a big hurry to do it."

Libby bit her lower lip. "Okay."

John rose from the coach and walked to the front door. "I'm going to take Whiskers for a walk."

"I think I'll get Brody's room ready while you're away," Sally said.

"Can you take the luggage back to the room before you leave?" Libby asked. "It's a bit heavy for me to carry."

"No problem," John said as he grabbed a handle on one piece and tugged. "Damn, this is heavy!"

"See?"

He followed Libby to the bedroom, clutching the luggage with two hands. Wendell was asleep, letting out occasional snorts.

"John, I'm so sorry," Libby whispered as he placed the suitcase at the foot of the bed. "About everything."

"Don't worry about it, Libby. We've been through it before. We'll survive."

After taking the remaining luggage to the room, he put a leash on Whiskers' collar and left the house. He glanced at Sister Cathy's residence on his way down the street and no one appeared to be there. The Ten Commandments sign was still next to the porch along with a white cross, and a large black ichthus symbol on the bottom panel of the white front door.

Two doors down, Tanya Martin was tending to her flower garden in front of her house, removing weeds and pruning plants.

"You're putting the rest of the neighborhood to shame," John said as he approached her.

Tanya stood and removed her gloves. "I don't know about that," she said with a weary smile. "I'm trying to fix up a mess from yesterday."

"Rufus'?" he said, smiling.

"No, some hooligans. Someone wrapped toilet paper all over the front yard and mashed some of the plants last night."

His smile faded like a wilted flower. "Are you serious? Did you call the police?"

"I wanted to, but Rufus didn't want to make a scene."

"But this is the second time your house has been vandalized."

Tanya shrugged. "Rufus thinks it was some kids."

"If it was some kids, why did they only target your house? I haven't seen other houses defaced."

"That's what I tried to tell Rufus."

"By the way, where is he?"

"The store."

"Would you mind if I contact a friend of mine in the police department?"

"I wouldn't mind but I'm not so sure about Rufus. You might want to talk to him first. He said he can handle it."

"How?"

"He went to buy a gun."

"I suspect he thinks it's more than kids then."

"He's got some other ideas about who did it."

"And?"

Tanya frowned. "I'd rather not say. You should talk to Rufus."

On the return from the park, John noticed lights in Sister Cathy's house and three vehicles in the driveway. Southern gospel singing drifted from the open windows. He stopped and contemplated going to the front door to let her know about Wendell's condition.

As he was about to leave, a young man in a light brown suit stepped out of the house. "Is there something I can help you with?"

"I was wanting to talk to Cathy, but I see she's probably busy right now," John said. "I can come back later."

"Is it about Sister Cathy's ministry?"

"No, it's something else."

The man approached John. "I'd be happy to relay the message."

John studied him for a second…a receding hairline on a nearly shaved head, pointed nose, and wearing a small confederate flag pin on his lapel. "Thanks, but I'd prefer to do it myself. It's somewhat personal. A family matter."

"We really don't like people coming up to the house unannounced. Kind of like trespassing. You know what I mean?"

"Really? I don't see any trespassing signs," John said, forcing a grin. "And isn't it supposed to be a church?"

"Oh, it's not a church," the man said, crossing his arms. "It's Sister Cathy's home where she invites people to share their love of the Lord."

"I'll keep that in mind the next time I'm walking my dog," John said as he turned from the man and walked away.

"Have a nice day, old man," the man said, revealing tattooed numbers 1-4-8-8 on four fisted fingers. "And be careful."

John turned back around, a twisted grin from the comment, and said, "Same to you, kiddo."

~ * ~

"Did you have a nice walk?" Sally asked, entering the living room as John removed the leash from Whiskers' collar.

"So-so."

Sally giggled. "How so-so?"

"I ran across this strange person at our new neighbor's religious sanctuary. He almost acted as if I were trespassing. I didn't get good vibes from him. Makes me wonder about Sister Cathy and her everlasting message of salvation."

"Wendell and Libby haven't complained about it." Sally sat on the couch and curled a leg underneath her.

"Maybe it was just me." John shrugged as he sat on the easy chair while Whiskers scampered to the water bowl in the kitchen. "I probably send off bad vibes to the righteous. They probably view me as a heathen."

"Silly man," she said. "Oh, I've got Brody's room ready. It might be tight quarters for a few nights, but it'll sure beat sleeping on the floor."

"Now that's some good news I can rest my head on. I've decided I'm too damn old to be sleeping on the floor or any hard surface. I don't have padding on my butt anymore. It feels like bone against whatever surface."

"It's been a while since we slept together in a real bed. Probably back in Budapest."

"Sure seems like a lifetime ago."

"It sure does." Sally smiled, as if to herself. "I don't remember the last time we slept in a full-size bed. Maybe after we first got married."

"It may have been a twin-size one, back in the dorm."

"I don't think so, John Ross. We never slept in a dorm room."

"Uh, are you sure?"

"Yes, I'm sure! You must be thinking of someone else."

"Nope. It was you. I'm sure."

"Did you sleep with someone else?"

"No!"

"You can tell me. It was so long ago and we weren't married," she said. "I forgive you."

"Now, wait just a minute. I didn't sleep around on you."

"I'm okay with it now."

"I remember now," John said, nodding his head. "It was at a homecoming a year or so after we graduated."

Sally sat motionless, staring at the corner of the room for a few seconds. "I sorta remember that. They opened several dormitories and rented rooms for the weekend. I think we stayed overnight in my old dorm."

"That's right," John said, a bright smile emerging on his face. "I knew I wasn't dreaming it."

"So long ago."

"Yeah, so long ago you accused me of sleeping with another gal."

"I'm sorry. I shouldn't have said anything."

"You were my only girl back in college. You should know that."

"I'll try to remember. I promise."

"Those are good memories."

"So are you ready to downsize tonight?" she asked.

"I think I can handle it as long as you don't try to nudge me off."

She gave a mischievous wink. "Moi?"

"Speaking of beds, is Wendell still in bed?"

"I haven't heard a peep. Even from Mother. But I did hear from rehab and they say Brody is doing fine."

"Why did you wait so long to tell me?"

"I just remembered."

"That's okay."

"I was going to tell you when you got back, but you started on something else."

"Sister Cathy's house."

"That's it."

"So everything's going well at rehab?"

"The counselor says Brody has been cooperating and in good spirits. They've been pleased with his progress."

"I hope it carries over to when he comes back. But let's not go there now. We have enough drama going on right now."

"Oh, almost forgot, Chloe called."

"Chloe called? Okay, how is she?"

"She sounded great. She says she's getting her strength back. I offered to go up there, but she says to stay put with Brody in rehab."

"Chloe is always thinking about others. I guess we did good raising her."

They heard a faint rat-a-tat on the floor, signaling Geraldine was up and about and would soon make an appearance. They sat quietly as she entered the living room.

"Did you have a nice nap, Mother?"

"I slept too long," she said, stifling a yawn. "I missed one of my shows on TV."

"You can watch it anytime on cable," John said. "There's a menu button on the remote control."

Geraldine glared at John. "I can? Why are you telling me now? Do you know how many shows I've wanted to watch but thought I had to wait until they were reruns?"

"I thought you knew."

Geraldine padded to the couch and sat next to Sally. "How was I to know? Isn't that assuming too much? How am I to know something if someone doesn't tell me? I was married to Harry Corman, not Harry Houdini."

"Point taken."

"Now what's that supposed to mean?"

"Please, Geraldine, I'm only agreeing with you. I'll show you how to access programs a little later. Okay?"

"Well, don't forget."

"I'm sure you won't let me."

"There you go again."

John shook his head and chuckled. "Whatever."

"Mother, is there anything special you want for supper tonight?" Sally asked

"I've been craving a hamburger," she said. "I don't know why. Maybe it's from some commercial I've seen on TV."

"How about if I went to some fast-food restaurant and bought hamburgers and fries?" John asked.

"I want a homemade hamburger."

"I'm not sure if we have any hamburger meat but we can run out and get some," Sally said.

"I'd like to have it on the grill. Do you still have one of those?"

"It's somewhere in the garage," John said. "I can get it out and fire it up, if that's what you'd like."

"Maybe Wendell and Libby would like hamburgers as well," Sally said.

"I'm sure they'll take anything you offer," Geraldine said. "Beggars can't be choosy."

"Anything you'd like with your hamburger?"

"Maybe some fries and coleslaw."

"We'll pick some up at the grocery. Anything else? Tomato? Lettuce? Pickles?"

"All those?"

"Anything else?"

"Eggnog."

"I don't think so, Mother. I don't believe you'll find this time of the year."

"Can you look?"

"We can do that," John said.

Libby sauntered into the living room rubbing her eyes and sat on the other side of Geraldine.

"How's Wendell?" Sally asked.

"He's awake now," Libby said. "Poor baby, he's still in so much pain."

"Want another Motrin?"

"Thanks, but we found his pain pills."

"Were there any missing?"

"Maybe a few. We don't count them but I guess those were the ones Brody may have taken."

"I'm going out to the garage and get the grill," John said as he rose from the chair. "I'll probably need to clean it up a bit."

Sally eased off the couch. "While you're doing that, I'll run to the grocery and pick up a few things for dinner. Anything special for you and Wendell?" Sally asked Libby.

"Whatever you think we'd like," Libby said. "Beggars can't be choosy."

Geraldine turned toward Sally and winked.

~ * ~

John rolled the gas grill out of the garage and to the backyard, in view of the kitchen window so he would be able to communicate with Sally once she started preparing the meal. Whiskers joined him, sniffing and marking the fences separating the properties.

John sprayed off spider webs and dust from the grill with a garden hose and wiped it off with a throwaway T-shirt, then brought out a lawn chair he'd stashed away for the winter. He sat and waited for Sally to return from the grocery with the ground beef and other hamburger fixings. He wished he'd called her cell phone and asked her to pick up a six pack of Sam Adams but figured she was probably on her way back.

After nearly an hour, he went back in the house and asked Libby and Geraldine, who were engrossed in a soap opera in the den, if they had heard from Sally. He had expected her to be away for only thirty minutes or so.

Wendell called out for Libby from the bedroom, saying he needed her to help him from the bed so he could go to the bathroom. John followed her and helped lift him to his feet. Libby held his hand as he inched toward the toilet, punctuated by minor moans and groans.

Another fifteen minutes passed, and John grew concerned about Sally. He picked up his cell phone from the kitchen counter and called her, perhaps even to ask her to purchase beer as the excuse for making the call. She answered after three rings, a tone of frustration in her shaky voice.

"What's the matter, hon? Are you having car problems?"

"You could say that," she said. "I can't find it."

"What?"

"I forgot where I parked it," she said.

"Maybe someone stole it," John said.

"Maybe. I don't know. I hope not." Her voice trembled.

"Go back in the store and I'll be there in ten minutes," John said. "Everything's going to be all right. Okay?"

"I'll be at the front entrance."

John told Geraldine he had to run a quick errand, not giving her any details for the reason he had to leave. He knew he'd never hear the end of it. And poor Sally wouldn't either.

"I hope you get back before Sally," she said. "You know we might be getting hungry around here."

John nodded and headed to the supermarket. He spotted Sally standing behind the automated glass doors, a bag of groceries in each arm. He rushed to her side, taking the groceries from her slumping arms.

"Now where did you park the car?" he asked.

"I don't remember."

John's brows crumpled. "Any idea?"

Sally pointed to her right. "I thought it was over there. That's where I usually park. I've walked all over there trying to find it."

"Let's put the groceries in my car and let me take a look," he said. "And you can get off your feet."

After placing the bags in the back seat and Sally getting in the front passenger seat, John took her fob key and strolled toward the rear of the crowded lot. He looked in the direction to where Sally said she'd parked her SUV, then the other direction. He took out his phone and was about to call the police when he remembered he could use the fob to honk the horn. Seconds later, he heard the vehicle's loud beeping about hundred feet away under a tree in the rear of the large lot.

"I found it," John said when he returned to his car. "It's at the back." He pointed in the direction.

"I don't remember parking it way over there. Do you think someone could have moved it?"

"That's highly unlikely. You just forgot. It was under a tree, so maybe you were wanting to park it in the shade. We get in the habit of doing something and lose track when we do something else."

"I feel so stupid."

John patted the top of her hand. "It's all right, hon. We've all done it. Let's go. I think some folks are getting hungry back there."

John dropped her off in front of her vehicle, waited while she pulled out of the space, and followed her out of the parking lot.

Along the way, John thought about the beer he could have purchased. He was tempted to stop at a liquor store but decided it wouldn't be the best idea, considering Sally's fragile state of mind.

~ * ~

"What took you so long?" Geraldine asked when Sally stepped inside the house with John, each carrying a sack of groceries. "People could starve to death around here. Does it take two to go to the supermarket, in separate cars no less?"

Sally stopped, and glanced down as John stood beside her. Geraldine sat between Wendell and Libby on the couch.

"Her car wouldn't start," John said. "I had to jump it."

Geraldine gave him a suspicious look. "So when are we going to eat? Another hour or so?"

Sally sighed and walked toward the kitchen, stopping at the corner of the couch. "Mother, how about if we just have breakfast for dinner?"

"It sounds like a good idea to me," Libby said. Wendell sat rigid and tight-lipped.

"I guess that'd do," Geraldine said, lifting her shoulders up and down. "But I had my heart set on hamburgers."

"We'll grill out for lunch tomorrow," John said. "It'll give me time to finish cleaning the grill."

"I thought you had cleaned it," Geraldine said. "You were going to fix our hamburgers on a dirty grill?"

"No, Geraldine," John said. "I was only going to wipe it down some more. It's fine as it is."

"John, can you give me a hand?" Sally asked from the kitchen.

"I'm on my way." John nodded at his starving houseguests and hurried to Sally's side.

John set the groceries on the kitchen counter and began putting things away in the refrigerator and cabinets.

"We don't have enough eggs," Sally whispered with a pained face. "And not much bacon. What are we going to do?"

"Gimme a minute," John said. "I'll check with the Patels. Go ahead and start the coffee and whatever you need to do."

John left through the garage and went next door. He was able to get eight eggs from the Patels but they didn't have any meat. He noticed Wilma Reliford sitting on her front porch reading the newspaper and scurried over there. Fortunately, she had an unopened package of bacon.

"You saved the day," John said. "I'll pay you back tomorrow."

"Is there any chance of you doing it later tonight?" she asked, her eyes pleading like a helpless child. "Bert loves his bacon in the morning. And you know how Bert is."

"No problem. I'll run to the grocery after we eat."

"Could you pick up a can of coffee as well? We're about out. And Bert has to start the day with coffee."

"I'll do it," John said, anxious to get back to the house. "I know how Bert is. Anything else?"

"That should do it."

"By the way, where's Bert?"

"He's at a Neighborhood Watch meeting over at the church. He was expecting you to be there."

"Damn," John said, his brows furrowed. "Sorry 'bout that. I forgot all about the meeting. Please tell him I'll be at the next one."

"I'll tell him you had some other things come up," she said. "He might not like it if I told him you forgot about it. You know how Bert is."

"That'll be our little secret."

John jogged back to the house, clutching the eggs and bacon close to his chest. When he stepped into the kitchen, Geraldine was coming in from the living room.

"What's going on in here?" she asked. "How long does it take to make breakfast? I don't even see anything on the stove."

John handed the eggs and bacon to Sally, standing next to the counter. "It'll be a few more minutes, Mother. Why don't you sit down and have a cup of coffee?"

"I needed to let Whiskers out for a minute," John said.

"I don't think so," Geraldine said. "The little mutt has been at my feet the entire time."

"That's why it took longer than usual," John said. "I was wondering where he was. Didn't you hear me calling for him?"

"No."

"You must have been talking to Wendell and Libby and didn't hear me."

"We haven't said a word. Just waiting for Sally to tell us dinner was ready. That's why I came out here."

Sally opened the package of bacon and lined the strips on a plastic tray to put in the microwave.

"Do you need any help, hon?" John asked.

"You can get the eggs ready to scramble."

John broke the eggs in a small bowl and began stirring them when Libby and Wendell meandered into the room.

"I heard you say scrambled eggs," Libby said. "Wendell prefers his to be fried."

"Oh, really?" John said with a chagrined expression. "We don't have any more eggs."

"Maybe the neighbors have some," Geraldine said.

"I don't think so," John said. "It's also getting rather late."

"What does that have to do with it? It's not even dark outside."

"I can run down to Sister Cathy's and see if she can spare a couple eggs," Libby said. "It wouldn't be a problem."

"Whatever," John said, shaking his head. "It's your call."

After pouring the eggs into a hot skillet, Sally put the bacon in the microwave and punched in the cooking time.

"If you want fried eggs, you need to get down to your sister's house," Sally said to Libby, breaking her silence. "John, can you start the toast?"

Libby hurried from the kitchen and out the front door, leaving Wendell sitting with a bewildered expression at the counter. A few minutes later, when everyone was seated at the dining room table with food on their plates except for Wendell, Libby returned breathless, clutching two eggs.

"You couldn't wait for me?" she asked.

"Do you like to eat cold eggs?" Geraldine asked before taking a small bite from her plate.

"Here's the eggs." Libby held the eggs toward Sally.

Sally was about to stand when Geraldine placed her hand on her forearm.

"Can't you see Sally's eating?" Geraldine snapped. "You make Wendell's eggs. You're his wife."

Libby's mouth puckered as she fought back tears, then moseyed to the stove.

"That's okay, baby," Wendell said as he rose gingerly from his seat. "I can make my eggs. You go ahead and eat your food before it gets cold. I know you like scrambled eggs."

Libby glanced at Geraldine. "No, I can wait. It won't take a couple minutes. I can warm mine in the microwave. I can eat with you."

"Suit yourself," Geraldine said. "Let's just eat."

~ * ~

After a tense but quiet dinner, Wendell rose from his chair hunkered over like frail old man in need of a walker and turned toward the den. Libby pushed back her chair to go with him, placing a hand on his lower back for support.

"Poor baby," she murmured.

"Why don't you help clear the table?" Geraldine said.

Libby was taken aback by the comment, squinting at John and then Sally.

"It's all right, Mother," Sally said. "I can take care of it."

"No, it's not all right. She's able to do a few things around here. You'd think you and John were their help."

Libby hesitated for a moment before gathering hers and Wendell's plates and silverware and carried them to the kitchen sink. Wendell looked pitiful, bracing the corner of the table.

Geraldine looked at Sally and John with a wide grin.

"Thank you, Libby," Sally said amiably. Libby began rinsing off the dinnerware and placing it in the dishwasher.

Wendell sauntered toward the den. John picked up his plate and carried it to the sink, then headed to the den, where Wendell was sitting in the rocker reading a magazine.

"I walked past Sister Cathy's house earlier, hoping to tell her about your condition," John said. "A young man came out and almost accused me of trespassing."

"I'll give Sister Cathy a call and let her know about my back," Wendell mumbled as if to accentuate his pain. "It slipped my mind. Maybe Libby mentioned it when she went after the eggs."

"It's not a very welcoming bunch, at least from the encounter I had."

"Probably one of the recent converts. They get a little over-zealous at times. I'll speak to her about it as well. Thanks for wanting to tell her, but it's best if me or Libby talks to her. Some of them don't seem to take too well to strangers."

"Seems kind of odd."

"Just between you and me, they are kind of odd."

"What do you want me to do with those two boxes in the living room?"

"Oh, shoot, I forgot about that. Could you put them in your garage until I can haul them down there?"

"No problem," John said. "Or I can deliver them."

"No thanks. I'll take them down after I'm better."

"John, why is Geraldine being so mean to me?" Libby asked as she entered the den. "I can't think of anything I've ever done to cause her to treat me like she has. She really hurts my feelings."

John glanced at Wendell, hoping he would respond. "She's been known to get on mine and Sally's cases once in a while. Right, Wendell?"

"Mama can be hateful at times. You kinda have to let it go in one ear and out the other."

"That's good advice," John said.

"And sometimes you just have to get up and leave the room when she's in one of her really bad moods. Heaven forbid!"

"I'll try," Libby said. "But she can be so hurtful. Certainly not Christ-like."

"Amen," John said.

"Dad used to say she was bipolar," Wendell said. "I don't know about that, but I think she's gotten worse since he passed away."

Everyone hushed when Geraldine entered den and sat in the recliner, her throne which no one dared to occupy, especially since John returned from Europe. She turned on the TV with the remote, just as *Jeopardy!* was coming on the air. Libby tip-toed out of the room as if to go unnoticed by Geraldine. But with the TV volume turned up, Geraldine had already tuned out everyone in the room.

John returned to the kitchen where Sally finished loading the dishwasher. He poured kibble and water into Whiskers' bowls, then walked up behind Sally and wrapped his arms around her shoulders.

"Everything okay?" he asked before pecking the side of her neck.

"I still can't believe I couldn't find my car in the parking lot. That's embarrassing."

"C'mon now, Sally. Don't fret over that. We forget where we put things all the time."

"But a car?"

"Yes, a car. The lot was packed, and you found the place under the tree. Then you got focused on what you needed to get in the store. It's not a big deal. I do it all the time."

"Please John, don't patronize me."

"I'm not. It's the truth. When I was working, I always had to think about where I parked my car."

"If you say so."

"It happened all the time."

"And then the dorm room."

"Let's not go there again," John said.

Sally turned around, her back against the counter, and John smooched her softly on the mouth. "I did remember to change the sheets on Brody's bed. It's going to be close quarters for us."

"I like it that way," John said. "The closer the better when it comes to you."

"I didn't have a chance to look around in his room."

"I doubt if there's anything there," John said. "At least I hope I'm right. I think he took what he wanted from Wendell's prescription bottle. But I'll check it out tomorrow to make sure."

"Do you want to go the den and watch TV?"

"Too much tension there unless you want to watch *Jeopardy!* Let's go for a short walk instead."

John put the leash on Whiskers, and they left the house without telling anyone, since Geraldine and Wendell seemed immersed in the TV program and Libby had retreated to the bedroom.

An orange glow from the fading sun enveloped the neighborhood. Several streetlights flickered on as they strolled down the street, with Whiskers setting the off-and-on pace. As they approached Sister Cathy's well-lit house, they heard an off-key singing of "The Old Rugged Cross" flowing from two open windows, triggering a sudden laugh from both of them.

"I'm sure the neighbors appreciate hearing that noise," John said. "That'd drive me nuts."

"I wonder if anyone has complained?"

"I don't know, but give it time. I may do it."

"Now, John, you'd better not."

"Just kidding, sweetie. Maybe Wendell and Libby will take charge of it when they move in there."

"I'm not counting on it."

Allen Boatwright, who lived next door, stepped out of his house and waved. "It's a nice evening for a walk," he said from his porch. Allen was also retired but spent most of his time at Herrington Lake.

"It's beautiful," John said. "I haven't seen much of you. I can imagine where you've been."

"I don't think I've seen you since your retirement party last year," Allen said. "My houseboat has become my main home since the weather turned warmer. I'll be heading back to Herrington Lake tomorrow."

"Sounds relaxing."

"Well, I'm going to Baskin-Robbins and get some ice cream. I've had a hankering for a banana split." Allen smiled and headed to the driveway to get in his car. "Enjoy your walk."

"We may have to do what he's doing," John said to Sally as Allen drove away.

"Buy a houseboat?"

"I was thinking ice cream."

"Let's get a few more walks in," she said. "I don't need those extra calories right now."

"Neither do I."

Whiskers wailed as the congregants started another song, "Trust and Obey," as if beckoning his masters to get moving again. They obeyed.

~ * ~

Wendell had already gone to the bedroom to be with Libby by the time John and Sally returned. Geraldine was in the den, stretched out in recliner, watching *Dancing With the Stars*, a foot bouncing to the rhythmic music.

"Anything exciting happen while we were gone?" John asked as he sat on the couch while Sally went to the bathroom.

"Does anything exciting ever happen around here?" Geraldine's eyes were focused to the television.

"You might want to give that some more thought."

Geraldine paused a moment and turned her head toward him. "You might be right."

"Have Wendell or Libby ever said anything about the ministry they belong to?" John asked softly.

"I try not to get them started, especially Libby. She babbles on about it so much it makes my ears ring."

Sally came in, sat next to John, opened a magazine and closed it after a few seconds. Her shoulders slumped. "I'm tired. I hope you don't mind, but I think I'm going to bed."

"I think I'll join you," John said. "It'll be nice sleeping in a bed for a change."

"It's your fault," Geraldine said, still eyeing the flamboyant dance moves on the TV.

"Our fault?"

"You didn't have to let them sleep in your room."

"But they were in the bedroom when I returned from Europe. And how were we to know they'd be homesteading?"

"Now John," Sally said, tapping his knee. "That's not nice. They're our guests, not homesteaders."

"But Geraldine does have a point."

"Thank you, John," Geraldine said, giving me a smarmy smile. "I'm glad you can agree with me on things once in a while."

"You're right...once in a while." John winked.

"Your old mother-in-law knows a few things."

"As you remind me from time to time."

Sally rose from the couch, grabbed John's hand, and gave a light tug. "Let's go to bed."

"Let us know if you need anything," John said to Geraldine. "Just tap on the ceiling with your cane."

"Very funny," Geraldine said. "But you can hand me the throw over on the rocking chair?"

Sally picked up the cover and gave it to Geraldine, then kissed her on the cheek. "Good night, Mother."

"Sweet dreams," John said to his mother-in-law.

"Don't let the bedbugs bite!" Geraldine snickered.

Sally didn't waste any time pulling back the covers on Brody's bed. They quickly undressed and got under the sheet.

"This ain't too bad," John said as he cuddled up and placed an arm around her.

"It sure beats the floor."

"I'm not sure Wendell and Libby would fit in this bed," John said. "There's not a lot of room for us."

Sally didn't respond, and within twenty minutes was snoring, when John lurched up. "Damn."

"What is it?" Sally asked in a startled tone.

"I need to go to the grocery. I promised Wilma I'd get some coffee and bacon."

"It can't wait until the morning?"

"Bert expects bacon and eggs in the morning. And you know he's an early riser." John slipped on his jeans and shirt in the dark. "I won't be gone long."

"Knowing Bert and Wilma, I understand."

"Go back to sleep," John said. "Don't wait up for me."

"I hope you're kidding."

"I am." He tapped her hip and left.

John glanced in the den on the way out, noticing Geraldine was already snoring with the throw hanging on the side of the chair. He tip-toed to her side and covered her, pulling the cover down over her bony feet and under her pointy chin, then turned off the TV and lights.

After the short drive on the quiet streets to the supermarket, John went directly to the meat department and grabbed a pound of bacon, then to an aisle for a of coffee. On the way to the checkout counter, he got sidetracked at the bakery section and contemplated picking up a dozen chocolate-iced donuts for his visiting homesteaders.

Standing next to the rack, he sensed someone close to him. He stepped to the side and without looking at the person said, "Oh, sorry. Didn't mean to block you."

"Training food?"

John turned his head in the direction of the voice. It was Officer Kate Washington in uniform.

"Well, hi Kate," he said. "I sure didn't expect to see you tonight. It's been a while."

"Yes, it has," she said. "What are you doing out so late?"

John held out the bacon and coffee. "Getting this for Bert."

"Bert?"

"You know, Bert Reliford, from Neighborhood Watch."

"So you do those kinds of things for neighbors? I bet they love you."

John chuckled. "I borrowed these from his wife and told her I'd get her some before the morning. But I forgot, so here I am at this time of the night. Believe it or not, I was in bed. What brings you here?"

"I was heading back to the station and thought I'd pick up some donuts for the guys," she said. "How's everything been? Brody?"

John grimaced. "He's back in rehab. Another drug overdose."

"I'm sorry to hear that. I thought he was on his way to recovery."

"We thought so as well." John shrugged. "But we've been told relapses are not uncommon."

"Sad, but true."

"I hate to rush off, but I need to get this to Bert's wife before they go to bed," John said as he finished placing a dozen assorted donuts in a container. "It was great seeing you, Kate."

"Same here," she said. "Don't be such a stranger."

Before he could take back the words, he spurted, "We need to get together for coffee sometime and catch up on a few things."

"I'd love that," she said. "Just let me know when it's convenient for you. You know where to reach me."

She gave John a tight hug, nearly causing him to drop his grocery items.

John let out a short breath as he backed away, clutching his groceries. "Good night."

Driving back to the house, John couldn't get his mind off seeing Kate again. He hoped he wasn't sending the wrong message to her because there were things he wanted to discuss with her, such as Sister Cathy and the escalated agitation of minorities in the neighborhood.

The living room lights were on at Bert's house when John pulled into the driveway. The front-porch light flicked on as John approached the steps. Bert opened the door, wearing a blue robe emblazoned with a UK patch and blue-striped pajamas.

"What in tarnation brings you here at this hour of the night?" Bert asked. "Isn't it past your bedtime?"

John handed the groceries to him. "Something for Wilma."

"Wilma?"

"I borrowed some bacon earlier and told her I'd get her some more in time for your breakfast in the morning."

Wearing a light green robe and matching cotton gown, Wilma came up behind Bert, peeking around his arm. "Oh, hi John. What are you doing here so late? I hope it's nothing serious with Sally or your mother-in-law."

Bert turned around and handed the groceries to her. "John said you needed bacon for my breakfast in the morning. So he went out at this late hour to get it for you."

"You didn't have to," Wilma said meekly. "You could have done it at any time."

"You said Bert has to have his bacon and eggs in the morning."

"You told him that?" Bert scowled.

Wilma took a step back. "I did?"

"It wasn't a problem," John said. "I would have been here sooner, but it slipped my mind. I guess I must be getting older."

"We know you're not getting any younger," Bert said.

"I'm reminded of every day."

Bert turned to Wilma, motioning her to the kitchen with his head. "You can put it in the refrigerator."

"Enjoy your breakfast in the morning," John said to Bert as he backed away.

"I can't believe she had you go out for this," Bert said. "I'll say something to her later about it."

"Please, Bert," John said. "It was my fault. I told her I'd go get it this evening. Don't blame her. Blame me."

"I'll think about it."

"Besides, she was thinking about you."

"Okay," Bert said with a slight grin. "I do like my bacon and eggs every morning."

"Anyway, good night and maybe see you tomorrow."

"One more thing, John," Bert said in a subdued voice. "We missed you at the meeting tonight."

"Meeting?" John said, tilting his head as if he didn't know what Bert was referring to.

"Neighborhood Watch."

John lowered his shoulders. "I don't know what to say. I'll be at the next one."

"Promise?"

"You've got my word."

"Really?"

"Scout's honor," John said, flashing a silly grin and the Boy Scouts' three-finger salute.

When John got back in his car, he noticed the lights were already turned off in the front of their house. He hoped he hadn't caused a tiff between Bert and Wilma, although knowing Bert as he did, he knew he probably had.

Whiskers was ready to go outside when he got back, greeting him at the door. He let the pooch out and waited on the porch. There appeared to be peace down at Sister Cathy's house, with only a porch light on and no cars in the driveway or out front in the street. Whiskers scampered back into the house and went directly to his pad.

John did the same but had to nudge Sally a little to get some room on the bed. She reluctantly moved over a few inches, even cornering the pillow, but he didn't mind as he drifted off to sleep within minutes.

Twelve

After a restful sleep on a regular bed, John took Whiskers outside in the quiet predawn hours for his morning routine. He'd thought about staying in bed, but years of getting up early to head to work at the newspaper put him in a habit almost impossible to break. He came to cherish it as his personal alone time to do whatever he wished, which was usually nothing much other than reading the newspaper or drinking coffee in solitude to think. Now it included time with Whiskers.

He glanced down the street and noticed two men carrying boxes into Sister Cathy's haven. Whiskers returned from the side of the house, and seeing the activity, let out several sharp barks. The men stopped in their tracks and looked toward John and his aroused doggy.

"Shhh!" John placed his forefinger over his mouth. "You're going to wake up the neighborhood."

Concerned Whiskers might dart down the street, John yanked him up and hurried into the house. After filling the pup's bowls, he realized he had forgotten to pick up the newspaper, if it was out there.

John went back outside, eyed the paper at the end of the driveway, and rushed over to get it. As he turned to return to the house, someone asked, "Were you watching us?"

John recognized the voice as the man who had spoken to him in front of Sister Cathy's house. He was wearing jeans and a T-shirt with a white lightning bolt over a black raised fist insignia emblazoned on the front.

"I beg your pardon?" John asked.

"Were you spying on us?" the man asked, stepping out of the darkness and into the porchlight, closer to John.

"Are you serious?"

"I saw you watching us."

"Listen, young man, I live here. In fact, I've lived here for more than thirty years. I don't owe you a damn explanation for anything. Do you understand?"

"Didn't I tell you to be careful the other day?"

"You'd better be careful as well," John said in a deliberate tone. "If you know what's good for you."

"Corley?" A woman's voice came from Sister Cathy's house.

"I'm warning you, old man." The man backed away into the faded darkness.

"And I'm warning you," John said as he walked toward his house. "Don't mess with this old man."

"Corley!" the woman boomed. "Get back here. Now!"

The man glared at John for several silent seconds, then turned around and trotted down the street. "I'm coming, Mom."

John's hands trembled from the unexpected encounter as he stepped back into his house. He could feel the blood pulsing through his veins. He stopped for a few seconds in the living room, taking several deep breaths, before proceeding to the kitchen.

He was startled for a moment when he saw Sally pouring coffee. As she spun to take the cups to the bar, John slammed the newspaper down on the counter.

"What's wrong?" Sally asked. "You look upset about something."

"That young prick from down the street gave me another warning," John said, grim-faced. "He thought I was spying on him."

"Spying? When?"

"This morning," John said. "What do you think? I just finished talking to him."

"Don't take it out on me."

"I'm sorry. I'm just angry."

"That's crazy what he did."

"I know it's crazy. I was outside with Whiskers. I looked down the street and noticed some guys carrying boxes into the damn Sister Cathy's house. And then the scrawny punk comes down and accuses me of spying on them and even threatens me again."

"Did you say anything?"

"Hell, yes, I did. I told him it was none of his damn business what I do and he'd better be careful, too."

"What did he say?"

"Nothing much. The hallowed Sister Cathy beckoned him and he returned to the flock."

"She was out there, too?"

"I assume it was she. And apparently she's his mother."

John could feel his blood pressure rising again, and took several more slow, deep breaths. He clenched his jaw as he sat at the counter.

"John, you need to settle down. You're going to have another heart episode."

"That's what I'm trying to do. He really ticked me off."

"Do you think we should call the police?"

"I'm giving it some thought," John said. "They're acting as if they've got something to hide. And who carries in boxes into a house at this time of the morning?"

Sally reached over and patted the top of his clenched hand. "Maybe we should say something to Wendell and Libby."

"What in the world could they do? They're wrapped up in that so-called ministry."

"They could say something to Sister Cathy."

"This Sister Cathy crap is getting old, too. I'd like to know more about her. I think I'll check with the neighbors, or better yet, call the county clerk's office and ask about the sale of the house."

"It sure wouldn't hurt to know something about it."

"Just when things seem to be settling down in the neighborhood after the rash of vandalism last year, this stuff pops up. If it's not one thing, it's something else. So much for a peaceful retirement."

"I know," she said. "That's when I think we should consider moving."

"One thing at a time."

"Just try to be calm."

"Please, Sally. I'm trying to do that."

Sally took a sip from her cup while John sat with a meditative frown. He wasn't in the mood for any more conversation.

She opened the box of pastries and set it in front of him.

He wasn't in the mood for eating either.

~ * ~

After the stressful breakfast, John took Whiskers out for a quick walk, in the opposite direction of Sister Cathy's house. When he returned, Geraldine was sitting at the bar drinking coffee with Sally. She was still in the clothes she had worn the previous day. A twisted look on her face made him wish he had taken a few extra trips around the block, gone on to the park, or gotten in the car to visit his buddies at McDonald's.

"Why did you let me sleep in the recliner last night?" Geraldine growled, rolling her thin shoulders. "I'm stiff all over. I'll probably end up like Wendell, thanks to you."

"You looked comfortable and I didn't want to disturb you," John said as he sat next to Sally. "Sorry 'bout that. I won't do it again."

"It's a little late now, but I accept your apology."

"Next time I'll pick you up and lay you on the couch. How'd you like that?" He grinned.

"You better not!" she replied with a slight smile. "Your back might go out."

"I think I could handle it. How much do you weigh? A hundred pounds?"

She rolled her shoulders in mock defiance. "That's none of your business!"

"Any plans today?" Sally asked John, breaking up the lighthearted banter.

"I may run over to McDonald's. It's been a while since I saw the guys."

"And sit around and gossip," Geraldine said.

"Yep, just like you old gals," John said.

"I heard from one of the girls in the book club," Sally said. "We're having a meeting in a couple days, so I may try to finish a book and go."

"How about you, Geraldine?" John asked. "Any plans?"

"Are you trying to be funny?" Geraldine narrowed her eyes. "The only time I ever leave the house is to go to the doctor. Sometimes I feel like I'm in prison."

"It's of your own doing," John said.

"Are you trying to be funny again? And what in the world are you talking about?"

"Mother, we'd be happy to take you anywhere you'd like," Sally said. "I'm told they have a lot of wonderful activities at the senior citizens center."

"You can't be serious," Geraldine said, crinkling her eyes. "Do you think I want to sit around all afternoon playing Bingo, or in a sing-along circle, or playing cards with a bunch of old biddies who are treated like children. I don't think so!"

"You're not exactly a spring chicken," John said. "It might be fun."

"There you go again." Geraldine pointed a finger at him. "I've got better things to do."

"Like sitting in the den and watching TV from morning to night?"

"If that's what I want to do, then I'll do it." she said in a cheeky tone. "And it's none of your darn business if I do. I don't need your permission."

"Then you shouldn't complain."

"You're the one who brought it up."

"But you're the one who whined about never leaving the house."

"First of all, I didn't whine about it. I don't whine. And second, let's just drop the subject. You'll spoil my breakfast."

"Mother, you might take a college course at the university," Sally said. "Or join a book club at the library."

"A book club? Why don't you ever invite me to go to your book club? Ashamed to be seen with me?"

"Now, Mother, you know better than that," Sally said, red-faced. "You've never asked."

"And you've never asked me."

"Maybe because you fractured your hip. And maybe because I was away in Europe, and then with Chloe in New York. I haven't exactly been around here much, have I? I haven't even attended the book club in months. But if you want to go with me, you are hereby invited."

"Well, I'll just think about it," Geraldine said, "even though I don't like your tone."

"You let me know," Sally said.

"I will."

"Do you care to go with me to McDonald's?" John asked.

"You'd better be careful. I may just take you up on your offer. How would you like that?"

"You know I was kidding you."

"Oh, really?"

"If you're ever up to anything, let us know, Mother," Sally said. "It won't be a problem. Maybe we could go to a movie."

Geraldine scrutinized them for a couple of seconds and opened her mouth as she were about to reply, but eased off the stool and proceeded to the den without another word. John and Sally looked at each other with their mouths shut firmly.

After taking his cup to the sink, John headed to his new bedroom to change his shirt before going to McDonald's. The door to his former bedroom was cracked open, and he saw Wendell moving around the bed in apparently no discomfort. Libby came into view wearing a pink see-through teddy, causing John to dart to Brody's room and close the door as quietly as he could. "Unreal," he said, sitting on the side of the bed to settle down from the unexpected exposure.

After putting on a polo shirt, he cracked open the door to make sure the area was clear to leave the room. He breathed a sigh of relief when he saw his bedroom door was closed. He scampered to the kitchen and sat at the bar.

"You wouldn't believe what I just saw," John said to Sally as she was wiping off the counter.

"Libby in her underwear?" Sally said with a light laugh.

"Huh?"

"I'm just kidding, sweetie. Remember when you told me about walking in on her?"

"Oh, yeah. Anyway, I saw Wendell in the bedroom, and he was moving about like a brand new man."

"No aches and pains and humping over?"

Before John could reply, Wendell and Libby entered the kitchen, with her leading the way. Wendell was hunkered and bore the contorted face of a beaten-down old man.

"Not feeling any better today?" John asked.

"I feel like...awful," Wendell muttered as Libby braced his back as he sat on a stool. "I don't think I slept more than an hour or so last night."

Libby had the expression of a pitiful puppy as she sat next to him. "Poor baby. I could hardly sleep either. He moaned and groaned all night."

"Coffee?" Sally asked, lifting the half-filled pot.

"Oh, please," Libby said. "Bless you."

"John picked up donuts last night at the grocery," Sally said.

John placed the box on the bar while Sally poured coffee. Libby reached in and got chocolate-glazed donuts for Wendell and herself.

"You may have to go to the doctor if it doesn't get any better," John said. "It could be serious."

"I want to give it another day or two," Wendell said like a grief-stricken child. "The pain's excruciating but it usually runs its course over a few days. At least it has in the past. I'm praying it'll be the same this time."

"You certainly have our thoughts and prayers," John said. Sally's eyes darted in his direction before she returned the coffee pot to the warmer.

"Wendell and me have been talking about going back to Alabama," Libby said after swallowing a bite of her donut. "We had a heart-to-heart about it last night. And we prayed on it, too."

"Prayed a lot," Wendell added.

"Really?" John said. "What brought this on?"

"We've heard from the kids and they really miss us and want us to come home. And we miss them, too. Especially our little grands. They are such blessings in our lives."

"I can imagine," John said. "We feel the same about Whitney. You let me know if there's anything I can do, hear? Don't you hesitate one minute. At least you have your bags packed."

"Yes, we do," Wendell said, raising his brows as his eyes suddenly brightened.

Geraldine tapped her way back into the kitchen and opened the box. "Why didn't you tell me we had these?"

"Sorry, Mother, it slipped my mind," Sally said. "We got discussing other things. Remember?"

"I remember. But I still would have liked a donut with my coffee this morning."

"There's still ten in there," John said. "So sit down, take one, and make yourself at home."

"I believe I will," Geraldine said, pushing up on the stool. "In fact, I think I'll take two."

"Help yourself."

Libby reached in the box and took two long johns for herself and Wendell and pushed the container toward Geraldine.

"Better hurry," John said, giving Geraldine a good-natured wink. "You have to be fast around here."

"There'd better be another long john in there," Geraldine said.

For Libby's sake, there were several remaining for her mother-in-law.

~ * ~

The usual gang was at McDonald's, occupying the tables at the rear of the dining area. They were gabbing a few decibels over normal since several were hard of hearing, causing others to raise their voices to be heard, even those with hearing aids.

"Welcome back, stranger," Curtis McKenzie said as John walked toward them with a steaming cup of coffee. "Been up to no good as usual?"

John chuckled as he sat next to Howard Brock and across from Curtis. "Kinda hard for me to avoid these days. I thought retirement was supposed to put me on easy street. I'm finding a few bumps in the road along the way. It ain't what it's cracked up to be, or at least how I thought it would be."

"Wishful thinking, Rossi," said Mel Snider in his vibrant radio voice. "The only headache I don't have is having to deal with work every day. The downside is I don't have a bi-weekly paycheck for me and my wife's healthcare's out-of-pocket expenses. But I'm still alive, so I guess I can't complain too much."

"We're not at that point yet, although I've had a couple scares with my ticker," John said. "I'm not taking anything for granted. I can hear your stories and know things can change without notice."

"Or read the obits," Curtis said.

"I was gonna say that. That's something I look at every morning. I can't say it gets my day off to a good start seeing the ages of the recently departed, but it keeps me grounded."

"It only gets worse the older you get," Mel said. "A sad aspect of life."

"I won't argue with that. I think we die a little when we hear about someone's passing."

"Unless there's some SOB who kicks the bucket. Then it's good riddance. It may add a day or two to your life."

"That's kinda harsh, Mel, but I hear ya," Howard said, raising his thick brows. "We've all had to deal with assholes in our lives. But I'm not sure I wish the death penalty on anyone I've known." He paused. "Well, maybe one or two."

Everyone laughed, several pounding their fists on the tables.

"Hey, John, I forgot to tell you Brandon Wilkes was here a couple days ago," Mel said. "He said you mentioned our meetings a few weeks ago. He was disappointed you weren't here."

"Well shoot," John said. "I guess he remembered. I hope you treated him well."

"It was great seeing him," Howard said. "He mentioned something about having to finish some work on a book he's working on, but promised to come back. I suppose we didn't scare him off."

"Maybe he'll be show up the next time," John said. "I'm sure he has some stories to share."

"You still have your in-laws at your place?" Curtis asked John. "Your brother-in-law is a piece of work. Has he toned down his rhetoric?"

"It's hard to say," John said. "He and his wife are Bible thumpers now. So what do you think?"

"Heaven forbid!" Howard said. "We have one of those in our family. Fortunately, he lives in Richmond and we don't see much of him. But he's one pious putz. Never gets off his pedestal. Even sends out Bible scriptures by email on a daily basis."

"I can feel the brotherly love in your voice," Mel said, laughing. "Hallelujah, brother!"

"Thank God for the delete button," Curtis said.

"Unless you have to deal with it, you don't understand how bad it can be. It's like some political nutjob who's always espousing some off-the-wall crap they've seen on Facebook or other place," Howard said. "You know what I'm saying?"

"I've heard about that," John said. "That's one reason I'm not using it. I get enough of nonsense when I come here."

"Hey! Watch what you say!" Mel said. "We resemble that remark."

"Just kidding, although you know as well as I do there are a few who will go unmentioned who fit the mold."

"And we won't go there," Curtis said. "Some things are better left unsaid."

"But getting back to my in-laws, Wendell told me before I left this morning they're moving back to Alabama to be with their children," John said. "They're getting homesick."

"I guess your prayers have been answered," Curtis said, grinning. "Right?"

"I suppose so. We'll also get our bedroom back."

"They've been sleeping in your bed all this time?" Howard cocked his head with furrowed brows. "I don't know if I would have let them do that. A bed is a man and woman's private sanctuary. At least that's the way my wife and I have always viewed it."

"Some extenuating circumstances," John said. "Plus, Sally is soft-hearted about those things. I mean, it is her brother."

"There's always a limit for me," Mel said. "I must be hard-hearted."

"You're just protecting your love nest," Curtis said.

"Smartass!"

"They haven't been too bad," John said. "I mean, I've known them for so long that whatever they say or do really doesn't surprise me. It can even be entertaining at times. But it wasn't until they ran across some extreme religious fundamentalists that things turned a little sour for us. Did I tell you we have some in our neighborhood?"

"Keep 'em there," Curtis said. "They can be a real pain in the ass."

"I hope they leave as well," John said. "Since they moved in, we've had some nasty things happen to a few minority families. So I'm beginning to wonder if there's a connection. I hope not, but you never know."

"Sounds like white-supremacy folks to me," Mel said. "They've been popping up all over the country in recent years. I'm sure you know that."

"From what little I can gather from Wendell and Libby, in their sermonizing, is that it's a white-only mission," John said. "I even had one of the followers accuse me of spying on them. Crazy stuff."

"Those so-called Christians can have a twisted set of values," Howard said. "Be careful."

John laughed. "That's the message I got."

"Yeah, one of those 'love thy neighbor' messages," Curtis said.

"And then they're worried about other religions espousing violence when that's what they're doing. It doesn't make any sense."

"Seriously, most of the religious folks I know are good people and devout in their worship," John said. "They're not seeking to harm or scare anyone. They just want to find some answers in their lives as well as some temporary refuge from all the bad things going on in the world."

"And they like to sing and go to church socials," Curtis said.

"Now, you're being sarcastic," John said, shaking his head.

"I confess." Curtis made a sign of the cross.

"It takes only a few zealots to create havoc," Howard said. "They twist the scriptures to their own liking."

"Hell, I think most of them use religion as a front to cover their hate," Curtis said, his voice rising. "It's total bullshit."

"Amen, brother!" Mel said with a big laugh. "Go tell it on the mountain!"

"And they're involved in politics with their holier-than-thou messages and their mega-churches."

"I agree," Howard said. "They need to be taxed. Folks have seemed to forget about separation of church and state."

"Those clowns want you to forget that," Mel said. "It's all about money and power."

"Damn straight," Curtis banged a hand on the table.

A young woman, sitting with two children, turned and looked at the guys with squinted eyes like a cat about to pounce.

"I think we'd better keep it down," Howard said. "We're getting some nasty looks."

"We are getting a bit rowdy for some old farts," Mel said with a light laugh. "There's nothing like religion and politics to get one's blood boiling."

"That's a reason we try to avoid those subjects," Howard said. "Remember?"

"You're right," Curtis said with a shrug. "But we keep falling into that trap."

"It's John's fault," Mel said.

"Me? Why do you say that?" John asked.

"You brought it up about your relatives."

"You're right, but it wasn't my intention. One thing led to another."

"You're forgiven," Curtis said.

"Anything else going on I don't know about?" John asked after taking a sip of coffee. "Any good news for a change?"

"I'm not sure this is the place for good tidings," Howard said. "You should know newspaper people talk of gloom and doom. It's in our blood."

"Unfortunately," John said. "For the most part we've peddled death, destruction, corrupt politicians, sports cheats, and catastrophes. Even obituaries."

"Yeah," Mel said. "In other words, life."

"Speaking of obits," Curtis said, "did you read about Wilbur Collins passing away? Only seventy-four. The notice said to give to some Alzheimer's disease organization, so I imagine he was a victim."

"Sorry to hear that," John said. "I hadn't seen him in several years. I think the last time was at the library and he wasn't his ebullient self then. Certainly not the person who penned witty columns for the paper. I even told Sally something didn't seem right. His eyes seemed somewhat dull."

"Like there was nobody home?" Curtis said.

"I sure as hell hope it doesn't happen to me," Mel said. "That's a sad, slow death."

"I think it's too late, Melvin," Curtis said, thumping his hand on the table. "We've been wanting to say something to you about it, but we weren't sure you'd remember."

"Smartass!"

"If you can't have a sense of humor, especially at our age, then your life is already a little empty," Howard said.

"Yeah, it kinda helps a person get over the sadness in their lives," John said. "Try to enjoy the day but know things could turn nasty without any notice."

"And they probably will," Howard said. "And then you die."

"Yep, here today, gone tomorrow," Mel said.

"Hey, guys, this is getting a little heavy," Curtis said. "Let's move on to something else."

"It is depressing," Mel said. "Makes you think more about euthanasia."

"What?" Curtis asked, rearing back his head. "Isn't taking your own life depressing?"

"I was just thinking about Wilbur," Mel said. "What a sad way to go. Would you want your final years to be live liked that? Only a shell of yourself? And how about those folks with terminal cancer. I spent time with my wife's brother after doctors said he only had a month to live. It dragged on for a few more weeks, and those weeks were awful for him and heartbreaking for the family. He was in lots of pain and practically starved to death. I wouldn't wish that on anyone. Even you, Curtis."

"Oh, thanks, buddy," Curtis said with a wry grin. "But I know what you mean, and I agree with you. People should be able to die with a degree of dignity. It's not like we're going to beat the system because in the end we all end up six feet under or in a cremation urn."

"That's what I'd want," John said. "We make all kinds of decisions during our lives, some even life and death, so we should be allowed to decide when to end it all. I know if I ever got like your brother-in-law, Mel, and couldn't do anything about it, I think I'd take matters into my own hands."

"Suicide?" Howard asked.

"Why not?" John said. "There's not a miracle drug out there that's going to save you when you're at that stage. And it'll help alleviate some of the grief and financial strain on your family. Some European countries allow it. Maybe that's when I'll return to Europe."

"It's a damn shame some folks who won't let a person die on their own accord have no qualms about executing a person in prison," Curtis said. "Or sending folks off to war to be killed in the prime of their lives. Makes no sense at all."

"Or abortion—" Howard said.

"Let's not go there now," Mel said. "At least not here."

"But we can agree that dealing with death is something we'll all have to face, in one way or another," Mel said.

"You're right," Howard said. "I try not to think about it. I'm going to live forever. So far, so good."

"You wish!" Curtis said with hearty laugh. "As the old Doors' song goes, 'no one here gets out alive.'"

"Morrison sure didn't," John said. "Or Manzarek."

"Well, guys, I hope to get out of here alive and run a few errands for the wife before going home," Mel said. "And if I don't, she's liable to send me to an early grave."

"Same here," John said as he stood. "Until the next time."

"If we make it until then," Curtis said as he led the old friends in single file to the rear exit.

~ * ~

When John returned, Wendell and Libby's luggage was back in the living room against the front wall next to the door. Sally was napping in the bedroom while Geraldine was in the den, in the recliner with the TV turned on to a baseball game.

"Where's Wendell and Libby?" John asked Geraldine as he walked to the couch. She was startled by his presence, shaking her head and raising her hands. Whiskers was curled on his pad, oblivious to everything.

"Sorry," John said. "I didn't mean to wake you up."

"I was just resting my eyes." Geraldine pulled the side lever to an upright sitting position. "Now what did you ask me?"

"Where's our houseguests?"

"They went to the store to pick up a few things to eat on the way to Alabama," she said, half looking at him and half keeping an eye on the TV as if trying to figure out why there was a ballgame on the screen. "He says they plan to drive straight through. Only going to stop for gas and bathroom breaks. Isn't he silly? Especially being down in his back."

"Maybe Libby will drive part of the way."

"No," said Geraldine. "He has to be in control when they get in the car. He's always been that way. Just like his father. And I think she likes to feel she's being escorted."

"It's still a long drive. When are they leaving?'

"For some reason, after dark."

"That's odd."

"That's what I think. But who listens to me?"

Geraldine flicked the channel to a soap opera and directed her attention to the program as if John had vanished from the room. He took it as a cue to leave and check to see if the mail had arrived.

Whiskers was at his feet when he opened the front door, so he let him out while sorting through the mail on the porch, most of which was the usual daily dose of charities and political groups seeking donations. He came to one from the reunion committee at his high school, which he left unopened while waiting for Whiskers to finish sniffing around a mulberry bush at the corner of the house.

Wendell and Libby returned a few minutes later, sitting in their car and talking before getting out and each carrying a sack of groceries for their drive back to Alabama.

"You must be taking a long way back," John stepped to the side and opened the door to let them pass into the house.

"We had to get a few other things," Wendell said. "Can you wait here for a minute? I need to talk to you about something." John sat on the porch steps, waiting for Whiskers to finish his snout scan over various points of the front yard.

"Sure thing." John noticed Wendell was moving about in no apparent pain, not even a wince when he stepped into the house carrying the groceries. Libby followed, looking downward to avoid eye contact.

Whiskers ran up and hopped in John's lap, rising up and licking his chin. John hugged the pooch and set him back down when Wendell returned and sat next to him.

"Your back is feeling better?" John asked.

Wendell let out a short breath. "That's one thing I wanted to talk to you about."

"I'm not a doctor or pain specialist, so I'm not sure you need my opinion."

Wendell let out a nervous chuckle. "My back's not bothering me."

"What?" John acted astonished by the admission, blinking his eyes several times, and overdoing it a bit as Wendell gave him a wary look.

"I didn't want to move down to Sister Cathy's house. There's some scary folks down there, especially since her son showed up."

"What do you mean?"

"I'm ashamed to say but it's a white-folks only church, if that's what you want to call it. I think it's more like one of those so-called alt-right groups. I think that's what they call them. The only thing they talk about there, when it's not Jesus, is Blacks, homos, and taking back the country, whatever that's supposed to mean."

"Everyone was okay at first?"

"I began to suspect something early on, but Libby seemed to enjoy getting involved with the mission stuff. Like I said, they wanted to bring in only whites. When I said something about it, they said they needed to grow the membership first with whites, then they would spread the mission to others. But I knew it wasn't going to happen after Corley and his friends showed up. That Christian One stuff is a bunch of hooey."

"So you faked your back injury?"

"Those folks scare me," Wendell said. "I had to come up with some excuse. Especially for Libby. I didn't want her involved."

"What does she think?"

"She's a little upset, but she doesn't know everything's that's going on there," Wendell said. "It's when the men are away from the women that some of this stuff comes out. All she hears about is the Bible study, singing, and mission work in the neighborhood."

"You could have been straight with us about everything," John said. "We might have been able to help."

"I didn't want to get you and Sally involved because of what they might do. It was easier this way."

"I see. And you're leaving after dark?"

"The reason we're leaving tonight is so we can get away before they know we're gone."

"Won't they follow you?"

"I don't think so. I mailed a note to Sister Cathy this afternoon, telling her we had to leave because of a family emergency in Oklahoma."

"Oklahoma? Who lives in Oklahoma?"

"I just told her in case they try to track us down. I don't think they will, but you never know."

"They won't get any information from me," John said.

"That's another thing. Please don't ever let on where we live. I'll call you once we find a new place."

"Don't you have a place in Alabama?"

"Uh, we had to leave," Wendell said, pressing his lips." I'll explain some other time."

"Anything else we can do?"

"Could you spare a little cash to tide us over while we get settled?"

"Uh, sure," John said. "How much do you need?"

"A thousand?"

John blinked several times...this time it was natural. "I'll have to go to the bank. I don't carry that much on me."

"I didn't want to ask Mama, although I'm sure she would give it to me. But you know how she can be. I'd never hear the end of it."

John nodded. "Understandable."

"Are you sure it won't be a problem for you and Sally? I don't want to deplete your savings."

"It won't be a problem."

"Are you sure?"

"Anything to help family. We keep a little back for emergencies and I think this qualifies as an emergency."

"We'll pay you back as soon as we can. I promise."

"That's good," John said. "At your convenience."

Wendell rose, a rare appreciation reflected in his moist eyes as he bent over and shook John's hand. "I knew we could count on you."

"Well, as Sally likes to say, family matters."

Whiskers began scratching at the door, letting John know he was ready to go back inside for food and water.

Sally entered the living room as they stepped into the house. She glanced at the luggage with a puckered forehead.

"Are you going back to Sister Cathy's?" she asked Wendell.

"Uh, no," he said. "It's kind of a long story. We're going to Alabama."

"Wow!" She sat in the easy chair. "What brought this on?"

"I'll explain later, hon," John said. "It has to do with Sister Cathy's ministry."

Wendell winced. "It wasn't what we thought it would be."

"Okay," Sally said. "I understand. You do what you have to do. That's what matters."

"How about me ordering a pizza for old time's sake?" John asked. "Just let me know what you want on it and when to place the order."

Libby sauntered into the room. "Did I hear someone mention pizza?"

"I'm going to order one before you guys leave. Just let me know what you want."

"Anything works for me as long as there's some meat on it," Wendell said. "And maybe some cheese sticks."

"Don't forget I like diet soda," Libby said. "There's not any in the refrigerator."

"I'll do that." John said. "Anything else?"

"Do they have desserts?"

"I think they have brownies. How's that? I'll get a tray of them," John said. "Along with the diet soda."

~ * ~

As darkness set in, and the loaded pizza and most of the brownies were completely consumed, the family gathered in the living room for hugs and farewells. Wendell peeked out the corner of the curtain toward Sister Cathy's house.

"It looks like it's safe to leave." He spoke softly as if someone there could hear him. "Doesn't seem to be like there's much going down the street."

"I don't understand why you just didn't leave in broad daylight," Geraldine bellowed. "You don't need to be driving at night. That's stupid. You could have been halfway there by now if you'd left earlier instead of taking your own sweet time."

"Could you keep it down, Mama?"

"Can't you answer me?"

"You wouldn't understand, Mama."

"Maybe if you'd tell me I would, instead of leaving me in the dark. I may be old but I still got my wits about me."

"Mama, please. I don't want to argue right now."

"And why are you looking down the street? And I thought your back was out. That was a fast recovery, if you ask me."

"Geraldine, I'll explain later," John said calmly. "Let's just get them on the road before it gets too late. They've got a long drive ahead of them."

"That's crazy," Geraldine said, shaking her head. "Well, give me a hug because there's something I want to watch on TV and I don't want to miss the beginning of it."

Wendell gave her a light hug and kissed her cheek. Libby used both hands to squeeze one of Geraldine's, then hesitated for a moment before bending over and pecking her cheek.

"We're going to miss you, Mama," Wendell said. "Let us know if you need anything. And try to come down and visit. The kids would love to see you. That's all they talk about."

"Sure," Geraldine said, looking toward the ceiling as she headed to the den. "Bye."

John and Wendell picked up the luggage, tip-toed to the car and placed it in the trunk. Libby and Sally followed, each carrying a bag of groceries they put in the back seat.

John glanced down the street at Sister Cathy's house, which was brightly lit with several cars parked out front and in the driveway. He could faintly hear "Softly and Tenderly" in the short distance. He felt somewhat foolish being so secretive, but understood Wendell's concerns.

"I haven't a clue what's going on there tonight," Wendell said, standing next to John. "They usually don't have Bible study this late."

"Maybe they're studying something else, since you and Libby aren't there," John said. "Didn't you tell me they have different groups?"

"Yeah, but those things are usually posted on the wall and—"

Corley stepped out on the front porch by himself and lit a cigarette. Wendell froze for a moment, then crept around to the side of the car and knelt as if in prayer.

"What in the world are you doing?" Libby said.

"Shhh! Corley's out front."

Libby, wide-eyed, put her hand over her mouth and squatted next to him. "This is so silly," she said.

"Not really. We'll talk about it after we get on the road."

"You bet we are. You have a lot of explaining to do."

John quietly closed the trunk and walked over to Sally. They watched Corley take a long drag off his cigarette, blow out a thin stream of smoke, then flick it in the front yard and return to the house. John wondered if Sister Cathy was bothered about cigarette butts on her lawn.

"The coast is clear," John whispered. "You guys better hit the road."

Libby gave Sally a quick hug and waved at John before slouching into the passenger seat. Wendell shook John's hand and stared at him for a moment.

"Did you forget something?" he asked with his brows lowered.

John looked at him, trying to think what he was talking about, then remembered the thousand-dollar loan. "Wait a second." He rushed back to the house.

"What's going on?" Sally asked.

"Oh, it's nothing," Wendell said. "There's something he wanted to give me for the trip."

John was back within thirty seconds and handed a puffy, white, sealed envelope to Wendell. "Sorry 'bout that. You should have said something earlier."

"Thanks, again," Wendell said. He tore open the envelope as if to see if the money was there. John wondered for a second if he was going to count it out, but Wendell flashed an appreciative grin, stuffed the packet in his front pants pocket, and got into the car.

"Drive safely," John said.

"We'll call when we get there," Libby said, leaning toward the driver's side window. "Gonna miss you folks. And thanks again for the leftover brownies. We'll eat them on the way. God bless now."

Wendell backed out of the driveway with the lights off and drove in the opposite direction of Sister Cathy's house. John and Sally watched as they turned the corner, the car lights flicking on, and the vehicle disappearing from view. They walked back toward the house, stopping at the porch steps.

"What was that all about?" Sally asked.

"What?" John said.

"The envelope."

"Oh, something to tide them over until they get settled back down."

"I'm glad we could help."

"I loaned them a thousand dollars. I didn't think you'd mind."

"You know I don't. I want the best for them."

"He assured me he'd pay us back."

"I guess we'll find out."

"Yep, one of these days. God willing."

Geraldine was in the den, leaned back in the recliner watching TV when they went back into the house. They sat on the couch, unsure what was on the screen, when the doorbell rang.

"Who in the world at this time of night?" Sally asked, her brows scrunched.

"I bet it's Bert." John rose from the couch and went to the front door. "He was probably wondering what was going on in the driveway."

There were two more rings before John opened the door. Corley took a step back as they made eye contact under the yellow porch light. John's eyes widened and he was sure the visitor could see the surprise on his face.

"Good evening, sir," Corley said with a smarmy smile. "I was wondering if Mr. Corman was around?"

John hesitated for a moment. "Wendell and Libby went out for a while. I'm not sure when they'll be back."

"I'm sorry I missed them. When they return, would you tell them Corley dropped by?"

"I surely will," John said with a strained smile. "Is there anything I can help you with?"

"We haven't seen them in a couple days and were a bit concerned."

"They're okay. I can tell you that."

"Just tell them Corley stopped by." He turned and walked across the lawn toward Sister Cathy's home, stopping to light up another cigarette when he reached the sidewalk.

John returned to the den and sat next to Sally, letting out a short breath.

"What did Bert want?" she asked.

"It wasn't Bert. It was Corley."

"From Sister Cathy's house?"

"Yup. He wanted to see Wendell and Libby."

"What did you tell him?"

"Being a person of the cloth, or related to one, I couldn't lie, so I told him they were on their way to Alabama."

Sally bumped her leg against his leg. "John, you're not serious."

"No, I'm not serious." He started laughing.

"Would you two keep it down over there," Geraldine scolded. "If you haven't noticed, I'm trying to watch TV."

"Yes ma'am," John said.

"And what's so funny?"

"I'll tell you in the morning. Go back to your show."

"You're being a smart aleck again." Geraldine turned up the volume.

"Let's go to bed," Sally said. "It's been a long day."

"Don't forget," John said, flicking his brows. "We've got our bed back."

"I forgot. We can sleep there tonight."

"I'll race you to the bed," John said as he stood.

"You think I ought to change the sheets?"

"Uh, never thought about that. You're right."

Sally got up and headed toward the bedroom. "Looks like I'll win."

"At least I've got something to look forward to."

"Would you two keep it down?" Geraldine said. "My goodness, you'd think you've never slept with each other before."

"It does seem like forever since we've been in our bed," Sally said.

"Well, it's your fault."

"I know, Mother."

"Then sweet dreams."

"Same to you, Mother."

"Do you want me to check on you later?" John asked Geraldine.

"What in the reason for?"

"Don't want you falling asleep in the recliner. Remember the last time?"

"Since you mentioned it, you might peek in on me before you go to sleep if it wouldn't be too much trouble," she said sweetly.

"Anything else?"

"Why did Wendell leave tonight?"

"Can it wait until the morning?"

"No."

"No?"

"You heard me."

"The short version is they weren't comfortable being around their religious friends so they decided to leave like thieves in the night."

"Are you trying to be funny, John?"

Thirteen

Sally's phone rang as she and John were driving to the rehab facility to pick up Brody. Her eyes brightened, and after she mentioned Chloe, John turned off the radio so he could catch parts of the conversation. Chloe said she'd left the doctor's office with a prognosis that the treatments had eradicated the lethal ovarian cancer cells.

Tears rolled down Sally's cheeks as she passed the reassuring information to John. He pulled the SUV to the side of the road and listened to the conversation before Sally handed him the phone.

"That's the best news I've heard in ages, sweetie," John said to his daughter. "I hope we can all get together soon and celebrate."

"We will, Daddy," Chloe said. "I feel like a ton of weight has been lifted off my shoulders. A person doesn't truly realize what cancer can do until they experience it. I wouldn't wish it on anyone."

"Believe it or not, we've silently gone through the ordeal with you."

"I know you have," Chloe said. "I appreciate everything you and Mom have done. I couldn't have made it without your love and support."

"That's sweet to say, but you're one tough cookie. I think you could have done it."

"I'm that way because of you and Mom."

"Oh, well, we're on our way to get Brody and I'm sure he'll be overjoyed with the news."

"Tell him I love him and want him to get better."

"Will do," John said. "Love you, sweetie. You've made my day."

John returned the phone to Sally and got back on the road, hoping the intense counseling would bring encouraging news for Brody's outlook as well. Sally ended the call, her face glowing for the first time in ages, at least since their time in Budapest.

"I feel like it's a brand new day," Sally said with a broad smile.

"Wouldn't it be nice if Brody had the same resolve and determination as Chloe?"

"I know what you mean, but they're dealing with different diseases."

"You're right," John said, shrugging. "One can only hope."

Ms. Farley, a counselor, briefed John and Sally in an office off the front lobby about Brody's progress. It had a positive ring since they were there to take him home.

"Is there anything we can do?" Sally asked.

"We want to minimalize a relapse," John added. "If that's possible."

"One thing I'd like for both of you to do, if possible, is attend support-group meetings for Brody," Ms. Farley said. "You can gain a lot of information while also showing Brody you're participating in his recovery."

"Just sign us up and tell us where to go for meetings," John said.

"I'll email a list of times and places for you," she said. "I'll tell you now those in the recovery phase appreciate it when family members and friends are involved and interested in them."

"We're all in this together."

Brody walked into the front lobby minutes after the counselor finished her assessment and recommendations. He hadn't shaved in the two weeks he was away, developing a full growth that, coupled with his tired eyes, made him look older than his thirty-seven years. He also appeared leaner and especially gaunt in the face.

Sally's eyes welled as she hugged Brody. John shook his wayward son's drooping hand, then took his one travel bag and led the way to their car. A light shower began from the gray sky.

As they drove on the narrow road, John and Sally didn't inquire about his stay. They weren't sure of Brody's attitude and didn't want any setbacks from his fresh new start. Brody didn't appear in the mood to volunteer any information about what had transpired in the facility. The swishing of the windshield wipers was the only sound for five minutes.

Sally cleared her throat when they reached a stoplight. "Chloe's finished with her treatments. The oncologist says she's cancer-free. She has to go back in three months for a follow-up exam. Isn't that great?"

"That's good," Brody said with a spent smile.

"And Wendell and Libby have gone back to Alabama," she said. "They left three days ago."

"That's nice."

"Your grandmother is about the same. I think she's getting around better. I know she's missed you."

"That's good to hear."

"And guess what?"

"What?"

"I think she's going to stay with us."

"Oh."

"Would you like to stop at Wild Eggs or someplace and get breakfast?" John asked.

Brody shrugged. "Nah. Not hungry. I had something before you got to the center."

"Are you sure?" Sally asked.

"I'm good."

Geraldine stood inside the front door. She held out her arms, holding the cane in one hand and tugged at Brody before he finally relented and bent over to receive a soft kiss on the cheek. Whiskers greeted him, brushing against his leg several times before receiving a reluctant pat between the perky ears.

"You going to the bathroom now?" Geraldine asked.

"No," Brody said with a forced smile. "What for?"

"Aren't you going to get rid of that beard? It makes you look so…I don't know. Rough."

"Thanks." Brody let out a short breath.

"I'll buy you a razor," Geraldine teased, brushing her hand against his bushy beard.

"Mother, please," Sally said. "Let's give him time to unwind."

Brody backstepped out of Geraldine's reach and sidestepped her as he headed toward his room without saying a word.

"What's his problem?" Geraldine clenched her teeth.

"He's tired," Sally said. "Just give him a little time to get settled."

"I don't know why he's taking it out on me. I didn't do anything. I didn't make him go away."

"He's not doing that. He's only tired and needs to gather his thoughts. He's been away for two weeks. He'll be back to his old self in no time."

"I'm not sure that's so good." Geraldine padded toward the den.

John looked at Sally. "She has a point."

"Don't say that, John. You know what I mean."

"I'll try."

"What the hell!" Brody's voice thundered from his bedroom.

"It seems like he's back to his old self," Geraldine said from the den.

John and Sally hurried to his room. "What's the problem?" Sally asked at his doorway.

Brody stood next to his bed, arms across his protruding chest. "You went through my belongings while I was gone?"

"What are you talking about, Brody?" Sally asked, her brows gathered as she took a small step toward him.

"What's all your shit doing in here?"

"We slept in here a few nights because Wendell and Libby had our bedroom," John said. "Remember?"

"Well, it sure looks like someone's gone through my things."

"Honey, even if we'd wanted to, we didn't have time," Sally said. "For most of the time while you were away, we slept on the floor in the living room."

"My back can attest to that," John said with an unconvincing laugh.

"Okay then," Brody said, letting out a light breath and sitting on the side of the bed. "I'm sorry. I guess I'm just stressed."

Sally sat next to him, placing an arm around his drawn shoulders. "We understand. It's going to take a while to get back into a routine."

"I'm going to walk Whiskers," John said, stepping out of the room. "Let me know if you need anything."

"I'll leave you be." Sally kissed Brody on the cheek and followed John out of the room. Seconds later, they heard the door close.

John stood in the living room, hands on hips. "Damn."

"What's the matter?" Sally asked, her head tilted.

"I wish we had gone through his room more thoroughly."

"Why do you say that?'

"Because he was so upset about us being in there while he was away. It makes me think he had something stashed away."

"You think so?"

"I hope I'm wrong," John said as he fastened the leash to Whiskers' collar.

They turned around when they heard Geraldine approach, her cane tapping on the hardwood floor.

"What was all the commotion about?" she asked.

"Please, Mother, Brody's stressed from being away for a couple weeks," Sally said.

"Stressed? He should be in a good mood, coming back here. I know I would be."

"Give him time," John said. "Actually, I think we're all a little stressed about what's been going on the past few weeks."

"I'm not stressed," Geraldine said, puffing her scrawny chest.

Sally touched Geraldine arm. "I forgot to tell you about Chloe. She's cancer-free."

"How do you know that?"

"She called while we were going to get Brody. Let's go to the kitchen. I'll make another pot of coffee and tell you about it."

John opened the front door. "C'mon Whiskers, let's take our walk."

"You and your dog," Geraldine said. "I'm beginning to think you go on those walks as an excuse to get out of here for a little while."

As John fastened the leash on Whiskers, he smiled at Geraldine, and left.

~ * ~

John and Whiskers were halfway down the block when someone shouted, "Hey, you!"

John stopped and turned around to see where it was coming from and if it was directed at him. Across the street, and marching toward him, was Corley Gibson.

"Yes?"

"Why did you lie to me about Wendell and Libby Corman?" Corley asked in a sharp tone as he got closer. "I don't appreciate it."

"Sorry to hear that."

"Where'd they go?"

"I'm really not sure."

"Cut the crap, old man. You know where they went."

"I beg your pardon." John felt the muscles in his arms begin to tighten as he glared at Corley. He turned and began to walk away. Whiskers let out a rare growl.

"You're a pussy, just like Wendell."

John bit his lower lip and continued walking down the street.

"We'll find out where he is," Corley yelled. "He'll regret ever running away, the fat-ass coward."

Rufus Martin stepped out on his front porch. "What's going on?" he asked John.

"Get back in the house, blackie," Corley shouted. "No one called for you."

"What did you say?" Rufus asked, eyes like a hawk, as he stepped off his porch.

"You heard me. Now mind your own fuckin' business, if you know what's good for you."

Rufus continued striding toward Corley, his fists clenched and eyes blazing with fire. John grabbed Whiskers in his arms and scurried between them.

"Let's cool it," John said, raising a hand.

"Fuck you, old man!" Corley, raising his head like a snake about to strike.

"Are you from across the street?" Rufus asked. "The so-called church group?"

"What's it to ya?"

"And behaving this way, and that language. You should be ashamed of yourself. And you call yourself a child of God?"

"Kiss my ass." Corley turned and darted back toward his house, slamming his fist on the hood of a parked car as he crossed the street. He glanced back one time, flipping his middle finger at them.

"He's nuts," Rufus said. "What's he so outraged about?"

"He's upset because I refused to tell him where my brother-in-law went."

"Your brother-in-law was part of that hate group? You've got to be kidding me."

John frowned. "I wish. He left it because it wasn't what he thought it was. You can say he was more of a sheep in a lion's den."

"I just don't understand these people anymore. They claim to be Christians and act just the opposite. It seems to be everywhere. It used not to be this way, or least not this bad. Now they think they can act any way they want to, as if they have the right to do so. Heaven help us."

"I hope I didn't get you drawn into this," John said as he set Whiskers on the sidewalk. "It's not worth it. I've been tempted to call law enforcement. I haven't seen anything like it since the sixties."

"I'm not sure what they can do unless there's some hate crimes involved and you can prove it. Anyway, being Black means you've heard and seen it before."

"It doesn't mean you have to like it or accept it," John said. "I'm white and I don't like it or accept it."

"I never said that. I've just been exposed to it through the years. I was born into it. It's almost like you can never let your guard down. Once you do, somebody says or does something to you. It's a way of life you can't escape."

"Well, please be careful until we get to the bottom of what's going on. Okay?"

"Don't worry," Rufus said with a snarky grin. "I was prepared if it got out of hand."

"Huh?"

Rufus patted his back pocket. "Some heat."

"I'm glad it didn't escalate."

"Me, too," Rufus said. "But I wasn't going to take any chances. Not anymore."

~ * ~

Brody was in the den, sprawled on the couch reading *Sports Illustrated* when John returned. Geraldine was in her usual spot, feet elevated, and immersed in a mindless talk show about entertainment celebrities. Occasionally she would join in the conversations, expressing her views, as if she were one of the panelists.

John sat on the rocker, not saying a word since they hadn't spoken to him, while Whiskers curled in his padded bed. Sally showed up, looked at the couch to see if Brody was going to make room for her to sit down, then turned around.

"Where are you going?" John asked, easing out of the rocker.

"The kitchen."

John followed her, and they both sat the bar. "Have you heard from Wendell?" he asked.

"Not a word," she said. "I hope he's all right."

"I'll try to reach him in a little while. I need to talk to him anyway."

"What for?"

"Sister Cathy's hooligan son was asking about him. He's a bit upset I didn't tell him Wendell left and wouldn't tell him where. He got a little confrontational about it. Even Rufus Martin came out of his house."

"Mild-mannered Rufus?"

"Mild-mannered Rufus packed with a pistol."

"You can't be serious," Sally said, head thrust back and wide-eyed.

"Some time ago, Tanya mentioned he was shopping for one. They don't feel safe anymore."

"That's a shame."

"I just don't want to see him looking for an excuse to use it."

"You don't think he'd do that, do you?"

"You never know what the breaking point is with people. I just hope he has it for protection."

"I don't understand what's going on in our neighborhood. It used to be so peaceful, quiet and everything. A nice place to live. I don't feel as safe as I used to."

"Neighborhoods change just like everything else. Folks move out and other folks move in. It's kind of a roll of the dice. We've been lucky for the most part."

"Oh, the objective side of the journalist."

"Well, you asked," he said with a chuckle. "Just providing the facts, ma'am."

"So our luck is changing?"

John sighed. "You could say that. Vandalism, drugs, punks."

"Maybe we should start looking into moving again."

"We can do that. Give it some thought."

"Sometimes I wonder if we should have left after the kids moved out."

"Things were going great then. We were both working and the neighborhood was a lot better than it is now. At least we thought it was."

"I guess you're right," Sally said. "It's kind of hard to think about the future when things are going well."

"Oh well, talking to others, I've heard similar stories about their neighborhoods as well, even those in affluent areas. I guess the drugs and vandalism are everywhere."

"That's sad. I wonder what kind of world we are leaving Whitney and other children?"

"It seems a lot of people don't really care. They're more concerned with accepting the present than trying to make changes for the future. I think it's selfish."

"This is depressing me," she said.

"Me, too."

Sally went to the counter and prepared a pot of coffee. John opened the newspaper, glancing at the obits, thankful he hadn't lost any more friends or acquaintances, at least until tomorrow's edition.

Sally set their coffee on the counter, stirring creamer into each cup while John folded the paper. "I can't understand how Wendell and Libby got involved with those people," she said. "It seems more like cult."

"Me neither," John said, shrugging. "I'm so tempted to call the police about it, but I don't want to cause more problems. I suppose I'm hoping things will blow over."

"Maybe they'll move out. We can only hope."

"And pray."

Brody walked into the room and sat next to Sally, planting his elbows on the counter. "Anything around here to eat?"

"I'm sure we have something," she said. "Anything in particular?"

"I don't care." He ran his fingers through his thick unkempt hair. "Whatever you can put together. I'm not choosy."

"I'll see what I can do." She went to the refrigerator and took a frozen lasagna from the freezer and placed it in the microwave.

"Dad, can I borrow the car?" Brody asked. "I want to go over to Ashley's apartment and let her know I'm back."

"You can't just call her?" John asked.

"Aw, Dad, I want to surprise her. We also need to talk. It's been two weeks." He leaned back on the stool, dropping his hands to his side. "It'd be nice to go out and get some fresh air after being cooped up in rehab. A person could go stir crazy there."

John made quick eye contact with Sally. "Sure."

Brody sprang off the stool, a wide grin replacing his sullen expression. "Well, I'm going to take a shower and get dressed. Let me know when it's time to eat."

"About ten minutes," Sally said. "But I can reheat if need be."

"Works for me."

"His mood has certainly changed since he got home," Sally said after Brody closed the door to his bedroom.

"Maybe because he wanted to borrow the car," John said. "Isn't there usually a reason for the way he acts? Getting what he wants usually brightens his mood. Don't ya think?"

"Now, John, don't be so harsh. Don't forget where he's been the past two weeks. It would put a lot of people in a sour mood."

"I'd think they'd be in a better mood. I thought those programs were supposed to put a positive spin on life. You know, getting your life together."

"But still, he's been away and it has to affect how you feel."

"Please, Sally, he's thirty-eight. It's not like we sent a child to summer camp."

"No, he's thirty-seven. He won't be thirty-eight for another month."

"Like that should make any difference?"

"Do you want something to eat?" she asked, letting out a light huff.

"Ah, changing the subject." John laughed.

"I'm not going to get into it with you over his rehab treatment. We just don't see things the same way. I think you're being too judgmental, so let's not discuss it. Besides, you're getting me upset now."

"Really?'

"Do you want something to eat?"

"I'm not hungry," he said, sliding off the stool. "I'm going to go mow the lawn."

"Be that way."

John shook his head. "I'll eat after I'm finished." He tossed his car keys on the bar. "Those are for Brody."

John went through the garage door and pushed the lawn mower to the side of the house. He pulled the starter rope several times, getting a mute response. He looked in the gas tank and saw it was empty. He walked back into the garage for the gas can and found it bone dry as well. "Shit."

John reached his hand into his pants pocket for his car keys, but realized he left them on the kitchen bar. He decided against going back into the house, not wanting to deal with Sally's current frame of mind. He went back outside to the mower.

"Problem?"

John looked around and saw Bert approaching from the driveway, hands tucked in his front pockets.

"Out of gas." John shrugged. "I guess I'll need to run out and get some."

Bert glanced at the lawn, long overdue for a mowing, unlike his neatly manicured yard which usually got cut twice a week whether it needed it or not. "I've got some gas at the house."

"Thanks. I'll repay you."

As Bert walked away, Brody came out the front door, munching on a peanut butter-and-jelly sandwich.

"You got the keys?" John asked.

"Yeah, thanks," Brody said. "Could you spare me a twenty or so?"

John pulled out his wallet and handed Brody a twenty-dollar bill. He then took out a ten and gave it to him.

Brody stuffed the bills in a front pocket of his jeans. "Thanks, Dad. I'll repay when I can."

John nodded. "Have a nice time. Give my regards to Ashley. And try to be back at a decent hour. Do your classes start tomorrow?"

Brody grimaced. "Yeah, ten in the morning. Every day. Back to the old grind."

"Let's hope they're more effective this time around."

"Yeah, I need to get my shit together. That's for sure."

"Did Mom tell you we were going to get involved in a support group?"

"Really? She never said anything about it."

"So we'll all be involved in your rehab."

"Won't that be fun." Brody puffed his cheeks. "Well, I need to run. See ya."

Before John could say anything else, Brody got into the car, smiled wide, and backed out of the driveway.

Sally poked her head out of the kitchen door. "Are you sure you don't want something to eat? I've got lasagna. Brody changed his mind."

"You can fix me a sandwich," John said. "I'm waiting for Bert to return with some gas for the mower."

She frowned. "I guess I'll eat the lasagna."

"Give it to your mother."

She smiled. "That's an idea. I really wasn't in the mood for lasagna either."

Bert returned a minute later with his gasoline can and poured the gas into the mower's tank while John watched. He filled it to the top without spilling a drop or any overflow. "That should do you. Your yard isn't as large as mine."

"I don't know why that would be the case," John said. "I thought all the property lines were the same in the neighborhood."

"Well, in a sense, but I made arrangements with my next-door neighbors to mow part of their front lawns."

"Why would you want to do that?"

"It makes my lawn look better when I mow past their lines," Bert said. "On one side I mow to the side of their house and on the other I mow to their driveway. It evens everything out. They don't mind."

"I guess not. You care to mow mine?"

"What benefit would it be to me?"

"Just kidding, Bert."

"Okay, then. I wasn't sure. Is there anything else you need before you start mowing? Have you checked the oil?"

"I'm good, Bert. Can I pay you for the gas or take some to you whenever I refill my can?"

"Just being neighborly. Someday I may need some gas and may have to ask you for some. But I doubt it."

"We'll just pay it forward then."

"Whatever works, John." Bert grabbed the can and returned to his house. When he was out of sight, John checked the oil level on the mower, thankful it was all right because he wasn't sure if he had any oil in the garage. He certainly didn't want to go begging to Bert for that.

John glanced down and noticed he was wearing the wrong shoes to mow the lawn and went back inside to change. Sally was sitting at the bar eating lasagna.

"Your mom didn't want lasagna?" John asked.

"She said it was too early in the day for it so I made her a ham-and-cheese sandwich."

"Ham?"

"Wendell left a few slices in the fridge," Sally said.

"That was nice of him."

"I think he did it for Mama. She likes ham."

"Still no word from them?"

"Not a thing. I hope they're okay."

"Give 'em time."

"That's all I can do."

~ * ~

After mowing the lawn, John took Whiskers for a walk around the block without incident. Bert waved as they passed his house and gave John a thumbs-up, an apparent approval of his yardwork. There wasn't any activity at Sister Cathy's house, although several cars were in the driveway. John was relieved not to be accosted by Corley, or one of Sister Cathy's dubious disciples.

Sally was in the den watching TV with Geraldine when he returned. He went to the kitchen, tossed a treat to Whiskers, and took a can of beer from the refrigerator. He sat at the counter, checking his cell phone to see if he missed any calls. He had a text message from Wendell, saying they'd had stopped for breakfast at a Denny's in northern Alabama. He gulped the beer and tossed the can into the recycle bin.

"I'm going to take a shower," he said at the top of the stairs.

"You don't need our permission," Geraldine said, followed with a giggle.

"I'll save you some water."

"What's that supposed to mean?"

"Just kidding, Geraldine."

"Are you insinuating I don't take showers or bathe?"

"Please, Geraldine."

"But I do stay clean. I wash myself off every morning when I get up. I'm afraid I'll slip and fall in the bathtub. You'd feel like I do if you were in my condition."

"I'm sorry, Geraldine. I wasn't making a comment about your cleanliness. I was only teasing. Okay?"

"If you say so."

"One question, though."

"What?"

"If you decided to take a shower or bath, would you want me to rescue you if you fell?"

"You're being a smart aleck again!"

John flicked his brows and headed to the bathroom.

Standing under the lukewarm flow, the steady warm stream tingling his face, John was lost in his thoughts for a couple minutes, only to be jarred by Sally's slender hands on his waist. He turned and kissed her forehead.

"I hope you don't mind," she cooed. "I needed a shower as well."

"Any time," he said. "It's been awhile since we've done this."

"We need to save some water for Mother," she said, snickering. "Wasn't that a slogan back in the day? You know, save water, shower with a friend."

"I recall us taking lots of showers together. And doing more than taking a shower."

"I wouldn't dare try it now. I'm afraid I'd end up like Mother, falling down and fracturing my hip."

"Hey, why didn't you come to my aid about her bathing habits?"

"I'm not crazy. It wasn't worth it. Anyway, I know it's been difficult for her."

"But I wasn't saying she was dirty or anything."

"She's been sensitive about it. I almost wish we could install one of those secure tubs for her."

"We can do that," he said. "Now that she's going to be with us for the long term."

"I'm not sure Brody would like it."

"Brody would like it? Are you kidding me? This is our house."

"But they still share the same bathroom. That's all I'm saying."

"Okay. I'm still hoping he'll be here for the short term. But I suppose that's wishful thinking."

"Would you mind washing my back?" Sally asked.

"And changing the subject?"

"That, too."

"I can take a hint."

"My back needs a good scrubbing."

"I can do more than that."

"You naughty man!"

John lathered a washcloth with soap and moved it gently over her neck, chest, breasts, and belly.

"How's that?" he asked.

"My back?" She turned around and he continued to stroke it across her smooth back before scrubbing her shoulders.

"Do you want me to continue?"

"This feels so good." She let out a soft breath as her shoulders slumped. "I didn't realize how tense I was. So please continue."

"I'm sorry for my little outburst over Brody earlier today. I was trying to make a point. I get so frustrated with him."

"I know how you feel," she said. "And I shouldn't be so defensive about him. I agree he needs to grow up. I just don't want him to rebel against us and do something foolish again. I think he's back in a fragile place."

"You're right," John stopped scrubbing her back and began massaging her shoulders. "I need to give him some space, at least until he's back on a routine again."

"If something happened to him, I don't know if I could handle it."

"What do you mean?"

"If he died from an overdose." Her voice quivered.

"Let's not think like that. He's back on the road to recovery. Let's be positive."

"I'll try."

He kissed the back of her neck. "We'll all get through this together. As a family."

"Now let me wash you off," she said, turning and holding out her hand for the washcloth.

His eyes sparkled wickedly. "I thought you'd never ask."

~ * ~

After the steamy shower, John put on gray lounging pants and a T-shirt and Sally donned powder blue pajamas. They crawled under a sheet for a quick nap, but ended up chatting about Brody's treatment, Wendell's predicament, and Chloe's condition. As the sunlight began to fade through the curtain, they ventured to the den to check on Geraldine.

"My, don't we look cute this evening," Geraldine said from the recliner as they proceeded barefoot to the couch. Whiskers was curled in his cushion, eyes barely open to see what was going on in front of him.

"Long day," John said. "And too early for bed."

"I thought you were sleeping," Geraldine said. "It's been so quiet around here for the past couple of hours."

"More or less resting our eyes and catching up on a few things," Sally said as she curled her legs on the cushion. "We haven't had much time to do that."

"It has been kinda hectic around here the past few weeks."

"Did I tell you Wendell and Libby made it to Alabama early this morning?" John said. "I'd guess they're probably home now."

"No you didn't. I was worried they'd turn around along the way and come back here because it was taking them so long."

"Why do you say that, Mother?" Sally asked.

"He just seemed to have a lot on his mind."

"I'll call him a little later and see if he arrived safely," John said. "Anything else?"

"Aren't we going to eat tonight?" Geraldine asked.

"I'll be happy to make something," Sally said. "Anything in mind?"

"How about pizza?"

"Pizza? Aren't you getting tired of pizza?"

"Never."

"Well, I guess we could order one."

"You know, I really didn't like pizza that much until I came here, and you have it all the time."

"We do?"

"If it's not you, it's Brody ordering a pizza. I'd have to say Libby loved it as well. Wendell, not so much, but never turned his nose up to a slice. We didn't eat it much in Arizona. Back there, it was tacos all the time. I got so sick of tacos."

"You might be right," Sally said. "I apologize. We should have more variety around here."

"That's okay. There are different varieties of pizza." Geraldine grinned. "We can try them all."

"Except anchovies." John said.

"Maybe."

"What would you like?" John asked.

"Surprise me."

"Are you sure?"

"I know it will have vegetables on it so that's fine by me."

John got his cell phone in his room and placed the order with a local pizzeria. He noticed he had received a call from Kate Washington while he was in the shower, but she didn't leave a message.

"It'll be about twenty minutes," John said when he returned to the den. Geraldine was already engrossed in *Jeopardy!* and didn't acknowledge him. Sally was scanning the newspaper.

"Any news?" John asked. "I haven't had a chance to look at it."

"Didn't you work with a Glen Johnson? The name kinda rings a bell with me."

"It was a while back, maybe twenty years ago. Why?"

"He died two days ago. It didn't give a cause." She handed the newspaper to him, opened to the page with the obit.

"I see," John said. "Only fifty-eight. I knew he was a few years younger than me."

"Are you going to his visitation?"

"No."

"No? How come?"

"I only worked at the newspaper with him. That's the only connection. We weren't friends by any stretch of the imagination."

"I didn't know that."

"There are lots of things you didn't know about the newspaper."

"I'm sorry for saying anything."

"Honey, I didn't know everything about what was going on at the school where you taught. I'm sure there were a few teachers you weren't friends with for various reasons."

"You're right."

"Glen Johnson would stab anyone in the back to get ahead," John said. "And he did it to me once. He tried to blame me on a botched story, telling others around the newsroom I let something slip by in the copy. He didn't think it'd get back to me, but it did. And when I confronted him about it, he backed off like a frightened kitten. Said there was some kind of misunderstanding. But it was something that I never forgot."

"That's understandable."

"He was always the type who talked behind people's backs. Those folks don't seem to realize people pick up on those things and know they're probably talking behind their backs as well."

"Okay, honey, you've made your point."

"I feel sorry for his family," John said. "But we won't be sending flowers."

"Okay, okay." Sally nudged him in the side. "I get your point."

"You didn't have a teacher or two in the school who was that way?"

"John, of course I did. It happens everywhere."

"More than you can imagine," Geraldine said, turning down the volume. "I can't count the times it's happened to me and Harry. Even to me in Arizona. That's another reason I don't want to go back. Thanks for reminding me."

"You're welcome, Geraldine," John said before taking a deep breath. "It wasn't my intention. I was simply making a point."

"And you've made it very clear," Sally said. "Now we know the rest of the story."

John chuckled. "I guess you do now."

The doorbell rang, prompting Whiskers to let out a sharp bark and causing Geraldine to jerk back for a moment.

"Must be the pizza," John said, easing up from the couch.

"Did someone say pizza?" Geraldine said, pulling up from the recliner with a huge smile.

"Saved by the bell," Sally said.

"Can you answer the door, honey?" John said. "I need to go the bedroom and get my wallet."

"I'm not dressed," she said. "And I don't have my robe."

"I'll do it," Geraldine said, tapping her cane on the floor.

John hurried to the bedroom, opened his wallet, and realized he'd given all his cash to Brody. "Shit!"

"John, the boy is waiting for you," Geraldine said, raising her voice to a light shrill at the front door. "Are you coming?"

John scampered down the steps to the living room, a frantic look on his face. "I don't have any money."

"What?" Geraldine said. "Then how are we going to pay for it?" She glanced at the delivery man, still holding the pizza.

"You don't have any?" John asked.

Geraldine let out a huff. "Well, let me go get my purse in the bedroom. I think I have some money."

"Stay here, I'll go get it." John grabbed the purse on the dresser and hurried back to the front door, handing it to her.

The order came to sixteen dollars and change, and she handed a twenty to the delivery person. After taking the pizza from him, she stood staring at him.

"Is something the matter, ma'am?" the man asked.

"Don't I have any change?"

John stepped to the door, nodding for the man to leave. "Keep the change, sir. Have a nice night." He closed the door before Geraldine could say anything.

"He owes me money," Geraldine said, her spine erect. "Nearly four dollars."

"I'll give you a twenty tomorrow," John said. "The change was a tip."

"All he did was carry a pizza to the door. It's not like he prepared it or anything."

"Please, Geraldine, let's go eat the pizza before it gets cold."

"I don't believe you, John. Throwing away money like that. At least he could have given me my money so I could give him a tip.”

“Next time I’ll charge it.”

“Why didn’t you charge it to begin with?”

“Because I thought I had the cash.”

“Well, next time you’d better be sure.”

Sally stood at the entry to the den, grinning at the exchange.

“What’s so funny?” Geraldine asked, clenching her jaw.

“Nothing, Mother. I’m just hungry.”

“That’s something we can agree on,” Geraldine said as they walked to the bar.

“I hope you like it,” John said.

Geraldine sat on a stool, watching John open the container. “I’m not so sure now after what happened. It kinda took away some of my appetite.”

“Really?”

“No,” Geraldine said with a sassy grin. “I’m just giving you some of your medicine.”

“Being a smart aleck?”

“Just like you!”

Fourteen

John was up before sunrise the next day, letting Whiskers outside while he searched the front yard for the newspaper, finding it under Sally's SUV on the dew-damp driveway. As he reached to get it, Brody pulled in, the car's bright beams startling him for a second.

"You're just getting home?" John asked as he got back on his feet.

"Yeah," Brody said. "We were watching TV and fell asleep on the couch. When I woke up, it was around two, so I figured I may as well as spend the rest of the night. I didn't want to bother you guys."

"I've heard that before."

"What?"

"Never mind. Is everything okay?"

"Gimme a break. I haven't taken any drugs or anything."

"Did I mention drugs? You could have called or texted."

"Like you or Mom would see it at two?"

"What time's your meeting?"

"Ten. Like I told you yesterday. It hasn't changed."

"I've got coffee brewing."

"Great," Brody said as he led John and Whiskers into the house. "I need something to clear my head."

As John took care of Whiskers' bowls, Brody poured a cup of coffee and sat at the bar. "Anything around here to eat?"

"I can whip up some eggs or something. I think there's some cereal in the cabinet. Your mom should be waking up soon if you want to wait. Oh, I think there's some leftover pizza in the fridge."

"Pizza's fine," Brody said. "I'll take a couple slices."

John looked at Brody for a second, then walked to the fridge, took out the box and handed it to his son. "Take what you need and pop it in the microwave for a minute or so. You can probably toss in the trash what you don't want."

Brody appeared confused, then grabbed three slices from the box and moseyed to the microwave. John got himself a coffee since Brody had neglected to pour him a cup.

Brody sat quietly for a couple minutes while chewing on the spongy pizza. John perused the newspaper while Whiskers finished eating and retreated to his pad in the dark den.

"I'm thinking about moving out," Brody said.

"What?" John closed the newspaper. "Why?"

"I need more space and breathing room."

"Brody, you don't even have a job," John said. "How in the world are you going to afford an apartment, food, and everything else?"

"Ashley invited me to move in with her."

John took a couple of short breaths as he looked away from Brody and gathered his thoughts. "Are you serious?"

"Yeah."

"You hardly know the girl."

"I've known her long enough. Several months, at least. We get along really well. She understands me. And she has a spare bedroom at her place."

"Spare bedroom?"

"Okay, Dad, I know what you're thinking," Brody said. "We're simply good friends. There's nothing serious going on."

"Oh."

"Believe what you want."

"I think we need to discuss this some more."

"Discuss what? I'm an adult. Remember?"

"Can we talk about this later? Maybe get Mom's opinion?"

"No problem," Brody said, easing off the stool. "I'm going to take a shower and get cleaned up for the rehab session."

"Can you hold it on the shower until your mother and grandmother wake up? It shouldn't be much longer."

"Sure thing," Brody said as he left the room.

John warmed his coffee and picked up the newspaper, glancing over the front-page headlines and then the obituary section.

"Mornin'," Sally said as she padded into the kitchen rubbing her puffy eyes.

"You may want to sit down after you pour your coffee," John said.

"What do you mean? I hadn't planned on standing up while drinking it."

"Figure of speech. You're getting as bad as your mom."

"And you."

"Touché."

Sally poured her coffee and sat on the stool, stirred in a teaspoon of creamer, and looked at John. "What now?"

"Brody says he wants to move in with his girlfriend."

Sally dropped her spoon, clanging on the bar's granite surface. "He what?"

"You heard me correctly," John said, unable to suppress a smile. "That's what he told me this morning, after spending the night at her apartment."

"What did you tell him?"

"Basically, I said we all need to discuss it."

"I don't think it's a good idea."

"I agree. But me telling him will set off some fireworks. He reminded me he's an adult and it's his decision."

Sally lifted the cup and took a sip. "Oh, John, what are we going to do? He's not ready to leave home."

"I don't think there's anything we can do except to reason with him."

"He doesn't even have a job," Sally said. "Or a car."

"I tried to remind him of that."

"This is crazy."

"I know it, and you know it. Try convincing *him* of that."

"Where is he now?"

"Up in his room. I asked him to wait before taking a shower until you and your mother woke up. I was trying to buy some time. I haven't heard a peep, so my guess is he's waiting to take a shower."

"What are we going to do about his car?"

"I guess we'll have to drive to Chicago. I assume it's at his apartment unless it's been moved to a compound."

"Are we still paying rent on his place?"

"Until the end of the month. That's when his lease runs out. More money down the drain."

"Regardless of what Brody does, I guess we need to take care of everything there."

"I'll make plans to drive up there," John said. "With Brody."

"Maybe moving out will be a good thing."

"How so?"

"He'll be forced to take on some responsibility."

"He needs to be accountable for his actions, good and bad."

Sally went over and poured another cup of coffee and topped John's. "I wish I knew more about the girl."

"Maybe we should invite her over?"

"That'll give us a chance to get to know her."

"And for your mother as well."

"You're giving me a headache," Sally said, shaking her head. "Can we discuss this later?"

"Ready to take another vacation?"

"You mean, to get away from everything here?"

"Yep."

"I heard Greece is nice this time of year."

"Did I hear someone mention grease?" They looked toward the dining room as Geraldine moved toward them. "I thought the pizza last night was a little greasy. I didn't sleep well because of it. Gave me some heartburn and put gas on my stomach."

"No, Mother, we were discussing Greece, as in the country of Greece."

"Why in the world would you be talking about that?" Geraldine sat on a stool next to John.

"It just came up about places to visit," Sally said.

"I don't see how you can even think about another trip with all that's been going on here the past couple of months."

"I don't mean now, Mother. We were just talking. Do you want coffee?"

"Yes, please," Geraldine said, then turned her face to John. "Did the pizza give you gas?"

~ * ~

Later came sooner than expected.

They heard the shower running. John picked up the newspaper and began reading again. Sally sat cradling her cup, staring across the room in silence. Geraldine retreated to the den to watch her morning programs on TV. Whiskers padded into the kitchen, lapped in his water bowl, then rested under John's stool.

Minutes later, Brody strolled into the kitchen, hair damp from the shower, shirtless, and wearing blue-and-white lounging pants. He plopped down at the bar as if in a restaurant and looked at Sally like she was a waitress. "Coffee, please."

Sally eased off her stool, poured the coffee and placed it in front of Brody. "Anything else, sir?"

"I'm good, Mom," he said with a perky smile. "Maybe cereal a little later. Or oatmeal. That leftover pizza didn't cut it. Too greasy. Yuck."

"Dad says you may have some moving plans."

"Oh, he already told you." Brody took a sip from his cup. "Yeah, I think it's about time I moved out. Ashley's got an extra bedroom."

"I don't believe you're thinking this through," John said. "She's going to let you stay rent-free? You're not going to have to chip in on groceries? Utilities?"

"We'll work it out." Brody shrugged. "It's not a big deal. We've got time. We're cool."

"You don't even have transportation," John said. "And, no, you're not using our vehicles so don't even ask."

Brody clenched his jaw. "That's fine. She has a car I can use. I think she even has a bicycle."

"Okay."

"Besides, I have my car in Chicago. We plan to drive up there in the next week or so and get my stuff."

"I had planned on doing that," John said.

"It's my business and my problem. Don't worry about it. Just chill. Ashley can take me."

"It'll save me a trip."

"Yep," Brody said with a smarmy grin. "I'll be out of your hair."

"Are you going to look for a job?" Sally asked.

"I'll find something, even if I have to flip burgers or deliver pizza."

"Flip burgers? Deliver pizza?" John said, letting out a small chuckle "Sure."

"What's so funny, Dad?"

"Oh, nothing. I guess it's just the idea of you working in fast food."

"It might be fun."

"Fun? Is that why everyone is knocking down the door to work in fast food?"

"Screw it," Brody tightened his lips. "You wouldn't understand."

"That's sure putting your college education to good use."

"Why are you being such a hard ass?" Brody pushed away from the bar. "You'd think you guys would be happy I'm leaving."

"There's a time and place for everything," John said. "I'm not sure if this is it. We'd still like to see you get through the rehab."

"I'm clean. Totally."

"We've heard that before, Brody," Sally said. "But you just completed two weeks in rehab. We're just concerned about you. I wish you'd understand that."

"Well, you don't need to be anymore, because I'm getting my shit together. Okay?" Brody kicked back the stool, nearly knocking it over, and stormed to his bedroom. Whiskers whimpered.

"That went as I expected," John said. "Can't accept advice, criticism, or anything that doesn't go his way."

"I just don't understand him anymore." Sally wiped a tear from her cheek.

"I don't believe he truly understands himself. Sometimes I wonder if we've got him in the right kind of counseling."

Minutes later, Geraldine padded into the kitchen, planting her cane in front of her with both hands gripping the handle. "What's all the ruckus about this time?"

"It's nothing, Mother," Sally said.

Geraldine pursed her mouth and took three more steps, standing next to Sally at the bar. "If it's nothing, then why are you crying?"

Sally dabbed a paper napkin on her eyes. "It's Brody."

"Like I couldn't guess? What's he up to this time?"

"He wants to move out," John said.

"Move out?" Geraldine said, easing up on the stool. "Where?"

"With his girlfriend."

"That colored girl?"

"Yes, Mother," Sally said. "The Black girl he brought here a few weeks ago."

"I remember her."

"Coffee?" John asked.

"Please," Geraldine sat on a stool and folded her hands on the bar.

John poured her a cup and sat back down. "Anything else?

"Not at this moment." Geraldine leaned over and patted the top of Sally's hand.

"We were trying to reason with him about not leaving and he got upset," John said. "Like he usually does."

"That boy doesn't know how to face problems," Geraldine said. "Always runs away from them. Kinda like Wendell."

"Has Wendell called since yesterday?" Sally asked. "I'm beginning to worry about him."

"He wouldn't be calling me," Geraldine said. "Unless he wanted something."

John said. "Maybe he'll call today. He should be there by now."

"Or tomorrow. Or the next day. Or next week," Geraldine said. "I can never keep up with him."

"What do you mean?" John asked.

"I don't know when he'll call. It's always out of the clear blue sky. Just like when you were in that foreign country."

"Hungary?"

"No, I'm not hungry!"

"I mean the country Hungary."

"If that's where you were at, then it's Hungry, or however you pronounce it."

"But I'd like to know something about Wendell. Even Libby," Sally said. "I'm a little concerned about them, leaving like they did."

"I'll try to reach him then," John said.

"Good idea," Geraldine said with a chagrined expression. "I'm glad you thought of that."

"Let's eat breakfast," Sally said. "Anyone care for pancakes?"

"Works for me," John said.

"Do you have any sausage or bacon?" Geraldine asked. "They break the sweetness of the syrup."

"I'm not sure if we have any," Sally said as she walked over to the refrigerator. "It looks like we're out."

"Which do you prefer?" John asked.

"Sausage," Geraldine said.

"I'll run to the convenience store and pick up a package," John said. "Anything else we need, hon?"

"Milk for Brody," she said.

"I'll be right back." John headed to the front door but turned around and returned to the kitchen.

"What's the matter?" Sally asked.

"Brody has my keys."

"Then go up there and get them," Geraldine said. "You're his father."

"I don't feel like another confrontation." He looked at Sally. "Where are your keys?"

"I believe in my purse," she said. "Let me go check."

Sally went to the bedroom and returned a minute later with her opened purse. "There're not here. I don't know where I put them."

"John, go up to Brody's room and get your keys," Geraldine said. "This is ridiculous."

"Anything else we need from the grocery?" John said, trying to ignore his mother-in-law.

"Did you hear me, John?" Geraldine said. "Go get your keys from him. You're the father."

John walked over to the refrigerator and opened the door. On the top shelf were Sally's car keys. He covered them in his hand and closed the door, then stepped over to the sink.

"Here they are," he said, reaching down to the counter and then holding up the keys.

"My goodness, I don't remember putting them there," Sally said.

"Doesn't surprise me," Geraldine said, raising her chin.

"Off to the store." John flashed a grin at Geraldine. "Want me to pick up something for your gas?"

She shook her head. "Smart aleck."

When he walked outside, he realized his car was parked behind Sally's SUV. "Damn!"

He returned to the house, and after ten seconds of hesitation, went to Brody's room and knocked on the door. "Son, I need the keys to back out my car so I can go to the grocery. Or you can back it out."

Brody opened the door, stared at John for a moment, and headed out the front door to move the car. John hurried to Sally's SUV and waited until Brody backed his car into the street. He smiled and nodded to his son as he went past him. Brody stared straight ahead as if in a trance and pulled the car back into the driveway.

As John drove to the store, his cell phone vibrated. A call from Sally.

"Forget something?" he asked. "Or Brody?"

"We don't have any pancake mix or syrup," she said in a distressed voice.

"No problem," he said.

"Don't tell Mother. I'll never hear the end of it."

"Your secret is safe with me. Scout's honor."

~ * ~

John hurried through the grocery, wanting to get back before Geraldine got on her high horse about Sally's forgetfulness and Brody pouting about being mistreated or misunderstood or whatever excuse he manufactured for the situation.

As John approached Sally's car in the parking lot, he noticed someone kneeling next to the rear bumper. "What are you doing?"

A young man wearing khaki pants and white shirt glanced up and dashed away before John could get a good look at his face. He walked to the back of the car and noticed a black-and-white "Black Lives Matter" bumper sticker Sally had placed there before their trip to Europe had been partially scraped from the vehicle.

"So much for equality around here," John muttered.

John looked around to see if the miscreant was anywhere in the lot, but he had vanished from sight like a cowardly ghost.

John noticed several cars parked in the driveway and on the street as he drove by Sister Cathy's house. Five men donned in khaki and white shirts stood on the porch, puffing cigarettes like mini-smokestacks, and chatting. They turned their heads and stared, as if in slow motion. He felt their gazes all the way to his driveway. When he got out of the SUV, he glimpsed back but they had disappeared into their private sanctuary. He assumed they returned to the house to study a different kind of scripture.

John walked into the kitchen, a semblance of peace restored to the household as Sally, Geraldine, and Brody were seated at the kitchen bar laughing.

"What's so funny?" he asked, placing the sack of groceries on the counter.

"Wendell called while you were gone," Sally said.

"Where is he?"

"All we know is Florida," Brody said. "He was very secretive about it."

"I had to put Brody on the phone because I could barely hear him," Sally said.

"Yeah, he was whispering like some guy in a spy movie," Brody said. "Some weird shit."

"What did he say that had you laughing?"

"It was Libby," Geraldine said. "She was shouting so loud in the background even I could hear her."

John chuckled. "What was she saying?"

"She told him to stop whispering and talk in a normal voice," Brody said. "So he got pissed off and hung up the phone."

"Are you serious?"

"He'll call back after he gets her settled down," Geraldine said.

"Or she gets him settled down," Sally said.

"But he sounded okay?" John asked.

"Except for Aunt Libby," Brody said.

"I can't believe they're in Florida," John said. "I wonder why?"

"I haven't a clue," Sally said.

"Maybe he didn't see the exit signs and drove right on through Alabama," Brody said, laughing.

"I bet it's because of Sister Cathy and her righteous following," John said. "I wonder if he heard from someone there."

"I sure hope not," Sally said. "That'd be scary."

"Let's just keep this to ourselves for the time being," John said.

"Is that why he left?" Brody asked. "Those religious nuts down the street?"

John gave Brody a rundown of what had transpired the past few days and why Wendell decided to leave. "Have you encountered run-ins with them?"

"Nope, other than Whiskers pooping in their yard," Brody said. "Sometimes I see people carrying stuff into the house but that's about it. I never gave it much thought. I'll be on the lookout from now on."

John diverted Geraldine's attention, discussing a celebrity item he'd read in the newspaper, while Sally removed the groceries from the sack and started breakfast. Brody played a game on his smartphone.

After everyone finished eating, Brody left to attend the rehab class while John took Whiskers out for their daily walk. He took a few steps in the opposite direction of Sister Cathy's house, but turned around, deciding he wasn't going to be intimidated in his own neighborhood.

All was quiet as John breezed past the house, pulled by Whiskers' eagerness to move on after spotting several pigeons on the sidewalk two houses down the street. He went to their usual bench in the park and unleashed Whiskers to torment birds minding their own business by the pond. There wasn't much else going on as John leaned back on the bench and crossed his legs, lost in thought. It didn't take long for Whiskers to tire from scampering and return to lie next to John, who stroked between the pooch's floppy ears while taking in the serene surroundings. John's tranquility was temporary as a thunderous cloudburst unloaded a torrent of rain. He grabbed Whiskers and dashed for cover under a maple tree about one hundred feet away, practically drenched by the time he reached the leafy canopy. Whiskers was spared the soaking as John tucked him under his arms.

When he reached the house, out of breath and soaked to the bone, Sally made him stand at the doorway while she fetched a bath towel. Whiskers shook off his wetness and scuttled to his pad in the den.

At the door, John disrobed down to his boxers, and darted to the bedroom to take a hot shower.

"Why didn't you come home before it started raining?" she asked, standing next to the bathroom sink.

"I beg your pardon?"

"You should have come home when you saw it was going to rain."

John turned off the shower and Sally handed him another heavy towel to dry off. "Like I'm supposed to know when it's going to rain of biblical proportions?"

"I'm just sayin'. Mother and I didn't expect you to be gone for so long."

"If you knew it was going to come down like that, why didn't you call me?"

"I wanted to but couldn't find it."

"Doesn't your mom have a cell?"

"I never thought to ask her."

"Did you try to call your number and see where it rings?"

"I never thought about doing that, either."

After John put on a pair of cargo pants and a polo shirt, he picked up his phone on the dresser and called Sally's. A moment later they heard it ringing in the bathroom. John found it in the medicine cabinet.

"Here ya go." He handed the phone to Sally.

"How did it get there?"

"I have no idea," he said. "It's your phone."

When they returned to the bedroom Sally said, "I did hear from Chloe while you were gone."

"Maybe she called when you were in bathroom."

Sally paused for a moment. "Maybe. Could be. I don't remember."

"What did she have to say?"

"She says she's feeling stronger every day and wants to visit us in a few weeks."

"That's wonderful," John said, sitting on the side of the bed. "It seems like ages since I saw her and Whitney. Is Sam coming along, too?"

"I don't know. She didn't mention it, so I doubt it. But you never know."

"That's something to look forward to. At least we won't have to give up our bed."

"Why is that?"

"Well, maybe Brody will have moved out by then."

She winced. "Have you given much more thought about Brody?"

"To be honest, no. One reason I went to the park was to clear my mind. He's going to do what he wants to do. There's nothing we can do to stop him. So maybe that's why I'm not giving it a lot of thought. Furthermore, I'm not going to lose sleep over it."

"I guess you're right. Maybe that girl will help straighten him out."

"I only hope she's not part of the problem, like the gal back in Chicago. He doesn't need friends like that. Or Arnold."

"I haven't heard him mention Arnold."

"He probably knows better than to do so in the house."

"Do you think he'll get a job?'

"Honey, I'm beginning to believe it's wishful thinking. He hasn't worked in more than six months, maybe a year. Who knows? I think he's beginning to enjoy early retirement." John chuckled.

"With no benefits?"

"We're his benefits. You should know that."

"Oh, I never thought of it that way."

Fifteen

There was a hard thump on the front door.

"I wonder who that could be?" John asked, folding the newspaper at the kitchen bar.

"Better go answer it so you can find out," Geraldine said as she stepped into the kitchen.

"Thanks, Geraldine. If it's Jehovah's Witnesses or some Mormon boys, I'll have you talk to them."

"You better not!" Geraldine rapped her cane on the floor.

Two more knocks before John reached the door and opened it. "May I come in for a few minutes?" Rufus Martin asked.

"Sure, have a seat on the couch," John said as he stepped to the side. "Care for anything to drink?"

"Thanks, John, but I can only stay for a few minutes."

John sat on the easy chair. "What's up?"

"It's that so-called church group on the street. I'm getting concerned about what's going on there."

"I feel the same way. As you know, it's bothered me for quite a while. Have they done anything?"

"We've had some more racist graffiti and some minor vandalism in the past week. A few other homes have had it as well."

"Uh, minorities?"

"Of course," Rufus said. "Have you seen or heard anything? I know you walk around the neighborhood every day."

"Not really. I was confronted by one person. The same guy we both talked to. Remember?'

"Yeah. I think he may be the ringleader, but I'm not sure."

"What do you want me to do?"

"I'm just asking a few of the neighbors to keep an eye out on what's going on and let me know. But I don't want to get you guys messed up in it."

"What do you mean, Rufus? We all live in this neighborhood so we all should be involved. I don't care what the issue is."

"I appreciate that, John."

"I'll make a few calls and see what I can do. Maybe Bert can do something with the Neighborhood Watch group."

"I've talked to Bert and he seems a little wary about getting involved in it."

"I wonder what his reason is?"

"I think it has something to do with it having to do with religion."

"I'll get with him," John said. "We'll put an end to this stuff, one way or another, and once and for all."

"I welcome anything you can do, John. But please be careful. Oh, by the way, I've noticed some of them carrying boxes into the house, usually late at night," Rufus said.

"That's interesting."

"It's probably nothing other than being sneaky about it."

"Let me know if you see or hear anything unusual."

"Will do."

John stepped on the porch and watched Rufus walk to his house, making sure there weren't going to be any incidents from their righteous neighbors. He noticed Rufus glance at Sister Cathy's house, stuff his hands in his pockets, and turn toward his home. John wondered if Rufus was carrying his gun. He wouldn't be surprised and wouldn't blame him.

Sally was in the living room when John returned. "Mr. Martin seemed very upset," she said.

"He should be." John walked past her to the refrigerator, where he took out a can of beer. She followed and sat at the bar.

"What's happened?"

"More racist graffiti and a few other things to his house and some of the minorities in the neighborhood."

"That's shameful."

"I know and we've got to do something about it."

"What do you mean?"

"I think we know where it's coming from," John said. "I need to get with the police and see what they can do. And I have to talk to Bert. From what Rufus told me, he's sort of shirking his duties with Neighborhood Watch."

"What has he done?"

"According to Rufus, nothing."

"But what can he do?"

"First of all, it's Neighborhood Watch. The neighbors need to be keeping a watchful eye on what's going on and report it, regardless of who's doing it. It shouldn't be too difficult. It's not like forming an armed militia or vigilantes. It's neighbor watching out for neighbor. That's pretty simple."

Without saying another word, John set his half-empty beer on the counter and walked to Bert's house. He found Bert on his knees, yanking weeds and spreading mulch at the side of his house.

"What's going on?" John asked.

"I'm working on my yard. What does it look like?"

"I'm sorry for asking the obvious."

"You're excused."

"I spoke with Rufus Martin a few minutes ago."

"Oh."

"He said he approached you about some problems occurring in the neighborhood and you seemed noncommittal."

"He did?"

"It's about some graffiti and vandalism targeting some minorities," John said.

"Yes, I remember," Bert said. "I told him I'd look into it."

"Why haven't you?"

"I will, eventually." Bert rose to his feet and removed his soiled gloves. "It takes time. You just don't jump into these things haphazardly."

"I don't know what you mean?"

"John, it's like pitting neighbor against neighbor. Rufus doesn't have any proof about who's doing those things."

"But he has an idea."

"I know, but it's just seems too far-fetched, involving Sister Cathy."

"So you know her pretty well now?"

"I've spoken to her a few times."

"And nothing seemed out of sorts?"

"A little, but I didn't see anything that egregious. Religious folks can be that way, you know."

"We need to have a talk," John said.

"Sure, John."

"How about after dinner tonight? Say, around seven?"

"Sure thing. My place or yours?"

"My house."

"Should I eat beforehand or are you going to have something?"

"How about if I order some subs?"

"Could you order pizza instead?"

John paused, thinking about how tired he was of pizza. "Will do."

"Sure thing, John. Can I bring Wilma? Maybe she can talk to Sally while we're busy discussing the neighborhood problems."

"Of course, Wilma is always welcome."

"One more thing," Bert said. "Could you make it a meat-lovers pizza?"

"Of course. Anything else?"

"Do they offer any kind of desserts with it"

"I'm sure they do. I'll see what I can do."

Bert beamed. "I'm looking forward to it."

"See you at seven." John turned and headed back, wondering how food figured into the discussion. And the thought of pizza made him wince.

"We're going to have company this evening," John said to Sally, who was reclined on the couch holding a book.

"What?" She bolted up and blinked several times as if something were in her eyes. "This house is a mess."

"Don't worry. It's an impromptu Neighborhood Watch meeting. I'm going to order a few pizzas."

"Why are we having it here? Doesn't Bert usually hold those meetings at the community room of the Methodist Church?"

"I told Bert we needed to talk about the racist graffiti and vandalism that's been going on the past few weeks. He's coming over at seven with Wilma."

"Wilma?"

John chuckled. "He believes she can keep you company. I think he's using it as an excuse to say he's taking her out to eat."

"Do we have to have pizza?"

John laughed. "That's what Bert ordered."

"I need to pick up some things in the den and dining room."

"I'm also inviting a few other folks if they can make it. Rufus and Tanya Martin, the Patels, and any others who've been subjected to any taunts or damage to their personal property."

"Is there anything you want me to do?"

"Keep Wilma company?"

"I can do that," Sally said with a sigh as she eased off the couch. "Anything else?"

"And your mother."

Sally frowned.

~ * ~

"Do I smell pizza?" Bert asked gleefully as he and Wilma stepped inside the living room. "I told you I had a surprise for you."

Bert stopped at the entryway to the dining room when he saw Rufus, Manny Patel, and several other people of color sitting around the table, chatting, and munching pizza. His wide smile evaporated into thin air.

"Have a seat," Manny said, scooting over for Bert to sit next to him. "Grab a piece before it gets cold."

"I didn't know you had company," Bert said, a weak smile crossing his face as he went to the chair like a disheartened child. John nodded and beamed.

Sally walked in, took Wilma by the arm and led her to the den. "I've got our pizza downstairs."

John sat at the head of the table and chewed on a slice, washing it down with a swallow of Coke. He looked at Bert with an impish grin. Bert responded with a scowl.

"I asked our neighbors to attend because they are the ones who are directly affected by what's been going on the past few weeks. I didn't think it was proper for Neighborhood Watch to do anything without their input," John said above the chatter.

Bert cleared his throat. "Uh, sure, John. Makes sense to me."

Before John could ask the men to tell what they'd experienced, their wives entered the room, carrying their food on paper plates.

"What's up?" John asked, tilting his head. "Out of pizza?"

"They believe they need to be in here to express their opinions," Sally said. "They live here as well."

"Well, they're right," John said as he stood. "Let me get the stools in the kitchen and folding chairs in the garage."

"I'll give you a hand," Bert said, following John to the garage.

"Mother, do you care to join us?" Sally asked at the steps to the den.

"*Jeopardy!* just came on," Geraldine said, turning up the volume.

"We'll try to keep it down as not to disturb you."

"What do you mean by that?"

"Never mind, Mother," Sally said, and sat next to Wilma.

Moments later, Geraldine seemed to get message and turned down the sound.

"You could have told me about inviting all these folks," Bert said as John handed him two folding chairs. "I could have prepared something to say."

"It was a spur-of-the-moment decision," John said. "We're all neighbors and we need input from everyone."

Bert called the informal meeting together and went around the room to get feedback from everyone about the recent problems facing the group. Most of them noted racist graffiti had been written on or near their homes, trash cans had been turned over, items in yards stolen, and air being released from tires. Several reported boxes had been removed from porches of various neighbors, regardless of their color or ethnicity.

"I didn't know it was this serious," Bert said. "I wish some of you had told me what was going on. Neighborhood Watch is only as good as the people involved. I hope all of you will think about joining."

"I can't prove it, but I didn't have any problems until that church group moved in," Rufus said. "Have you noticed you never see people of color in their house? The whole thing seems kinda fishy to me."

"I've talked to Sister Cathy a few times and she seems to be on the up and up," Bert said. "I think you may have her wrong."

"It's not the so-called Sister Cathy," Rufus said. "It's those young thugs who hang around the house. I think there's more going on than meets the eye."

"Aren't you being a little harsh?" Bert asked. "I haven't heard of them doing any vandalism."

"Maybe if you'd get out of your yard once in a while," Manny said.

Bert flinched.

"I'm sorry, Bert, I didn't mean to be so harsh, but there's a lot going on here. We just haven't been able to catch the culprits."

Bert's lower lip pushed out. "I'm just one member of the neighborhood. I don't wear a badge."

"It sure sounds like you're defending them," Rufus said.

"I don't mean to," Bert said, his face flushed. "I just don't think it's right to accuse someone without the evidence. That's all I'm saying. I'm trying to be fair."

"But you're not being fair to us," said Tanya Martin. "This has been going on for several weeks. It's not like it started yesterday."

"She's right," said Asha Patel. "We're tired of it."

"Yeah, before it's too late," said Wilma, raising a fisted hand to make her point. "We need to reclaim our neighborhood."

"Wilma?" Bert said, surprised his usually quiet spouse had spoken up.

"Let's stay focused," John said, sensing escalating tension. "I'm going to get in touch with law enforcement and see what can be done. In the meantime, keep an eye on what's going on around your homes."

After the meeting broke up, Bert and Wilma stayed around until after the others had left.

"John, I must tell you I didn't appreciate you sending me into the lions' den," Bert said. "Like I told you earlier, you could have warned me."

"I didn't mean for it to get heated," John said. "But I thought it was important for you to hear what some of our neighbors are saying."

"John's right," Wilma said. "We all need to know how our neighbors feel about it."

Bert glanced at Wilma for a second before turning toward John. "You should know me better than that. How long have we been friends? Thirty years or longer? I would have listened to you."

"But you haven't. You keep defending Sister Cathy. By the way, can't we just call her Cathy Gibson or Ms. Gibson? I don't consider her a sister."

"Whatever works for you, John."

~ * ~

"What a noisy bunch," Geraldine said when she entered the living room less than a minute after Bert and Wilma left. "I could hardly hear my TV."

"I'm sorry, Geraldine. There's some things going on in the neighborhood and folks wanted to air their concerns."

"Any pizza left?"

"I'll look in the boxes but I don't believe so, Mother," Sally said.

"They were loud and ravenous."

"Sure looks that way," John said as he gathered paper plates and cups from the table and stuffed them in a large black plastic bag.

Seconds later, Brody came in the front door with Ashley by his side.

"What's going on?" Brody asked as they entered the dining room. "Did you have a party?"

"We had an informal Neighborhood Watch meeting," John said.

"About what we talked about earlier?" Brody asked.

"That and more," John said as he headed to the garage to dispose of the trash.

"It's nice to see you again, Ashley," Sally said. "We're out of pizza, but I can offer you something to drink."

"Thanks, Mrs. Ross, but we stopped at Arby's and got a bite to eat," she said.

"Have you guys got a few minutes?" Brody asked as John returned to the room. "There's something I want to tell you."

John motioned everyone to sit at the dining room table while Sally hurriedly wiped it off with a paper towel. They sat for several seconds, looking at each other as if to see who was going to open the discussion.

Brody took Ashley's hand. "We've been talking and I want to come clean about something."

"You don't have to do that," Geraldine said with a small smile. "We understand you've had problems and everything will get better. It's like starting fresh."

"Please, Mother, let Brody talk."

Brody cleared his throat. "It has to do with the drugs I used. I stole them from Uncle Wendell."

"What?" John asked, his brows furrowed.

"When they came here, I saw their pill bottles on the dresser. When they weren't around, I went in the room and took a few. That's how I got high those times. I didn't get them from Arnold or anyone else. It was from a little stash I stole from Uncle Wendell."

"They mentioned about missing Vicodin when he hurt his back," Sally said.

"It was me who took them." Brody glanced at Ashley. Her warm smile was a look of approval and support for his confession.

"That certainly explains a few things," John said.

"If you don't mind, Mr. Ross, something that's encouraged is being forthcoming about things," Ashley said. "Brody and I have talked about a lot of things since we met."

"Things went sorta sour between us the past week or so," Brody said, looking again at Ashley. "She said she wouldn't see me if I wouldn't tell you where I got the drugs. So, that's what I'm doing."

"That's a big step forward," John said. "And Ashley, I appreciate what you've done for my son."

"Is there anything we should be doing for Brody?" Sally asked Ashley.

"I think everyone needs to be more open about Brody's problem," Ashley said. "I know that's difficult because Brody and I have gone round and round about his addiction. Needless to say, you need to keep any temptations locked and out of sight."

"I'll try to be more forthcoming about everything," Brody said. "It's hard. I've come to the realization I can't lick it by myself."

"That's good to hear," John said. "That's what we've tried to stress all along. I guess we didn't do a good job at times."

"You can say that again," Geraldine piped in. "He couldn't do anything right to please you."

"Now wait a minute," John said.

"That's okay, Dad," Brody said. "I need to take responsibility for my actions."

"And Sally should stop enabling you all the time," Geraldine said.

"Now, Mother," Sally said.

"Mom has done the right things, for the most part," Brody said. "She's always provided me with support, even when I didn't deserve it."

"I think we're already making progress," Ashley said. "Please feel free to call me if you need someone to help you deal with this."

"She's good," Brody said, reaching over and squeezing Ashley's hand. "She helps me stay on the straight and narrow path to recovery."

"The main thing is to be there when you stray," Ashley said. "Tough love."

"That's what grandmothers are for," Geraldine said. "Right?"

"We're family and we look out for each other," John said.

"Are you sure there's no more pizza?" Geraldine asked.

Sixteen

The following morning, while on a walk to the park with Whiskers, John texted Kate Washington about setting up a meeting to discuss the increased crime in the neighborhood. She responded within a minute, noting that she was on patrol near the park and could meet him there. He mentioned the picnic shelter by the parking lot, and when he reached the destination, her blue-and-white patrol car was already there.

They shook hands, rather than their usual hugs, and sat on the wood picnic table. She fussed over a frisky Whiskers for a few seconds before pulling out her notepad and pen. "That's a cute pup you've got," she said.

"Whiskers appears to like you," John said. "He's been known to growl at those he doesn't care for."

"Speaking of bad guys, what's been going on in your neighborhood?"

John gave her a rundown of the racist graffiti, vandalism, stolen items, and other activities, including Sister Cathy's church. He told her about Wendell's concern about Sister Cathy's followers and her son, Corley Gibson. Kate took copious notes as he talked, asking numerous questions for clarification.

"Several neighbors have been hesitant in notifying the police for fear it would exacerbate the situation," he said. "And to be honest, I think a few felt the police wouldn't respond because of their race."

Kate shook her head. "I wish people would get that notion out of their heads. We respond to every report. We have to prioritize at times because of manpower, but I'd say we're basically color-blind when it comes to crime, especially hate crimes."

"So what should I tell them?"

"Continue to monitor what is going on and notify me when there is another incident or occurrence. I'd like for you to give me names, addresses and other contact information so I can follow up. I'll also run a background check on Sister Cathy and her son and check crime reports to see if there's any correlation between their activities and any criminal acts."

They stood, shook hands, and walked toward her patrol car. "I appreciate what you're doing," John said.

"That's my job," Kate said as she opened the door to her squad car. "Protect and serve."

"I know, but I want you to know it doesn't go unnoticed."

John watched as she pulled out of the parking lot and headed toward his neighborhood, apparently to refresh her mind about the area. John and Whiskers went on to their usual place by the pond, where he sat in tranquil surroundings and gave more thought about helping his neighbors. Whiskers was content romping around in the space between the bench and pond.

He was interrupted by an unexpected phone call from Wendell.

"I'm sorry I wasn't able to talk to you when I called before but I had a connection problem," Wendell said, without mentioning the problem was between him and Libby. "We're in Dunedin, Florida, for a few nights."

"How long do you plan to stay there?" John asked.

"I'm not sure. I guess once I feel it's safe to go back to Mobile. Have you heard anything since we left?"

"Corley Gibson came around."

"Oh, darn. I was afraid of that. What did you tell him?"

"I didn't know where you were going."

"Please don't say anything about our whereabouts."

"Don't worry about that," John said. "We know you're in hiding."

John proceeded to tell him about bringing in the police to investigate Cathy and Corley Gibson and recent crimes in the neighborhood. Wendell seemed relieved to hear the news but tensed up when John said Officer Washington might get in contact with him.

"I don't think that's a good idea," Wendell said. "I'm afraid she'd let it leak where we are."

"Don't worry about that," John said. "Let's be concerned about getting to the bottom of what's going on. She'll protect you."

After ending the call, John called for Whiskers and they walked back in the relative quiet surroundings. He couldn't help but feel somewhat optimistic about the new day.

~ * ~

Sally was pulling up weeds around the foundation of the house when John returned.

"What's got into you?" he asked, unleashing Whiskers.

"I think I'm getting a little stir crazy," she said. "I also needed a little distance from Mother. She was asking all kinds of questions about Brody and wondering about the whereabouts of Wendell and Libby."

"We can tell her Wendell is in Dunedin, Florida. He called while I was at the park."

"You were gone a long time. He must have had a lot on his mind."

John sat on the porch steps. "I also spoke to a cop about our neighborhood situation."

"At the park?"

"I had sent a text to Kate Washington about our problems and she was in the neighborhood so we met at the shelter. She's going to start moving on some type of investigation."

"I did see a police car while you were away."

"It was probably Kate, checking out the neighborhood."

Sally stood and removed her soiled gardening gloves. "I think I'm finished for the day. I'm not used to bending over like this."

"Let's go inside and I'll fix us some iced tea while you get cleaned up," John said as he got up and opened the door. Whiskers dashed inside to his water bowl.

"Where have you been?" Geraldine asked at the top of the steps leading to the den.

"I went for a walk with Whiskers," John said.

"I know where you've been because you're always walking with your mutt. I mean Sally."

"I was out front working in the yard," Sally said.

"I've been calling for you," Geraldine said.

"Is anything the matter?"

"No," she said. "I wondered where you were."

"Didn't you look out the front door or go up to the bedroom?" John asked.

"I hollered for her, and when she didn't answer, I grew concerned."

"I'll let you know if I ever go too far away," Sally said.

"Maybe you two should carry your cell phones with you in case you need to contact each other?" John said.

"John, would you stay out of this?" Geraldine said. "This is between Sally and me."

"That is a good idea, Mother," Sally said. "You never know when there could be an emergency."

"I'll think about it."

"Would you care for a glass of iced tea? I'm going to prepare some for Sally and me." John headed toward the kitchen.

"That'd be nice," Geraldine said as she followed him.

"By the way, I heard from Wendell."

"You did? Why are you taking so long in telling me? I've been worried sick."

"Because you were asking about Sally."

"Well, John, what did Wendell have to say?"

"Not a lot—"

"What then?"

"Let me finish. He and Libby are in Dunedin, Florida. They're going to stay there for a few days."

Geraldine sat on a stool. "How come?"

"They want to wait until things get settled down around here."

"That doesn't make any sense. What does that have to do with us?"

"Not us, but with those people at the Bible study they attended. I told you Wendell was concerned about what they were doing."

"I don't remember you telling me."

John set a glass of iced tea in front of Geraldine. "There were some things going on there Wendell was concerned about, so that's why he and Libby left."

"We're all concerned about that so-called ministry," Sally said as John handed her iced tea. "That's the reason we had neighbors over here the other night."

"You mean that wasn't a pizza party?"

John nearly spewed tea from his mouth. "What?"

"Weren't you paying any attention?" Sally asked.

"I was watching my program on TV. You know that."

John sat across from her and calmly explained what the meeting was about and how the police were going to get involved.

"I'm glad you finally decided to tell me," Geraldine said. "You always leave me in the dark."

"I thought you were listening."

"Now why would you say that?"

"Because you seem to hear everything else going on here."

"Are you being a smart aleck?"

Seventeen

The next day, Sally headed off to a book club meeting while John dropped Whiskers off at the groomer and went to have an oil change on his car. Geraldine declined an offer to go with Sally, deciding instead to do laundry and organize and clean her bedroom.

John reminded her to plug in her cell phone in case something came up for her to reach one of them. She balked at first but went ahead after seeing it on top of her dresser.

Geraldine put a load of dirty clothes in the washer and went to the den and turned on the television. After finding a channel showing *The Golden Girls*, and settling into the recliner, the doorbell rang.

She turned down the volume and sat for a few seconds, hoping if she remained quiet the person would go away. But the doorbell rang again.

"It's probably the mailman with a package," she said to herself. She pulled up out of the chair and grabbed her cane. "Coming! Coming!"

When she opened the door, a man in a short-sleeved white shirt and khaki pants stood several feet away with a pleasant smile.

"If you're selling something, I don't want any," she said curtly.

"Oh, I'm not selling anything, ma'am. I'm doing a neighborhood census and need to ask a couple of questions."

"Who's it for?"

"Uh, a group is trying to determine emergency medical services for the community, especially for seniors."

"Well, you'd better be quick because I'm missing my TV program."

"It won't take long. I promise, ma'am. First, how many people live here?"

"Three. Me, my daughter and her husband."

"How long have you lived here?"

"I've only been here since before last Christmas. My daughter and her husband have lived her for about forty years, give or take a few years."

"And finally, what is your name?"

"I'm Geraldine Corman."

"And the others?"

"Sally and John Ross."

"We had a report someone else lived here."

"Oh, I forgot, their son Brody. He comes and goes so much I hardly know if he's here or not." She laughed.

"Hmm, that's odd because a neighbor reported another couple lived at this residence."

"They must have thought my son and daughter-in-law lived here. It sure seemed like it for a while, but they were visiting me."

"That explains it," the man said with a smile. "And their names?"

"Wendell and Libby Corman. Her real name is Elizabeth but she goes by Libby."

"I understand." The man closed his pad. "That should do it. I thank you for taking the time to answer these questions, ma'am. I'll let you get back to your TV show."

"That wasn't too bad."

"Oops, one more thing," the man asked. "Did your son and daughter-in-law move somewhere here in Lexington?"

"I wish they had, but they're down in Florida now."

"Wow. My parents live in Florida. Did they move near Disney World?"

"No, someplace called Dunodin, Dunnodin, something like that."

"Dunedin?"

"That's it. I need to go." Geraldine flashed a grin and closed the door before the man could ask another question. She checked on her laundry and returned to the den.

Several minutes later, she heard the ringtone on her phone playing the opening stanza of Dolly Parton's "9 to 5." She waited until it came on the third time before getting up from the recliner.

"Who in the world can that be?" she said as she headed to her bedroom. She was able to pick it up on the fifth ring. It was Sally.

"What in the world do you want?" Geraldine snapped "I was watching TV."

"I was checking on you and making sure everything is okay," Sally said. "I'll be back in about forty-five minutes or so. Is there anything you want me to pick up on the way home?"

"If I needed anything, I would have told you before you left. I should have never turned on this phone. You and John are going to bug me every time you leave the house now."

"That's because we love you and want to make sure you're okay."

"If you say so. Is there anything else? I'd like to get back to my TV program."

"Anyone call or drop by since we've been gone?"

"No," Geraldine said. "I've got clothes in the washer and I need to check on them."

"I'll let you go do that. I'll see you in a bit."

"I just remembered, someone stopped by doing some kind of census. He had a few questions and was gone in about a minute."

"Sounds good, then."

Geraldine laid the phone back on the dresser and went to check on the laundry, waiting two minutes for the washer to end before putting the clothes in the dryer.

"Now for a little peace and quiet," she said, returning to the den. "I've probably missed most of my program."

~ * ~

Sally was in the den chatting with Geraldine when John returned from his errands. Whiskers ran up to Sally, jumping on the couch, seemingly proud to show off his new haircut and nail trim.

"How was the book club meeting?" John asked as he sat on the rocker.

"It was nice to get out of the house and spend time again with the girls," Sally said. "I didn't realize how much I missed it."

"And how was your day?" John asked Geraldine, who had muted the volume on the television, a rare occurrence for her. "Did you get much accomplished?"

"A load of laundry and I cleaned up my room," she said with a wide smile.

"It looks like we all had a productive day. Has anyone heard from Brody?"

"Not a word since he dropped by yesterday," Sally said. "I guess he's going through with moving in with Ashley."

"I suppose we can't stop him," John said. "He's going to do what he wants to do. We might well accept it and make the most of it. She does seem to be a nice person."

"I sure hope she can keep him focused on his recovery," Sally said.

"She certainly has the background," John said. "Let's hope love doesn't get in the way."

"What do you mean by that?" Sally asked.

"I don't want her blinded by affection, and tries to remain objective as possible under the circumstances. You know, be professional."

"We can only hope," Geraldine said. "That boy sure needs some direction in his life."

"I think Brody coming forward about taking Wendell's meds is a positive sign," Sally said.

"Only time will tell."

"I'm hoping Bert will drop by so I can tell him about the police investigation," John said. "He didn't show up while we were away, Geraldine?"

"Don't you think I would have told you if he did?"

John raised his hands, palms out. "I'm sorry. I know you would have."

"The only person who showed up was some kind of survey taker while I was watching TV. But he didn't stay long."

"Survey taker?" John asked. "What did he want?"

"He asked about the number of people living here. He said it was about some kind of programs for old people. He was a nice young man. He asked a few questions and left."

"That's interesting. I haven't read anything about it in the newspaper or heard anything on the local TV news."

"Not everything is in the newspaper or TV," Geraldine said. "You know that."

"You're right. I was merely curious."

"You do have some nosy neighbors."

"Why do you say that?" Sally asked.

"The man thought that Wendell and Libby lived here."

"How did that come up?" John asked.

"The man thought five people lived here. But I set him straight. I told him they were visiting me."

"Did he ask for any other information about them?"

"No," Geraldine said. "I told them they left a few days ago and went to Florida."

"You what?"

"I told him where they went. He said he has relatives in Florida. I think it's his parents."

John glanced at Sally, then looked back at Geraldine. "What did this person look like? Have you seen him before?"

"Of course not, John. I never get out of the house. You know that."

"But do you remember what he looked like?

"Let me think," Geraldine said, her squinty eyes looking toward the ceiling. "He had short hair and was wearing a white shirt and nice brown pants. He was a nice-looking boy and very respectful. That's about it."

John took a deep breath and rose from the rocker. "I'm going to fix a glass of iced tea. Does anyone else care for any?" He motioned with his head for Sally to follow him to the kitchen.

"I would like some," Geraldine said. "You know I like mine real sweet." She turned on the TV sound as John and Sally were leaving the room.

"I'm worried your mother talked to one of Sister Cathy's disciples," John whispered to Sally in the kitchen. "The description she gave fits the way some of the outfits the men wear. It could be Corley."

"Oh, my goodness," Sally said. "Do you think we should call Wendell?"

"I think I'll notify Officer Washington first and see what she thinks about it. I don't want to alarm Wendell, but I don't want to see him in harm's way."

"Where's my tea?" Geraldine shouted from the den. "You're sure taking your own sweet time."

"Now hold your horses, Geraldine. I want to make it sweet enough."

"You might want to let Sally handle that."

"Are you saying I may not make it sweet enough for you?"

"You may not be sweet enough to do it."

~ * ~

After preparing Geraldine a glass of sweet tea and Sally an unsweetened tea, John sat on the porch steps and called Kate

Washington. He informed her about Geraldine's possible meeting with Corley.

"To be on the safe side, I'd advise you to let your brother-in-law know about what happened. I'll alert Dunedin police about the situation," she said.

"Have you found out anything here about the group?"

"Nothing so far, but we're in the preliminary stages. I'll let you know if we learn of anything going on."

After ending the call, John immediately dialed Wendell's number but there wasn't an answer. "Why doesn't it surprise me?" he mumbled to himself before going back inside.

Sally was on the couch in the living room, reading a book, while Geraldine was watching a soap opera in the den. Whiskers was on the easy chair, but since he was curled and asleep, John didn't have the mettle to shoo him to the floor.

"I talked to Officer Washington and there wasn't any news on our holy neighbors," John said as he sat on the opposite end of the couch. "I also called Wendell, but there was no answer. I'll try again later."

"Is there anything we can do in the meantime?" she asked.

"Dunedin police will be told about what's happened. I think he'll be relatively safe for the time being."

Sally bookmarked the book and laid it beside her. "What are we going to do about Brody?"

"What do you mean?"

"Did I hear someone mention Brody?" Geraldine said as she entered the living room.

"Yes, Mother," Sally said. "I'm wondering if we should say something to Brody about leaving and moving in with his girlfriend."

"He's not a child, even though he can act like one at times," Geraldine said as she moved toward the easy chair, prompting Whiskers to jump to the floor before being ordered to by the matriarch.

"You're right about that," John said. "There's really not anything we can do about it, regardless of how we feel. As far as I'm concerned, it's a moot issue."

"This would never have happened fifty years ago," Geraldine said. "Good society frowned on people who did that."

"But some folks still cohabitated," Sally said. "John and I knew a few couples back in college who lived together."

"But you and John didn't," Geraldine said. "At least you better not have."

"We knew you would frown on it," John said with a laugh. "So we were a good boy and girl."

"Sally wasn't raised that way," Geraldine said. "And neither was Wendell."

"I wasn't either. But I don't have a problem with it now."

"Me either," Sally said.

"I believe it gives people a chance to really know each other and see if they can live together before making a long-term commitment of getting married."

"They only do it for sex," Geraldine said.

"Couples can discover if they're sexually compatible," Sally said. "It's all part of a relationship."

"I can't believe what you're saying, Sally," Geraldine said, shaking her head.

"With the divorce rate as high as it is, people need to make sure they can live together, especially if they plan to have children," Sally said. "You know how bad it is for children from a broken home."

"I know some older couples who live together because they'd lose Social Security benefits if they got married," John said. "I bet you knew a few of those back in Arizona."

"I did, but some of my friends didn't say anything, although we didn't approve of it,." Geraldine said. "We just minded our own business."

"Would you get married again if the opportunity came along?" John asked.

"What makes you think I haven't been asked?" Geraldine asked with a smirk.

"I didn't know that," Sally said.

"I don't tell you everything that goes on in my life. I've got some privacy, you know."

"Have you had any boyfriends?" John asked, raising a brow.

"Now that's none of your business either."

"What would you do if you had a chance to remarry or live together?"

"That's not a fair question and I'm not going to answer it."

"I was just curious," John said. "I won't pry anymore."

"What are we going to do about Brody?" Sally asked.

"I don't think it's our decision, because he has made up his mind about it."

"I wish I hadn't even brought it up," Sally said.

"Why?" John asked.

"Because the more I think about it, it's really none of our business. I think we should want him to be happy. And if Ashley brings him happiness, then that's what I want for him, too."

"That's what I want as well for him. If it helps him overcome his drug problem, all the better."

"I wish Wendell were here," Geraldine said out of the blue. "I worry about him. Even Libby."

"We'll let you know once we hear back from him," John said.

"What does that mean? Have you tried to call him?"

"I called less than an hour ago but he didn't answer. He was probably busy doing something. I'll try again later."

Geraldine seemed satisfied with the answer as she held out an empty glass. "Can I have some more sweet tea? Maybe a little sweeter this time?"

Eighteen

John was awake earlier than usual the following morning, easing out of the bed as not to disturb Sally and venturing to the kitchen to start the coffee. Whiskers didn't bother to show up, opting to get more shut-eye before starting his regular routine.

As the coffee was brewing, John opened the front door to see if the newspaper was anywhere to be seen in the dimly-lit yard. Before getting ready to turn on the porch light, he noticed activity at Sister Cathy's house, where three men carried boxes stealthily from a white van to the front entrance. He didn't flip the light switch, knowing the sudden brightness might attract their attention.

After it appeared the men had finished their pre-dawn chore, John closed the door, returned to the kitchen and poured a cup of coffee. He sat at the bar, lost in thought as to what was going on down the street. He wondered if other neighbors besides the Martins had noticed the surreptitious behavior from their self-righteous neighbors.

Before making another cup of coffee, John went back to the front door to see if anything was going on. This time he flicked on the porch light. The van was gone, but his newspaper had arrived in the middle of the yard. He summoned Whiskers with a quiet command to go outside with him. Whiskers wasn't enthusiastic about leaving his padded cushion but eventually sauntered out the front door, going to the side of the house while John fetched the newspaper. John glanced at Sister Cathy's house and noticed a tiny orange glow coming from an indistinct person on the porch inhaling cigarette smoke.

"Let's go back inside, little buddy," John uttered to Whiskers, who had finished his business and was already headed toward the front porch.

John took care of Whiskers' food and water bowls before sitting back down at the bar with a steaming cup of coffee and thinly-folded newspaper. He was tempted to call Officer Washington but changed his mind since it was only four forty-five. Even if she were on duty, he realized men carrying boxes didn't merit getting in touch with the police. And they would probably need a search warrant.

He took a sip of coffee before unfolding the newspaper. Nothing attracted his attention on the front page. The newspaper seemed thin on news and advertising. As he was about to put the paper aside for others to read, a headline on the city page caught his attention. The story noted a police report about an increase in porch thieves, those individuals who steal packages delivered to homes by private carriers. Some had been recorded on security cameras, resulting in several arrests and postings on social media.

When Whiskers went back to his pad in the den, John put his cup in the sink and headed toward the bedroom, thinking he could grab a short sleep before Sally and Geraldine woke up. But he was startled as turned the knob on the bedroom door when Sally appeared from the other side.

"Are you trying to give me a heart attack?" he asked.

"Were you going back to bed?"

"I thought I would, but I guess I'll stay up with you. There's still hot coffee in the kitchen."

"You can go on to bed if you want to," Sally said. "I'll read the paper and eat a little breakfast."

Geraldine opened the door to her bedroom, stepping out in her pink bathrobe. "Did someone mention breakfast?"

"How about if I make pancakes?" Sally asked.

"I think I'd like eggs and hash browns," Geraldine said.

"I'm not sure if we have any hash browns. I'll have to check."

"Pancakes sound good to me," John said.

"I thought you were going back to bed," Sally said.

"Since I'm up, I'll take a few."

"But Mother wants eggs and hash browns." Sally turned to her and smiled.

"What if we don't have any hash browns?"

"Couldn't you run to the supermarket and pick up a bag?" Geraldine asked.

"Are you serious? At this time of the morning. It's only six-twenty."

"I really had my heart set on hash browns." Geraldine said with softhearted eyes.

John looked at the mother and daughter for a few seconds, hoping they'd change their minds. "Sure, why not. I've got nothing better to do this time of the morning."

"Can you get some prune juice, too?" Geraldine said. "I haven't been regular the past few days."

"Will do," he said. "No sausage or bacon?"

"It wouldn't hurt to get some," Sally said. "And maybe some milk and bread."

"Biscuits would be nice," Geraldine said. "Do we have any honey?

"I don't believe so," Sally said. "We can add it to the list."

John took out his cell phone, touched the "note" app and began typing the grocery list. "Anything else? Going once...twice...three times... that's it. I'm outta here."

John didn't waste any time in the supermarket picking up the items on the list and headed back home. Several cars were parked in the driveway and in front of Sister Cathy's house but he didn't see anyone on the premises.

Sally and Geraldine were seated at the kitchen bar drinking coffee as he placed the groceries on the counter, taking out the items destined to go in the refrigerator.

"You weren't gone long," Sally said as she eased off the stool. "I'll get started on the hash browns. John, can you get the eggs?"

John looked on the shelves and door, but there were no eggs to be found. "Damn," he mumbled.

"What's the matter, hon?" Sally asked.

John mouthed, "No eggs."

Sally squeezed her eyes shut for a second.

"Is something the matter?" Geraldine asked, somehow picking up on the sudden stillness in the room.

"Uh, we're good," John said. "I'm just trying to figure out where to put all these groceries."

"You didn't buy that much stuff."

"I think I left something in the car," he said as he closed the refrigerator door. "I'll be right back."

John hurried out the front door as Sally began pouring the frozen hash browns in large skillet. From the sidewalk, he looked both ways and saw the light on in Allen Boatwright's house, a bachelor who lived next door to Sister Cathy.

He dashed over to the house, rang the doorbell, and waited a few seconds before Allen creaked open the door.

"Who is it?" Allen whispered.

"It's me, John Ross."

Allen opened the door and invited John to come into the house. "I thought you might be one of those nutjobs from next door."

John laughed lightly. "No, I'm the nutjob from across the street."

"Not compared to my neighbors."

"I was wondering if I could borrow a few eggs from you."

"Are you serious?"

"We're out of eggs and my dear mother-in-law wants some for breakfast. For some reason, we're always out of eggs."

"I think I have a few," Allen said. "Let me go check."

He returned holding four eggs but slipped and dropped one as he was about to hand them to John. "Shoot!"

"That's okay," John said. "Three will do."

"You might want to go down to Bert's house and see if he has any."

"I borrowed from them before. I didn't want to hit them up again."

"Anything else?"

"If you don't mind, why are you upset with your neighbor?"

"They seem to be up all hours of the night, loading and unloading boxes. It's outside my bedroom so I can hear it all. I haven't had a decent night's sleep in weeks. And then there's the gospel singing. It seems like the same songs, over and over."

"Any idea what they've got in the boxes?"

"I assume it's their religious propaganda, er, literature. I'd never heard of Christian One before."

"It's new to a lot of us."

"I'll let you know if anything out of the ordinary goes on."

John nodded. "Again, thanks for the eggs. I'll repay you when I go to the grocery."

"Aw, don't worry about it. I've borrowed enough eggs in my life, especially when I go boating. So I'm just paying it forward."

John clutched the three eggs, attempting to open the door. "Have fun on your next outing. Do you still spend time at Herrington Lake? I know you like the outdoors."

"Let me get that," Allen said as he grabbed the doorknob. "I won't be going anywhere while these folks are around. I don't trust 'em."

"Can we discuss this some time?" John said as he stepped on the porch. "Sally is probably wondering what's taking me so long."

"Anytime, John."

~ * ~

Sally was standing at the stove fixing the hash browns when John entered the kitchen holding the eggs.

"Did you go to a hatchery to get those eggs?" Geraldine asked. "It's sure taken you long enough."

"Mother, we ran out of eggs so John went to a neighbor's house," Sally said.

"Three eggs? We're going to have one each?"

"I don't want any eggs," John said as he set them on the counter by the stove. "They're for you and Sally. I'm not hungry."

"Why didn't you buy more eggs when you went to the supermarket? Wouldn't that have been easier? Or did someone forget?"

"Did you?" John asked.

"What's that supposed to mean?"

"I see you at the refrigerator several times a day. Didn't you notice we were out of eggs?"

"I wasn't looking for eggs."

"Maybe we weren't either."

"Please, let's stop this arguing," Sally said as she cracked open the eggs in a bowl. "Can't we just eat breakfast in peace?"

"Works for me," John said.

After scooping the hash browns onto to plates, Sally poured the beaten eggs into a skillet to be scrambled.

"What are you doing?" Geraldine asked. "I wanted fried eggs."

"You should have said something, Mother," Sally said as she stirred the eggs.

"But you didn't ask."

"It hasn't stopped you in the past."

"Sally, I can't believe you're talking to me this way."

"Well, I'm sorry."

Sally carried the eggs and hash browns to the bar, placing one in front of Geraldine and the other across from her.

"Am I supposed to eat with my hands?" Geraldine asked.

John opened the drawer and took out forks and knives and placed a pair by each of the plates. "They're you go. Anything else?"

Sally and Geraldine gave sly glances at each other and ate in silence. John poured another cup of coffee and read the newspaper, peeking a few times to see if the detente was still in place between mother and daughter.

When everything appeared quiet and settled, Brody entered the house without knocking, provoking a few barks from Whiskers until everyone realize it was a friendly intruder.

"Good morning," he said as he walked into the kitchen, smiling, and then kissed his mother and grandmother on the cheek.

"What brings you here this fine morning?" John asked as he put down the newspaper.

"Am I too late for breakfast? Everything sure smells delicious."

"Unless you brought some eggs," Geraldine said.

"Coffee'll do," Brody said as he sat next to Sally.

"Are you sure?" John asked. "I can run out and get some pastries."

"And eggs too," Geraldine said.

"Thanks, but I only stopped by to pick up some clothes and a few other things," Brody said.

"So you're moving in with Ashley?" Sally said, raising her brows.

"I told you I was. It'll make things easier on all of us."

"So rehab will continue?" John asked. "We think that's important."

"Sure, Dad," Brody said before taking a sip of coffee. "Believe it or not, Ashley is more insistent about it than you."

"I sure hope so."

"Me too," Geraldine said. "Maybe someone can give you proper guidance."

John looked at Geraldine. "What?"

"You know what I mean. Brody hasn't been given the proper attention here."

"Please, Mother, let's not discuss that right now."

"You don't want to hear the truth?"

Sally turned to Brody. "Do you need some help packing your clothes?"

"Do you have any empty boxes or a suitcase you aren't using?"

"I have a few empty boxes in the garage," John said as he stood. "I'll go get them."

"Have you heard from Uncle Wendell and Aunt Libby?" Brody asked.

"Not a word," Geraldine said. "I'm worried about them."

"How come?"

"I don't know," Geraldine said, her eyes moist. "Something isn't right."

"Now Mother, I'm sure he's doing okay. We'll try to get in touch with him today. He's probably busy finding a job or a permanent place to live."

"What do you mean? I thought he had a home in Alabama. And what's he doing in Florida?"

"We tried to explain it to you the other day," Sally said.

"I don't remember."

"We'll discuss it later, after we take care of Brody."

"I need to get some stuff together and get to my daily counseling," Brody said.

John returned with three medium-size boxes. "Will these do?"

"Beggars can't be choosy," Brody said with a chuckle.

"Why don't you use my suitcases?" Geraldine said. "I won't be going anywhere."

"The boxes are fine. Like I said, I'm in hurry. Maybe next time."

John handed the boxes to Brody. "Let me know if you need anything else."

Sally followed Brody to his room but was stopped at the door. "I don't need any help," he said as he tossed the boxes on the floor.

"Are you sure?"

Brody clenched his jaw. "Mom, I don't have any drugs in here if that's what you're thinking."

"Brody, I'm just trying to offer a hand. That's all."

"You and Dad have probably gone through my room anyway looking for drugs and stuff."

"So?"

"You think that's right?"

"If you had a child with an addiction, what would you have done?"

Brody tightened his mouth for a moment. "Yeah, I guess I'd do the same."

~ * ~

Sally walked across the hall to the bedroom and sat on the bed, hands in her lap and eyes closed. John was in the bathroom, trimming his beard.

"Are you into meditation now?" John asked as he walked past her to the dresser.

"I should be," she said, with a weary expression.. "I'm concerned about Mother. She's been acting odd lately."

John turned around and looked at her. "You know, I thought the same thing this morning but didn't want to say anything. I thought I was imagining it."

"I don't think so."

"Do you think it's because of Wendell being away? Or Brody moving out?"

"I'm not sure. Something just isn't right."

"What do you want to do? Should we sit down and talk to her and ask what could be troubling her?"

"I guess it wouldn't hurt."

"Does she have any doctor appointments coming up?"

"She has a follow-up for the fractured hip. It'll be a few more months before her annual wellness check-up."

"We'll keep an eye on her and see if there's anything merits more attention. Maybe she's just upset about Wendell and Brody."

Brody, holding the three boxes, tapped on their door with his foot. "You guys in there?"

John opened the door. "Let me give you a hand with that."

"I'm okay," Brody said. "Wanted to let you know I'm leaving. I'll be back in a day or so to pick up the rest of my belongings."

"We're going to miss you," Sally said from the bed.

Brody laughed "Even though I'm not around that often?"

"I hope you won't be a stranger," John said. "Don't forget your grandmother enjoys your company."

"I'll be around."

"Oh, can you give us Ashley's address and phone number in case we need to reach you for some reason?" John asked.

"My hands are full," Brody said, raising the boxes. "But I'll text you after a while and let you know."

Brody turned and headed toward the living room. John hurried up to him and opened the door.

"I'll be in touch," Brody said as he stepped out of the house. "Tell Grandmother I'll give her a call."

"You can't say something to her now?" John asked, brows furrowed. "She's in the den."

"I'm in a big hurry, Dad. I need to get Ashley's car back to her and get my ass to the rehab session."

John followed him to the car, taking the boxes so Brody could unlock the trunk. Brody didn't waste any time loading the boxes and opening the driver's door.

"We hope all goes well," John said. "Let me know if there's anything you need."

"Uh, could you spare twenty dollars so I can put some gas in her car?" Brody asked. "I'll pay you back."

John took out his wallet and handed Brody two twenty-dollar bills. "Don't worry about it."

When John returned to the house, Sally was sitting on the couch with Whiskers lying by her side. He sat in the easy chair and let out a sigh.

"I wanted to give him a set of sheets and some towels and washcloths, but he seemed in a hurry to leave," Sally said.

"He said he had to return the car to his friend and go on to rehab class," John said. "I suppose he's telling the truth."

"He couldn't even manage to say 'goodbye' to his grandmother."

"Oh, so you noticed."

"Mother did as well. She came in here and peeked out the

curtain. When he got in the car and backed out, she went up to her room."

"Have you checked on her?"

"I will in a few minutes. I want her to get settled down a bit. She had a hurt look."

"He said he'd give her a call later on. We'll see if it happens."

"I'm not counting on it."

John's cell phone vibrated. It was a call from Kate Washington.

"It's the police," he said to Sally. "I need to take it."

"About Brody?"

He gave her a calming gesture by palming a hand. "No, it's about the neighborhood."

Sally left the room as John answered the phone.

~ * ~

"I really don't have anything new to tell you," Kate said. "I was able to run a few checks but nothing came up. Has anything else happened in your neighborhood?"

"Actually, it's been relatively quiet," John said. "I did speak to a neighbor and he told me about people bringing in boxes after dark."

"There's no crime in that."

"I know. I'm just passing along some information."

"Keep me posted if you hear of anything else."

"I'll do that. Thanks for your interest."

"John, we'll continue to investigate, but until there's something firm to go on, there's not much we can do. I hope you understand."

"You know I do. Oh, by the way, I remembered something about Corley Gibson. He had the number 1-4-8-8 on four fingers. Is that a birthday or something because I figured him to be around thirty something?"

"It's a hate symbol," she said.

"Huh? How so?"

"The one and four represent fourteen words—we must secure the existence of our people and a future for white children."

"And the two eights?"

"The eighth letter in the alphabet is h. So it stands for Heil Hitler."

"What a crazy world we live in."

"I see it practically every day."

"And I seem to learn something new every day."

~ * ~

John went to look for Sally, finding her in the den talking to Geraldine. Whiskers ran up to him, an indicator he needed to go outside.

"What did the police have to say?" Sally asked.

"To be honest, nothing," John said, kneeling to pat Whiskers' back. "They'll keep a watch on everything. That's all they can do at this point."

He told her about the numbers and what they represented to white supremacists. She shook her head in disbelief. "There's so much hatred in the world now."

"Are you finished?" Geraldine asked. "In case you didn't notice, Sally and I were talking."

"I'm sorry about that, Geraldine," John said, tilting his head back. "I was passing on some information Sally probably wanted to know."

"It doesn't sound like any information if the police didn't have anything."

"That's very observant. But no information is still information."

"That makes no sense."

John took a quick look at Sally. "I'm going to take Whiskers out for a few minutes. We can discuss this later."

"What is there to discuss?" Geraldine asked. "The police didn't tell you anything."

"Please, Geraldine, there are other things to talk about. I'll leave you be so you can continue your conversation with Sally."

Sally sat tight-lipped in the rocker, apparently unwilling to get drawn into the back-and-forth. She gave a semi-wink to John before he left the room.

John put the leash on Whiskers and they left the house, heading in the opposite direction of the park. They had walked six blocks when John noticed a man carrying a box from three houses away and running to a blue late-model pickup truck as if pursued by a wild animal. He waited behind a parked car on the street a few seconds as the vehicle sped away before approaching the house. He didn't know the residents but decided to knock on the door. There wasn't an answer, but he noticed a next-door neighbor painting a fence between the houses.

John introduced himself to the man, who looked to be in his mid-60s and wearing baggy cargo shorts, a paint-splattered T-shirt, and flip-flops. He gave an apprehensive look, like John might be selling something until he saw Whiskers lifting his leg on some petunias. He looked again at John, raising a brow. He introduced himself, coolly, as Jack Seitz.

"Mrs. Kleine planted those flowers last weekend," he said.

"So that's who lives here?" John asked.

"Yep. Rich and Frankie Kleine."

"Do you know if they're home?"

"What's it to you?" Jack narrowed his eyes.

John let out an exasperated breath. "I was walking down the street when I saw a person run from their house carrying a package. They got into a truck and left rather quickly. I thought it was strange. You've heard of porch pirates, I assume. That's why I'm asking."

A faint smile came over the man's ruddy face. "I'm sorry about that. We kind of keep an eye on each other's house and property. They're both at work. He's a plumber and she works at a doctor's office. You've got to be careful nowadays about what you tell people."

"I understand completely," John said. "You may or may not know but we've had some vandalism and some hate crimes in the neighborhood in recent weeks and I was curious about what I saw. I'll come back later and see if they were expecting anything or if someone was simply picking up a box."

"They're usually home around five or so," Jack said. "If I see them, I'll let you know. Got a phone number?"

"I appreciate that." John removed an old business card from his wallet, jotted his phone number on the backside, and handed it to Jack.

John gave Whiskers a slight tug and they headed back home. Sally was sitting on the front-porch steps, talking on the phone to Chloe. John unleashed his pooch and sat next to her.

Geraldine stuck her head out the door. "Are we going to have lunch anytime soon? A person could starve around here."

"What would you like for lunch?" John asked. "Your wish is my command."

"Pizza."

"Really?" John blurted, then added, "Sure thing. What do you want on it?"

"The works."

"Anything else?"

"Diet soda."

"Diet soda?"

"Nope. I'm just seeing if you remember Libby. She always wanted diet soda."

"I do remember," John said with a warm smile.

"I wouldn't mind some kind of dessert."

"I'll see what they offer."

"Just surprise me." Geraldine closed the door.

"What was that all about?" Sally asked after ending her call with Chloe.

"Your mother wants pizza for lunch," John said. "She's in a better mood from this morning."

"We talked while you were away. She said she's been having slight headaches."

"Has she thought about seeing a doctor about it?"

"Believe it or not, she asked me to set up an appointment. I'll take her tomorrow afternoon."

"That's good. I hope it's nothing serious. How about Chloe?"

"Everything is going well. There's really no news to report, as you would say."

"That'd mean no news is good news."

"Smarty."

~ * ~

Late in the quiet afternoon, while Geraldine was watching TV and Sally was reading in the bedroom, John leashed Whiskers and headed back up the street to the Kleines' house. Rich was sitting on the porch swing drinking a bottle of beer. He appeared to have talked to his neighbor since he seemed to be waiting for John's arrival.

"My wife ordered some snacks from one of the companies and we were told they'd be arriving today," Rich said with a sardonic grin. "I'm a guessing it won't be happening."

"I thought it looked suspicious when I was walking up the street. I've been told it's somewhat of a problem now. People apparently cruise the streets, looking at houses to see if there are any packages from a delivery service."

"Mr. Ross, they're doing more than that. I don't know if Jack told you, but I'm a plumber and I spend my workdays going to houses all over town. It seems anything that ain't tied down is getting stolen. You know what I'm sayin'? Things like bikes, lawn chairs and such. We've ordered stuff before but this is the first time it's happened to us. I guess we'll have to be more careful and make sure we're around when we're expecting something."

"Have you had any other problems? Or your neighbors?"

"Someone stole some tools from my truck one night, but it was my fault for not locking it up. I should have known better."

"I remember the days when folks could leave their cars unlocked, even their houses, and nothing would happen."

"Those days are gone, Mr. Ross."

"Please, call me John."

Rich took a swig of his beer. "Weren't you the sports editor of the paper?"

"I retired last year," John said.

"I thought you looked familiar. I've done some work for the newspaper in the past. I liked the sports section when you were there. Ain't much to it now."

"The paper is shrinking. The Internet cut into advertising in a big way. Now a lot of newspapers are struggling to exist."

"I sure hope they see some daylight. I think they're important. And not just sports stuff. They keep some of those crooked politicians in line."

"I agree with you, Rich."

Rich's wife Frankie stuck her head out the door and told him dinner would be ready in ten minutes. Rich introduced her to John as the person who witnessed the theft.

"I don't know what the world's coming to," Frankie said, stepping out the front door. "You just can't trust anybody these days."

"That's what I was telling Mr., er, John," Rich said.

"I wish I could have been closer to the house," John said. "Maybe if they'd seen me it wouldn't have happened."

Rich stood and finished his beer. "You live down there near those religious folks?"

"You mean Sister Cathy?"

"That's it," he said. "They're something else."

"What do you mean?"

"They came around here a couple times passing out literature," Rich said. "They wanted us in some kind of Bible study."

"Do you remember who they were?"

"An older couple. Don't recall their names. She was kind of on the chubby side."

"Wendell and Libby?"

"That's them," Frankie said. "He didn't say a whole lot but she was really filled with the spirit, if you know what I mean."

"Do you know 'em?" Rich asked.

"My brother- and sister-in-law," John said, feeling his face flush. "I hope they didn't cause any problems."

"Nah, they were okay," Rich said. "Just a bit too religiousy for me. Especially Libby. She was a hoot."

"We went to a couple of those Bible studies," Frankie said. "They started talking about whites being the superior people so we quit going. We didn't agree with those teachings."

"Did you hear those things from Wendell and Libby?"

"No," Rich said. "In fact, they weren't there the last time we went."

"It's been great talking to you," John said. "I need to be heading back."

"It's been a pleasure meeting you, too," Rich said.

"I wish it could have been under better circumstances."

"Oh, heck, that's the way things are nowadays."

John mentioned the Neighborhood Watch program. Rich and Frankie appeared interested in attending if it didn't include going door-to-door recruiting people, like they'd been asked by Sister Cathy's group. John typed their phone number into his cell contact list.

Whiskers led the way back as John called Wendell's number. He was transferred to the voice mail.

Nineteen

John was awakened from sleep by soft knocks on the front door. He grabbed his cell phone from the night table and saw it was a two-fifteen. "Who in the world can it be?" he mumbled.

"What is it?" Sally asked, turning around in bed to face him.

"Someone's at the front door. I better check it out. It's probably Brody or the police."

"Be careful," she said, bracing herself on her elbows in the darkened room.

John eased out of bed, put on his pants, and tip-toed downstairs to the front door. There were two more taps before he gradually opened the door. Before he could say anything, two people pushed their way inside the house. It was Wendell and Libby.

"Hurry and close the door before anybody sees us," Wendell said in a hushed tone. Libby clung to his arm, tight-lipped and bedraggled.

They followed John to the dining room, sitting at the table while he turned on the light, then turning it down to a low luminosity with the dimmer switch.

Seconds later, Sally padded into the room, holding her bathrobe closed in the front after seeing the houseguests. "My goodness, what are you doing here?" as she stood between them, patting their shoulders.

"We just couldn't stay away," Wendell said. "After what we saw and heard, we knew it wasn't right to run away like we did."

"It wasn't fair to you and John after all the hospitality you showed us," Libby said.

"Can I put on a pot of coffee or get you something to eat or drink" John asked.

"Coffee would be nice," Wendell said. "We've been on the road the past fourteen hours."

"Do you have any diet soda?" Libby asked.

"Believe or not, but I do have two cans of diet soda from when you were here," John said.

"Oh, you remembered," Libby said with a warm smile. "That's so sweet."

After John started brewing the coffee, he gave Libby her drink and sat at the table with everyone. Before he could say anything, a light switch flicked on the in the upper level.

"What's going on down there? Do you know what time it is?" Geraldine said as she went down the steps. Her eyes brightened when she saw Wendell and Libby at the table. "Oh, my goodness. What a surprise!"

Wendell rose and hugged her as she wrapped her thin arms around him. Libby reached over from her chair and patted Geraldine's shoulder. "We thought we'd pay another visit, Mama," Wendell said with a light chuckle. "I hope you don't mind we didn't call beforehand."

"This is so nice," Geraldine said. "I've been worried sick about you. Just ask Sally."

"Everyone has been in our prayers," Libby said. "That's a reason we decided to come back."

As Sally poured coffee into their cups, Wendell explained why they had left so suddenly for Florida. He said they were concerned about the white-only doctrine Sister Cathy's group was espousing, something that crept into the discourse several weeks after they become involved. By accident they had noticed packages stacked in a back room, with various addresses on them, and didn't want to become implicated if it were stolen property, which they suspected could be the case.

"I'm really ashamed about how I acted," Wendell said, his voice breaking. Libby, her eyes welling, placed a hand over his hand.

"We knew it wasn't the Christian thing to do," Libby said, wiping a big tear off her cheek with her forefinger.

"We had some visits from Corley Gibson," John said. "They wanted to know where you were."

"They found us," Wendell said. "One of his friends showed up the other night at the motel. We were in the pool when we saw him knocking on our door. Libby pretended to be someone else and he told her he was Corley's buddy and was checking to how we were doing."

"That's when we decided to skedaddle from there," Libby said.

"We knew it wasn't' safe." Wendell said. "After he left, we packed our bags and hit the road. I asked the motel clerk to tell anyone who asked about us that we went to Disney World."

"I'm glad you decided to come back here," John said. "Maybe we can do something about them. I've talked to the police."

"You have?" Wendell said, eyes open wide.

"Don't worry, I didn't mention your names."

A look of relief flowed over Wendell and Libby's faces.

"It sounds like you were high-tailing it out of Florida," Geraldine said.

"Oh, we were, Mama, but we knew we had to do the right thing back here."

"We were doing both," Libby said. "Doing what Jesus would do."

Geraldine gave Libby a questioning glance but didn't say anything.

"I suppose you're worn out," Sally said.

"I feel I could drop right here and go to sleep," Libby said, letting her tongue out. "I hardly slept any of the way. Too much was on my mind."

"Let me get your bed ready," Sally said.

Libby pushed her chair back and turned toward the stairs. "Are we going back to your bedroom?"

Sally grinned. "You get Brody's room. He's moved out since you left."

"Will the bed be large enough for Wendell and me?"

"If it's not, you can sleep on the living room floor, like Sally and John did while you were here," Geraldine said. "Remember?"

Libby frowned. "Oh."

~ * ~

Early the next morning, before the break of day, Brody crept upstairs to his bedroom, opened and closed the door, and flipped on the light switch. Libby, lying on top of the covers with a leg draped over Wendell, shrieked. Wendell nearly rolled out of the bed, reaching his hand against the floor to keep from tumbling down.

"What are you guys doing here?" Brody asked. "I thought you left."

Wendell righted himself in bed while Libby yanked a sheet over her exposed body. "We got back a few hours ago," Wendell said in a dry voice. "We had some things to take care of."

John came out into the hall in a T-shirt and boxers and saw light from under Brody's bedroom door. He knocked once and turned the doorknob.

"What's going on?" he asked, blinking his eyes from the overhead light. "And what are you doing here?"

"I came by to pick up a few more things," Brody said softly. "I didn't know you had company."

"At five in the morning?" John asked. "You're never up at five."

"I had some things to do today. I wanted to get a head start."

"If you say so." John pressed his lips together.

Sally sauntered into the room, rubbing her eyes as she looked around. "Is that you, Brody?"

"Hi, Mom," he said brightly. "I'm running some errands before counseling."

"But it's still dark outside. What time is it?"

"A little after five," John said.

Seconds later, Geraldine padded to the doorway in a pink bathrobe, an eye mask on the top of her head as she surveyed the room. "Is this a family reunion or something?"

"We were waiting for you," John said.

"Are you trying to be funny?" Geraldine said, cocking her head. "I was sound asleep."

"Uh, do you mind if I get some more of my stuff?" Brody asked, inching toward the closet.

"Go ahead," Wendell said with a trace of irritation. "You're already here."

"I'm going to make a pot of coffee," John said. "I might as well stay up."

"Do we have any pastries?" Geraldine asked, wide-eyed.

"No, but I suppose I can go out and get some."

"You know I like long johns."

"We do, too," Libby said, wiggling her brows.

"I think my car is blocking yours in the driveway," Brody said. "Wait a few minutes and I'll back it out."

As John turned to leave the room, Geraldine said, "John—"

"What?"

She giggled. "You may want to put on some pants."

John looked down and scampered to the bedroom. A minute later, he stepped back out wearing jeans and went to the kitchen to prepare the coffee. Sally and Geraldine followed, leaving Brody with Wendell and Libby.

"I hate it when you have to go out," Sally said as John scooped coffee into the basket.

"I won't be gone long," he said. "Anything we need?"

"Make sure you get enough long johns with the creamy filling," Geraldine said. "Those are my favorite."

"Sure thing," John said as Whiskers moseyed up to him. "Tell Brody I'll be out front when he comes down. I'm going to let Whiskers out for a few minutes."

Whiskers ran to the side of the house while John searched the front yard for the newspaper. He glanced down the street and saw several people gathered on Sister Cathy's front porch. A minute later, a white panel van backed into the driveway. The front porch emptied as they marched around to the back of the house.

"Hey, Dad," Brody said as he walked out of the house. "Ready?"

John's body stiffened, wondering if those down the street heard Brody. He turned toward his son. "Sure. Are you wanting long johns, too?"

"I can't stay," Brody said. "I need to do a few more things before I go to counseling."

"This time of morning?" John asked. "It's only five-thirty."

"You think I'm looking for pills or something?" Brody asked.

"No, Brody, it's just that you've never been an early bird like me. I'm curious to see you out this early. That's all."

"Okay, then."

"And one other thing," John said. "I don't think you're searching for pills or whatever whenever you come to the house."

"Well, if you want to know, I'm going to a restaurant over on Winchester Road. I got a job there, washing dishes and busing tables."

"You what?"

"Dad, it's four hours every morning. It's something I can do to get on my feet while in counseling. Ashley thought it was a good idea and it will help out with the expenses."

"I don't know what to say," John said.

"You don't have to say anything. It's only temporary while I get my act together."

John watched as Brody got into the car and backed out. They both gave reluctant waves as Brody drove away.

John walked to his car and got in. He turned on the ignition and lights, then saw Whiskers staring at him from the driveway. He opened the door. "Come on, little buddy. Let's go for a ride." Whiskers jumped to his lap.

John drove down the street toward Sister Cathy's house and didn't see any activity. Seconds later, a blue pickup truck parked in front of her house.

~ * ~

When they returned twenty minutes later, the sun was peeking low on the horizon. The blue truck was gone as well as the van and there didn't appear to be anyone in Sister Cathy's house.

"I hope you got cream-filled long johns," were Geraldine's first words when John entered the dining room with the box of pastries.

"Were you serious?" John asked, handing the box to Sally. "I got glazed and jelly-filled donuts. I did get a couple plain long johns for Wendell and Libby."

Geraldine glared at him. "You can't be serious."

"No, I'm not serious. You've lived here long enough so I have a good idea what you like to eat." John glanced at Wendell and Libby. "And you guys, too."

As they delved into the pastries, John took care of Whiskers' needs in the kitchen. After pouring a cup of coffee, he nearly spilled it when he turned around and Wendell was standing two feet away.

"I didn't mean to startle you," Wendell said softly. "After breakfast, I'd like to discuss Sister Cathy and what's going on down there."

"Sure thing," John said. "Would you like me to invite several others from the neighborhood?"

"Gee, I don't know. I don't want to get things stirred up too much."

"Don't you think it would be a good idea? From what you've already told me, wouldn't it be the right thing to do to share it with others?"

"I suppose I should," Wendell said, the corners of his mouth turned downward.

"Before Sister Cathy came along, this neighborhood was rather inclusive. We have families of many ethnicities living here. For the most part, we all get along."

"Let's do it then."

"I'll make a few calls. If there's enough interest, we'll have it over at the Methodist Church community room a few blocks over."

They walked back to the dining room and sat at the table. "Any jelly-filled donuts left?" John asked, grinning at Geraldine.

"We saved you one," she said, handing him a plain long john sliced down the side. When he took a bite, he realized it had been filled with grape jelly.

"You got me, Geraldine!"

Everyone's laughter stopped by a banging on the front door. Whiskers dashed to the living room barking.

"Who in the world can it be this time of the morning?" John said as he rose and headed toward the front door. "Hush, Whiskers."

Rufus Martin, sweat beads on his brow, backed away as John opened the door. "You wouldn't believe what just happened. The police raided Sister Cathy's house!"

John walked out to the front yard and looked at several police cruisers in front, red-and-blue lights flashing as officers stacked boxes on the front porch. "I just drove past there no longer than thirty minutes ago and didn't see anyone around."

"I saw it as well from my house," Rufus said as they walked toward Sister Cathy's house. "They hightailed it out of there a few minutes before the cops arrived."

John glanced around at the cops and saw Kate Washington toting a medium-size package from around the house. She placed it on the porch, walked to the property boundary and waited for John and Rufus.

"What happened?" John asked as he shook her hand.

"We got a tip that stolen merchandise was being stored here," she said, pointing toward the rear of the house. "And sure enough, there's quite a few boxes in a back room."

"That's unreal," Rufus said. "I've seen some people going back there quite a bit lately but I thought it was religious stuff."

"I thought the same," John said. "But I've heard about some of the so-called porch pirates in the neighborhood; even saw one down the street."

"It's not just your neighborhood," Kate said. "They've been all over the place, but especially around southwestern Fayette County."

"How did you track it here?"

"Someone with a security camera caught one of the thieves who happened to live here," she said. "Although he was wearing a face covering, we were able to see the numbers 1-4-8-8 on his hand."

"Corey Gibson."

Kate gave a knowing smile.

"I guess you can say you had his number," John said.

"With a little help from a friend."

"So where's Sister Cathy?" John asked.

"You mean Cathy Gibson? She's inside getting dressed. We'll be taking her downtown for questioning in a few minutes."

"There were a couple of trucks here earlier this morning," John said.

"Yeah, they left a few minutes before you guys arrived," Rufus said.

"They're now on their way downtown to be booked, if they're not already there," Washington said. "We apprehended them near Alexandria and Versailles."

"Thanks for the information," John said.

"Yeah, and thanks for busting this operation," Rufus said. "I think we'll all feel a little safer now."

John noticed Kate was holding a thin binder with "addresses" written on the cover.

"Was that found in the house?" he asked.

"It was on the kitchen table," she said. "It appears to be a master list of addresses. We'll examine it more to see what it all means."

"You might want to interview my brother- and sister-in-law. I think they were contributors to it."

"I'll get back with you a little later on that. I need to get back to work here." She turned and returned to the porch.

John and Rufus watched from the sidewalk as the police carried more packages to the front porch. Everything halted for a minute when Sister Cathy walked out of the house, handcuffed, and escorted by two officers to a squad car. She turned her head toward John and Rufus, an empty expression on her face.

"I must say this is quite a bit of excitement for the old neighborhood," John said as others from nearby homes came out to see what was happening.

"What's all the racket?" Allen Boatwright said as he approached them in pajama shorts and a T-shirt.

"Your neighbor has been busted," Rufus said. "They've been stowing away stolen goods."

"So that's what's been going on the past few weeks," Allen said. "I wonder how the police found out."

"One of the officers said they received a tip," John said.

"Gee, I wonder who that could have been?" Allen said as he flicked a half-wink to John while turning to return to his house.

~ * ~

Wendell was on the porch when John got back to the house. He unleashed Whiskers to do his business and sat on the top step.

"What was that all about?" Wendell asked as he stepped down to the walk, still watching the police activity going on down the street.

"It seems Sister Cathy's house has been a hiding place for stash taken by porch pirates," John said. "The police found the loot."

"My God. It's worse than I ever imagined. I knew there was stuff in the back but I thought it was more of their racist literature in those boxes."

"So that's the reason you fled the flock?"

"Please, John, don't try to be witty. I'm hurting inside."

"I'm sorry. I didn't mean to offend you."

"That's okay. I should have known better."

"So what happened?"

"I accidentally opened the door to the back room and saw the boxes and whatever," Wendell said. "Corey thought I was snooping around."

"So that's why they wanted to track you down after you left?"

"I think that's the reason."

"I guess it's safe to assume Sister Cathy knew what was going on?"

"I never saw her with any of the boxes, except those with literature for our Bible studies or handouts in the neighborhood. But it's hard for me to believe she didn't know what was taking place. I'm really disappointed in her."

Whiskers sauntered back from the side of the house, ready to go back inside. John opened the storm door for the pooch, but Wendell remained on the walk with a pensive look.

"Is there something else you want to discuss?" John asked as he closed the door.

"Do you think I still need to talk to your neighbors?"

"That's up to you. They would probably like to hear what was going on down there. You could give them a first-hand account."

"I suppose I should do that. It would be like a cleansing for me."

"If you believe so."

"I also want to apologize to you and Sally. You've been gracious to us, taking us in when we were weary. We inadvertently misplaced some trust when Brody got into my meds."

"Those things happen. We should have forewarned you about that."

"You probably should have, but we still bear some of the responsibility. It's a lesson Libby and I learned. I hope our children are never addicted to pills."

"It touches all families."

"I also want to thank you for your generosity in loaning us the money to make our getaway. It took us out of harm's way for a period of time."

"Do you plan to return to Alabama now this is about over?"

"I'll have to discuss it with Libby. To be honest, and I mean this from the heart, we've enjoyed being here in Lexington, living with Mama, Sally, and you. We didn't realize it until we were in Florida. It brought joy to our hearts."

"So you're thinking about relocating here?" John's forehead creased. "Permanently?"

"Is that a problem?"

"Of course not," John said. "It just surprised me. We'll be able to help you in any way we can."

Wendell and John watched as the police cruisers slowly left the Gibson house. Officer Washington looked at John and waved as she drove by. He raised his hand and smiled.

"I wonder if there's any pastries left?" Wendell asked as he stepped toward the house.

"I hope so," John said as he followed him inside. "That jelly donut concoction Geraldine gave me didn't satisfy my hunger." They both laughed.

"What's so funny?" Geraldine asked as they entered the dining room.

"I was hoping you'd have another jelly donut for me," John said.

"Really?"

"Just kidding. Are there any long johns left?"

Sally opened the box. "There's a few. I'll fix you guys fresh cups of coffee."

John and Wendell sat at the table and explained what had transpired at Sister Cathy's house. Sally returned, sitting between Geraldine and John and across from Wendell and Libby.

"That's so sad to hear," Libby said, reaching in for another long john.

"Why do you say that?" Sally asked.

"It's sad because they did it in the name of God's work. They should be ashamed of themselves. It's an abomination. God will punish them in the end."

"No room for forgiveness?" John asked, arching his brows.

Libby glanced at Wendell as if begging him to respond. They remained tightlipped.

"It is sad about what happened," Sally said. "But nothing really surprises me anymore. People seem to believe they can get away with anything these days."

"I've got some other news," John said.

"What's that?" Geraldine asked. "I hope it's good for a change."

"Wendell and Libby are thinking about moving to Lexington." John nodded at the smiling couple.

"Now that's funny," Geraldine said with twinkling eyes. "You're not serious."

"Mama, that's not nice," Libby said. "Don't you want us to move back and be near you?"

"Wendell doesn't even have a job," Geraldine said. "And you've never had a real one."

"I was raising our children, your grandchildren," Libby said. "That's a full-time job. Right, Sally?"

"Uh, sure," Sally stammered. "There's a lot of responsibility in being a full-time mom."

"But your children aren't children anymore," Geraldine said. "And you've always stayed at home."

"I've helped babysit our grandchildren. I've been there for my children when they didn't seem to want us. Doesn't that matter? Doesn't that count?" Tears filled Libby's eyes.

Geraldine shook her head back and forth. "Excuses, excuses."

"Please, Mama, we'll just go back to Alabama if you don't want us here," Wendell said, taking a deep breath. "I thought you'd be pleased to have us back. You seemed so happy when you saw us. I don't understand sometimes."

"Wendell, I just want you to stand on your own two feet," Geraldine said. "I hate to say it but you've gotten lazy since you've been here. You just don't seem to have the gumption to do anything other than walk around the neighborhood handing out brochures."

"I'll find something, Mama," Wendell said, a touch of hurt in his voice. "These have been turbulent times for us. For all of us. I'll get back on my feet. I promise. We don't want to be a burden on anyone."

"I don't want you living off Sally and John. They've been pushovers for too long."

"Now, Mother," Sally said with a thoughtful expression. "Wendell and Libby are our guests and they're family."

"Bless you, sis," Wendell said as Libby rested her head on his shoulder.

John put an arm around Sally's shoulders while she gently touched Geraldine's arm.

"There's always room for family," she said lovingly.

Epilogue

Later that afternoon, Wendell addressed an overflow crowd of the Neighborhood Watch group at the Methodist Church, moved from the community room to the main sanctuary. Bert had encouraged members to invite their neighbors to learn about the so-called Christian One ministry which had infiltrated their lives in various ways.

Although nervous at first, his voice quivering and hands shaking, Wendell grew stronger the longer he stood at the lectern. He explained what had transpired in Sister Cathy's Bible studies, moving from simple life lessons to subtle teachings of exclusion. He apologized for his initial actions in going door-to-door handing out literature, saying he had been naïve in their overall mission. And with the religious fervor of an old-time revivalist at a tent meeting, Wendell said fear drove him away, but love brought him back to them. A few of the assembled shouted, "amen." Libby wept tears of joy from the front pew at the reawakening for her and Wendell.

When it was announced that Sister Cathy had been released from custody and was back at her house, Rufus Martin led more than three hundred people on a march from the church to her house. They stood outside her home under a purple sky, shouting

"Love trumps hate" for several minutes before, "Leave our neighborhood." It grew louder.

Minutes later, two police cruisers slowly moved through the congested street and stopped in front of Gibson's house. Kate Washington walked to the front steps and asked the outraged throng to disperse. It was after Rufus, Bert, and John Ross came to her side, providing a calming presence, they returned to their homes without incident. Kate knocked on the door, went inside and spoke to Cathy Gibson, reassuring that she would be safe. A cruiser patrolled the neighborhood through the night.

Mid-morning of the next day, a small moving van backed up to Cathy's front door. Within an hour, the house was vacant and quiet. All that remained was the Ten Commandments plaque, tipped to its side in the flower garden by the porch steps.

~ * ~

A month later, the house had new occupants. Wendell and Libby, after receiving the blessing from neighbors and a cash advance from John and Sally, started a ministry for the poor, homeless, and disabled. They were lauded for their efforts, interviewed on TV and in the newspaper. But over time, the house fell into disarray as Wendell wasn't inclined to mow the lawn on a regular basis, Libby wasn't into maintaining the flower garden, and a few converts deemed by some neighbors to be somewhat unsavory had been accused of littering the area with items such as empty beer and wine bottles, cigarette butts, and drug paraphernalia.

A year later, while Wendell and Libby were conducting a fellowship picnic at Shipley Park, the house burned to the ground. The cause was undetermined by the state fire marshal, noting it could have been a faulty water heater or gas stove. Unbeknownst to John, Wendell, Rufus, Manny, Allen, Bert and other neighbors, a blue pickup truck was seen leaving the vicinity about the time of the fire.

Meet Michael Embry

Michael Embry is the author of 14 books including 10 novels, three nonfiction sports books, and a short-story collection. He spent more than 30 years in the news media, working as an award-winning reporter, sportswriter, and editor for two newspapers, a national news service, and a regional magazine as well as a book editor. He is listed in *Who's Who in America.*

Embry is co-founder, along with fellow Wings author Chris Helvey, of the Bluegrass Writers Coalition. He is a member of several environmental, human rights, animal rescue, and wildlife organizations. His interests include reading, travel, and photography. He lives in Frankfort, Ky., with his wife, Mary, and two rescue dogs, Bailey and Belle.

Other Works From The Pen Of Michael Embry

New Horizons - John Ross and his wife Sally take a long overdue vacation, traveling to Budapest for a guided tour. It turns out to be an unforgettable trip, mainly for the wrong reasons.

Darkness Beyond the Light - John Ross and his wife Sally learn their self-centered son Brody has been leading a double life and must navigate uncharted territory during the Christmas season to lead him out of the darkness of drugs.

Old Ways and New Days - Retired sports editor John Ross discovers there are many adjustments he must make in this coming-of-old-age novel.

The Bully List - Dealing with bullies isn't an easy thing to do so Josh and Sam try to come up with a list of things to do to get even with a gang of bullies.

Shooting Star - Basketball standout Jesse Christopher finds most of his challenges away from the gym as he tries to fit in as the new kid in school.

A Long Highway - A random act of violence in the workplace forces sports columnist Micah Stewart to hit the road in search of meaning to his life.

The Touch - Sports editor Blake Williams, a widower trying to raise three children, is careful to open his heart to another woman, fearful of the pain he might suffer again.

A Confidential Man - Sports columnist Chase Elliott is known as a trustworthy friend who can keep confidences. But can keeping some confidences prove to be deadly?

Foolish Is the Heart - Sports columnist Brandon Wilkes discovers there are important things going on in his life other than covering the big games.

Letter to Our Readers

Enjoy this book?

You can make a difference

As an independent publisher, Wings ePress, Inc. does not have the financial clout of the large New York Publishers. We can't afford large magazine spreads or subway posters to tell people about our quality books.

But, we do have something much more effective and powerful than ads. We have a large base of loyal readers.

Honest Reviews help bring the attention of new readers to our books.

If you enjoyed this book, we would appreciate it if you would spend a few minutes posting a review on the site where you purchased this book or on the Wings ePress, Inc. webpages at: https://wingsepress.com/